D0388916

A Million Suns

RAZORBILL

Published by the Penguin Group
Penguin Young Readers Group
345 Hudson Street, New York, New York 10014, U.S.A.
Penguin Group (USA) Inc., 375 Hudson Street, New York, New York 10014, U.S.A.
Penguin Group (Canada), 90 Eglinton Avenue East, Suite 700, Toronto, Ontario,
Canada M4P 2Y3 (a division of Pearson Penguin Canada Inc.)
Penguin Books Ltd, 80 Strand, London WC2R 0RL, England
Penguin Ireland, 25 St Stephen's Green, Dublin 2, Ireland (a division of Penguin Books Ltd)
Penguin Group (Australia), 250 Camberwell Road, Camberwell, Victoria 3124, Australia
(a division of Pearson Australia Group Pty Ltd)
Penguin Books India Pvt Ltd, 11 Community Centre,
Panchsheel Park, New Delhi – 110 017, India
Penguin Group (NZ), 67 Apollo Drive, Mairangi Bay, Auckland 1311, New Zealand
(a division of Pearson New Zealand Ltd)
Penguin Books (South Africa) (Pty) Ltd, 24 Sturdee Avenue,
Rosebank, Johannesburg 2196, South Africa

Penguin Books Ltd, Registered Offices: 80 Strand, London WC2R 0RL, England

10 9 8 7 6 5 4 3 2 1

ISBN 978-1-59514-398-3

Library of Congress Cataloging-in-Publication Data is available

Printed in the United States of America

DEDICATION:

Michelangelo said,
"Every block of stone has a statue inside it
and it is the task of the sculptor to discover it."

This book is dedicated to
Merrilee for providing me with the stone
and
Ben and Gillian for giving me the chisel.

Dei gratia.

A MILLION SUNS

BETH REVIS

razor
bill

An Imprint of Penguin Group (USA) Inc.

1
ELDER

"THIS ISN'T GOING TO BE EASY," I MUTTER, STARING AT THE solid metal door that leads to the Engine Room on the Shipper Level of *Godspeed*. In the dull reflection, I see Eldest's dark eyes, just before he died. I see the smirk on the corner of Orion's mouth as he relished in Eldest's death. Somewhere, beneath my cloned features and the echoes of every Eldest before me, there has to be something in me that's mine alone, unique and not found in the cloning material two levels beneath my feet.

I like to think that, anyway.

I roll my thumb over the biometric scanner and the door zips open, taking with it the image of a face that has never felt like mine.

A very mechanical smell—a mixture of metal and grease and burning—wraps around me as I enter the Engine Room. The walls vibrate with the muffled heartbeat of the ship's engine, a *whirr-churn-whirr* sound that I used to think was beautiful.

The first-level Shippers stand at attention, waiting for me. The Engine Room is usually crowded, bustling with activity as the Shippers try to figure out what has crippled the lead-cooled fast reactor engine, but today I asked for a private meeting with the top ten Shippers, the highest-ranking officers beneath me.

I feel scruffy compared to them. My hair's too long and messy, and while my clothes should have been recycled long ago, their dark tunics and neatly pressed trousers fit perfectly. There is no uniform for the Shippers—there's no uniform for anyone on board the ship—but First Shipper Marae demands neatness of everyone she has authority over, especially the first-level Shippers, who all favor the same dark clothing worn by Marae.

Marae's in the twenty-year-old generation, only a few years older than me. But already lines crease at her eyes, and the downward turn of her mouth seems permanent. A carpenter could check the accuracy of his level by the line of Marae's shorn hair. Amy says that everyone on board *Godspeed* looks the same. I suppose, given that we're monoethnic, she's right in a way. But no one could ever mistake Marae for anyone else, nor think she's anything less than First Shipper.

"Eldest," she says by way of greeting.

"I've told you: just call me Elder."

Marae's scowl deepens. People started calling me Eldest as soon as I assumed the role. And I'd always known I'd *be* Eldest at some point, although I'd never dreamed that I'd be Eldest so soon. Still, I was born for this position. I *am* this position. And if I can't see it in myself, I can see it in the way the Shippers still stand at attention, the way Marae waits for me to speak.

I just . . . I can't take the title. Someone called me Eldest in front of Amy, and I couldn't stand the way her eyes narrowed and her body froze, for just a minute, just long enough for me to realize that there was no way I could bear to see her look at me as Eldest again.

"I can be the Eldest without changing my name," I say.

Marae doesn't seem to agree, but she won't argue.

The other first-level Shippers stare at me, waiting. They are all still, with their backs erect and their blank faces turned to me. I know part of their perfection is due to Marae's strong hand as First Shipper, but I also know a part of it comes from the past, from Eldest before he was killed and the exacting way he expected everyone to perform.

There is nothing of me in their stoic obedience.

I clear my throat.

"I, uh, I needed to talk to you, the first-level Shippers, about the engine." I swallow, my mouth both dry and bitter-tasting. I don't look at them, not really. If I look into their faces—their older, more experienced faces—I will lose my nerve.

I think of Amy. When I first saw Amy, all I could see was her bright red hair swirled like ink frozen in water, her pale skin almost as translucent as the ice she was frozen in. But when I imagine her face now, I see the determined set of her jaw, the way she seems taller when angry.

I take a deep breath and stride across the floor toward Marae. She meets my gaze head-on, her back very straight, her mouth very tight. I stand uncomfortably close to her, but she doesn't flinch as I raise both my arms and shove her shoulders, hard, so she crashes into the control panel behind her. Emotion flares on the faces of the others—Second Shipper Shelby looks confused; Ninth Shipper Buck's eyes narrow and his jaw clenches; Third Shipper Haile whispers something to Sixth Shipper Jodee.

But Marae doesn't react. This is the mark of how different Marae is from everyone else on the ship: she doesn't even question me when I push her.

"Why didn't you fall over?" I ask.

Marae pushes herself up against the control panel. "The edge broke my fall," she says. Her voice is flat, but I catch a wary tone under her words.

"You would have kept going if something hadn't stopped you. The first law of motion." I shut my eyes briefly, trying to remember all I had studied in preparation for this moment. "On Sol-Earth, there was a scientist. Isaac Newton." I stumble over the name, unsure of how to pronounce a word with two *a*'s in a row. It comes out as "is-saaahk," and I'm sure that's wrong, but it's not important.

Besides, it's clear the others know who I'm talking about. Shelby looks nervously at Marae, her eyes darting once, twice, three times to the mask of Marae's unnaturally still face. The steady stoniness of the other first-level Shippers' postures melts.

I bite back a bitter smile. That seems to be what I always do: break the perfect order Eldest worked so hard to make.

"This Newton, he came up with some laws of motion. It seems frexing obvious, this stuff he wrote about, but . . ." I shake my head, still somewhat shocked by how simple his laws of motion were. Why had it never occurred to me before? To Eldest? How was it that while Eldest taught me the basics of all the sciences, somehow Newton and the laws of motion never came up? Did he just not know about them, or did he want to keep that information from me too?

"It's the bit about inertia that caught my attention," I say. I start pacing—a habit I've picked up from Amy. I've picked up a lot of things from Amy, including the way she questions everything. *Everything.*

Right at the top of my questions is a fear I've been too terrified to voice. Until now. Until I stand in front of the Shippers with the limping engine churning behind my back.

I shut my eyes a moment, and in the blackness behind my eyelids, I see my best friend, Harley. I see the hollow emptiness of space as the hatch door opened and his body flew out. I see the hint of a smile on his lips. Just before he died.

"There are no external forces in space," I say, my voice barely louder than the *whirr-churn-whirr* of the engine.

There was no force that could stop Harley from going out that hatch door three months ago. And now that he's in space, there's no force to stop him from floating forever through the stars.

The Shippers stare at me, waiting. Marae's eyes are narrowed. She won't give this to me. She's going to make me pull the truth from her.

I continue, "Eldest told me that the engine was losing efficiency. That we were hundreds of years behind schedule. That we had to fix the engine or risk never reaching Centauri-Earth."

I turn around and look at the engine as if it could answer me. "We don't need it, do we? We don't need the fuel. We just need enough to get to top speed, and then we could shut off the engine. There's no friction, no gravity—the ship would keep moving through space until we reached the planet."

"Theoretically." I don't know if Marae's voice is wary because she's unsure of the theory or because she's unsure of me.

"If the engine's not working—and hasn't been working for decades— then the problem should be that we're going too *fast*, right? That we're going to just zoom past the planet . . ." Now there's doubt in my voice— what I'm saying goes against everything I thought I knew. But I've been researching the engine problem since Eldest died, and I just can't cor- relate what Eldest told me with what I've learned from Sol-Earth's books. "Frex, our problem should be that we're going to crash into Centauri- Earth because we can't slow down, not that we're going to float aimlessly in space, right?"

I feel as if even the engine has eyes, and it's watching me too.

Looking at the Shippers, I can see that they all—they *all*—knew that the engine's problems did not lie in fuel and acceleration. They knew all along. I haven't told them anything new with this information. Of course the first-level Shippers know of Newton and physics and inertia. Of course they do. Of course they understood that Eldest's words about inefficient fuel and limping through space behind schedule were entirely false.

And what a frexing fool I am for thinking differently.

"What's going on here?" I ask. My embarrassment feeds my anger. "Is there even anything wrong with the engine? With the fuel?"

The Shippers' eyes go to Marae, but Marae's silently watching me.

"Why would Eldest lie to me about this?" I can feel myself losing control. I don't know what I expected—that I'd figure out the big problem and the Shippers would jump up and fix it? I don't know. I never really thought past telling them that the laws of physics go against the explanations Eldest gave me. I never thought that I'd say what I came to say and they would look to the First Shipper, not me.

"Eldest lied to you," Marae says calmly, "because we lied to him."

2
AMY

A DROP OF WATER SPLASHES AGAINST THE METAL FLOOR.

I keep my eyes squeezed shut, ignoring the cold and focusing instead on the black behind my eyelids. "Riding in the car down a long empty highway," I say aloud, my voice echoing, bouncing off the high, rounded metal walls. "With the windows down. And the music playing. Loud." I struggle to remember details. "So loud that you feel the music vibrating the car door. So loud that the image in the rearview mirror is blurry because it's vibrating too. And," I add, my eyes still clamped shut, "sticking my arm out the window. With my hand flat. Like I'm flying."

Another drop of water splashes, this time against my bare foot, sending a shiver all the way from my toes to the roots of my hair.

"Riding in the car. That's what I miss the most today," I whisper. My eyelids flutter open. My arms, which I'd raised foolishly while imagining driving down the road, flop to my sides.

There are no more cars. No more endless highways.

Just this.

Two melting cryo chambers on a spaceship that grows smaller every day.

Drip. Splash.

I'm playing with fire here, I know it. Or, rather, ice. I should shove my parents back into their cryo chambers before they melt any further.

But I don't.

I fiddle with the cross necklace around my neck, one of the few things I have left from Earth. This—sitting on the floor of the cryo level and staring up at my frozen parents and remembering one more thing I miss—is the closest I can come to prayer now.

Elder mocked me for praying once, and I spent an hour berating him for that. He ended up throwing up his hands, laughing, and telling me I could believe whatever I wanted if I was going to hold onto my beliefs so hard. The ironic thing is that now everything about me, including whatever it was I once believed in, is slipping through my fingers.

It was simpler before. Easier. Everything was all laid out. My parents and I would be cryogenically frozen. We would wake up after three hundred years. The planet would be there, waiting for us.

The only thing on the agenda that actually happened is that we were all frozen. But then I was woken up early—no. No. *He* woke me up earlier. Elder. I can't let myself forget that. I can't let myself ever forget that the reason I'm here is his fault. I can't let the three months that have passed between us wipe out the lifetime he took away.

For a moment, I think of Elder's face—not handsome and noble like I know it now, but blurry and watery like the first time I saw him, as he crouched over my naked, shivering body after pulling me from the dredges of the glass coffin where he found me. I remember the warm cadence of his voice, the way he told me everything would be okay.

What a liar.

Except . . . that's not true, is it? Of everyone on this ship, even the frozen bodies of my parents, Elder's the only one who handed me truth and waited for me to accept it.

The watery image of Elder comes into sharp focus in my mind's eye. And I'm not seeing him through the cryo liquid anymore; I'm remembering him in the rain. That night on the Feeder Level, when the sprinklers in the ceiling dumped "rain" on our heads so heavy that the flowers bent under the force, when I was still scared and still unsure, and droplets trailed from the ends of Elder's hair across his high cheekbones, resting on his full lips . . .

I shake my head. I can't hate him. But neither can I . . . Well, I can't hate him, anyway.

The one I can hate? Orion.

I wrap my arms around my knees and look up at the frozen faces of my parents. The worst part of being woken up early, without your parents, on a ship that's as messed up as this one is, is that there's nothing to fill your days but time and regret.

I don't know who I am here. Without my parents, I'm not a daughter. Without Earth, I barely even feel human. I need *something*. Something to fill me up again. Something to define myself by.

Another drop splashes down.

It's been ninety-eight days since I woke up. Over three months. And what should have been fifty years before we land has become nothing but a question mark. Will we even land?

That's the question that brings me down here every day. The question that makes me open my parents' cryo chambers and stare at their frozen bodies. *Will we ever land?* Because if this ship is truly lost in space with no chance of ever reaching the new planet . . . I can wake my parents up.

Only . . . I promised Elder I wouldn't. I asked him, about a month ago, what was the point of keeping my parents frozen? If we're never going to land, why not just wake them up now?

When his eyes met mine, I could see sympathy and sorrow in them. "The ship *is* going to land."

It took me a while to realize what he meant. The ship will land. Just not us. So—I keep my promise to him, and to my parents. I won't wake them up. Not when there's still a chance their dream of arriving at the new world is possible.

For now I'm willing to let that chance be enough. But in another ninety-eight days? Maybe then I won't care that the ship might still land. Maybe then I will be brave enough to push the reanimation button and let these cryo boxes melt all the way.

I lean up so my eyes are level with my father's, even though his are sealed shut and behind inches of blue-specked ice. I trace my finger along the glass of the cryo chamber, outlining his profile. The glass, already fogged from the heat of the room, smooths under my touch, leaving a shiny outline of my father's face. The cold seeps into my skin, and I flash to the moment—just a fraction of a second—when I felt cold before I felt nothing.

I can't remember what my father looks like when he smiles. I know his face *can* move, his eyes wrinkle with laughter, his lips twitch up. But I can't remember it—and I can't envision it as I stare through the ice.

This man doesn't look like my father. My father was full of life and this . . . isn't. I suppose my father is in there, somewhere, but . . .

I can't see him.

The cryo chambers thud back into place, and I slam the doors shut with a crash.

I stand slowly, not sure of where to go. Past the cryo chambers, toward the front of the level is a hallway full of locked doors. Only one of those doors—the one with the red paint smudge near the keypad—opens, but through it is a window to the stars outside.

I used to go there a lot because the stars made me feel normal. Now they make me feel like the freak that nearly everyone on board says I am. Because really? I'm the only one who truly misses them. Of all the two-thou-sand-whatever people on this ship, I'm the *only* one who knows what it is to lie in the grass in your backyard and reach up to capture fireflies floating lazily through the stars. I'm the only one who knows that day should fade into night, not just click on and off with a switch. I'm the only one who's ever opened her eyes as wide as she can and *still* see only the heavens.

I don't want to see the stars anymore.

Before I leave the cryo level, I check the doors of my parents' chambers to make sure they locked properly. A ghost of an *X* remains on my father's door. I trace the two slashes of paint with my fingers. Orion did this, mark-ing which people he planned to kill next.

I turn, looking toward the genetics lab across from the elevator. Ori-on's body is frozen inside.

I could wake him up. It wouldn't be as easy as pushing a reanimation button, like waking my parents would be, but I could do it. Elder showed me how the cryo chambers were different; he showed me the timer that could be set for Orion's reanimation, the order of the buttons that needed to be pushed. I could wake him up, and as he sputtered back to life, I could ask the question that hollows me out every time I look at his bulging eyes through the ice.

Why?

Why did he kill the other frozens? Why did he mark my father as the next one to kill?

But more importantly, why did he start killing now?

Orion may believe that the frozen military personnel will force the people born on the ship to be soldiers or slaves . . . but why did he start unplugging them when planet-landing is impossibly far away?

He'd hidden from Eldest for years before Elder woke me. He could have stayed hidden if he hadn't started killing.

So I guess my real question isn't just why, but . . .

Why *now*?

3
ELDER

I STARE AT MARAE, MY MOUTH HANGING OPEN. "WH-WHAT the frex do you mean?" I finally stammer.

Marae rolls her shoulders back, straightening her spine and making herself appear even taller. My eyes flicker to the other Shippers, but I notice that hers do not. She doesn't need them to affirm who she is or what she believes. "You have to understand, Eld . . . Eld*er*," Marae says. "Our primary duty as Shippers is not to fix the engine."

My voice rises with anger and indignation. "Of course your frexing duty is to fix the engine! The engine is the most important part of the whole ship!"

Marae shakes her head. "But the engine is only a *part* of the ship. We have to focus on *Godspeed* as a whole."

I wait for her to continue as the engine churns noisily behind us, the heartbeat of the ship.

"There are many things wrong with *Godspeed*; surely you've noticed." She frowns. "The ship isn't exactly new. You know about the laws of motion, but have you studied entropy?"

"I . . . um." I glance around at the other first-level Shippers. They're all watching me, waiting, and I don't have the answer they want to hear.

"Everything's constantly moving to a more chaotic state. A state of disorder, destruction, disintegration. Elder," Marae says, and this time she doesn't stutter over my chosen name. "*Godspeed* is old. It's falling apart."

I want to deny it, but I can't. The *whirr-churn-whirr* of the engine sounds like a death rattle ricocheting throughout the room. When I shut my eyes, I don't hear the churning gears or smell the burning grease. I hear 2,298 people gasping for breath; the stench of 2,298 rotting bodies fills my nose.

This is how fragile life is on a generation spaceship: the weight of our existence rests on a broken engine.

Eldest told me three months ago, *Your job is to take care of the people. Not the ship.* But . . . taking care of the ship *is* taking care of the people. Behind the Shippers are the master controls, monitoring the energy sources applied to the rest of the ship's function. If I were to smash the control panel behind Marae, there would be no more air on the ship. Destroy another panel, no more water. That one, light. That other one, the gravity sensors go. It's not just the engine that's the heart of the ship. It's this whole room, everything in it, pulsing with just as much life as the 2,298 people on this level and the one below.

Marae holds her hand out, and Second Shipper Shelby automatically passes her a floppy already blinking with information. Marae swipes her fingers across it, scrolling down, then hands it to me. "This past week alone we've had to perform two major fixes to the internal fusion compartment of the solar lamp. Soil efficiency is way below standard specs, and the irrigation system keeps leaking. Food production has barely been sufficient for over a year, and we'll soon be facing a shortage. Work production has decreased significantly in the last two months. It's no small thing to keep this ship alive."

"But the engine," I say, staring at the floppy, full of charts with arrows pointing down and bar graphs with short stumps at the end.

"Frex the engine!" Marae shouts. Even the other Shippers break their immobile masks to look shocked at Marae's cursing. She takes a deep, shaky breath and pinches the bridge of her nose between her eyes. "I'm sorry, sir."

"It's fine," I mutter, because I know she won't go on until I say this.

"Our duty, *Elder*, is clear," Marae continues, clipping her words and holding her temper in check. "Ship over planet. If there is a choice between improving the life aboard the ship and working on the engine to get us closer to Centauri-Earth, we must *always* choose the ship."

I grip the floppy, unsure of what to say. Marae rarely reveals what she's feeling, and she never loses control. I'm not used to seeing anything on her face beyond calm composure. "Surely we could make *some* sacrifices in order to get the engine back up to speed. . . ."

"Ship over planet," Marae says. "That has been our priority since the Plague and the Shippers were developed."

I'm not going to let this go. "That's been . . ." I try to add up the years, but our history is too muddled by lies and Phydus to know exactly how long that's been. "Gens and gens have passed since the 'Plague.' Even if the ship is the top priority, in that amount of time, we *must* have come up with *some* way to improve the engine and get us to the planet."

Marae doesn't speak, and in her silence, I detect something dark.

"What aren't you telling me?" I demand.

For the first time, Marae turns to look to the other Shippers for assurance. Shelby nods, a tiny movement that I almost don't notice. "It was before I was named First Shipper. Before you were born. The First Shipper then was a man named Devyn." Marae's eyes flick to Shelby one more time. "Information about the engine has always been—selectively known."

Which means, of course, that as few people as possible know the truth.

"I was apprenticing then," Marae continues, "and I remember that Elder—the other Elder, the Elder before you—"

"Orion," I say.

She nods. "Eldest sent him to do some maintenance on the ship, and when he came back, he didn't report to Eldest. He went straight to Devyn. Whatever he said then . . . it made an impact on Devyn. All research ceased for a while after that."

"The Shippers went on strike?" I lean forward, shocked. Of everyone on *Godspeed*, the Shippers are the most loyal. I don't know if it's because we trusted them even without Phydus, or if it's because they're genetically engineered to be loyal, or if it's simply because they, like Doc and a handful of others, *like* the Eldest system of rule, but whatever the reason, the Shippers are unswerving in their loyalty.

"They didn't strike exactly, not like the weavers did last week. They did all their duties as normal. Except for engine research."

"What made them start researching the engine problems again?" I ask. I'm vaguely aware of the other Shippers in the room, the deep silence, the uncomfortable way they hold themselves, but my attention is focused on Marae.

"Elder died," she says simply.

She means Orion—when Orion was Elder, he faked his own death to avoid a very real death at the hands of Eldest.

"After that," Marae goes on, "First Shipper Devyn resumed research on the engine. Although . . . the research was even more closely hidden than before. Fewer Shippers were allowed access to the engine, and Devyn was not exactly, well, not exactly *forthright* with Eldest. When I took his place, I carried on as he trained me. But . . . I started to notice . . . irregularities."

"Irregularities?"

Marae nods. "Things didn't add up. Some of the engine's problems seemed new—as if intentionally done, and recently. All records of past research were gone—destroyed, probably, as we've never been able to discover them."

So Devyn had misled his apprentice, Marae. Whatever Orion had told him had made Devyn change everything, even going so far as to hide information from his own Shippers and Eldest. Orion once told me that *Godspeed* was on autopilot, that it could get to Centauri-Earth without us. Why would he say that if he's the one who knew the problems with the engine went deeper than anyone else thought?

"Eldest started to realize this too, didn't he?" I ask.

Marae looks down at her hands. "The Eldest's job is to take care of the people. The Shippers' job is to take care of the ship. But before he . . . before he died, I think, yes. He'd realized something wasn't right."

I rub my face with both my hands, remembering where I first heard those words. Remembering the way Eldest had spent more and more time on the Shipper level, in those last weeks before Orion killed him.

How long has this been going on? Eldest told me my focus had to be on the people, but we can't have been the only Eldests to realize that we had to focus on the engine too. What happened to them? It all connects at the so-called Plague, the beginning of the lies, the beginning of Phydus. Somewhere between the Plague and now, the truth was lost, and we, all of us, me and Eldest and the Shippers and everyone else, whether we were on Phydus or not, allowed ourselves to believe blindly what others told us.

"I'm . . . *done*," I say, throwing my hands back down. "I'm done with the lies, with the ways things used to be. What *exactly* is wrong with the ship's engine? If it's not a matter of fuel efficiency, what is it? Are we going too fast? Are we going too slow? *What?*"

Now Marae slouches. "We're not going too fast or too slow." She looks sad, worry in her eyes. "We're not going at all."

4
A M Y

I CHECK THE CLOCK ON A FLOPPY WHEN I GET BACK TO MY room in the Hospital. Crap. It's later than I'd thought it was. Every day I've been spending more and more of the morning in the cryo level. At first it was to run. But then I quit running. Now I just go and force myself to remember one thing I miss from Earth, one thing in as great detail as I can. And then, eventually, I force myself to say goodbye to my parents. Again.

The solar lamp clicks on, illuminating the entire Feeder Level. Even though I have the metal shade pulled over the only window in my room, a sliver of light slices across the floor.

Morning has officially sprung. Great.

I slam my hand against the button on the wall by the door. *Beep!* A few moments later, a little metal door in the wall slides open, and a waft of steam floats into the room.

"That's it?" I say to the small pastry that lies inside. I pull it out. Wall food has never been very appetizing, but this is the first time I can say that it's small. The whole thing fits in my palm in a flat, depressed sort of way. Two bites later, and breakfast is over.

Someone knocks on my door. Even though the door is locked, unreasonable panic flares in my heart.

"Amy?"

"Doc?" I ask as I zip open the door to my bedroom. His solemn face greets me.

"I wanted to check in on you," he says, stepping inside.

"I'm fine," I say immediately. Doc has offered, more than once, to give me pale blue med patches. They're for "nerves," he says, but I don't want to bother. I don't trust the little patches he doles out instead of pills; I don't trust any medication made on this ship that also once made Phydus.

"No," Doc says, waving his hand dismissively. "I mean—well. Hrm. I'm worried about . . . about your safety."

"My safety?" I plop down on my unmade bed. Doc glances at the only chair in my room, the one at my desk, but he doesn't sit down. A jacket is slung over the back of the chair, and floppies and books I've pilfered from the Recorder Hall clutter the desktop. He probably wouldn't want to sit anywhere without an antiseptic wipe and some Lysol.

Not that there *is* any Lysol here.

Doc's stance is awkward; he keeps his arms close to his body, and his back is too straight. But his face is very serious. "I'm sure you've noticed the increased . . . Well, it's clear now that there are no more traces of Phydus in the people's systems. And now we're left with . . . The ship's not especially safe at the moment, especially for someone who . . ."

"Someone who looks like me?" I ask, flicking my long red hair over my shoulder.

Doc flinches, as if my hair is a curse word shouted in church. "Yes."

He's not saying anything new. I am the only person on this ship who wasn't born here. And while the residents of *Godspeed* had the individuality bred out of them so they're all monoethnic, I've got super-pale skin, bright green eyes, and red hair to mark how different I am. The former ship's leader, Eldest, did me no favors, either, telling the residents that I was a genetic experiment gone wrong. At best, most people here think I'm a freak.

At worst, they blame me for the way things have been falling apart.

Three weeks ago, I went for my regular morning run. I stopped near the chicken farm to look at the baby chicks. The farmer came outside with the feed—he's a huge man, his arms as thick as my legs. He set the bucket of feed on the ground and just . . . just *stared* at me. Then he walked to the gate and picked up a shovel. He hefted it up, testing the weight of it and running one finger along the sharp and shiny blade. I started running then, looking over my shoulder. He watched me, shovel in hand, until I was out of sight.

I haven't been running since.

"I'm not stupid," I tell Doc, standing up. "I know that things aren't exactly peachy around here."

I sling open the door to my wardrobe and pull out a long piece of cloth that's such a dark shade of maroon it's almost brown. The material is thin and a little stretchy. Starting behind my left ear, I drape the cloth over my forehead, then under my mass of red hair, then back around, wrapping up my hair so it's completely hidden behind the dark cloth. When I get to the end, I twist the wrapped hair into a bun and tie the ends of the cloth into a knot. Then I grab the jacket from the desk chair and sling it over my shoulders, pulling the hood up over my head. The last thing I do is tuck my cross necklace under my shirt so no one can see it.

"It's not perfect," I say as Doc inspects my apparel. "But if I keep my head down and my hands in the jacket pockets, it's hard for anyone to notice how different I am unless they get up close." And I don't really plan on getting up close to anyone.

Doc nods. "I'm glad you've thought of this sort of thing," he says. "I'm . . . well, I'm impressed."

I roll my eyes.

"But I don't think it's enough," he adds.

I push the hood out of my face and stare at Doc, making a point to meet his eyes. "I. Will. *Not*. Stay locked up in this room forever. I know you don't think it's safe, but I *won't* be even more of a prisoner than I already am. You can't keep me here."

Doc shakes his head. "No. You're right. I can't. But I think you need—" His hand moves to his neck, where his wireless communicator is embedded beneath his skin.

"No!" This is another argument we've had plenty of times before. Doc—and Elder too—neither of them understands why I refuse to get a wi-com. I know Elder wants me to have one because he cares and worries about me. And—it would be nice, to be able to talk to him whenever I like. Touch a button and I could ride the grav tube up to Elder's level, com him, or just find out where he is on the ship.

A wi-com is the ultimate cell phone, always keeping you plugged in.

Always keeping you tied to this ship, this ship that is *not* my home. I won't get a wi-com any more than I'll lock myself up in this room. Wi-coms are just too . . . too . . . too *not*-Earth. I can't just let myself be wired into the ship. I can't let them cut me open and implant something not-Earth *into* me, beneath my skin, wiggling into my brain. I can't do that.

Doc reaches into his pocket and pulls something out in a fluid motion that seems contrary to his usually stiff persona. He holds the thing out to me.

"This is a"—Doc pauses—"it's a special wi-com."

I force myself to look at the thing in his hand. It's essentially a tiny button, not any bigger than a dime, with three wires coming from each side. In a regular wi-com, the button's hidden underneath the skin behind your left ear and the wires burrow into your flesh. But Doc has braided the wires into a circle, making a bracelet. Tiny words are printed along the red wire, so small I can barely see them.

"Give me your hand."

I raise my arm obediently, then hesitate, drawing it closer to me. Doc snatches my wrist before I have a chance to object and slips the bracelet wi-com over my hand. He tightens it quickly—not enough to cut off my circulation, but enough to stop it from slipping off my wrist. Before I can say anything, Doc secures the wires with a metal cinch.

"You'll have to hold it to your mouth to speak," he says. "And then hold it to your ear to hear coms. There's an amplifier there." He points to the tiny black mesh that circles the button. This whole thing is smaller than the earbuds I used when I went running before school, but it's clearly far more powerful. When Doc tests it by sending me a com link request, it beeps loudly enough for me to hear from my wrist. Intrigued, I raise my hand to my ear and listen to the tiny electronic voice of the wi-com say, "Com link req: Doc."

"You made this?" I ask, awed.

Doc hesitates. His unease is so unnatural that I stop staring at the bracelet wi-com and instead turn my gaze to his nervous face. "No," he says finally. "I didn't make this. I found it."

"Where?" I ask. Dread wriggles through my veins like worms writhing in mud.

"In the Recorder Hall."

I glance down at the wi-com on my wrist in revulsion. All I can think about is the angry, spiderweb scar that marred the side of Orion's head, just under his left ear. I imagine the wires braided around my wrist being ripped from his flesh, dripping in blood and gore. "This was *his?*" I hiss.

Doc nods. "I found it among his possessions. He altered it himself. I don't know why he kept it, even—but the design works perfectly." Doc pauses. I didn't know it was possible, but he looks even more uncomfortable as he meets my eyes. "There was . . . a note. He made this wi-com specifically for you."

"For me?" I ask, peering down at the thing entwined around my wrist.

"He wrote that he feared for your safety, if something happened to him and the Eldest system faltered, as he thought it would. As it did."

I don't know what to do with this information. That Orion, who tried to kill my father, who *did* kill other people from Earth, helpless, frozen, and defenseless, that he would care enough about me to remake his wi-com . . . A twisted sort of emotion, part gratitude, part revulsion, snakes around my insides.

"Not that I really want a wi-com, but can't you just make another one? A *new* one? One that wasn't under someone's *skin?*"

"We don't have unlimited resources. There are more babies coming than we have wi-coms ready for, and the Shippers are already scrambling to make more. Besides which, I can't program a used one for a baby; it runs a greater chance of wearing out over time."

I fiddle with the metal clasp, trying to get the blasted thing off.

Doc's hand twitches, but he doesn't reach out to stop me. Instead, he says, "Amy, you need a wi-com. It's this or get one implanted."

"You can't make me—" I start.

"No," he says, "but Elder can. And we both agree—and you know it too—that you need to be able to call for help if . . ."

My hand stills. *If.*

Frex. He's right.

Doc nods, satisfied that I'm not going to rip the thing off and throw it away. "Well. I just wanted to give you this. Let me know if . . . if you need anything." He walks away, shutting the door behind him.

But me, I remain as frozen as when I lay in the glass coffin and the ice stilled my beating heart.

Frex is one of *their* words.

I am not one of them.

I, with a wi-com on my wrist, am not one of them.

I'm not.

I'm not.

5
ELDER

The words take a long time to sink in. "We're . . . stopped?" I say. I scan the Shippers' faces, hoping for some hint that this isn't true, but the grim set of Marae's jaw is evidence enough for me.

Oh, *frex*. How am I going to tell Amy *this?*

"How long have we been stopped?" My voice rises. I sound like a tantrum-throwing child, but I can't help it.

"We're . . . not sure. For some time. Maybe since the Plague." Marae bites her lip.

"There was no Plague," I say automatically. She knows this; she's just used to calling the mutiny that happened so many gens ago the Plague, perpetuating the lie the Eldest system is based on.

Behind me, the ship's heartbeat continues: *whirr-churn-whirr*. "How can we not be moving?" I ask. "The engine is still working." Even to me, I sound desperate, a child refusing to believe the fairy tales aren't real.

"We've been diverting energy since the Eldest system began, actually. We need it for the internal function of the ship. The solar lamp alone isn't strong enough anymore."

I force myself to meet Marae's eyes. "So where are we?"

Marae shakes her head, thrown off by my question. "What do you mean?"

"How far away are we from Centauri-Earth? If we've been stopped for . . . for so long, then our projected planet-landing is . . . inaccurate, to say the least. So, how far away are we?"

"We don't know," Marae says. "We cannot be concerned with planet-landing now. We have to hold *Godspeed* together."

The authority in her tone—the way *she* has given *me* an order—claws up my spine. "Here's what we're going to do," I command. "One of you will be assigned to navigation. Exclusively. If we know how far away we are, we'll know how big a fix we need to do on the engine. Maybe we can make the ship limp along, long enough to reach the planet. Maybe eventually we'll have to discuss more drastic measures." I level my gaze on Marae. "But we *are* going to focus more on making this ship actually reach Centauri-Earth."

Second Shipper Shelby opens her mouth to speak, but Marae throws her hand up first to stop her. "I'll do it myself," she says, "but first, we want to make a *request* of you."

The way she says "request" makes it feel much more like a demand, but I nod anyway.

"We want the Feeders to be put back on Phydus."

My hand slips into my pocket. For a moment, I wonder if Marae knows that I've carried the wires from the Phydus machine with me every day since Amy ripped them out three months ago.

"*No*," I say, firmly, as much to myself as to them.

"It wouldn't be hard to fix the Phydus machine," Marae says. "In fact, Second Shipper Shelby has already done a preliminary repair report—"

Marae holds her hand out, and Shelby gives her another floppy already flashing with a mechanical diagram.

I glance down at the floppy. It would be an easy fix. An easy fix—and an easy solution. A little bit of Phydus—maybe not even as much as Eldest used before . . . we could eliminate a lot of the conflicts we're having . . . get people back to working without fuss . . .

"No," I say adamantly, my voice low. "We're not using the pumps."

"It doesn't have to be through the pumps," Marae says. "Doc's been working on some med patches for us using the Phydus compound."

I cut her off. "No one *needs* Phydus."

Marae's lips tighten. She reaches across me and swipes her finger across the top of the floppy. The mechanical diagrams are replaced with a line chart. "Productivity decreased by ten percent the first week the Feeders were off Phydus. It's down to nearly thirty percent now, and there seems to be no indication that it will rise again." She offers me the floppy, but I don't take it. "Our food supplies are dangerously low. This is a primary concern, but we're running out of other necessities, such as clothing, as well."

I open my mouth to speak, but she continues in an even voice. "We have crime now. Never had it before. But now we do. Domestic violence, theft, vandalism. With Phydus—"

And there it is. Doubt. They trust the drug more than me.

"I'll take care of the people," I say, my voice firm. "You take care of the ship."

"But Eld—Eld*er*," Marae says, resting one slender hand on my arm. "Why bother? They don't need to be anything but workers. We don't need them to be anything else."

"I understand what you're saying." I grip the edges of the floppy.

I don't tell her that I've thought of all of this before.

I don't tell her that's why I carry the wires to the Phydus machine around in my pocket every day.

Instead, I say, "What we need is a police force. Like they had on Sol-Earth. I need people who I can trust, who can help me ensure that everything runs smoothly."

Marae stands straighter. "A poe-leez force?"

This time, I'm the one who swipes the floppy and starts tapping on the screen. After a moment, I hand her an article about police and social sciences. She scans it briefly, then hands it to Shelby.

"Basically, I need people who can help enforce the rules. Investigate crime, stop people from doing wrong. If there's trouble, I'll need backup."

"The Shippers have always been obedient to the Eldest system. We will make sure the system does not fail. In whatever capacity it becomes." She means: she's willing to try using police instead of Phydus. I'm not confident enough in her words or my position to ask what will happen if my latest suggestion fails.

I know the first-level Shippers better than nearly anyone else on this ship, even though I've only worked with them in the months since Eldest died. I can read their faces. Haile and Jodee and Tailor are nodding along with Marae, eager to accept this role. Prestyn, Brittne, Buck, and even Second Shipper Shelby look wary. I know they will follow Marae, though, even if they wouldn't follow me. And while Marae sometimes still tries to boss me around because I'm younger, she never truly forgets my position as Eldest, even if I won't take the name.

This might just work.

And, as soon as I think that, Shelby makes a noise of surprise. We turn to her. In her hands is the floppy she'd taken earlier. She holds it out first to Marae, but then she thinks better of it and hands it to me. The Shippers break their ordered line and crowd around me as I read the giant white words flashing across the black screen.

DO NOT ACCEPT THE OPPRESSION OF THE ELDEST SYSTEM

THERE IS NO LEADER

LEAD YOURSELF

"Someone has hacked into the floppy network," Marae growls. Her fierce eyes meet mine. "Is this what you meant by needing a poe-leez force?"

"Yes." My voice lacks her passion. These words flashing across the screen say I am nothing, and for the first time since Eldest died, I think they may be right.

Marae slides the floppy from my fingers and tries to swipe the screen clear. The last two words—**LEAD YOURSELF**—grow larger, filling the whole screen. Marae slides her fingers across the screen again. Nothing happens.

"Frex!" I've never heard her curse before.

The Shippers gather close to the screen. They look worried—Haile and Jodee start whispering to each other, and Brittne's hand moves to her wi-com. Shelby's eyes keep reading the phrase over and over, mouthing the words silently.

"Calm down," Marae snaps, and I—and every Shipper—focus our attention on her. "This is our first task as poe-leez. And we will *not* fail the Eldest."

She hands the floppy to Fourth Shipper Prestyn. "This is a good hack," he says after a moment of examination. "I'll get my group started on breaking it right away."

Marae nods curtly, and Prestyn heads to the door, already barking orders into his wi-com.

"I'll check all our security feeds," Second Shipper Shelby says.

"And we'll need to start researching methods to add increased security to the floppy network," Marae says. The rest of the Shippers break away from the group, a buzz of activity already drowning out the sounds of the churning engine behind me.

Marae touches my elbow and draws me aside. I can still see the bright white words on the floppy, mocking me.

"What are you going to do, Elder?" she asks.

I meet her eyes. "I really don't know."

6
AMY

THIS WI-COM IS SUPPOSED TO CONNECT ME TO THE SHIP, BUT all it does is make me feel even more *disconnected* from my past. But . . . I *do* need it, like Doc said. Because I'm not safe here.

My hand clenches around my wrist. The bruises are long gone, but other hands once held my wrists, forcing me down to the ground. . . .

I release my hand and suck in a huge breath of air. I won't let myself think of that. I can't let myself think of that.

Instead, I look at the wi-com. I imagine the braided wires slithering apart, sliding under my skin, burrowing through my flesh. I'm wearing something that was once *inside* someone else. It's like wearing a tooth on a necklace or making earrings from toenails. It's even worse that it came from Orion. I want nothing more than to rip this thing that was once his off my wrist and destroy it . . . but something stops me.

At least, with the wi-com, I can reach Elder. In the past few weeks, I've seen him less and less—and I get it, really I do, I know he's busy. But . . . I can't help but smile. It *will* be nice to be able to talk to him.

I push the button on the wi-com and say Elder's name. I raise it to my ear, waiting to hear his voice. *Beep!* "Com link denied," a pleasant female computer voice says.

Well, it *would* be nice to talk to Elder. If he'd actually answer my com.

I look closer at the wi-com—small black letters are printed along one of the wires. I wouldn't really notice them if I wasn't inspecting the wi-com so closely. I dig my finger into the braided wires, separating the red wire from the others so I can see the letters more clearly.

It's one phrase, three words repeated over and over and over in tiny print: *Abandon all hope*.

My first thought is, how did Doc miss this? He said he cleaned the wi-com. But, I suppose, this is just another mark of how disturbed—by which I mean downright psycho—Orion was. I wouldn't be surprised if Doc saw the message and gave the wi-com to me regardless—words printed on a wire don't actually change whether or not the stupid thing works. Doc cares more about practicality than whatever leftover bits of Orion's insanity are braided up into the thing.

Beyond that, the phrase is apt. If there's one thing I don't have any more of, it's hope. It's almost like Orion left that message just for me.

And then I realize: he did.

Doc said the wi-com came with a note. It is, in a way, my inheritance.

My mind spins. Orion doesn't have to tell me there's no more hope for me aboard *Godspeed*; I figured that out on my own. But . . . maybe he meant something more . . . Because—I know where this phrase comes from. It is, according to my tenth-grade English teacher Ms. Parker, one of the most recognizable lines in literature, right up there with Rhett not giving a damn about Scarlett and Hamlet waffling on about whether to be or not to be. *Abandon all hope* is the phrase written above the gates of hell in Dante's *Inferno*.

And, since books were pretty much off-limits until Elder took over as ruler of *Godspeed*, that's not something Doc would have known. Of everyone on the ship, I'm probably the only one who knows about books from Earth.

Other than Orion, that is, who spent most of his life hidden in the Recorder Hall with only words and fictional characters for company.

The more I think about it, the more convinced I am. These aren't just some casual words Orion doodled somewhere. "Abandon all hope" is a specific phrase from a specific book written on a wi-com that Orion left specifically for me.

Maybe I'm reading too much into this. It's probably nothing. But I've had "nothing" for far too long, and I'm ready for *something*. Anything. I'd rather go to the Recorder Hall and look up the phrase in Dante's *Inferno* than just sit here and stare at the walls some more. I zip my jacket all the way up, leave my room, and head to the elevator. I'm excited, and my legs want to *run* . . . but instead, when I get outside, I remember how running only makes me more noticeable and walk with my head down and the hood of my jacket pulled up. As I mount the stairs to the Recorder Hall, I glance up out of habit. In a cubby by the door hangs a painting of Elder, one of Harley's last works. This is the closest I've come to seeing Elder in days; the more time that passes, the more wrapped up he is in running *Godspeed*. In a lot of ways, he's more trapped than I am.

Painted Elder peers out from the hall at his enclosed kingdom, and I turn, following the path of his painted eyes.

The solar lamp's glare blinds me for a moment, and in that split second of darkness, I realize something I didn't know before: I don't need to see the landscape to know every inch of the Feeder Level spread out before me. I close my eyes, and I can still see the rolling fields in perfectly spaced hills. I know the precise pattern of colors of the trailers that make up the City on the far side of the ship. I know the exact point in the metal sky when the rivets holding the roof together get so far away, I can't really see them anymore. I know the shape of each painted cloud.

I try to dig into my memories for what my house looked like in Colorado, but I can't remember exactly. The shutters on the windows—were they more brick red or burgundy? What kind of flowers did Mom plant in the front yard?

I know *Godspeed* now better than I can remember Earth.

"Outta the way, freak," a hefty woman says, shouldering past me as she leaves the Recorder Hall. I must look like even more of a freak than normal—wearing a jacket when everyone else has short sleeves, standing in the doorway of the Recorder Hall like an idiot.

A young man, slender and tall, stares at me openly as he follows the woman toward the path leading to the Hospital. I pull my hood farther down. He turns his head to look at me as he steps off the stairs, and something in his eyes makes me turn on my heel and rush into the Recorder Hall.

Godspeed has not just replaced Earth in my mind; it's replaced my home. And it's inhabited with people who hide dark thoughts behind staring dark eyes.

I shake my head, willing thoughts of both my old home and the man to fall from my cluttered mind. There's no use thinking about either.

Inside the Recorder Hall is dark and quiet. There are people here, but they ignore me in a way they wouldn't outside, where the false sunlight streams across my pale skin and the red hair peeking out from under my scarf. They're focused on the information they're seeing and understanding for the first time. They're not concentrating on me.

That's why I like it here.

There are crowds of people at each of the giant digital screens hanging from the walls. Even though Elder has opened up the entire Recorder Hall to everyone on board, most Feeders stick to examining the floppies—if they come at all. Few venture into the rooms past this one, filled with books; fewer still go to the second and third floors to visit the galleries.

Here, each of the wall floppies is labeled with a different subject—**History**, **Agriculture**, and **Science** are the most popular ones. A crowd of nearly a dozen people peer up at a diagram of a nuclear reactor on the *Science* wall floppy, arguing in soft tones about some detail in the schematics.

The least popular wall floppy is *Literature*. Only a handful of young women are scrolling through a copy of Shakespeare's *Romeo and Juliet*. They're struggling with the language more than my classmates did in ninth grade, but I wonder if, when they do get past the *thees* and *thous* and *I bite my thumb at you, sirs*, will they walk away thinking *that* is love? I consider pausing here and telling them about the debate we had in class where I argued that Romeo and Juliet weren't really in love. In ninth grade, I was so sure of myself I won the debate (and a prize of a free homework pass), and I remember shooting down the opposing side so passionately that the entire class was in an uproar. But now . . . now I can't remember a single argument from the debate on either side, and I can think of nothing to say to these people. How can I argue that *Romeo and Juliet* doesn't *really* show love to a group of people who have no concept of what love really is? When *I* don't know what love really is—just what it isn't.

Suddenly, all the wall floppies go black.

"Hey!" one of the girls reading Shakespeare shouts.

"What's going on?" a burly man at the *Agriculture* wall floppy growls.

Giant words in bright white letters scroll across the darkened screens, filling the hall with one phrase, repeated over and over.

LEAD YOURSELF

My eyes widen, and I pull my hood even farther down over my face, so hard that the seams strain against the back of my head. While everyone else is distracted, reading the words and puzzling about how they flashed on their floppies, I rush to the back of the hall, toward the book rooms. Something like this was bound to happen. Elder's been spending all his free time with me in the Recorder Hall, reading up on civics and police forces, but I don't think he really understood that some people are going to want to rebel just because, for the very first time, they can.

"Who did this?" A male voice cuts through the mutterings of the crowd. He sounds wary, scared even, but also aggressive, as if he'd like to find and punish whoever hacked the floppy network.

"What does it mean?" a woman near me says. Her friend shakes her head violently, her hair whipping her cheeks, her eyes wide with fear.

A woman at the *Science* floppy starts tapping the screen, trying to make the message go away. The crowd around her starts whispering uneasily as nothing she does changes the message. Whoever hacked the floppies did a good job, apparently.

"Eldest needs to fix this," the first man says. It takes me a moment to realize he's talking about Elder. Many of the people around him nod, their eyes on the screen, their mouths gaping.

"Those floppies didn't change until the freak walked by," one of the women who had been reading *Romeo and Juliet* says in a clear, loud voice. She starts searching the crowd in the entryway for me. I duck my head and run into the back hall.

I don't breathe until I'm in the fiction room and the door zips shut behind me. There's no lock—hardly any of the rooms on the entire ship have locks—but if I can lie low here, the people in the entryway might eventually forget their anger and forget me.

The fiction room is smaller than the others on this floor; clearly, the ship's makers decided that history and science were more important than novels. I wish it looked more like my library back home, with huge plush beanbags scattered across the floor, dark carpet, posters of famous authors on the walls, and tiny square dusty windows filtering in the sunlight. Instead, the fiction room looks like all the rest—cold and sterile and entirely too clean. It's like a hospital room with books instead of beds: white tiled floor, stark paneled walls, silvery-metal table.

Even though the room is sparkling clean, there is an ever-present scent of dust and old paper rising from the tomes. Everything here is in alphabetical order regardless of subject matter. Chaucer is beside Agatha Christie; J. K. Rowling beside Dr. Seuss beside Shakespeare. When I get to the end of one row and look down the next, I see unreadable titles, some written in languages I can guess at—French, German, Spanish—and some I can't even begin to decipher—Chinese? Korean? Japanese?

I could get lost here, but I need to see if Orion really did leave a clue for me to follow in the phrase printed on my wi-com. I quit wandering among the fairy tales and poetry (Grimm and Goethe) and head to the first row of books, running my fingers along their bumpy spines. I head to the first bookcase, scanning the titles—*The Pilgrim's Progress, Ender's Game, Mousetrap*—until I get to the one I'm looking for.

Inferno, Volume I of the Divine Comedy, by Dante Alighieri, shelved beside a slender volume of Shakespeare's sonnets. Ironic—a book of love poems beside a book about hell. I pull out the poetry collection and toss it on the metal table near the door so it can be reshelved with the *S*s; then I hook my finger on the spine of Dante's *Inferno*.

Just the title makes me remember those weeks in Ms. Parker's English class. I can feel the hard seat of my class desk; I can remember laughing with Ryan and Mike as we worked on our final project.

Funny how a book about hell reminds me of home.

As I slide *Inferno* off the shelf, something slips out, wafting to the floor. I bend over to pick it up—a paper-thin sheet of rectangular black plastic, about the length and width of my open hand. The feel of it reminds me of a floppy, but it's smaller, and there is a fingernail-size bit of raised hard plastic in one corner. I slip it in my pocket; Elder will probably know what it is. I stand back up and reach for Dante again.

The door bursts open. I get a glimpse of a panicked woman's face— eyes wide with fear, dark hair swinging. She races past me to the far side of the room and throws herself behind the last bookshelf.

I run over and drop to my knees beside her trembling body. "What's wrong?" I ask, reaching for her. Now that I have a chance to really look at her, I realize who she is: Victria. Harley and Elder's friend. The girl who writes, stories or novels, I think. The last time I spoke with her, I told her about the sky on Earth and how it never ended, and she spit in my face, denouncing me in front of everyone.

She snatches her hand away. Sweat beads on her face and arms, and she's panting hard. "Luthe—Luthor. He's . . ."

Him.

My stomach drops.

He's the one. The one who held me down three months ago, who used the Season as an excuse to try to rape me. He was like Harley and Elder— aware of the world around him without Phydus dulling his mind. He knew what he was doing when he slammed me to the ground and pressed his weight against me. When he watched hope leave my eyes. When I gave up struggling.

He told me his name was Luthe, but Victria called him Luthor. Like

Lex Luthor, Superman's arch-nemesis . . . but the exploits of a bald super-villain seem comical compared to the evil that lies behind this Luthor's skin. I realize then—Luthe is his nickname. The name his *friends* call him. The idea of calling him that fills me with revulsion. I don't like to think of him in the same terms his friends do.

The door zips open again. Victria whimpers softly, hiding her face. I jump up.

He stands in the doorway, scanning the room.

His eyes lock on me.

And he smiles. Slowly.

Seductively.

7
ELDER

THE DOOR IS LOCKED. JUST THE WAY I LEFT IT.

After—after everything—after
Orion was frozen and
      Amy found out the truth and
            Eldest died and
                  I watched him die . . .

I watched him die.

After all of that, I crawled back up to the Keeper Level. The empty, hollow Keeper Level. And I broke into Eldest's room, and I found his stash of alcohol, and I stayed drunk for two days straight. Then I threw up for two more days, and then I relocked his door, one of the few doors that even has a lock.

And I put a table in front of it.

Now I shove the table out of the way so forcefully that it tips over on one side and crashes to the ground.

Before, the Keeper Level seemed too big, big enough for everyone on the ship to stand in it at one time so they could be lied to while they looked up at the ceiling and gasped at the light bulbs called stars.

When it was Eldest and me, this place felt huge, the space between us filled with emptiness and silence. Now that it's just me, the Keeper Level feels claustrophobically small.

My wi-com beeps. I jab it with my finger to silence it.

And before I can talk myself out of it, before I can walk away and promise to go into his room later—

—I unlock Eldest's door.

Dust particles swirl in the light as I enter. I breathe deeply, expecting to smell Eldest's musky soap, but instead it smells like mildew. My feet stick to the floor. Near the door lies one open and spilled alcohol jar, dried into a gummy mess. That's my mark on Eldest's room.

The room itself is messy and cluttered, but that's the way Eldest kept it. The bed's unmade, the blankets a swirl of cloth at the foot. Spilling out from underneath the bed is a pile of wrinkled clothes. A dirty plate that's still littered with a few crumbs rests perilously close to the edge of his nightstand.

I feel like an interloper, a trespasser in Eldest's private space, but I remind myself that, technically, *I'm* Eldest now, and this is more my room than a dead man's.

On the desk are the scattered remains of a model engine. I pick up the small resin nuclear reactor core, wiping the dust carefully from the surface. The first time I saw the frexing thing was when Eldest hid it from me. I weigh the model engine in my hand. He knew something was wrong, even then. If he had just *told* me the truth from the start, maybe we could have worked together to solve the engine's problems. If everyone would just be frexing honest, we'd probably be at Centauri-Earth by now!

I hurl the model engine across the room. It crashes over Eldest's bed, sprinkling cracked resin across his pillow, still dented from where he laid his head.

Shite.

I rub my hands across my face.

Shite.

With the hacked message on the floppy network and Marae's eagerness to form my police force, I'd pushed from my mind the hardest truth of all.

We're not going anywhere.

Stopped.

Staring at the broken engine bits on Eldest's bed, I realize something. I'm not going to tell the rest of the ship. I'm not. I never thought I'd get tangled up in the lies Eldest wove around *Godspeed* . . . but I can't tell them. I can't tell them we're not just going slowly. We're stopped. If just taking them off Phydus has calls for revolution leaking through the floppy network, then surely they'll rip this ship apart if I tell them we're not going anywhere; they'll tear through the metal with their teeth and let themselves be swallowed into the black of space.

Just like Harley.

I run my fingers through my hair, snagging them on tangles. What am I doing here? Eldest might have suspected we were stopped, but it's not like he hid the secret to reviving the engine in his bedroom.

A floppy on Eldest's desk flashes. The bright white words fade to black. The floppy beeps and reboots itself. After a moment, it shows the start-up screen as normal. Whatever Marae and the first-level Shippers did worked, and the hacker's message is wiped from the screen.

My wi-com beeps again.

I start to answer the com when I notice something—another door. I silence the beeping in my left ear and move toward the door, stepping over piles of Eldest's dirty clothes. Why is there another door here? There's the one to the bathroom, of course, but I've never noticed this one before— I've only been in Eldest's room twice, and both times I was focused on finding something else: first the model engine, and then later the alcohol.

There's a rainbow scratch along the floor; Eldest used this door frequently. My hands shake as I reach toward the old-fashioned knob—it's metal, from Sol-Earth. It won't twist, but when I pull, the door opens anyway. I stare curiously inside.

A closet.

Closets are rare; most bedrooms have wardrobes instead, but I must admit I was hoping for something more here. Disappointed, I turn away, but something catches my eye. A rag pokes out from the top box on the floor of the closet. It's an odd sort of greenish blue, a color I remember in the deepest part of me.

I suck in my breath, then forget to breathe out again. When I reach down and pull the scrap of cloth from the box, my hands are numb.

When I first moved into the Keeper Level, one of the only things I brought with me was a blanket. Small, stained, and worn threadbare in spots. A particular shade of greenish blue.

This blanket was the oldest thing I owned. At the time, I thought that it had come from my parents. As Elder, I was never allowed to know who they were, because otherwise I'd be biased toward them. Or so Eldest told me. In reality, I'm a clone, manufactured, not born.

Eldest had me moved from family to family until I was twelve—six months with the shepherds, six months with the butchers, six months with the soy farmers.

And with all that moving, I never knew which family belonged to me. But the blanket was mine.

My earliest memory is hiding under the blanket when I was told I'd have to move again. I don't remember which family I was with or which I was moving to, but I remember cowering under the blanket and thinking that maybe, when I was a little baby, it had been my mother—my *real* mother—who had wrapped me in it and held me against her.

After the first few days on the Keeper Level, Eldest and I got in a fight, and he called me an impossible child, babied and spoiled. I promptly stormed into my room and punched the walls, knocking everything in sight off my shelf—and then I saw my blanket. The epitome of being a baby.

I'd tried to rip it in half but couldn't, so I chucked it in the trash chute.

And, somehow, Eldest saved this piece of me. Kept it for years. I press it now against my face and think about all Eldest was, and all he wasn't.

The only thing hanging from the rod in the closet is a heavy robe, the ceremonial robe Eldest only wore on important occasions. I drop the blanket back into the box and reach for the robe. It's much heavier than I expected. Definitely wool—I've carded and spun enough from my time before Eldest began training me to recognize the waxy-rough feeling of the cloth. The embroidery spans the entire length and breadth of the robe. Stars dance along the top, crops grow along the hem, and between them is a band of horizon that never ends.

The clasp opens at my touch, and I slide under the robe. The weight of it pushes my shoulders down, makes me hunch over. The hem drags the floor by a good inch or two, and my chest isn't broad enough to fill out the robe; the stars cave in around me.

I look ridiculous.

I pull the robe off and shove it back into the closet.

8
AMY

I HAVE TO GET OUT. I HAVE TO LEAVE. *NOW.* I CAN'T STAY here. Not with him. Escape. Must escape. *Now.* NOW. But there's nowhere to go. He crosses the threshold and is at me in two strides. Luthor draws closer to me, so close that I can feel the heat of his body burning my skin. When I suck in a lungful of air to scream, I suck in some of his exhaled breath too. Luthor reaches toward me, and the scream in my throat dies, choking me and leaving me breathless.

Luthor flips the hood away from my face. He grabs hold of my maroon head wrap, and I jerk away, my hair spilling out over my shoulders. The bookshelf behind me is an unyielding wall. Luthor slides his hand down the side of my face and grabs a fistful of my hair. He yanks it, hard, pulling me closer to him. I strain against his grip. I don't care if he rips the hair out of my head, I am not going to let him control me. I reach behind me and grab two books from the shelf by their spines. As Luthor twines my hair around his hand, forcing me to face him, I whip out the books, slamming them on either side of his head.

"*Augh!*" Luthor shouts, an inhuman roar of pain. He clutches the sides of his head, a string of curse words—some I know, some I don't—following me as I drop the books and duck under his arm.

"Come on!" I yell at Victria, who is still hiding behind the last bookcase. She steps out and I grab her wrist and drag her behind me, out of the fiction room and toward the hall.

Luthor follows quickly, but we've got enough of a head start that we make it to the crowded entrance hall before he reaches us. I stop when we reach the center. The message that had filled all the screens before is gone, and the floppies have returned to normal. A short woman wearing the immaculately starched dark clothing favored by the Shippers stands near the *Science* floppy, deep in conversation with the group that had been studying the engine schematics earlier. A few people look up, startled by our sudden entrance, but for the most part, no one notices us.

Luthor stands with both arms gripping the doorway that leads to the hall, glaring at us. He won't do anything now. Not with everyone else here. It's not the Season anymore; there's no more Phydus. He doesn't have an excuse.

Victria yanks her hand out of my grasp. "Thanks," she mutters, the sound more like a growl.

"Hey!" Luthor's voice echoes throughout the entrance hall. Most people turn to look at him, but Victria dips her head low and hurries for the exit, abandoning me in the center of the hall as Luthor pushes up from the door frame and heads toward me.

"You think you can just walk away from me?" Luthor shouts.

"I know I can," I say, and I actually make it a few steps closer to the exit before he grabs me by the elbow and spins me around.

I scan the entrance hall. Everyone's watching us. A few have drawn closer, and from the worry in their eyes, I can see that they're on the verge of coming to my aid. Still—they hesitate. Because he's one of them. And I'm not.

"Things are different now," I hiss at Luthor, yanking my arm out of his grasp. "You think you can take whatever you want, but you can't."

I step away quickly, determined to escape this room without him laying another finger on me. His laughter rings out, a disgusting sound that sends chills down my spine. "Things *are* different!" he bellows after me. "We haven't got a leader anymore!"

I spin on my heel. "Elder is leader!" My voice is high and loud; it comes out as an angry screech. I can't help but remember the message that flashed across the floppies earlier.

Luthor snorts in contempt. "You think that boy can stop me? You think that boy can stop any of us?" He sweeps his arms wide, indicating the entire crowd of people who are now staring avidly as we scream in the middle of their usually silent hall.

"We can do anything we want," Luthor says in a low voice only I can hear. He grins broadly and looks around him, then lifts his voice in a mighty roar, "We can do anything we want!"

I see it in the faces of the people around us.

The realization that what he's said is true.

9

ELDER

"ELDER?" A VOICE CALLS OUT AS ELDEST'S DOOR ZIPS SHUTS behind me.

"The frex?" I mutter, peering around. No one has access to this level but me.

Red hair swings around the door frame of the Learning Center. "Amy?" I ask, shocked, rushing forward.

She smiles—not a grin, just a gentle curve of her lips that doesn't quite reach her eyes.

"I hoped you'd be here," she says.

"How—how did you get here?"

She steps all the way out of the Learning Center and into the Great Room with me. She raises her left hand.

"Doc gave it to you!" I say, examining the wi-com encircling her wrist.

Amy nods. "I figured . . . it used to be Orion's, so it would probably give me access to the Keeper Level, and . . ." She shrugs. "It did. I tried to com you before, but you didn't pick up. Or did I do it wrong?"

"No, I got some coms that I ignored."

Amy punches me lightly on the shoulder. "Ignoring me, huh?"

"I couldn't if I tried," I say.

She smiles again, another wry twist of her lips with no light behind it. We stand a few feet apart—her near the Learning Center door, me closer to the middle of the Great Room, and the silence falls between us like a tangible, awkward thing. She pulls her necklace out from under her shirt and twists the charm in her fingers.

"What's wrong?" I ask.

"Nothing," she says immediately, dropping the necklace.

I narrow my eyes but let the moment slide by.

"I haven't seen you in a while," she finally says. She hasn't moved away from the Learning Center door, so I move closer to her. She puts one hand in her pocket and looks for a moment as if she's going to pull something out.

"I had to go settle some problems in the City and then . . . on the Shipper Level."

"Now it's my turn to ask you," Amy says, withdrawing her empty hand from her pocket. "What's wrong? Did you see the message that was on the floppies?"

"Yeah," I growl. "The Shippers were able to reverse the hack, but . . ." I shrug, and although I mean to appear nonchalant, even I know the gesture is bitter. "Damage done. I've asked Marae and the first-level Shippers to serve as my police force."

"*Good*," Amy says with such vehemence that I stare at her. "It's just— I'm glad you're finally doing it. Getting police I mean," she adds when she notices my look.

"I should have done it a month ago." I say, then wait for her reaction.

Her hand twitches, as if she'd like to reach out to me, but she doesn't. "You're still not telling me something," she says softly.

Neither are you, I think, but I can tell from the hardness of her eyes that she won't tell me whatever it is that's bothering her. Instead, I confess my truth. About the engines. And the lies. How we're not moving, and we don't even know where we are. I tell her what I haven't told anyone else on board.

"And we can't tell them," I add. "If the Feeders knew . . ."

Amy bites her lip but doesn't argue. For now.

I run my fingers through my hair, trying to pull my answer up through the roots. "We've been stopped a long time. The ship's not going to last forever. It's . . . *Godspeed* is falling apart."

When I say it now, to her, I finally realize the truth. And I finally see the things I've never seen before, and what they really mean. The dwindling food production, despite the fact that we're pumping all the fertilizer and nutrients we can into the fields. It's true that most Feeders haven't been working as hard as they did while on Phydus, but even their lack of productivity can't excuse the way the crops barely have enough strength to push their way up through the soil.

That year when we had so much rain—was it just for research, or did the irrigation system break? The chemically derived meat substitute used in wall food at least twice a week—is it really a better source of nutrition or just the best Doc and the scientists could make when the livestock was no longer enough to feed everyone?

I'm starting to see why Eldest was so . . . so desperate.

I think of the sound of the engine, even if its energy is just being diverted to the internal functions of the ship: that *churn* amid the *whirr*s. It's not a healthy sound.

When I'm done talking, I realize how silent she's been the whole time.

"Amy?" I ask softly.

She meets my eyes.

"Does this mean . . . can I wake my parents up now?"

"What? No!" I say immediately.

"But . . . if we're not going to land—if there's no hope at all that we'll ever land—then, why not?"

"We might still land! Frex, give me a chance to fix this problem."

"Maybe one of the frozens can fix it. There are scientists and engineers frozen too, you know."

"Amy—no. No. My people can handle this."

She mutters something I don't catch.

"What?" I demand.

"It's not like they've done that good of a job so far! Hell, Elder, how long have the engines been dead? Since before you were born! Maybe even decades—or *longer!*"

"I don't need this!" I roar. "Not from you too! I don't need you telling me what to do or that I'm not good enough."

"I'm not *questioning* you!" Amy hurtles the words at me. "I'm just saying, someone from Earth could probably fix this problem!"

"You're just *saying* that we should wake your parents up!"

"This isn't about them!"

"With you, it always is! You can't just wake up your parents because you're a scared little girl!"

Amy glares at me fiercely, an angry flush staining her cheeks. "Maybe if you'd admit you weren't good enough to do everything on this effing ship yourself, you could see that you have people who could actually help you right underneath your feet!"

I know she said it in anger—that I wasn't good enough. But her words *do* hurt, like a hot knife slicing through the center of me. "Haven't you figured out that half my problems are because of *you?* If I didn't have to watch out for the freak, maybe I could get something done!"

As soon as the words slip past my lips, I wish I could grab them with my hands and crush them in my fists.

But I can't.

The words are there.

I've called Amy a freak, the one thing I swore I'd never do.

I was the only person on the whole ship who hadn't called her that.

And now I have.

Amy jerks her head, almost as if the words have struck a blow against her cheek. She spins on her heel and storms toward the Learning Center door—and the grav tube that would take her away from me.

"Amy!" I shout, racing after her. She ducks her head away from me, hair swinging down to cover her face, and darts through the door. I grab her by the elbow, spinning her around and pulling her back into the Great Room. She jerks out of my grasp, but at least she doesn't keep running from me.

"I'm sorry," I say immediately. "I didn't mean that. I'm sorry, I'm sorry, I'm sorry." I raise my hand again, but she flinches from me, and I drop it immediately.

She doesn't meet my eyes.

"You're right," she finally says, blinking rapidly and looking up at the artificial stars.

"No, I'm not, I'm sorry, you're not a freak, you're not."

She shakes her head. "Not about that. About . . . I'm scared," she whispers.

She twists the wi-com round and round her wrist, leaving a red mark.

I've seen her silent before, brooding. There have been times when we'd be talking and she'd suddenly drop from the conversation, retreat within herself for a few moments before returning to me. Before, I'd always thought it had something to do with me—that she'd remembered my betrayal, or I'd said something to trigger a memory of the past she could no longer have. Now I'm wondering if it's something else.

"What's wrong?" I ask, my voice lower, the fight in it gone, replaced with concern.

She jumps at the question.

"Has someone hurt you?" I ask. "Or threatened you?"

I move closer to her. I want to reach out, take her hands in mine, draw her closer to me. But she looks as hard as stone.

10
AMY

WHAT AM I SUPPOSED TO SAY? THAT I STILL HAVE NIGHTMARES about something that happened three months ago? How lame would that sound? If I was going to say something, I should have said it *then*. But then everything else became much more important—Harley and Eldest's deaths, Orion's capture, the elimination of Phydus. Elder has over two thousand people who all have a problem they expect him to fix. How could I burden him with one more from me? If there was anyone I could tell, it would be him—but I can't. I can't. It's not just that three months have passed, or that he's busy with the ship, or that I'm afraid he won't believe me.

It's that, when it happened, he wasn't the one to save me.

And if he couldn't save me then, how can he save me now?

"I could protect you," Elder says, moving closer to me but not meeting my eyes. "You could move in with me . . ." His words fade to silence.

We're so close we could touch. All it would take is for me to reach out my hand. But neither of us makes a move.

"I don't need to," I say automatically. I have control. I don't need to run away and hide. I will *not* let Luthor turn me into a simpering child.

And I don't want Elder to believe he has to take care of me. Because if he thinks I want his protection, he's also going to think I want more.

I start pacing, but it just makes the walls feel closer.

Elder runs his fingers through his hair, making a rumpled mess of it. "You don't have to stay here just to be safe," he finally says, standing up too. "You could stay for—for other reasons. . . . "

"No," I whisper, knowing and dreading what he's going to say next. I can't—I'm not ready—I don't . . . I don't know. I don't know what I want, but I know that I don't want to hear what he's going to say, just as surely as I know he's going to say it anyway.

He grabs my arms, not in an angry grip like before, but in a gentle, soft way that invites me closer to him. I don't move.

"Amy—I—" He looks down, takes a deep breath. "I . . . I care about you. I want you to want to be here." He doesn't quite meet my eyes. "With me."

He lets go of me, raising one hand to brush the hair from my face. I can't help it; I close my eyes and lean into his hand, feeling the warm roughness of his fingers against my cheek. His breath shudders.

I step closer.

I look up, and he's searching my eyes, just like he did after kissing me for the first time in the rain. "What are you looking for?"

He doesn't answer.

He doesn't need to.

I know what he wants.

And it's not fair.

"Just because we're the only two teenagers on this whole ship doesn't mean I have to love you. Why can't I have a choice? Options?"

Elder steps back, stung.

"Look, it's not that I *don't* like you," I say quickly, reaching for him. He jerks away. "It's just . . ."

"Just what?" he growls.

Just that if I was back on Earth instead of on this damn ship, if I had met Elder at school or at a club or on a blind date, if I had my choice between Elder and every other boy in the world . . . Would I love him then?

Would he love me?

Love without choice isn't love at all.

"Just that I don't want to be with you just because there's no one else."

11
ELDER

"BUT . . ."

But she's already gone.

12
A M Y

THE NEXT MORNING, I GO STRAIGHT TO MY PARENTS. I STARE at their icy faces until my eyes hurt, then I squeeze them shut. But whether I see them or not, the truth remains: They are frozen. I am not. And *Godspeed* is stopped.

Stopped.

I force these thoughts from my head. Instead, I try to think of something to say to my parents, some memory I miss. But I can't concentrate. I sigh, stand up, and slam my parents back into their cryo chambers. Nothing's been right since Elder's fight with me, and I can't dwell on both their past and ours.

It's strange. On Earth, I've been called a lot worse than *freak*. But here, that word carries a different meaning, and when shouted at you by one of the few people you trust, it carries a different hurt.

As I straighten, something digs into the side of my leg. I reach into my pocket and pull out the small rectangle of black plastic that I found yesterday in the Recorder Hall. I almost showed it to Elder, but . . . I couldn't. When I got to the Keeper Level, I just wanted to be with him, without ominous messages from Orion to distract us. And then all I wanted was to escape from him.

The black rectangle looks like a small version of a floppy, so I swipe my fingers along the top of it. A glowing box lights up in the middle of the screen. Words flash across it: **RESTRICTED ACCESS**.

I glance up. Without meaning to, I've meandered past the cryo chambers and toward the gen lab on the far side of this level. Beyond that door are vats of genetic material Doc and Eldest used to manipulate pregnancies during the Season, the water pump used to distribute Phydus . . . and Orion. What's left of him. A frozen shell like my parents.

I roll my thumb across the biometric scanner that locks the door to the gen lab and step inside once the door zips open. Someone's placed a chair right beside the closest cryo chamber in the room, facing the thick glass window, like a Father positioning a chair to speak to the bedridden ill. I kick the chair out of the way so that I'm face-to-face with the man behind the glass.

Orion.

"I *hate* you," I say.

His eyes bulge, his fingers claw, but he can't reach me. He can't respond, he can't blink, he can't even move. He's frozen, as good as dead.

But I still hate him.

This is Orion's punishment. For the murders of the frozens and for the death of Eldest. When—if—the ship lands and the other cryogenically frozen people awake, they are to judge him for his murders and do with him as they see fit. That is the sentence Elder laid on him when he pushed the button to freeze him. But I know—in ways that no one else on this ship does—the real punishment is in being frozen. My mind remembers what it's like to be asleep but not asleep. My body recalls the way my muscles wouldn't—couldn't—move. My heart will never forget what it's like to fade in and out of time, to never know if one year or a thousand have passed by, to torture yourself with the idea of your soul trapped behind ice for all eternity.

I know what torture there is behind ice.

Behind the glass window in the cryo tube, I can see the red veins popping in Orion's eyes. I imagine myself mirrored in his pupils, but he's blind. His hand is pressed against the tiny window in the cryo freezing tube. For a moment, I place my warm, living hand over his. Then I glance at his eyes and snatch my hand away.

In my other hand, I still hold the small floppy thing I found in the Recorder Hall. I look at the handprint I left on the glass in front of Orion's face, then back at the box on the screen and the words across it: **RESTRICTED ACCESS**. Some information on the floppy network is restricted—Elder has to use his thumbprint, like on the biometric scanner, to unlock it. I doubt my thumbprint will be enough, but . . .

I press my thumb against the glowing box.

The entire screen lights up.

And I find myself looking into Orion's face.

<<begin video feed>>

On the screen, Orion looks exactly as I remember him just before he was frozen: unkempt dark hair that could do with a wash, eyes that seem oddly kind given his quickness to kill, and an easygoing, friendly curve of his lips that belies the lines in his face. He sits on the bottom of a staircase so large that it extends past him well out of view, up and up. I've never seen that staircase before, a fact I find oddly comforting. I like that there are still some things about *Godspeed* I don't know.

The image wobbles as Orion adjusts the camera.

ORION: If you're seeing this, then something went wrong.

I glance up at the frozen Orion. Yeah, something went wrong. The ship is stopped, Elder's already hiding the truth from everyone else, and I don't know how much longer we can survive.

ORION: I hope that no one ever sees this. I hope that all went as I had planned, that Elder joined my side, and that together we defeated Eldest and started a new system of rule on *Godspeed* based not on tyranny, but on working together.

Orion sighs heavily.

ORION: But I'm not certain Elder's on my side, and I know Eldest isn't, and there's too much at stake to leave anything to chance. I have to have a contingency plan. And Amy—you are my contingency plan.

Orion turns toward me, as if he knew I'd be a little to his left, his eyes boring into mine.

ORION: I hope Elder's the leader I need him to be—that this ship needs him to be. But if he isn't and if I'm . . . well, if I can't be there to help, all that I have left is this video and the hope that you, someone from Sol-Earth, will know what to do. I can't leave this information for just the shipborns. They don't know enough. They can't make a choice about what to do when they only know one thing. But you—Amy—you know both the ship and a planet. You can be objective. You will know which is the greater evil. When you know all that I know, all that Eldest tried to keep hidden, then you will also know what to do.

I stare up at frozen, immovable Orion, then glance back at the screen.

ORION: Amy, you're going to have to make a choice. And soon. Look around you. The Eldest system has been dying for generations. I was not the first Elder to rebel, and Elder won't be the last. Whatever control the Eldests had before is slipping away. The ship is dying. You can see that, can't you? You can see the rust. You can see how the solar lamp isn't as bright as it should be. How the plants take longer to grow . . . if they grow at all. How the only thing that had been keeping the people calm and in check was Phydus. I know Elder. I know he's going to try to rule without Phydus. And nothing could be more dangerous. When the Feeders are off it, when they see what is becoming of their world—then you'll have a true rebellion on your hands.

I think of the way Luthor's voice rang, loud and angry, throughout the Recorder Hall. *We can do anything we want!*

ORION: *Godspeed* won't last much longer. It wasn't designed to last forever. It's a miracle it's lasted as long as it has. Here's the thing—here's why I need you, Amy, and I need you to make the choice that, for whatever reason, I can no longer make. I know you hate, you must hate me.

Orion leans forward, his face filling the entire screen.

ORION: But did you ever ask yourself why I was unplugging frozens now, of all times?

I suck in a shaky breath; I'd forgotten to breathe.

ORION: Why didn't I just wait and let some future gen take care of that problem?

Even though he's on the screen and not really here, I can feel the urgency in his voice all the way deep inside me, in my very bones.

ORION: The choice is coming! And it is a choice. And you—you must decide for everyone.

For a long moment, Orion pauses.

ORION: But I can't tell you what it is. You're going to have to find it.

Orion runs his fingers through his hair, in exactly the same way Elder does when he's worried.

ORION: It took me years to discover the truth, and just as long to accept it. When I met you . . . I know you must hate me because I left people from Sol-Earth to die. . . .

Left them to die? It was so much more than that. He pulled them from their chambers and *watched* them die. There's a big difference there. He killed them.

My eyes narrow so that Orion's recorded face is nothing but a blur. I glance up at the real Orion, frozen behind the glass of the cryo chamber. *You have no idea how much I hate you,* I think. I could lay at his feet everything that's wrong in my life now.

ORION: But Amy, you are so special. You're from Sol-Earth. But you don't have an agenda like the others . . . like your parents. You didn't come here with a mission. You—and only you—will be able to determine what choice needs to be made, if the risks are worth it. I can't trust anyone else to make this choice, not even Elder or those I once counted as friends. I'm going to hide the clues so that only you, someone from Sol-Earth, could find them. Trust no one, Amy. Not Elder, not Doc, not anyone from my past. They're from *Godspeed*, not Sol-Earth. They won't know—they can't know—that there even is a choice to be made.

I don't like the way Orion tells me not to trust Elder. I don't like it at all. But—I think back to yesterday, and the way I have kept my darkest secrets from him. I am already doing what Orion wanted me to do before he asked it of me, and I hate myself a little for that.

ORION: You'll need to begin with the first piece of the puzzle. But here's the thing, Amy. I already gave it to you. So: go find it. Find all the clues I've left for you. And I have to hope that when you do, the choice you make is the right one.

Orion looks straight behind him, then back to me.

ORION: Because you're running out of time.

<<end video feed>>

13
ELDER

I FEEL ALONE.

I don't mean I feel lonely; I mean I feel alone, the same way that I feel the blanket resting on my body, or the feathers of my pillow under my head, or the tight string of my sleep pants twisted up around my waist. I feel alone as if it were an actual thing, seeping throughout this whole level like mist blanketing a field, reaching into all the hidden corners of my room and finding nothing living but me. It's a cold sort of feeling, this.

When I finally get out of bed, the only thing I want to do is to go straight to Amy and demand her forgiveness. Maybe we can at least go back to what we had before our fight, even if all we had was an awkward friendship punctuated by significant silences. I have to figure out what to do about the ship's engines—if anything even *can* be done—but I can't fix the ship without first fixing whatever I broke in Amy.

I'm so intent on this idea that it's not until I'm halfway down the grav tube to the Feeder Level that I remember the look in her eyes as she left me yesterday—a combination of anger and hurt and sad—and I realize that she probably doesn't even want to see me. The solar lamp clicks on as my feet land on the dais under the grav tube. I trudge down to the path. The morning mist evaporates before my eyes.

Instead of going to Amy's room in the Hospital Ward, I veer left to the Recorder Hall. Maybe if I give Marae some of the books I've read on police forces and civics, she'll have a better idea of how to organize the Shippers in this new duty. That's what I tell myself, anyway. But the reality is I dread seeing Amy, knowing that she'll still be mad at me. And that she has every right to be.

I'm surprised that when I enter the Recorder Hall, there are already people here, gathered around the wall floppies in the entryway. Most of them crowd around the *Science* section. Second Shipper Shelby points to the generator in a diagram of the ship's engine as she lectures to the crowd gathered at her feet. She meets my eyes and nods at me. I knew Shelby had, with First Shipper Marae's and my permission, begun a class for interested Feeders on the technical aspects of the ship, but it hadn't occurred to me that these lessons would begin just fifteen minutes after lamp-on.

I hesitate before I go down the hallway into the book rooms. Isn't Shelby's lecture futile? The engine is dead, even if the Feeders don't know it yet. Frex, we're not even sure how far we are from Centauri-Earth. Even if these Feeders *do* garner enough information to get the ship moving again, chances are that they won't see the planet in their lifetimes.

One of the Feeders listening to Shelby rubs her stomach in a slow circle. She's three months pregnant now, but her tunic hides her rounding belly. Her movement, as unconscious as it is, reminds me—that's what this is about. Shelby's lectures aren't meant to solve the engine problem—not really—but to give these people hope.

That's the one thing Eldest did right. He may have lied—but in the end, he gave them a reason to keep going.

That's what everyone's missing now.

I duck silently into the hallway and head to the book rooms. I throw open the door of the room dedicated to works on civics and social studies.

"What the?" someone shouts from inside.

I jump back, startled, my heart racing. "You scared the shite out of me!" I exclaim, collapsing in the chair at the table across from Bartie.

Bartie's laughing too hard at his own response to reply. For a moment, this feels like old times. Bartie and I were friends when I lived in the Hospital for the year before moving to the Keeper Level with Eldest. There was a whole gang of us, then: Harley, Bartie, Victria, Kayleigh, and me, counting my lucky stars that, for the first time ever, I had friends.

We would spend our days in the Hospital or the garden. Harley would paint while Bartie played guitar and Victria wrote. Kayleigh was always flitting around, trying to tinker with everything. She made a metal canvas stretcher for Harley that nearly bit his fingers off, and she once tried to figure out the old Sol-Earth schematics for an electric guitar that very nearly electrocuted Bartie.

Those times were all laughter and happiness.

The smile slips off my face, and Bartie's grin fades. I don't have to look at him to know we're both thinking the same thing: everything changed after Kayleigh died. Kayleigh was the glue that held our friendship together, and with her gone, we were nothing. Harley spiraled into darkness that only Doc's meds got him out of. By the time he'd started recovering, I'd moved to the Keeper Level, and Bartie and Victria had drifted in different directions. Victria spent her time in the Recorder Hall with Orion, and Bartie, as far as I could tell, found friendship only in his music.

"How have you been?" I ask, leaning forward.

Bartie shrugs. A stack of books surrounds him, but they're all thick, regal-looking tomes from the civics section of the book room, not music books.

"It's odd to see you without Amy," Bartie says.

"I—it's just—we—" I heave a sigh, running my fingers through my hair. Amy and I have spent a lot of time lately in the Recorder Hall, in this very room, actually, developing a plan for a police force. I know she's wary of me, hesitant to trust me after I confessed to being the one to have woken her up, but . . . she'd quit flinching at my touch, she used to smile at me easier.

Until I called her a freak.

Frex.

"Everything okay?" Bartie asks, a hint of real concern in his face.

"Yeah," I muttered. "It's just . . . Amy . . ."

Bartie frowns. "There are more problems on this ship than a freak from Sol-Earth."

"Don't call her a freak!" I say, snapping my head up to glare at Bartie so violently my neck cracks.

Bartie leans back in his chair, throwing up both hands in a gesture of either defense or dismissal. "I was merely pointing out that you have more important things to worry about."

My eyes narrow, reading the title of the thick book Bartie had been scrutinizing. On the cover is a woman with skin paler than Amy's and a dress so wide I doubt she'd fit through the doorway. I read the title—a history of the French Revolution.

"Why are you reading that?" I ask. I try to laugh in a genial sort of way, but the sound comes out like a garbled snort. I look at Bartie with new eyes, wary eyes. A lot of time has passed since we would follow Kayleigh and Victria to the Recorder Hall and race rocking chairs across the porch.

And the French Revolution isn't a topic I would have thought Bartie would study.

Was he interested in the frea—I stop myself from even thinking the word—was he interested in the *unusual* woman on the cover of the book? Or was he interested in the guillotine cutting off the king's head? I mentally shake myself. I'm being paranoid.

"Food," Bartie says.

"Food?"

He nods, pushing the volume closer to me and picking up a slender book bound in green leather. "I thought it was . . . interesting. That 'let them eat cake' bit—I wonder if they would have even revolted if there hadn't been the shortage of food."

"Maybe they were just revolting from dresses like that," I say as I point to the voluminous swaths of silk pouring off the woman's skirt on the cover of the book. I'm trying for levity again, but Bartie's not laughing and neither am I—my mind is remembering the red line in the chart Marae showed me, the line that showed the decreasing food production. When the rest of the ship sees how quickly the food's disappearing—that the ship is dead in the empty sky, and that soon we will be too—how long will it be till they, like the people in Bartie's book, turn their farm tools into weapons and revolt?

Bartie doesn't answer me, just flips open the smaller green book. His eyes don't move over the letters, though, and I get the feeling he's waiting for me to say or do something. I'm not so sure I'm just being paranoid anymore.

"Something's going to have to change, and soon," Bartie says, his eyes on the book. "It's been building for months, ever since you turned them."

"I didn't—" I say automatically, defensive even though there was no real accusation in his voice. "I just . . . I mean, I guess I changed them, but I changed them *back*. To what they're supposed to be. What they are."

Bartie looks doubtful. "Either way, they're different now. And it's getting worse."

The first cause of discord, I think, *is difference.*

Bartie turns the page of the slender green book. "Someone's got to do something."

The second cause of discord: lack of a strong central leader.

What does he think I've been doing? Shite, all I do these days is run from one problem to the next! If it's not a strike in one district, it's complaints from another—and every problem is just a little worse than the one before it.

Bartie glares at me. There's no question about it now: there's contempt and anger in his eyes, although his voice remains soft-spoken. "Why aren't you stepping up? Why aren't you keeping the order? Eldest might've been a chutz, but at least you didn't have to worry about getting through the day when he was in charge."

"I'm doing what I can," I protest.

"It's not enough!" The words bounce around the room, slamming into my ears.

Without thinking about it, I pound my fist onto the table. The noise startles Bartie; the shock of it makes me forget my anger. I shake my hand, pain tingling up my arm.

"What are you reading?" I growl.

"What?"

"What are you frexing reading?"

When I glance up, Bartie's eyes meet mine. Our anger melts. We're friends—even without Harley, we're still friends. And even if the ship hasn't exactly been a friendly place lately, we can still hold onto our past.

Bartie lifts the smaller book for me to see the title: *The Republic,* by Plato.

"I read that last year," I say. "It was confusing as frex. That bit about the cave made no sense at all."

Bartie shrugs. "I'm at the part about aristocracy." He pronounces it "a-risto-crazy." Eldest told me it was "ah-rista-crah-see" but he probably got it wrong too, and besides, what's the difference?

I know the part he's talking about well—it was the center of the lesson Eldest had prepared for me. It was also, essentially, the base of the entire Eldest system. "An aristocrat is someone born to rule," I say. "Someone born with the innate talent to guide everyone else."

Bartie can't be thinking what I'm thinking: that the only reason I was born to rule was because I was plucked as an embryo from a tube full of other genetically enhanced clones whose DNA had been modified to make the ideal ruler.

"But even Plato says that the ideal state of an aristocracy can decay," Bartie says.

The word *decay* reminds me of the entropy Marae mentioned, how everything is constantly spinning out of control, including the ship. Including me.

"An Eldest is like an aristocrat," Bartie adds. He's searching my eyes now, the book forgotten, as if he wants me to pick up some deeper meaning to what he's saying. I pull my mind away from the broken engine and Marae's lies and back to the conversation at hand.

"But the Eldest system isn't decaying," I say. "It works. It is working."

"You're not Eldest," Bartie points out. "You're still Elder."

I shake my head. "In name only. I can rule without taking on the title."

"Titles confuse me." Bartie picks up *The Republic* again, closing it and staring at the cover. "This book talks about aristocracy and tyranny like they're two different things, but I don't see a difference." He slides it across the table. "There are other forms of government, though."

"What are you saying?" I ask warily.

Bartie stands and so do I. "You don't have to be alone in this," he says. "Look at the reality of the situation. Even if you are the one aristocrat on this ship, the one leader—you're sixteen years old. Maybe you will be a great leader . . ."

"Will be?" I growl.

He shrugs. "People don't respect you now. Maybe in another five or ten years."

"People respect me because of what I am!"

Bartie drops the book on the table; its thud echoes on the metal surface. He heads toward the door, shouldering past me when he nears. "You've given us all the chance to think, to choose for ourselves what we want." His voice is quiet, almost a whisper. "I respect *that*. But you've got to realize that maybe, when we've had a chance to think about it, we're not going to choose you as our leader."

Bartie picks up two books from the table—the history of the French Revolution and a book from the science room, *Technical Instruction on Communication Systems*. He abandons Plato's *Republic* on the table and carries the other books across the room without speaking. When the door zips closed after him, though, it feels as if there are a lot of words drifting through the silence he leaves behind.

The last cause of discord. Individual thought.

He has no idea that I haven't slept a full night in three months. That I do nothing *but* try to figure out how to keep a ship full of angry, passionate, self-aware people from self-destruction. That now, on top of everything else, I have the dead engine to worry about. All he sees is my failure.

If I can't rule without Phydus, that's all any of them will ever see.

Failure.

For giving them back their lives and not being able to save them from themselves.

When I step back outside, I have to blink to adjust to the brightness. Everything seems calmer here, more still, almost reverent. The Recorder Hall wasn't loud, exactly, but it wasn't quiet, either.

Something catches my gaze. I turn slowly.

Beside the door to the Recorder Hall is a painting, a portrait of me, held in a place of honor. It was one of the last paintings Harley ever made.

And someone's shredded it.

It looks as if a giant claw of knives ripped through the canvas—five long gashes slice through my face and chest, spilling out strings and dried paint like bleeding wounds. The background behind me in the painting—a mirror of *Godspeed*'s fields and farms—is mostly untouched. Whoever did this took care to dismantle my face and leave the rest of the painting unharmed.

And it wasn't like this when I entered the Recorder Hall. Whoever did this waited for the perfect opportunity—to make sure I saw, and to make sure I knew it was done when I was nearby.

I force myself to turn. My eyes dart around the fields and down the path. There's no one here. The vandal fled already . . . or simply strolled into the Recorder Hall to fade among the crowd, watching me as I walked past.

14
AMY

BACK IN MY ROOM, I CAN'T QUIT PACING. ORION LEFT CLUES—
for me? About something important, something life or death, apparently.
Could it be about the death of the ship? The stopped engines?

And—how has he already given me the first clue?

I stop pacing and stare at my bedroom wall, catching sight of the chart
I'd painted there. It's been three months since Elder stopped Orion from
murdering the frozens in the military. Before that I'd tried to identify the
murderer by painting the list of victims on my wall. I trace the sloppy
letters, the paint so thick that the edges leave tiny shadows on the white
wall. Thin lines of black drips have dried like witches' fingers reaching for
the floor. One line is longer and thicker than the others. It cuts through
the dusty ivy Harley had once, long ago, painted for his girlfriend, whose
room this once was.

Black scrawls on a dirty wall. That is all Orion ever gave me, other
than the bodies of victims.

I close my eyes and breathe deeply, remembering the way the paint
smelled as I dipped Harley's paintbrush into it.

Paint.

Harley.

That's what Orion gave me. The only thing he ever really gave me. Harley's last painting. When Harley was in the cryo level, piecing together bits of wire so he could open the hatch and slaughter himself in the vacuum of space, he gave his last finished painting to Orion—who gave it to me. After Harley's death, I was too sad to look at it and asked that Elder take it to Harley's room for me.

Which is where it must still be. . . . I race out of my room and down the hall. Harley's room is easy to find—smudges of color create a rainbow path straight to his door.

His room smells of dust and turpentine, like old mistakes. The slats over his window stream artificial light over a small plant in a homemade pot that has long since died. Speckles of dust glitter in the bars of light.

It feels like a violation, stepping into this room. My hand lingers by the door frame, my thumb still resting on the biometric scanner.

I step inside slowly, still holding onto the door frame with one hand, reluctant to dive fully into this den of Harley's past. My fingers slide from the wall to the dresser pressed against it, leaving four shiny paths in the dust on top. Is this three months worth of dust, or more? I never saw Harley in his room, only saw him leaving it once as we passed in the hall. I cannot picture him in it now. It is too small, too cramped. This is more like storage than a home.

But Harley was an artist, a true artist, and his storage is more precious than anything I've seen in a museum. Canvases are stacked against the wall. I flip through a row of them, all facing the room. One is nothing but splatters of paint and black ink, an experiment failed, I think. There's another koi fish, the same kind of painting Harley did for me, but this one is more cartoonish and less realistic, with lighter colors that would be pastel if they weren't so brightly clashing.

The last painting faces the wall, but even before I turn it around, I see the rips in the canvas, ragged edges leaking threads.

It's a painting of a girl. There's a smile on her lips, but none in her deep and watery eyes. She looks like she's just emerged from a bath or a swimming pool; her hair is dripping wet, and droplets leave dark stains trailing down her face.

The cuts on the canvas were made in anger—they're jagged and rough. Someone—Harley?—has gone back and tried to repair the canvas, but no one could put her face back together again.

Kayleigh. It has to be. My fingers run down the thick paint of her hair. This is the girl Harley lost, the one that made him lose himself.

Suddenly, I feel like a trespasser, violating Harley's sanctuary. It doesn't matter that he's gone: this room is still *his*, and I do not belong.

I came for the painting. I should get it and go. I scan the room, looking for the one painting that belongs to me. There, *there*, under the window— the black black sky. The silver-white sprinkles of stars. The orangey-gold koi swimming around his ankle. Harley.

I rush across the room toward the canvas, and my hip knocks into a ruler on the edge of the table, sending the papers stacked on top of it flying. I drop to my knees and try to gather as many as I can. I can see sketches—a girl swimming, a girl floating, an empty pond filled with belly-up fish—but while I want to take my time and look, really look, at the drawings, I feel like I shouldn't, that it's forbidden to even be touching them.

"What are *you* doing here?" a voice hisses from the doorway, and all my fears are confirmed. The wrongness of being in this room tugs at my navel.

I look up. Victria is outlined by the light of the hall. She steps inside, and a blanket of shadows falls over her.

"Well?" From the angry impatience of her voice, I can tell that whatever happened between us in the library doesn't count. What counts is that I've violated the sanctity of one of her only friends' rooms.

She clutches a small leather-bound book so tightly that her knuckles are white. I can't understand this girl—she hates me for telling her about the sky; she ignores the fact that I saved her from Luthor; she despises me for just being in Harley's room.

"You shouldn't be here," she spits out.

"I know—I—"

Victria crosses the room and snatches the papers from my hand, gripping them so forcefully that the thin sheets crumple and a few rip. "These aren't yours!"

My eyes narrow. "This is." I draw the canvas closer to me. It *is* mine.

"Whatever." She gingerly starts to pick up Harley's scattered drawings. I could not be more clearly dismissed.

I start to leave, lugging the canvas with me. When I turn around at the door, Victria's ignoring me. She's replaced the papers on the table and is smoothing one down. I glance over her to see the sketch. It's supposed to be Elder, I think, but he looks older, and there's a smirk on his charcoal lips that I've never seen on Elder's real lips. It's odd for Harley's drawings not to be spot-on.

She doesn't notice me as I step closer. I have never seen that look of longing on Victria's face before. I haven't seen it on anyone before—except when Harley told me about Kayleigh.

"Victria?" I ask.

She jumps, jerking her hand and sending Harley's sketch of Elder skidding across the table. "You have your painting, now go!"

I study her face. Her eyes flick once more to the table and the drawing, betraying the love I see hidden there.

I go without saying another word.

It's not until I'm back in my room, dipping the brush into the thick white paint, that I realize the sketch wasn't of Elder at all. The wrinkles at his eyes, the crooked twist of his lips—that had to be Orion.

15

ELDER

Doc coms me as I leave the Recorder Hall.

"Where are you now?" he asks.

"Recorder Hall."

"Good. Come out to the wall near the garden."

"Why?"

"I can't explain it. Just come on out."

"But—I wanted to speak with . . ."

"Speak with Amy?" he asks, biting off each word.

Yes. I did. All Bartie's outburst and the slashed painting have done is remind me that Amy is one of the few people on this whole frexing ship who isn't waiting for me to fail. I *have* to apologize—again—for calling her a freak. I want to tell her that I don't care what she needs to feel safe on *Godspeed*, I'll give it to her. I want to tell her that if the only thing that will bring the smile back to her eyes is waking up her parents, maybe we should do it. And even if I know I can't actually tell her that last bit, I want to look her in the eyes and make sure she knows that I would if I could.

My silence is answer enough for Doc.

"Elder, this is your *job*. You can't decide when you're Eldest and when you're not. You. Are. *Always*. Eldest. Even if you don't take the title." Ah. There's the berating I'd been waiting for.

I sigh. "Fine. Be there soon."

Doc's apprentice, Kit, meets me in the garden. Doc didn't want to take on an apprentice, but he's of the age that he will need a replacement, and I insisted. Of all the nurses that applied for apprenticeship, Kit was the best. Not the best with medicine—Doc constantly complains about what a slow learner she is—but she's the best with the people, and I decided that Doc needs someone more human beside him as he works. Doc wasn't happy with my decision, but he accepted it.

"Thank you," Kit says. "We just weren't sure what to do."

"What's going on?" I ask, following her down the path, past the hydrangeas and the pond to the metal wall behind the garden.

Doc crouches on the ground, for once negligent about the dirt and grass stains that must be seeping into his pants.

A woman kneels in front of the wall. She looks a little like some of the pictures of people praying on Sol-Earth—her hands rest on the ground, palms up, and her body bends forward, her face resting on the metal wall.

"She won't get up," Doc says.

I squat down beside her. "What's wrong with her?"

Doc shakes his head. "She just won't get up."

I put my hand on the woman's back. She doesn't flinch—she doesn't acknowledge my presence at all. My hand creeps up to her shoulder, and I apply as gentle pressure as I can until her body weight shifts back. She leans away, sitting on her ankles.

I know her.

I try to know everyone on the ship, but I can't. There are too many of them, and no matter how hard I try, I can't know them all. But I do know this woman.

Her name is Evalee, and she works in the food storage district in the City. I stayed with her family when I was a little kid; I don't remember exactly when. I don't think she was on Phydus when I lived with her family, but she definitely was on it later, when I visited her before moving to the Keeper Level. Even so, she was always kind to me. She put salve on my hand when I burned it while learning how to can string beans, and she ignored the way I cried even though I was old enough to know that such a small burn didn't deserve tears.

"Evie," I say. "It's me. Elder. What's wrong?"

She looks at me, but her eyes are as dead as if she was still drugged. Deader. Evie doesn't turn away as she reaches one hand up and scratches against the wall in front of her.

"No way out," she whispers.

She turns her head, slowly, to the wall. Like a child sinking into her pillow, Evie rests her face against the metal. Her fingernails scrape slowly down the wall, so softly I can barely hear it. Her hand hits the dirt and relaxes, palm up.

Doc watches us with a grim expression on his face. I look up at him.

"What's wrong with her?"

Doc's mouth tightens as he breathes a heavy sigh through his nose, then he speaks. "She's one of my depression patients. She went missing yesterday; I think she was just walking along the wall until she got exhausted and wound up here."

I glance at Evie's feet. They are stained reddish brown, even in the arches, and dark lines of mud cake under her toenails.

"What can we do?" I ask. But what I really want to know is: Will everyone else react this way when they find out that the ship is stopped? I always thought the worst that could happen was a rebellion, but this dead-inside depression makes me feel hollowed out too. Would it be better for us to rip the ship apart in rage or silently scratch at the walls until we simply quit breathing?

Doc glances at his apprentice. Kit reaches into the pocket of her laboratory coat and pulls out a pale green med patch.

"This is why I commed you," Doc says as Kit hands the patch to me. "I've developed a new med patch for the depression patients."

I turn the patch over in my hand. Doc makes them himself, with the help of some of the Shippers in the chem research lab. Tiny needles adhere to one side like metal filings stuck to tape; when you press the patch into your skin, the needles stick to you and inject medicine directly into your system.

"So use it," I say, handing it to Doc.

Doc takes the patch, holding it carefully. "I have to ask you—I wanted you to see why it's necessary, but then I have to ask you—I made the patches using Phydus."

I stare at Doc. Phydus? I'd told him to destroy all the stores of the chemical. Clearly he hasn't—and he doesn't fear me enough to lie and say he has.

But he does have enough chutz to ask my permission before using it.

Kit shifts nervously behind us. Even Doc looks worried about my reaction to the illicit drug. Only Evie, her face mashed against the metal wall, her feet muddy and calloused, doesn't care.

"Use it," I say, standing. Doc rips the med patch open, and I can hear the sigh of submission from Evie as the chemical seeps into her system.

Doc asks her to stand and follow him to the Hospital, and she silently obeys.

I trail behind them. Evie's emptiness was worse than the mindlessness I'd seen in the Feeders when they were still on Phydus. I think back to Amy's dull, Phydus-drugged eyes—Doc said she had a bad reaction to it. Is Evie having a bad reaction to being off it?

"Take her up to one of the rooms on the fourth floor," Doc tells Kit.

I shoot Doc a look as Kit walks Evie to the elevator.

"The fourth floor just holds regular patient beds now," Doc says firmly. He knows what I'm thinking—about the grays, and the clinical way Doc killed them under Eldest's orders to make room for more younger people. "Would you like me to give you my weekly report now, while you're here? We can go to my office."

I nod and follow him silently into the elevator. When it reaches the third floor, we both get off, leaving Kit and Evie to continue to the fourth floor. Doc leads me to his office. I pause at one door—Amy's. I want to turn right and go to her. I just want to give her my apology over and over until she accepts it. But instead, I turn left and enter Doc's office.

"The Hospital's been so busy lately," Doc says. "This is the first time I've had a chance to come to my office in two days. I'm sorry for the mess."

I snort. The office looks immaculate, but that doesn't stop Doc from immediately straightening the papers on his desk.

The Hospital *has* been busier than usual, though. Bruises and cuts from fights. Injuries from farm equipment when the operators were distracted from their jobs by senseless daydreaming that never would have happened had they still been on Phydus. A few people just doing stupid things to show how much chutz they had. And some . . . some pretty strange cases. Where people hurt themselves or each other, just because they suddenly had the capacity to feel, and they didn't care what they felt as long as it was something.

Amy said that she could mark how quickly the effects of Phydus wore off the Feeders by how many more people would come to the Hospital each day.

My gut twists at the thought of Amy. She's just down the hall, probably sitting in her room, hating me.

"My report," Doc says, sliding a floppy across the desk as he sits down.

Before I look at it, I say, "Will Evie be okay?"

Doc nods. "The Phydus patch is just like any other med patch—it's just that the meds inside it are a variation of Phydus. It's strong enough to act quickly, but I've also developed an antidote patch, just in case."

I'm still hesitant about using Phydus in any form, but at least there's an antidote. I let the subject drop.

For a moment, I consider telling Doc what I now know about the ship, how we're stopped. If Eldest had known, he would have told Doc. But I'm not Eldest, and Doc's not my friend. Instead of speaking, I examine the report Doc handed me.

SHIP HEALTH EVALUATION REPORT

Previous ship population: 2,298

Current ship population: 2,296

Fluctuations in population: -2

Jordy, Rancher: suicide

Ellemae, Greenhouse Keeper: complications in external injuries

Disease and injuries:

+3 infection due to previous wounds

+18 gastroenteritis due to improper food preparation

+6 workplace injuries

+9 self-inflicted injuries and violence

+43 alcohol-related problems (poisoning, injuries, etc.)

+24 malnourishment

+63 overfeeding

Psychological and health issues

-1 depression

+8 hoarding

+6 hypochondria

+2 deviant sexual behavior

Medical notes:

+2 pregnancies

I click on the deaths and read the names carefully, memorizing them. Because here's the simple truth—if I hadn't taken the ship off Phydus, people like Jordy and Ellemae would still be alive. And while I could say that a shorter life with feelings is better than a longer life without, the dead can't tell me their side.

I pause at the malnourished and overfed. Some of this is linked with the hoarding, I'm sure. People are afraid they won't have enough food later, so they're saving it now rather than eating it. Or they're eating as much as they can before supplies run out.

I can't help but think of Bartie's warning. The way to a revolution is through people's stomachs.

When I get to the end of the report, I ask, "Two new pregnancies?"

Doc takes the floppy back and reads over it, even though he must know what's on it. "Oh, yes," he says. "Both had lived in the Ward and chosen not to participate in the Season. They have, however, since decided to procreate."

"Doc," I say, curiosity making my voice rise. "If we wanted to increase the ship's population, then the Season's not very effective, is it?"

Doc swipes the floppy off and sets it on his desk, poking one side until it's square with the desk mat. "I, er, why do you say that?"

I lean forward, sitting on the edge of my chair. "I used to think that the Season was just the way things were, like how the animals mate on schedule. But it's pretty obvious now that the Season *isn't* natural. And if it's something engineered by you and Eldest, and if we're still trying to rebuild our population from the so-called Plague . . . well, the Season doesn't make sense, does it? One mating Season per gen? That would *reduce* our population, not recoup it. . . ."

My voice trails off, but Doc doesn't answer right away. The more I speak, the more I realize how right I am. The Season is just a frexing loon method to rebuild a population.

"Well, for some gens we had two Seasons," Doc says defensively. "And we've engineered it so many couples have multiple births."

For a moment we both stare at each other.

"It started a few gens ago," Doc says finally. His voice is hollow; it's like he's confessing a sin to me. "We figured it would be best to slow the population growth. We're having trouble producing enough food as it is."

"What happens when we can't produce enough food?" I ask.

Doc looks at me silently, and I can tell he's evaluating whether or not he will tell me. With the Shippers, I can demand truth and be assured they'll give it. But with Doc, I have to wait and hope. Doc was in favor of

Eldest's use of Phydus, and he was in favor of Orion's methods—after all, he was the one who kept Orion alive when Eldest ordered him killed. But I don't think Doc has made up his mind yet on whether or not I'm a good enough replacement for either of these men.

Apparently, though, I can be trusted with the truth. At least in this case. He finally says, "Eldest had thought of that. We have in storage a supply of over 3,000 black med patches."

"Black?" I ask. I'd never seen patches that were black.

Doc nods curtly. "In the event that the ship is no longer capable of sustaining life, the black patches will be distributed to the ship's population."

And now I understand what the black patches are for. A quick death, rather than a slow one.

16
AMY

I PROP HARLEY'S LAST PAINTING UP ON MY BED AND STAND back. His laughing eyes are even with my own, but there's no Mona Lisa–like illusion that he's looking at me.

"So," I say aloud to painted Harley, "just where is this clue Orion says is here?"

I'm hesitant to touch the paint—I don't want to do anything to damage it. Instead, I scan the painting with my eyes, looking for some hidden message from Orion.

I get lost in the image—there's Harley's face, and the stars, and the tiny koi fish swimming around his ankle. There are all the memories. How can someone I knew for so short a time have left such an indelible print on my soul? Seeing him look this way, so happy and free, makes me remember that something about Harley, that spark, that joy, that *something* that makes me wish he was still here, now.

I force my eyes to unfocus, to look past the image and into the paint. But there's nothing there.

I run my hands along the paint-splattered sides of the canvas. Nothing.

Then I flip it over.

I've never really looked at the back of the painting before. But now that I do, I notice a faint, almost invisible sketch made with a piece of charcoal or pencil from the looks of it. I squint, lean in closer, then pick the whole painting up and hold it up to the light.

A small animal—this isn't Harley's sketching; his pictures were much more realistic. This cartoonish creature looks a little like a hamster, but with huge, exaggerated ears . . . a bunny. And beside it, a circle . . . or, rather, a flattened circle that's more of an oval. In the center of the circle is a tiny square that looks like one of those super-thin memory cards Mom had for her fancy camera. It's stuck to the canvas with something tacky, but when I slip my fingernail under the edge of it, it pops right off.

I hold the object up on the tip of my index finger. Black plastic encases a thin gold strip of metal woven with silver threads of circuitry. What is this? It seems so familiar. I turn it over, but the other side is just hard plastic.

And then it hits me—I *have* seen something like this before. I rush to my desk and pick up the small screen that showed Orion's first video. Connected to a small port in the corner of the screen is an identical piece of square black plastic. The thing from the back of Harley's painting *is* like a memory card . . . if I could just figure out how to swap it with the one already there.

I squint at the back of the painting again, hoping for some other clue. And there, just under the sketch, are tiny words, barely legible.

Follow me down the rabbit hole.

"Curiouser and curiouser," I say.

It takes Elder about 2.5 seconds to reach my room after I com him.

"What's wrong?" he asks, skidding through the door.

I laugh at the way his eyes search my room, looking for a dragon to slay for his damsel in distress. "How'd you get here so quick?"

"I was in Doc's office."

The laughter fades. In the quiet, I'm reminded of the name he called me, *freak*, and the shape of Elder's lips as he formed the word.

"Listen, Amy, I'm sorry." I start to open my mouth, but Elder continues. "Seriously. I never meant to say that. I'm really sorry."

"I'm sorry too," I say, looking down at my hands. It's silly for me to dwell on one word said in anger when we have the whole ship to think of.

Silence spreads between us, but at least he doesn't look away from me.

"So," Elder says finally, "what's wrong?"

"Nothing's wrong," I say. "Just . . . strange. I found this."

I hold out the small black chip I peeled from the back of Harley's painting and the screen I found in Dante's *Inferno*.

"A mem card and a dedicated vid screen!" Elder says, laughing. "I haven't seen these in years! Floppies pretty much replaced them."

"How do you use this mem card thing?" I ask, offering it to him.

"A dedicated vid is just a digital membrane screen," Elder says as he gently pops out the original memory card and replaces it with the new one. The square chip snaps to the screen as if there was a magnetic pull between them. "It's like a floppy, but you have to have a mem card in the back to make them work." He places the old mem card on the edge of my desk, then flips the dedicated vid over and swipes his finger across the screen. A glowing square pops up.

"Here, let me," I say, taking the video screen from him and pressing my thumb onto it. The glowing box fades away, replaced with a video that starts playing automatically.

"That's . . . that's the cryo level," I whisper. The angle makes it look like security camera footage.

Elder shakes his head. "That's not possible; the cams down there were destroyed before Orion started to . . ."

Started unplugging the other frozens.

For several moments, nothing happens on the screen. I'm just about to ask Elder if it's paused or broken when there's movement at the corner of the video.

A shadow first, snaking across the floor like a clawed hand.

And then . . .

"That's me," Elder whispers.

I glance at him, unsure of why his tone is so high and worried.

"Let's—uh. Let's not watch this. I don't think we should watch this." His hand moves to stop the video, but I snatch it away.

"Why?" I demand.

Elder bites his lip, worry smeared across his face.

The Elder on the screen creeps forward. There's no sound to the video, which makes it even weirder when on-screen Elder stops as if he's heard something. After a moment, he turns to the square door that looks like it belongs in a morgue. He twists it open and slides the tray out.

And then I'm not looking at Elder anymore. I'm looking at *me*.

That's *me*, frozen in ice. So still. I look dead. Horror curls my lip. That's my flesh, my body. Naked. That's Elder, looking at my *naked* body.

"Elder!" I screech, and smack him upside his head.

"I didn't know you then!" he says.

"I didn't know you were such a creeper!" I shout back.

"I'm sorry!" Elder ducks away from me.

The Elder on the screen looks up suddenly, drawing our attention back to the video. But after listening, head cocked like a worried bird, the Elder on-screen dips his attention back to me. He raises a hand—I notice that it's shaking slightly—and places it on my glass box, just over where my heart is. Then he jumps—clearly startled by whatever sound he's hearing in the background—and dashes off-screen.

"You just left me there?" I ask. I knew he had, he'd confessed it to me already—but to see it like that. To see me, left there so carelessly, helplessly.

Elder looks miserable. He's not watching the screen at all; he's just watching me, this look on his face like he wishes I'd scream and punch at him and just get it over with.

But I'm not mad anymore . . . at least, I'm not as mad as I am sad. And slightly disgusted. I don't know how to put into words that sick, bile taste on the back of my tongue, so I don't say anything, I just turn back to the screen.

For several minutes, nothing happens. I watch as a thin trail of condensation leaks from the edge of my glass coffin and drops with a tiny, silent splash on the floor. I'm already melting.

Suddenly, I don't want to see this. I don't want to watch myself wake up. I can't relive drowning in cryo liquid, gagging on the tubes in my throat. I shut my eyes and turn my face away, even though it will take much, much longer for the me on-screen to melt all the way. But then Elder sucks in a breath of surprise, and my eyes fly back to the screen.

There's another shadow there, wider and longer, creeping slowly toward my frozen self. A shaft of light highlights the side of his neck, the part where a spiderweb of scars reaches behind his left ear.

Orion.

The first thing he does is slam me back into the cryo freezer. He locks the door shut and turns to leave.

But then he pauses.

He stares for a long moment off-screen, in the same direction Elder had walked away in, and he taps his fingers across the top of the cryo chamber, thinking. Then, slowly, deliberately, he pulls me back out of the cryo chamber. He looks down at me for a moment.

And then he walks away.

Orion told me that he got the idea to unplug the frozens from watching Elder unfreeze me. And this is it. This is the moment when he realized how easy it would be to kill people who can't fight back.

Static fills the screen.

"That's why he destroyed the cams in the cryo level," Elder says.

That's one reason, anyway.

Elder drops the vid screen on my desk and stands. Hair flops into his face, but I can still see his eyes shift to me. Waiting for me to react.

But I don't know how to respond. I don't know how I feel about this. About the way Elder looked at me, about the way Orion didn't. My brain can't process this.

"Amy?"

Elder's head whips up, panic in his eyes. He wasn't the one who spoke.

We both rush to the vid screen on the desk. The static has faded. Orion's face fills the screen, so close up that the camera must have been just inches from him.

Before the screen fades to black, Orion's voice rings out clearly. "Amy? Are you ready for this? Are you ready to find the truth?"

17
ELDER

THE SCREEN GOES BLANK. ORION'S LAST QUESTION HANGS IN the air, but the image Amy saw of me pulling her out of the cryo chamber fills her eyes.

"Amy?" I whisper, hesitant.

She swipes her hand across her face. Her eyes are red.

"Amy?"

"It doesn't matter," she says, her voice cracking in the middle. "What's done is done."

And that's what kills me inside. Because what's done was done by *me*. And as much as I wish Amy could see me the way I see her and want me the way I want her, she will never be able to forget the image of me pulling her out of her cryo chamber and walking away. No wonder she doesn't want to be in the Keeper Level with me.

I could punch whoever made Amy see this. My fists clench involuntarily. It's not like I'm so brilly on my own, but I certainly don't frexing need someone *showing* Amy what a chutz I was! "Who gave you this?" I demand.

Her clear green eyes meet mine, her voice steady now. "Orion did."

"*What?*"

"Orion did. Kind of. I mean, he left the wi-com for me. It has lettering on it, see?" She holds the wi-com out for me. "It's from a book. The book led me to the painting, the painting led me to . . . this."

"Why did he leave messages for you? What's he playing at?"

Amy hesitates, then hands me the mem card that was originally attached to the vid screen. When she presses her thumb against the ID box, the video plays. Orion's voice calls Amy his contingency plan, seeks her aid for a mission should he have failed, and—I can't help but notice—if it looks like I am failing too.

"Where did you get this?"

"I told you," Amy says. "Orion left me these clues."

"And you think—if you play his little game and solve these clues, then . . . what?"

"I don't know," Amy says. "But the way he keeps saying someone from Sol-Earth has to make the decision, it makes me think . . ."

I remember First Shipper Marae telling me about how Orion influenced the decision to hold back information about the ship's dead engine, how Eldest tried to have Orion killed soon after. If he made these videos as a way to get the word out on whatever it was that he discovered that led to Eldest trying to kill him, then there really might be a way to get *Godspeed* flying again.

This is *huge*. This—maybe at the end of this loons' hunt for clues and codes is the solution for the ship's engine! In which case . . .

"We should wake him up," I say.

Amy looks at me as if I've suggested we give the ship another Season.

"We *could*," I insist. "Wake him. Force him to tell us what he knows."

"He doesn't deserve to be woken." Amy spits the words out with more vehemence than I'd have expected.

"But Amy—"

"Besides," she adds quickly, "we couldn't trust him if we do wake him. This"—she jabs a finger at the vid screen—"might be the closest thing to truth we'll ever get from him."

I chew on my bottom lip. I know she wouldn't like the way I think about Orion. That maybe he was partly right. Not in killing the others, not right like that. But right in attacking Eldest, in learning what he could about the ship and acting on that knowledge. That took chutz, and I sort of envy him for it.

I'm glad Amy can't read my mind.

"This last video, it didn't have a clue. I think we're supposed to find the clue in this." Amy picks up the canvas of Harley's last painting and flips it over, showing me the sketch of the rabbit fields and the words *Follow me down the rabbit hole.*

"You think he hid something in the rabbit fields?" I ask doubtfully. After all, the rabbits don't burrow holes, they make nests—they're larger than the rabbits native to Sol-Earth, closer to hares.

"Yes, exactly," she says. "Or, maybe he's referring to another book."

Ah. There it is. I'm not a chutz. Amy doesn't actually think the clue is in the rabbit fields at all—she's just trying to distract me. She's probably already got the book she wants in mind.

But if she needs space, that's the least I can give her, even if the space she needs spreads out between us like flooding water.

I watch as Amy silently prepares to face the people outside the safety of her room. She wraps a long length of material around her hair and twists it in a low bun. She drops her cross necklace under her tunic with one hand while reaching for a long-sleeved hooded jacket with the other. She does all of this in a quick, fluid motion, as if she's done it many times before. I hate the way that hiding who she is has become a habit for her. But I don't tell her not to bother.

We don't really speak again until we're on the path heading to the Recorder Hall. "Are you sure you don't want me to go with you?" I ask.

"I'm sure," she says, and I don't know if her voice is small because it has to weave its way through the shadows under her hood or if it's because she's hiding her fear. Whatever it is she's not telling me, though, she's determined to meet it herself.

Amy starts down the path toward the Recorder Hall, leaving me to go left, to search for rabbit holes when we both know Orion's next clue is probably in whatever book she's thinking of. She looks so . . . defeated, with her hood pulled up, her shoulders hunched, and her eyes on the ground.

"No." I stride forward and in a few steps am by her side. I grab her by the elbow.

"No?" she asks.

"I know you're still mad at me," I start.

"No, not really—"

"You are, and that's okay, I deserve it. And I know you're trying to show how strong you are, to prove that you don't need me, but there's no reason for us to split up. You're being stubborn. And listen." I falter, and my voice drops. "I also know you're not telling me something. And it's fine—keep your secrets. But whatever it is that you're not telling me scares you, and I'm not going to let you be scared *and* alone. So you're sticking with me, and I'm sticking with you."

Amy opens her mouth to protest.

"No arguments," I say.

And for the first time in a long time, her smile reaches her eyes.

We visit the rabbit field first, even though I'm fairly sure Amy thinks we'll find the answers in the Recorder Hall. We don't talk after my outburst, but somewhere between the soy and the peanuts, we ease into a kind of mutual, friendly silence. It's not awkward or weird or anything—we're just strolling along the path next to each other.

The path narrows just before turning off to the rabbit field, and we both move toward the center at the same time. The back of my hand brushes hers. I snatch it away too quickly and shove it into my pocket, to make sure I don't accidentally touch her again. When I glance down at Amy to see if she noticed, she glances up at me at the same time. She smiles, and I smile, and she bumps into my shoulder, and I bump into her shoulder, and we both sort of laugh without making a sound.

Then we see a rabbit hop across our path.

"That's odd," I say. "How did this one get loose?"

"The fence has been ripped down," Amy says, pointing to where the flimsy chicken wire has been ripped from a post and trampled, leaving a gap in the fence wide enough for a man to just stroll through.

"Do you think something's happened?" Amy whispers.

I don't answer her. I don't have to. The body sprawled out in the middle of the field is answer enough.

18
AMY

THE RABBIT FARM WAS WHERE I FIRST FELT HORROR. NOT fear—I've been scared many times in my life, both on this ship and on Earth. But I didn't know horror until I looked into the eyes of the girl on the rabbit farm and realized that she was empty inside.

Now, when Elder rolls the body in the field over so we can see the face, I can see that, once again, the girl at the rabbit farm has empty eyes.

I drop to my knees beside her. Elder has his hand on his neck; he's comming Doc and his police force, but it's already too late. Much too late.

My mind takes note of the details in a detached way, even though the revulsion is bubbling up inside of me. The girl's arms are spread wide, with deep purple bruises at her wrists. Finger marks encircle her throat. Her skirt has been pulled up. Her eyes are wide and stare unblinkingly at the metal sky. A large rabbit nuzzles her bare foot. The bottoms of her feet are grass-stained, her knees muddy, as if she ran and fell more than once.

I gently pull down the hem of her skirt so that it rests straight against her knees, almost covering the mud, and then I push her eyelids closed.

"Who would do this?" Elder asks.

We can do anything we want, Luthor said.

I open my mouth to speak, but no words come out. I try to force them from me, but all that comes out is an almost inaudible sound of fear.

"What happened?" Doc calls as he rushes forward through the field. His assistant Kit follows him.

Doc starts to examine the body. I'm in the way, I know it, but I can't seem to move until Kit puts her hand on my elbow and pulls me up. She draws me away from the body and faces me toward the walls, away from death.

"Here," she says, offering me something. A small green med patch.

"No," I say automatically. I never trust any of the medicines made on this ship.

"It will calm you," Kit insists.

"No."

I turn back to the body. Elder and Doc are both kneeling beside the girl, talking in urgent tones. Arguing.

"Elder!" A voice calls from the other side of the field. I see a female Shipper—tall and slender with immaculately cut hair—running toward us.

Elder stands. "Marae, thank you for coming."

"You told me to come," she says simply.

The three of them stand over the body without a second glance at me. Elder and Doc discuss an autopsy as Marae taps on a floppy rapidly, her fingers dancing across the screen. Kit runs off at Doc's order to begin preparing an examination room. Soon other people come—each wearing the crisp, dark clothing that the top-ranking Shippers wear. They consult with both Elder and Marae before moving off to obey orders—one goes to gather the rabbits that got loose, another fixes the fence, another brings an electric cart and starts to load the girl's body.

The whole time, I stand to one side. I can't help but stare at the girl's face, at her closed eyes, and remember how once she cried and didn't know why.

Elder moves with swift efficiency. He's the youngest person on the whole ship, younger even than me by almost a year, but every time he gives a command, the people rush off to obey. Even though I've been so sure that Elder's the leader *Godspeed* needs, I've never actually *seen* him take charge. Not like this. And while this only proves that he can lead this entire ship like I always said he could, it also makes me feel even more detached. I don't know him. Or—I know him, but only one him. I know the Elder who's kind and almost like a puppy dog in his devotion, but I don't know this Elder who commands people older than him, who issues orders that are immediately obeyed. This Elder has never been more alien to me.

"I will try to collect as much DNA as I can during the autopsy," Doc says as two Shippers lift the body onto the electric cart.

I want to say: I think I know who did this.

"Do you think there will be enough to identify the murderer?" Elder asks. "I'll grant you access to the biometric scanner database."

Doc starts to follow the cart. "There might be something under her fingernails I can use. If not, I believe there will be seminal fluid present in this case. It may take a couple of days to process and run it through all the records."

I want to say: I only met her once, but I feel like I knew her better than any of you.

As Doc leaves, Elder gathers the Shippers together. "Shelby, see if there's any kind of vid feed of this area from when the girl was attacked. Buck, I'd like you to track down any Feeders in the area and question them; maybe there were witnesses to what happened here."

I open my mouth. I want to say: I'm breaking, and I need someone to hold me together.

But no sound comes out. I feel the hands around my throat, crushing my windpipe. I swallow dryly. *He's* not here. Not anymore. He killed her and left.

I try to speak again. I *should* speak, I have to speak.

But I can't.

Instead, I run.

My body thrills at this—I haven't run in ages. I've been too scared to go on my daily runs, but now I'm not running as I would for exercise. I'm running as if the force of the wind whipping around my body will be enough to keep all the pieces of me from crumbling.

Past the fence, down the path, past the soy fields. When I get to the main road that connects the Recorder Hall and the Hospital, I go straight to the Hall. I don't know why. I should hate this place. The last time I saw Luthor, it was here, in the Recorder Hall. But I'm certain, more certain than anything else, that the clue Orion left for me is here, and maybe if I can find that clue, I can also find something to make things right again.

I'm still running as I enter the Hall, pass the groups of people pouring over the wall floppies, and head straight to the fiction room. I throw open the door so hard that it bounces off the wall, and I don't pause until I reach the shelf that holds the book I'm looking for.

I slide the heavy book off the shelf, panting in an effort to catch my breath. An image is pressed into the front cover. A girl, a tree, and a smiling cat. The binding is cracked with age, the illustration faded. My heart races as I carry the book to the table in the middle of the room. I collapse into a chair and let the book thunk heavily on the metal tabletop. I can imagine Elder's look of disdain at the way I let it slam against the surface. He treats books like treasured, rare things, and I guess they are, but my father used to dog-ear books and read them until they fell apart, and I like his method better.

I flip the book open and read the title page.

Alice's Adventures in Wonderland
by
Lewis Carroll
Collector's Edition
Annotations & Literary Criticism © 2022

I've seen this book before. Not this exact one, but copies of it. It was required reading for the AP Literature class at my high school in Colorado. I planned on taking that class my senior year.

We left Earth before I had a chance to finish eleventh grade.

Those textbooks were brand new at school. Now this one is falling apart from age, despite the climate-controlled room it's stored in.

I snap the book shut, and a tiny cloud of dust rises up. As I breathe in the musty scent of old pages and dry ink, the thing inside me that I've been trying to keep together breaks.

I let my head fall down to the book, pressing my face against the illustration of the Cheshire Cat's wicked grin, and I sob, great, gulping sobs that choke me. And I think about the last time I choked, on tubes as

I emerged from the slushy ice when I melted, and then, later, as Luthor's arm pressed into my neck. And then all I can think about is how the girl at the rabbit farm choked too. And suddenly, I can't get enough air into my lungs, just like she couldn't get enough air into hers.

She died, alone and scared. I'm not dead, but I'm still alone and scared.

19
ELDER

"FOUND YOU," I SAY, PUSHING OPEN THE DOOR.

Amy sits in the middle of the gallery on the second floor of the Recorder Hall. Her knees are pulled up to her chin and her arms wrap around her legs. A thick, old book rests beside her, open-faced but ignored. The art room is cluttered, sculptures and paintings from last gen's artists stacked on one side and rows of canvases propped up on the other—mostly from Harley, but a few from some other artists. Art isn't exactly respected here on *Godspeed*, and although Orion had made something of an attempt to turn the collection into a proper gallery, he'd been much more focused on books than paintings.

"How did you find me?" Amy asks as I plop down beside her.

I tug at the wi-com around her wrist. "They have locaters, you know."

She nods silently. Her head falls against my shoulder, her long red hair spilling down my arm.

"I'm sorry you had to see that," I say.

"I'm just sorry it happened. Do you . . ." Amy doesn't look at me as she says this. "Do you know who did it?"

"We have some suspects. Second Shipper Shelby said she saw a Feeder shouting yesterday in the Recorder Hall. Something about doing whatever he wanted . . ."

I watch her closer. Shelby also said that the person the Feeder was shouting at was Amy. She gives no indication of that now, although I can see the secret behind her eyes, clawing to get out.

"Why did you run off?" I ask softly.

The last I'd seen of her was a blur of brown clothing. I didn't like the idea of Amy running off alone, but I couldn't abandon the investigation, not in front of the Shippers, and not before I knew they had everything they needed to find the killer. I tracked the location of her wi-com until I could escape.

"I thought I'd go ahead and get started on that clue Orion left me," she says, her voice cracking.

"Did you find anything?" I ask, pretending not to notice that she's been crying. The death of the girl in the rabbit fields seems to have affected her more than it did the shipborns.

Amy shoves the book over to me. I wince at the idea of a book—a *book!* From *Sol-Earth!*—being pushed across the floor, but I pick it up silently. I read the title and flip through some pages. "Why would there be a clue here?"

"Alice follows a rabbit down a rabbit hole," she says, turning the pages in my hand to a chapter near the beginning. She somehow avoids touching me, just as she's shying away from eye contact. "I thought it fit. But I guess not."

I look at the illustration that accompanies the chapter: a girl in a poufy skirted dress, staring curiously down a hole under a tree.

"Why did you come to the gallery?" I ask, closing the book and setting it gently beside me.

"No one else comes here," she says softly. "I didn't want to stay in the fiction room, and I figured nobody would find me here."

I wonder if she includes me as a nobody.

Amy twists the wi-com round and round her wrist. Her skin is pink there. I want to reach out and stop her. Instead, I turn the book over in my hands. I can't figure Amy out, but maybe if I can figure out the clue, I can take her away from whatever place in her mind she's retreated to.

"Huh," I say.

Amy jerks her attention to me. "What? Huh, what?"

I hold up the back of the book to her. "'Other works by Lewis Carroll,'" I read aloud. "*Through the Looking-Glass.*"

"So?" Amy eyes me curiously.

"The first clue was on the back of a painting, right?" I ask. Amy rolls her hand for me to go on. "Well, maybe the second clue is too."

"*Through the Looking-Glass* is a book," Amy says. "Not a painting."

Instead of arguing, I jump up and head to a stack of paintings. Harley did so many and the gallery is so small that not every single one is hanging from the walls. I flip through the canvases quickly—I know exactly which one I'm looking for.

"Harley did a painting right after his girlfriend, Kayleigh, committed suicide. I remember when he finished it—Orion said it was his 'greatest achievement.'" Amy looks at me doubtfully. "What's wrong?"

"Do you really think he'd use another painting for the next clue?" she asks.

"Maybe?" I shrug, still sifting through canvases. "He left those clues specifically for you, but let's be honest—he didn't know you that long. I guess he saw how close you were to Harley in that short amount of time and figured the best way to leave the clues was with his paintings." Amy doesn't notice the bitterness in my voice; even Orion could see that she was closer to Harley than she was to me.

"So where is this painting?" Amy asks.

"Don't know. It used to be on the wall."

"Where?" Amy calls. She's moved to the center of the room, examining the only wall that isn't decorated with art.

"Over there, actually," I say. I get to the end of the first row of Harley's canvases and start in on the second. "Anyway, Orion told Harley that good paintings all have titles. Harley said he didn't think paintings needed names, but Orion made a big deal out of it and called the painting—"

"*Through the Looking Glass*," Amy says.

"Yeah." I glance back at her. She's bending in front of the blank wall, reading a tiny placard.

"*Through the Looking Glass,* Oil Painting by Harley, Feeder," she reads. She turns back to me. "But where is it? There's a hook here for the painting, but no painting."

"It's not here, either," I say, pushing aside the stack of paintings.

"This must have been an important painting—it's the only one that has a placard."

Amy's right. The rest of the room is a bit of a mess, but this blank wall is neat, clearly sectioned off. It's obviously meant to be the center of attention, even if there's nothing left to direct one's attention to.

"Orion names the painting, he hangs it in the center of the room, he bothers to get a placard made that shows the title of the painting—this has to be the next clue he wanted us to find." Her green eyes search mine, as if she could see Harley's art in them.

I move to stand beside Amy, staring at the empty wall. "But where's the painting?"

20
AMY

"WHO WOULD TAKE IT?" I ASK. "SOMEONE CLOSE TO HARLEY?"

"He didn't have many friends. Me—Bartie, Victria."

"One of them?"

Elder shakes his head. I believe him—Bartie's too serious to think of stealing a painting, and while Victria would have no qualms about it, she'd pick a painting of Orion, not Kayleigh, judging by the sketch she stole from Harley's room. "And I know Doc wouldn't."

I snort. No, Doc wouldn't.

"Unless . . ."

"Yeah?" I ask.

"Harley's parents might have. . . ."

For some reason, this surprises me. I didn't really think of Harley having parents. He just . . . was. And while I know that the people living in the Ward were separated from the rest of the Feeders on purpose, it just didn't occur to me that there was anything of Harley outside of the Hospital and the stars.

"Come on," Elder says. "Let's try it."

In all my time on *Godspeed*, I don't think I've ever actually walked the entire length of the ship. I've run it dozens of times—or at least, I did before the Phydus wore off—but I've never walked it.

We start down the same path we took to get to the rabbit fields. When we reach the fork in the road, we go left instead of up and over to the fields. I glance back—the fence has been repaired, and the entire area looks undisturbed. I can see a couple of rabbits, lazily hopping about, sniffing the ground where their owner lay dead just a few hours before.

"Tell me about the painting," I say, desperately trying to replace the image in my mind of the rabbit girl's death with anything else.

"It's really frexing good," Elder says. "But, I don't know . . . weird, I guess. Usually Harley paints real-life things, but this one is . . . different. It's a picture of Kayleigh right before she died."

Somehow, it doesn't surprise me that the painting Harley did in memory of Kayleigh's death is weird—after all, the only other surreal painting he did was of his own.

"Her death—it surprised us all. Of all of us, I always thought that it would be Harley. . . ."

"You thought Harley would kill himself?" I ask.

"He'd tried a couple of times. Once before Kayleigh. Twice after. Three times after," he adds.

He'd forgotten the third attempt, the one that actually worked.

"Right after Kayleigh died," Elder says, "Harley started that painting. I mean, *right* after she died—he began stretching the canvas the same day we found her body, painted through the night. Eventually, Doc drugged him with a med patch. Once he was asleep, I lifted the wet brush from his hand. His fingertips were dented from his grip." Elder's voice is far away.

Freshly hatched puffy yellow baby chicks cheep up at us as we pass them. The solar lamp is bright and straight above us, making our shadows disappear on the dusty path. The City is far enough in front of us that while I can see people bustling about, I can't make out their faces, and the Recorder Hall and Hospital are far enough behind us that I don't feel their beady stares. I lower the hood of my jacket and unwind the strip of cloth around my hair, relishing the cool air against my scalp.

Here, in this one small part of the ship, with no one here but Elder, I'm not afraid.

Elder plods along down the path, his eyes down and his face troubled. I know the way silence and secrets can eat at you from the inside.

I touch his elbow and he stops, startled.

"Tell me how she died," I say.

2 1
ELDER

I WAS THIRTEEN AND STILL LIVED AT THE HOSPITAL. THE SHIP was going to land in 53 years and 147 days, and by that point, I would be the one to lead everyone off *Godspeed* and onto the new world. I'd been at the Hospital long enough to know that Harley was my best friend, that Doc was mostly okay, and that it would not be too long now before I would—finally—start my training as Elder.

Life was good.

Then.

Harley had dared me to climb the statue of the Plague Eldest that stood in the Hospital gardens. I hadn't gotten past the pedestal, but he was hanging from the Plague Eldest's benevolent left arm, gazing down the path to the pond near the back wall of the ship.

"Something big is floating in the water," Harley said. He swung his body and released his grip, landing with a thud in the fake mulch beside me. He left a purple paint stain on the Plague Eldest's elbow. "Let's go see."

Harley was taller than me and walked with longer strides. Even so, I was tempted to ask him to race. But Harley was also four years older than me, and racing was for children.

"Race ya," Harley said, kicking up mulch as he leapt away. He looked over his shoulder, laughed, and almost tripped over a blooming hydrangea spilling out onto the path. Little blue petals went flying, whipping past my ankles before drifting to the ground.

I had almost caught up with Harley, was reaching for his shirt to jerk him back and throw him off course so I could speed past him—

—when he stopped cold.

Harley threw his arm out. It caught me in the chest, painfully, winding me and bringing me to a stop.

"What the frex was that for?" I gasped, bent over.

Harley didn't say anything.

His face was sweating from the race, but underneath he was pale, giving him a deathly sheen. I turned from Harley to the pond.

I knew immediately the girl floating facedown in the still water was dead. Her hair was pulled over her head, the long dark strands of it sinking beneath the surface as if they were anchors being dragged along the silty bottom of the pond. Her arms lay relaxed on either side, palms down, and as I watched, they slowly disappeared under the depths.

There was something about her—

—something familiar . . .

All along the hem of her tunic were tiny white dots.

Almost like the tiny white flowers that Harley had painted for his girlfriend, Kayleigh. The ones he painted on her favorite tunic, the night he'd spent eight hours straight covering her room with ivy and flowers.

Kayleigh's flowers.

Kayleigh's tunic.

Kayleigh.

Harley made a barbaric noise and lunged toward the water's edge, leaving a deep brown-red scar in the earth from the force of his foot. He swept the water away with his arms as he threw himself into the pond, as if he could wipe away everything he saw before him.

The water didn't want to give her up. Her head sank lower.

Harley dove and grabbed Kayleigh by the wrist. He turned her over in the water and slapped her face as if to awaken her, but her head just bobbed gently. He swam a little, then jerked her body forward, then swam some more, then jerked her again. She floated willingly by his side, her arms and legs dancing like a wooden puppet's when all its strings are yanked at once.

Harley slipped, going to one knee, then found footing on the wet bottom of the pond and trudged through the thick mud. With one final, mighty heave, he tossed Kayleigh's body onto the bank and collapsed beside it.

A dribble of muddy water trickled from the left corner of her mouth, just where she used to twitch her lips up in a laughing smirk. Grime slid down the side of her face, pooling at the edge of her cheek and falling unceremoniously into the ground below.

Harley was shouting and sobbing something, but I couldn't understand the words.

All I could do was stand there, a witness, my mouth hanging open a little.

Like Kayleigh's mouth.

Her left leg was twisted backward, her ankle under her backside and her knee jutting forward in a sharp angle. One arm was thrown across her stomach, the other stretched out as if it were pointing up the path toward the Hospital. It suddenly became very important to Harley to position her body just right. He straightened her leg and smoothed her trousers down.

He placed her arms by her sides and rubbed his thumb over the palm of her right hand, like he used to do when he thought no one was watching, just before he'd lean in for a kiss, and they forgot about everything but their love.

"Harley," I said, breaking the spell. I took a step forward, squelching the mud by the banks. I knelt down and felt the warm water seep into the legs of my trousers and reached—toward him or Kayleigh, I'm not sure.

"Don't touch her!" Harley snarled.

I didn't move quickly enough. Harley lunged at me and threw the full force of his fist against my jaw. My teeth snapped over my tongue, and I tasted blood. I let myself fall away into the mud and cowered behind my arms.

When I dared look again, Harley was staring up. One hand still held hers, his thumb going methodically over her cool, lifeless palm, back and forth, back and forth.

"Why did she leave me?" he whispered to the painted metal sky above us.

Because this wasn't an accident.

It couldn't have been an accident.

Kayleigh loved the pond. Loved to swim with the koi. She'd dive under with handfuls of feed in her grip and uncurl her fingers underwater so the shy fish would dance up to her and nibble from her hands. She could hold her breath longer than anyone I knew. No one could catch her when she swam, not even Harley, who always tried.

Kayleigh couldn't have died by accident. Not in the water.

I stared at what was left of her.

Pale yellow square patches lined the inside of both her arms. Doc's med patches—the ones that made you fall asleep. This—this was what killed her. Not an accident. A choice. Kayleigh put herself into a watery bed and made sure she would never wake up. Suicide. We knew it must have been suicide. She'd been talking about how much she hated living, trapped on this ship, for weeks. Months. Just little things, a comment here, a snide remark there. Nothing we noticed. Not until—

My eyes drifted from her body to the lapping, almost-still waters behind her. I looked farther, over the reeds and lotus flowers on the far edge, my eyes skimming across the bright green new grass.

Where they crashed against a metal wall.

A hard, cold, relentless metal wall, studded with rivets and stained with grease and age. My eyes burned as I followed a seam in the wall up, up, curving higher up, until it met with the bright solar lamp in the center of the ceiling. Above that, I knew, was the Shipper Level, and above that, the Keeper Level.

And beyond that—beyond tons and tons of impenetrable metal—was a sky I had never seen.

A sky Kayleigh had never seen.

And she couldn't live without the sky.

22
AMY

ELDER FINISHES HIS STORY AS WE ENTER THE CITY. I WANT TO say something to comfort him, but this memory happened years ago, and there's nothing to really say, anyway.

I've never been this far into the City before. The whole Feeder Level looks different now, in the middle of the day, even though there's not that much difference in the solar lamp between morning, when I used to run, and day—this false sun doesn't move across the sky, doesn't paint the horizon with pink and orange and blue.

The City is bigger than it looks from the other side of the Feeder Level. When I look at the City from the Hospital or the Recorder Hall, it seems like it's made of Legos. The buildings are brightly colored boxes stacked one on top of the other, and the people are almost too tiny to see.

But here, it's different. The streets are crowded. Men—and a few women—pull carts, running through the paved streets and pulling their loads behind them as if they were nothing. Produce, meat, boxes, bolts of cloth—all fly from one street to another. It's louder than I expected. People call to each other across the street, and a couple at the corner are shouting at each other, waving their arms about. I smell smoke, and I'm worried that something bad has happened, but no—it's wafting from an outdoor grill.

The City itself seems more chaotic too. There are so many *people*. And for the first time, I really think of them as individuals, each with their own story. I try to imagine their lives. The man behind the window, slamming his cleaver into a rack of ribs. Is he bored or hiding anger behind the brutal attack on the meat? The girl leaning against the building, sweating and fanning herself—what's made her want to leave the comfort of her home to just stand there? What's she waiting on?

And what will they all do when they find out the truth? How much of the City will be destroyed when they discover, as they inevitably will, that *Godspeed* isn't even moving?

Although I keep my head down, wary of these people who could so quickly turn on me, Elder greets them all with a smile. He seems to know everyone, and they grin back at him.

Their grins fade when their eyes slide to me, though. They hiss "freak" so softly that Elder doesn't notice. I carefully pull my hood back up over my hair, making sure all of it is hidden.

"Harley's family lives in the weaving district," Elder says, leading me down the street. "That's in the middle of the City."

Each block is named for what the people there do. We must be in the meat district—there's a lingering scent of blood in the air mixed with a trace of rancid fat. Flies buzz in the windows and drift lazily over the slabs of meat waiting to be processed.

"Can you wait here a moment?" Elder asks. "I see something I should take care of."

I nod, and he walks into the butcher's on the corner. I creep closer to listen. Two men, both of the older generation, are working, even though there are five workstations in the building.

One of the men looks up when Elder enters. He nudges his partner.

"Oh, um, hello, Eldest," he tells Elder, wiping his bloody hands on the stained smock in front of him.

Elder doesn't bother telling the man that he prefers to be called Elder. "Where are your other workers?"

The men glance nervously at each other. The first turns back to the cow he's butchering, sawing away at a leg bone with a hacksaw. The other man stands at his counter, unsure of what to do. "They—well—they didn't come in today."

"Why not?"

The man shrugs. "We told them yesterday we would need help, that Bronsen was bringing in at least three head, but . . ."

"But they didn't come in."

The man nods.

"Why didn't you do something about it?"

He keeps wiping his hands on his smock, but they're as clean as they're going to get against that dirty thing. "It's . . . it's, uh . . . it's not our place."

"Not your place to do what?"

"To tell others to come to work."

Elder's jaw clenches. He leaves, letting the bell at the door say his farewell.

He storms down the street, and his scowl wards off any further greetings from those who pass us. "Eldest never had these problems," he growls at me in an undertone. "People just not working. Lazy. He *never* had to deal with that. People obeyed him, and they didn't dare miss work. Eldest made sure that everything on this ship ran smoothly."

"Eldest didn't do that," I say. My words startle Elder enough that he stops in his tracks. "He didn't," I insist. "Phydus did."

Elder smirks, and some of the anger in him fades. We pass a group of spinners sitting on the sidewalks, chatting merrily with each other as the threads slide through their fingers. In the next block, though, the buildings that house the looms are dark and quiet, no weavers in sight. Elder glowers at it as he leads me to an iron staircase set against the side of a series of brightly painted trailers stacked on top of the working area.

"The yellow one," Elder says, pointing to a trailer three flights up. "That's where Harley used to live."

I follow Elder up the steps. The higher we go, the more paint splatters there are on the railings and steps. Even here, Harley has left his mark. Elder hesitates before knocking, his fist poised over an aqua blue smear of dried paint.

No answer.

He knocks again.

"Maybe they're not here?" I ask. "It is the middle of the day."

When no one answers on his third knock, Elder pushes the door open.

2 3
ELDER

IT'S DARK INSIDE, AND IT STINKS OF SOMETHING SOURED. There are traces of Harley here still—the inside is painted white with yellow swirls along the top. A table sits in the center of the room, but all but one of the chairs have been stacked in the corner, and the top of the table is littered with scraps of cloth, scissors, and tiny bottles of colored dye—accouterments of being a weaver.

"Hello?" Amy calls. "I think someone's back there," she adds, nodding at the cloth covering the doorway that leads deeper into the trailer.

I step in front of her and peel back the curtain. This room is darker still and smells of musk and sweat. It's the main bedroom—beyond this room is another curtained door leading, I know, to a bathroom and a smaller bedroom.

Curled in a tight ball in the center of the bed is Harley's mother, Lil. Her hair is messy, but she's fully dressed, although her clothes are stained.

"What are you doing here?" Lil asks, her voice quiet and defeated.

"Where's—" I struggle for the name of Harley's father. "Where's Stevy?"

Lil shrugs without getting up.

Amy moves forward, hesitates, then sits on the edge of the bed. "Is everything all right?" She reaches for Lil, but Lil, startled by Amy's fair coloring, cowers back. Amy's hand drops into her lap. After a moment, she gets back up and moves behind me.

"Where's Stevy?" I ask again.

"Gone."

"For how long?"

Lil shrugs again.

From under the covers, I hear her stomach growl.

"Let's get you something to eat," I say. I step forward, reaching down for her hand. Although Lil doesn't flinch from me, she doesn't respond to my offer, either.

"No point," she says. "No food."

"No food?" I ask. I instinctively look to the curtained door; the wall food distributer is in the main room of the trailer. "Is it broken? I'll have maintenance come and check on it."

"No point," she says softly. I ignore her and com the Shipper level, requesting they send someone as soon as they can.

Once I break the com link, I turn my full attention back to Lil. "What's wrong?" I ask. "Why aren't you working? Should I com Doc?"

She stares at the ceiling. "I can't work. The dyes remind me of him. The colors. Colors everywhere."

"Lil," I say, making a mental note to com Doc later, "did you take any of Harley's paintings from the Recorder Hall?"

Now she sits up. "No!"

But her eyes dart to the curtain.

She notices my glance in that direction. "They're mine. He's my son. He was my son. It's all I have left of him."

"We just want to look," Amy says in a small voice from behind me.

Lil flops back into her pillow. "What's the point? He's not coming back. Neither of them is coming back."

She doesn't look up again, so Amy and I creep around the bed to the curtain on the far wall. I lift it up, and Amy follows me into the room.

A bathroom. The toilet's unflushed and the sink is stained. We move quickly to the side, where another curtain blocks a doorway.

This is Harley's room—or, at least, it was until he moved out to live in the Ward. There are traces of what the room used to be—a narrow mattress against one wall, a small nightstand that still holds a clock—but clearly in the years since he left, the room has become something of a storage space for his family. I maneuver past the boxes until I see what we came for: Harley's painting, *Through the Looking Glass.*

"It's beautiful," Amy breathes. I suppose she's right, but when I see it, I only remember the way it really happened, not the way Harley painted it.

The painting is vividly bright, even though in my memory everything was dark: the water, the mud, her eyes. Five figures stand at the top of the painting, looking down into the pond—me, Harley, Victria, Bartie, and, behind us, Orion. Harley had used some sort of reflective paint on the surface of the pond—but just beneath the mirror-like surface of the water, a girl swims, floating on her back, her laughing eyes peering up toward the surface. Koi swirl around her fingers, and a lotus plant's roots tangle in her loose, thick black hair.

"He really liked koi," Amy says.

"They were Kayleigh's favorite."

I can taste the murky pond water. I can feel the clamminess of Kayleigh's skin. I can see the bloated way her face squished under Harley's touch.

"Let's look for the clue," Amy says gently, pulling me away from the edge of the pond. "It's probably on the back, like the other one."

I lift the canvas up to the light, then flip it over.

"Look," Amy says.

A rectangle is sketched in light ink on the back and, in the center of it, another tiny mem card. I pry it off with my fingernail. Another message is written on the back of the painting in the same faint handwriting as the first clue:

1, 2, 3, 4. Add it up to unlock the door.

"Does he mean the door on the fourth floor of the Hospital? The one that leads to the elevator that goes down to the cryo level?" I ask.

"I don't think so. He told you about that door; he knows I've seen what's behind it. If he left these clues for me to find, then he must mean one of the other locked doors."

"There aren't any—" I start, but I stop abruptly. There are few locked doors on the ship—and fewer doors still that my biometric scan can't break through. But there *is* one area that is full of locked doors, doors locked with a keypad whose code even Eldest didn't know.

"The doors on the cryo level," I say. "The ones near the hatch."

Amy nods. "It has to be."

"Still got that vid screen with you?" I ask. Amy pulls it out of her pocket, and I snap the mem card into it. Amy runs her finger on the ID box on the screen. The screen comes alive with Orion's face. After hesitating a moment, Amy leans in closer to me, close enough to see the screen, but not so close that she touches me.

<<begin video feed>>

Orion is barely visible, hidden in shadow. He sits on the fourth step of a large staircase extending out of view behind him. His right hand taps against his knee in a jittery, almost nervous way.

"Where *is* that?" Amy asks.

I shake my head, intent on the video.

The camera wobbles as Orion adjusts the image. He speaks softly, almost kindly.

ORION: First, I want to say I'm sorry about Kayleigh. I never meant for her to die.

"He killed her?" Amy gasps.

I say nothing, but a heavy stone sinks in my stomach.

ORION: I didn't kill her. But I might as well have. She figured it out. Eldest's biggest secret. The one he doesn't want anyone to know.

"What could that be—"

"*Shh.*"

Orion pauses, swallowing hard as if overcome with emotion.

ORION: Amy, you should know this—if you decide to keep looking—Kayleigh's murder was a warning. Eldest may have killed Kayleigh, but there are things I can do. Locks I can change. Fool that he is—he hasn't thought to check them.

Orion stops abruptly. His eyes lose focus.

ORION: I don't know what's right or wrong anymore. Not since Kayleigh died. I don't know if what she knew was something the whole ship should know. I don't know if she should have found the truth.

Orion shifts on the steps.

ORION: I don't know if killing her was worth saving the ship.

He shrugs, as if there's a possibility that killing her was excusable, or even understandable.

ORION: Maybe it was. Maybe Eldest is right. This truth . . . I don't think anyone wants it.

Orion tucks a piece of hair behind his ear.
I tuck a piece of hair behind my ear.

ORION: That's why I need you, Amy. You will know. Because you were born on a planet, but you've lived on *Godspeed.* You're the only one on the whole ship who can know what to do with this truth.

Orion turns to face the camera, and his eyes seem to lock with mine.

ORION: I've seen the armory. Eldest showed it to me once. Just before . . . Anyway, I started asking questions. Like: If we are on a peaceful, exploratory mission like Eldest says, why are we armed for war?

I glance at Amy, but her attention is focused on the vid screen. Inside me, the stone grows larger. Amy never believed Orion had a reason to kill the frozens—she thought he was crazy and that his theory that the frozens would exploit those of us born on the ship was a delusion. I don't think she believes there even *is* an armory behind one of the locked doors, even now, seeing Orion talk about it.

Orion looks over both shoulders, fear filling his face. He looks guilty or afraid or both.

ORION: So here's what you need to do, Amy. You need to see the armory for yourself. You were from Sol-Earth, your father was in the military. You should know what is a reasonable amount of weaponry a ship like ours should have. So, go to the armory. See for yourself.

Orion shifts out of focus, then leans forward, his face filling the screen.

ORION: Oh, right. You need the code to get past the locked door, don't you? Well, I'll say only this, Amy. Go home. You hear me? Go home. You'll find the answer there. GO HOME.

The screen fades to black.

<<end video feed>>

24
AMY

GO HOME? *GO HOME?* WHAT THE HELL IS THAT SUPPOSED
to mean? Earth? Yeah, I wish. The new planet? Just as impossible.

"Maybe he means the next clue is hidden inside an atlas or something?" Elder says.

Ha ha, Orion, funny joke. My home is nothing but a book of maps to
places that I can't even reach anymore.

"Maybe," is all I say aloud. "I guess it's worth checking into."

Elder places the painting down on the ground gently, reverently, and
looks over his shoulder at it as he follows me out of the tiny bedroom,
through the bathroom, and into the next bedroom. Lil's still on her bed.
She sits up when she sees us.

"You're taking it, aren't you?" she spits.

"No," Elder says. "It's yours."

Lil blinks, and her eyes focus on him. She glances at me, but her eyes
dart quickly away again, unable to bear the sight of me, I suppose.

"And I'll make sure food is sent to you," Elder says. "I'm going to send
Doc over here too. He's been working on some med patches I think will
help."

Lil nods, but she doesn't get up as we leave her home. Part of me wonders: will she jump out of bed, race to her precious painting? Or does she care enough to even do that?

As we head down the stairs back into the City streets, Elder pushes his wi-com and starts issuing orders, first for food delivery, then for medication. He's so intent that he doesn't notice the angry man who spots us as we descend.

"Where is she?" the man demands. The man leans forward so close that Elder backs away until he bumps into the handrail of the stairs.

"Who?" Elder asks.

"Lil. You gonna make her work? 'Cause it ain't fair I'm working if she's not!"

"Stevy, she's sick. She needs some time. I've commed Doc—"

"She ain't sick! Just lazy!" the man roars.

Elder puts up both his hands. "Stevy, I'm doing what I can. She can go back to work when she's read—"

But he doesn't have a chance to finish his sentence. His eyes widen with shock as Stevy rears back his fist and slams it straight into Elder's jaw. Elder crashes to the ground. As soon as he manages to get back on his feet with the help of the handrail, Stevy slams his fist into his face again. Elder staggers back, but this time, he doesn't fall.

I don't realize I've screamed until the sound is out of my throat. Behind us, the group of spinners who were outside plying yarn have all noticed—they're standing up; they're rushing forward; they're screaming too; they're holding back; they're whispering to each other behind their hands.

I spin around. "Someone do something!" I shout at them. I've witnessed enough high school fights to know that a girl like me would be stupid to rush between them—they're both at least a foot taller than me, and one of Stevy's punches could easily knock me out.

Three of the spinners—two men and a woman who's not that much bigger than me—rush forward. But before they reach us, Stevy falls to the ground, clutching his head. The spinners stop short, staring.

Elder wipes his bleeding lip with the back of his hand.

"Make it stop," Stevy says, his voice somewhere between a whine and a demand.

"It will automatically stop in about two minutes." Elder speaks calmly, but there's a cold impassivity to his voice that frightens me. "By that point, I think you should have learned punching me is a very bad idea."

"What have you done?" I ask.

His lip won't stop bleeding; his teeth are outlined in red. "Something I told myself I'd never do," Elder mutters. "Come on."

He doesn't continue down the main street. Instead, he veers down an alley that heads toward the Greenhouses.

"It was something with his wi-com," Elder says even though I've dropped the question. "Eldest did it to me once. It's pretty effective at stopping someone."

"Elder!" a voice bellows after us. Elder freezes, then turns slowly back to the scene of the crime.

Stevy is lying on the ground, whimpering and clutching his head. Bartie looms over him, pointing at Elder. "What right do you have to punish this man like this?" he roars. "You said you were *so* much better than Eldest, but look at you! The first time someone protests against you, you punish him so severely he can't even stand!"

Elder narrows his eyes and storms back to Bartie and Stevy. "Okay, first? He can stand. It's just a thing that makes your wi-com make noise. And second? *He* punched me. He *punched* me."

Even though Bartie and Elder are close enough now that they could talk in normal tones, both of them are yelling. Bartie has his guitar strapped to his back, and for a crazy moment I think he's going to grab it by the neck and swing it at Elder's head. Instead, he just shouts, "What will you do the next time someone disagrees with you? Kill them?"

"Oh, come on! Quit exaggerating!"

But no one else seems to think Bartie's exaggerating. They're all watching Stevy moan and writhe on the ground.

"It's not that bad," Elder tells Stevy. "And besides, it should be over now." But Stevy doesn't get up. I wonder, is he playing up the pain to get attention, or does it really hurt as badly as it seems?

"We can't trust you, Elder," Bartie says, still shouting loudly enough for everyone to hear. He's drawing a crowd—the spinners have all hopped up from their spinning wheels to see what's going on. The bakers, covered with flour, are poking their heads out of their shop windows. The butchers walk out, meat cleavers still in their hands.

"When have I lied?" Elder says. "When have I proven dishonest?"

I try not to think about how Elder hasn't told everyone that the ship's stopped. It's not a lie, after all, just . . . not quite telling the *whole* truth.

"Everything I've *ever* done has been for this ship!" Elder bellows.

"Even her?" Bartie asks, pointing past Elder. At me.

"Don't bring Amy into this."

I stand, rooted to the spot, as everyone, even Stevy, turns their gaze on me.

When I first woke up on *Godspeed*, I went running and found myself in the City—but it was a different City from this. The people had hollow eyes and seemed robotic; they were frightening because they were so empty inside. Now their emotions are boiling over, and the fear and anger and distrust all writhe together inside them, spilling out in narrowed gazes and snarling lips and clenched fists.

"Get out of here, Amy," Elder mutters, casting a worried glance at me. I reach up and he grabs my hands, giving them a gentle squeeze before releasing me. "Go back to the Hospital. Go to where it's safe."

But I want to stay here. I want to show Elder that I'm not another mistake that Bartie can use against him. I want stand behind him and prove my loyalty.

That is, until someone in the crowd moves forward.

Luthor.

Just an anonymous face in an angry crowd. Bartie shouts something else, and Elder snaps back, and everyone's attention shifts to their argument.

Except Luthor's.

His eyes are locked on mine. His lips curve in a smile that twists at the corners, reminding me of the Grinch who stole Christmas.

He mouths something, and although I can't tell what he's soundlessly saying to me, I can guess the words. *I can do anything I want.*

I run—I race—I flee.

25
ELDER

I'M GLAD AMY LEFT—I DON'T WANT HER INVOLVED IN THIS argument. I hate how quickly Bartie drew her into it.

And I hate how quickly the crowd has grown.

I touch the wi-com on the side of my neck. "Marae, get down here. Bring your police force."

She starts to respond, but I cut off the com link. I need to focus on Bartie.

"Oh, calling for backup?" Bartie sneers.

"Why are you doing this?" I ask. "I thought you were my friend."

"This isn't about friendship." His voice isn't raised now; these are words for just me, even though the entire crowd is listening. "This is about having a chance to turn this ship into the kind of world we want to live in."

"And there's no place for me, huh?"

"There's no place for an Eldest. Even an Eldest who calls himself Elder."

From the corner of my eye, I can see blurs of dark blue and black zipping through the grav tube at the City. Marae will be here soon, along with about a half-dozen Shippers.

Stevy groans and struggles to his feet.

"Okay," I say. "It's all over. Let's just get back to work."

Some of the people in the crowd start to break away. The tension is already diffusing.

"Everyone break it up!" Marae roars, rushing forward.

And there's the tension back again.

"Ah, here comes Elder's latest idea—the *police force*," Bartie sneers, his voice raised again. "Here to make sure we work like good little boys and girls *or else*."

"It's not like that," I say—to both him and Marae.

"Can't anybody see what's going on?" A new voice cuts through the mass of people surrounding us. It's Luthor. Of course it is. He always has been one to revel in a fight, even years ago, when we were living in the Ward. Only now he doesn't bother to hide it. "He's *scared*. Our Elder is *scared*. He's scared of you! You! You have the power. He can't control all of us!"

"We can do what we want!" another voice from the crowd shouts.

"We can lead ourselves!" Bartie calls back.

The call becomes a cheer. *Lead ourselves! Lead ourselves! Lead ourselves!*

Marae and the other Shippers try to drown out the chant with their own shouted orders for silence. Expletives mingle with the chant—sneers and threats. The Shippers respond in kind. Their threats lead to action. Marae shoves a man twice her size back as he draws too close to us; another man takes a swing at Shelby.

I slam my hand against my wi-com. "Communicate area: within fifty feet of my location," I order. As soon as the wi-com beeps that the connection has been made with every other wi-com in the area, I say, "Everyone, *calm down*. There's no need for this."

A few people stop; they're listening to their wi-coms, I can tell. But not enough. "EVERYONE STOP," I shout, and my voice echoes in all of their ears. "Look around you!" I order, and most of them do. "These are *your* friends, *your* family. You're fighting *each other*. And there's no need for that. Stop. Fighting. Now."

I take a deep breath. For the most part, the crowd has stilled.

"And what about Food Distro?" Luthor roars through the quiet.

"What?" My head whips around to Marae. "What's going on at Food Distro?"

"Don't you know?" Bartie says, disgust in his voice. "How *can* you call yourself a leader if you don't even know that food distribution stopped?"

I turn again to Marae. "We were aware of the problem," she says apologetically. "We were just about to com you."

I don't bother waiting for another answer. I take off down the street toward Food Distro. The crowd around us is surprised—they weren't expecting me to suddenly start running straight for them. A few don't get out of my way fast enough, and I bump into them but don't stop. I can hear their voices and the thudding of their feet on the pavement following me, but I'm so frexing angry that I can barely think straight. I do *not* need Food Distro, of all things, added to my problems.

Frex. Frex, frex, *frex*.

The Food Distro is a giant warehouse so far on the edge of the City that it butts against the steel walls that encase the Feeder Level. Food distribution is automatic—or it's supposed to be. When I get to the huge steel-and-brick building, the manager, Fridrick, has chained the doors shut. He stands in front of them, arms crossed, eyes trained on me, waiting for a fight.

Everything in me tenses—my fists, my teeth, my eyes.

"What's going on?" I growl. The crowd that had gathered around Bartie and me now presses against me and Fridrick—and it is even bigger than before. Marae and the Shippers try to move around the edges, urging people to leave and let us take care of the problems, but they're not listening. Instead, the crowd is growing.

"I'll distribute food manually," Fridrick says. "I'll make sure everyone gets their *fair* share."

"What's that supposed to mean?"

"He's keeping the food for himself!" a woman shouts.

"It's not right!"

"Let's break down the doors!"

"Calm the frex down!" I bellow, spinning on my heel and glaring at the crowd. They don't calm—but at least they quit shouting. "Now," I say, turning back to Fridrick, who's been in charge of Food Distro since before I was born. "What's the problem with food distribution?"

"No problem," Fridrick says. "Once everyone leaves, I'll begin distributing the food."

I cast a doubtful look at the chain on the doors.

"He's only going to give food to some of us!" a deep male voice calls out from the crowd.

"For the ones who *deserve* it!" comes another voice.

I risk another glance behind me. Marae and the Shippers are all directly behind me, keeping the crowd from surging forward. There's at least two hundred people here, maybe more. They move in waves, not as individuals, and the waves are pressing closer to Fridrick and me.

"You don't own the food," I say to Fridrick. Now I speak loudly on purpose, intending everyone to hear.

"I do." He glares at me.

"You can't dictate who gets to eat and who doesn't," I shoot back.

"The storage levels are low."

I know they are.

"So what do I do?" Fridrick demands in a mocking tone. "Give everyone less? Or do what should be done—just distribute food to the ones who've *earned* it?"

Angry shouts, cheers of agreement, curses and screams erupt around us.

"There's enough for regular distro for several more weeks. After that, we can discuss rationing."

Fridrick narrows his eyes. "I ain't feeding the ones who won't work."

"Everyone works!" I shout, exasperated.

This was not the right thing to say. Fridrick doesn't answer—the crowd answers for him. They shout names: the names of their neighbors, their family, their enemies, their friends. People who aren't working. The weavers, who only went back to the looms because I mandated their strike to end but who continue to work at a slower pace. The greenhouse producers, who have been caught more than once hoarding produce for themselves. And individuals—specific people who have just decided to *not* work, either because they're lazy or because of depression, like Evie and Harley's mother, Lil.

Rising above it all is a new chant: *No work? No food! No work? No food!*

"And what about the Hospital?" a shrill voice rises above the chant.

"I work!" a voice near the back of the crowd shouts back. My eyes skim over the people and I see Doc, looking nervous and anxious to hear his precious Hospital called into question.

"What about all them at the Ward?" Fridrick says. What he doesn't say is, "What about Amy?"

Shite.

"You're right." Bartie shoulders his way past Marae—who looks very much as if she'd like to punch him right in the neck. "I'm going to apply myself to productive work from this point on," he says loudly.

Silence falls. Every eye is on him. I stare in wonder: how did he do it? How did he command everyone's attention so absolutely? While everyone quieted down to hear Fridrick and me, they weren't respectful. They were waiting for one of us to slip up; they were searching for ammunition to throw back at us. But every single person is focused on Bartie now, waiting for his next words.

He doesn't speak. Instead, he raises his guitar high over his head and stretches the neck of it toward Fridrick. "Consider this payment for this week's food," Bartie says. "And, as there is no longer a Recorder at the Hall, I will take that job."

Fridrick takes the guitar and stares at it, unsure of what to do. Finally he nods, once. He will accept this payment.

"And," I add in as loud a voice as I can muster, "we *will* continue food distro for everyone."

Fridrick narrows his eyes.

"There will be no further discussion," I add in a quieter tone before he can open his mouth. "Food distro will carry on as usual."

I turn to go, not giving him the chance to disagree. When I reach Marae, though, I can hear Fridrick's muttering slicing through the crowd.

"For now."

I turn back, my mouth already open, though I'm not sure what I'm going to say, when a scream rises up from the back of the crowd. The mob shifts—everyone's focus moves from Fridrick and me to the woman on the other end of the block, kneeling on the ground next to a man's body.

I squint.

That's Stevy's body.

2 6
AMY

I'M OUT OF BREATH BY THE TIME I MAKE IT BACK TO THE
Hospital. I'm not as in shape as I was when I ran track back on Earth. Kit
stops me at the door.

"What's going on?" she asks. "Doc just commed me from the City."

I shake my head. "Some people were causing trouble. Bartie and
Luthor and some of the Feeders."

"Doc says it's getting pretty bad," Kit replies. My face must have shown
my worry, because she very quickly adds, "But some Shippers are with
Elder, and I'm sure everything will be fine."

She rushes over to help when a nurse calls to her, leaving me with my
worried thoughts. I start to head to the elevator—I could go to my room,
but I remember Orion's words from the last video: "Go home. You'll find
the answers there. *Go home.*" And while I don't know for sure what he
means, I do know one thing: that little square bedroom in the Ward may
be where I sleep every night, but it is not my home.

Instead, I head back to the Recorder Hall. Maybe Elder's right and
the clue is hidden in an atlas, but I don't think Orion would have done

something that simple. Still, now's probably one of the safest times to go, especially since Luthor is busy in the City.

As I mount the stairs to the Recorder Hall, I notice that the little cubbyhole where Elder's painting once hung is empty. I glance behind me. From here, it's impossible to see what's going on in the City, but I don't like the way Kit assured me that everyone was fine. When people say that, they usually mean that nothing is.

There are fewer people than normal in the Recorder Hall, and most of them aren't watching the wall floppies or heading to the book rooms. Instead, they're gathered in clusters, talking in low, anxious tones. Several look up at me as I enter, and I realize that I'm not wearing my head scarf or my hood. I move to cover my hair, but it's too late. One of the men near the door approaches.

"Were you in the City?" he asks.

I nod. He looks more curious than threatening, but my leg muscles still tense, ready to run if I need to.

"Is it true what they're saying? That there's a riot?"

"I wouldn't call it that," I say. "Look, it was just a handful of people causing trouble."

A woman ducks her head down, listening to her wi-com. Their information is much more current than mine. They can com anyone in the City and get info, but I've only got Elder. My finger hovers over my wrist wi-com . . . but then I remember Bartie and Luthor riling up the crowd, bringing *me* in as evidence of Elder's ineptitude. He'd be better off without me bugging him now, that's for sure.

The others don't look convinced at my dismissal of the City's problems, but I pull my hood up anyway and go to the book rooms in the back of the Hall. It takes me a while to find what I'm looking for, but eventually I discover one oversized book with a map of the world on the cover. I realize, as I pull the book off the shelf, that there really would not be much need for an atlas of Earth here on this ship or when we land on the new planet. This is just for records, I suppose, nothing else.

There's a whole section in the atlas on America. I flip first to Florida—that's where I spent most of my childhood. I run my hands over the pages, but I can already tell there's nothing unusual there, not a floppy, not a mem card, not a handwritten note. I flip next to Colorado. That was the last place I called home. Cold winters. Clear skies. Eternal starry nights.

But empty pages—there's nothing here either.

I wonder if there's anything else with echoes of Earth on this ship—a globe maybe—I remember seeing one on the Keeper Level. But this was a clue Orion left for *me*, and I don't think he'd hide something on Elder's level for me to find.

I wander back out of the book room. I don't notice the silence until I reach the main entryway. The entire Recorder Hall is, weirdly, empty. The few people who were here earlier are gone, leaving the entrance hall to me. I slip out of my jacket, and the cool air makes my arms prickle. It feels almost dangerous to be here, alone, without even the jacket to protect me—but freeing, too.

I gaze at the wall floppies, wondering idly if I should bother trying to look at maps on them, and then my gaze drifts up. Hanging from the ceiling are two giant clay models of planets. A small model of the spaceship *Godspeed* flies between them on a wire.

The planet Earth is smaller than the model of Centauri-Earth and so detailed that I can pick out the long arm of Florida, the bumpy ridges of the Rocky Mountains. I jump up to reach it, but my fingers can't even brush against the South Pole. I briefly contemplate finding a ladder, cutting the Earth down, and smashing it open like a piñata, but I doubt any of Orion's secrets will spill out like candy. The model was there when the ship launched; how could Orion have slipped something inside it?

I glance at the model of *Godspeed*. That one actually looks like it could come down—it would be simple enough to lift the model off the hook it hangs from, and I could probably reach it if I stood on a chair. But . . . *Godspeed* is definitely not my home. Home may not be Florida and it may not be Colorado, but I *know* it's not *Godspeed*.

I hear a soft *beep, beep-beep*. Then again: *beep, beep-beep*.

My wi-com! I raise my wrist to my ear and press the button on the side.

"Com-link req: Elder," the wi-com says.

"Accept!" I say eagerly.

"Amy?" Elder's voice sounds frazzled.

"Yeah. What's wrong? What's happening in the City?"

Elder ignores my questions. "Where are you now?"

I look around me at the empty hall. "The Recorder Hall. I thought it would be a good idea to look into Orion's next—"

Elder cuts me off mid-sentence. "Can you get somewhere safer? Go to your room, okay?"

"What's going on?"

"I just want to make sure you're safe. Lock your door." Elder had my door fitted with a biometric scanner lock the first week I was on the ship, making it one of the few truly private rooms on board.

"Elder, what's wrong?"

"I just . . . I want you safe. I've got to go—" The com link disconnects before he's got the words fully out.

27
ELDER

"DON'T CROWD AROUND! GIVE US SOME AIR!" DOC'S BELLOWING does no good at all; if anything, the crowd presses closer.

"I'm glad you were already here," I say, dropping to my knees beside Doc as he examines Stevy.

Doc touches Stevy's neck, shakes his head, and leans back.

"What happened?" Bartie says. There's no more bravado in his voice. He's my old friend again, the one who used to race rockers across the porch of the Recorder Hall. And he's scared. "What did you do?"

"I didn't do anything," I say.

"You did something to his wi-com. Then he ends up dead." His voice is louder now. He's no longer my friend—he's my adversary. "Is this what happens to people who protest against you, Elder? They die?"

"Don't be a chutz," Doc says. He peels something sticky off Stevy's arm. A small pale green med patch. Our eyes meet briefly. This is a Phydus patch—one of the patches Doc developed recently.

"What kind of med patch is that?" Bartie demands. Behind us, I can feel the others' gazes. Marae, as efficient as ever, has organized her Shippers into a sort of barrier around us, keeping the crowd largely at bay. But it won't last.

"It's a specialized patch," Doc answers Bartie. He looks at it closer, forgetting about Bartie and everyone else as he mutters to me, "Someone's written something on it."

He holds the patch out. Bartie tries to snatch it, but I beat him to it. "Follow," I read aloud. In heavy black ink, just that one word: *follow*.

"But how did this patch kill Stevy?" I ask.

"This one didn't," Doc says. He pushes up Stevy's sleeve, exposing the patches hidden under his clothing. "One patch is harmless. But two more is an overdose." He peels the remaining patches off Stevy's arm.

I frown: med patches are supposed to be fast-acting, but the concentration of Phydus in these med patches seems too strong if just three will instantaneously kill a man.

"What's written on those patches?" Luthor calls out, trying to shove Marae aside so he can get closer.

Doc starts to hand the patches to me, but Bartie snatches them from his outstretched hands. "The," he reads off the first one, loudly so the whole crowd can hear. "Leader." He looks up at me, and there is real fear in his eyes. He thinks I've done this. "Follow the leader. These patches—the *special* patches that *killed* Stevy—are a command. A warning. To *follow the leader.*"

Before I can explain that none of this is my fault, that I didn't write those words or put the patches on Stevy, Bartie turns to the crowd. "This is what happens when you don't follow the leader." He spits out the words and throws the used patches on Stevy's cold body.

"This is what happens!" Luthor cries out, picking up the charge from Bartie. His words ring across the City. "This is the price you pay if you don't follow the leader! Don't follow Elder—and he has you killed!"

"Wait a minute," I shout, jumping up. "No I didn't! No I don't!"

But it's too late. Bartie's and Luthor's words have spread like poison. I can see the fear and revulsion in people's eyes as they break past the human barrier created by Marae and the other Shippers. They spill out, sweeping past me—knocking me down and shoving aside Doc as they scoop up Stevy's lifeless body. They chant—*follow the leader*—but it's a sneering, angry sort of chant. It's mocking me.

It's a battle cry.

More and more people—those who'd been waiting on the sidelines— join the shouting crowd. Stevy's body becomes a banner of revolt. His lifeless form is passed around, raised over the crowd, roiling over the hands of the people like waves.

"Enough," I say.

"They can't hear you." Doc's eyes are flashing, but his face is stony.

I press my wi-com. "ENOUGH!" I roar, and this time, every single frexing person on the ship hears me.

"The ship is now on curfew. Go to your homes. Do not leave them. The Shippers will be enforcing this curfew tonight. Everyone—*everyone*— is to leave the City streets, leave work, and retire to their own homes." If Eldest were giving this sort of order, he would have spoken with cold authority. But not me. I'm so mad I'm shaking, and I can't keep the quiver of anger from my voice. I turn my attention now to the mob in front of me, even though this com is going out to every single person on board the ship, "Look at what you're doing. Look at how you're treating the body of one of your own. This is disgusting. Leave him here so Doc can send him to the stars."

Silence.

"Go. Now," I say, and my voice sounds exactly the way Eldest's voice used to.

They go.

They grumble, and they scowl, and they mutter curses . . . but they go.

Marae moves silently beside me. "They still fear you," she says.

"They fear the past. They still remember Eldest."

"It's enough. It worked, didn't it?"

But I don't know if it did. Because I might have just enough authority in my voice to send them all home, but now what will they talk about behind their closed doors?

28
AMY

WHEN I GET TO THE ELEVATOR AT THE HOSPITAL, MY HAND hovers over the 3 button, but at the last second, I press 4 instead. I don't want to hide in my room. If something is wrong, if I need to be somewhere safe . . . I'd rather be with my parents. Besides, the cryo level is one of the safest places for me on the ship. Although Elder told everyone about the level after he took the ship off Phydus, few of them cared to see it, and fewer still can access it with their biometric scan. On the fourth floor, I race down the hall and roll my thumb over the scanner. As the elevator to the cryo level opens, my wi-com beeps.

Even though his voice has to travel all the way from my wrist, I can hear Elder's roar of "ENOUGH!" through my wi-com. I raise the communicator to my ear, but the sinking feeling in my stomach has more to do with Elder's message than the descending elevator. Someone has *died*.

Someone else. First the girl in the rabbit fields. And now, whoever was killed in the City.

I *have* to figure out what Orion's clues mean. He hasn't told me what choice I'll have to make or what he's ultimately leading me to, but it can't be worse than the rage and fear and anger that's going to keep growing until the people pull the ship apart—especially once they learn the ship's not even moving.

I bite my lip, thinking. Orion knew this would happen. He had this planned from the start, from the moment he pulled me back out of the cryo chamber. Whatever secret he's kept, he knew we'd need it now.

So why the hell did he give me such a confusing clue? Go home? What does he mean by that? Doesn't he realize that I don't have a home anymore?

The elevator doors slide open, and I go straight to cryo chambers 40 and 41, just as I have every morning for the last three months. Then I pull out my parents and sit down on the ground. It's not like they can give me answers, but if I focus my eyes on their frozen faces, maybe I can focus my mind on Orion's puzzle. Just as I start to sift through my muddled thoughts, though, the elevator dings.

My heart drops.

Someone's coming.

My first thought: *Elder.* But no. He's in the City.

My second thought: *My parents.* I jump up and slam them back into their cryo chambers, my heart racing. The doors to their chambers click closed just as the elevator doors slide open.

Victria.

"What are you doing here?" I snarl. I shouldn't—there's no reason for me to act like that—but I'm on edge.

Victria doesn't bother answering me—she gives me one quelling look, then strides straight across the room to the genetics lab.

When she reaches the door, I call out, "It's locked."

Victria doesn't bother turning around. She just runs her thumb over the biometric scanner, types in the password, and walks straight into the lab.

"Hey!" I say, jumping from the table. "How did you do that?"

I jog over to the lab door. Victria leans against the workbench where Eldest and Doc used to store DNA/RNA replicators.

"How did you know the password?" I ask. "And how did you get past the biometric scanners? The only ones who can unlock this door are Elder, Doc, and some of the Shippers."

"And you." She says this as if it was an accusation. It's true—but I don't bother to reply to her sneer. Instead, I wait for her explanation. "Elder gave me access more than a month ago," she admits.

"He . . . did?"

Victria finally turns her attention to me. "You know, Elder did exist before you came along. Frex, he even had friends and a life, all without *you*."

"I . . . I know."

Victria's face is stony, but I can see the muscle in her jaw clenching from how hard she's keeping her emotions in check.

"Can you please go?" she asks. But she doesn't look at me. She's looking at the cryo chamber where Orion's frozen, his eyes bulging, his hands clawing at the glass. I shut the door to the gen lab, giving her privacy.

Elder said he and his group of friends broke apart after Kayleigh died. Victria, I think, as the only other girl in the group, lost more than any of them, with the exception of Harley. I can see her, the writer who loved books, spending most of her time in the Recorder Hall. Where Orion was.

She must hate me. First I took away Elder and Harley, two of her last childhood friends. Then I took away Orion.

I somehow never thought of anyone caring about Orion. My memories of him revolve around the last time I saw him alive. Even though I thought when I first met him that he was kind and gentle, generous and friendly, all I can really remember about him is the crazed look in his eyes as he shouted at Elder to let my parents and the other frozens die. But of course, Victria never saw that. All she saw was her friend, the Recorder, with his face twisted and frozen.

And, on a day when Elder locks down the entire ship, when she must be scared because we're all scared—on a day like this, she ignored the command to go to her room. She goes, instead, to Orion.

I realize then: she didn't disobey Elder's order. He told her to go home. Well, sometimes home is a person.

I turn back to the cryo chambers. Victria has unwittingly given me the answer; I finally understand what Orion meant. He told me to go home. And I did, even before I understood what he meant.

I put my hand on the handle of cryo chamber 42. It's where I should be. It's the only home I have left.

I pull open the door.

I talk to my parents every morning, but this time, the lingering scent of the cryo liquid brings bile to the back of my throat. I gag, my body remembering how it felt to drown in the sickeningly sweet liquid. I can't breathe, and then I'm breathing too much, and with every breath comes the scent of the cryo liquid, and that scent is killing me.

I remember the way the liquid burned my nostrils, the way my vision blurred cornflower blue.

The glass box inside is missing a lid—it broke in pieces when Doc and Elder dropped it in their haste to rescue me from drowning in my chamber.

I'm thrown back into that time. I remember being in pain, but my memory of what hurt and how has faded with time. Instead, I remember Elder's deep soothing voice. I was so scared, so disorientated, and his voice pulled me through the fog of terror.

I force myself to quit thinking about waking up and instead focus on the actual cryo chamber. The glass is cool to the touch, and I marvel at how slender the box is, how my arms and legs pressed against the glass as I struggled to escape.

My hands stop.

There—right where my heart would be if I were lying in the box now—is a single piece of paper, folded in half.

My hand shakes as I unfold it.

MILITARY PERSONNEL ABOARD *GODSPEED*

1. Katarzyna Bergé
4. Lee Hart
12. Mark Dixon
15. Frederick Krasczinsky
19. Brady MacPherson
22. Petr Plangariz
26. Theo Kennedy
29. Thomas Collins
30. Ximena Roge
33. Alastair Potter
34. Aigus Wu
38. Jeremy Doyle
39. Mariella Davis
41. Robert Martin
46. Grace Spivey
48. Dylan Farley
52. Iñes Gomez
58. Aislinn Keenan
63. Emma Bledsoe
67. Jagdish Iyer
69. Yuko Saitou
72. Huang Sun
78. Chibueze Kopano
81. Mary Douglass
94. Naoko Suzuki
99. Juliana Robertson
100. William Robertson

29
ELDER

AFTER REMINDING DOC TO STOP BY LIL'S HOME BEFORE taking Stevy's body away, I help the Shippers inspect the City streets. Faces peer through windows as I pass. Sometimes I catch a meek glance marred by worry and fear, but more often the people glare down at me. They may have obeyed my curfew, but their eyes are defiant, angry.

My stomach roars—my last real meal was yesterday—and I only stop to eat when Marae insists. The streets are empty, but we don't leave until the solar lamp clicks off. As I ride the grav tube up to the Shipper Level, I can't help but notice that nearly every light is on in the City. I'm pretty sure I can guess what they're staying awake to talk about.

Most of the Shippers remain in the City—they make their homes here, after all, only coming to the Shipper Level to work—but Marae follows me up the grav tube. As our footsteps ring out across the metal floor, I realize that tonight, after Marae leaves the Shipper Level and I return to the Keeper Level, I'll be even more separated from the rest of the ship—two empty levels, all for me.

We make our way toward the *whirr-churn-whirr* of the engine. It's dark inside the Engine Room, but the engine still casts a shadow. It smells of burnt grease, but it seems smaller in my eyes, now that I know it's not moving the ship. Marae doesn't look at it at all as she crosses the floor and goes straight to a thick, heavy door with a seal lock.

The Bridge.

I remember Eldest's words for me before I started training—the Bridge is for the Shippers. I take care of the people, not the ship.

Marae opens the door and waits for me to enter first. An arched metal roof curves over the Bridge. The room is a pointed oval, drawing me to the front of it. There are two rows of desks with monitors protruding from them. A giant V-shaped control panel is built into the front of the room.

I sit down at the control panel and try to imagine what it would be like to steer this massive ship down to the new Earth.

But I can't. . . . The idea is so impossible to me that I can't even imagine being the triumphant leader who lands the ship.

I jump up from the chair. Eldest was right. I don't belong here.

Marae stands in front of one of the control panels. There are two screens there, both blank. One is labeled COMMUNICATION, the other NAVIGATION. "I was working on this today, as you requested, when you commed me to help with the . . . with the trouble," she says, brushing her fingers over the metal navigation label.

"Have you had a chance to figure out where we are?" I ask, interested.

Marae scowls. "It's a mess." She lifts up a hinged panel below the screens, showing me a jumble of wires and circuitry. "If I had to guess, I'd say this was deliberate, probably as far back as the Plague—after all, we did lose communication with Sol-Earth at that time."

"So someone, probably the Plague Eldest, cut communication with

Sol-Earth and that destroyed the navigation equipment too?" I ask, noting how both operations were housed in the same control panel.

Marae shrugs, hiding the ravaged electronics under the metal panel again. "I've been trying to sort it all out."

Even though she tries to disguise it behind an even-toned voice, I can still hear the disdain. "I'm sorry about today. I know the Feeder Level problems interrupted your work."

Marae eyes me. "You did well today," she says finally.

"Did well?" I snort. "That was one step away from a riot. Next time it *will* be a riot. But—thank you. It really helped that the Shippers stood on my side."

"The Shippers always stand on the side of the Eldest," Marae says simply, in the same tone she'd use if she were to tell me that the name of the ship is *Godspeed* or that the walls around us are steel. "But . . . I hope you realize, Elder, that we wouldn't have needed to be down there if you'd put the ship back on Phydus. If we didn't have this kind of trouble, then the Shippers and I *could* focus on the problems with the engine and the nav system."

"No Phydus," I say immediately, but the determination that's usually in my voice is gone. Even if Stevy was poisoned by Phydus, Marae's still right. How much time was wasted—not just in the Shipper level, but across the whole ship—today? We *have* to work, or we'll all die. We can't afford to break down like this.

"Eldest," Marae starts.

"Elder," I insist.

"Without Phydus, things are going to keep getting worse. They don't care what kind of leader you are—they want someone else. Anyone else. Or no leader at all. People are, at their heart, constantly moving toward a state of entropy. Much like this ship. We're all spiraling out of control. That's why we need Phydus. Phydus is control."

I sigh. "I admit, the way I've run things—or not—in the past three months hasn't worked well. I thought I could trust everyone to keep doing things the way they were."

"Can't you see?" Marae asks gently, like a mother talking to her child. "That's *exactly* why we *need* Phydus. That's the first thing you need to do, if you want to control the ship like Eldest."

"I don't."

"You don't what?"

"I don't want to control the ship like Eldest," I say. "Amy—" Marae narrows her eyes at the mention of Amy's name. I continue anyway, a growl in my voice now. "*Amy* helped me see that Eldest never controlled the ship anyway; he just controlled the drugs. I think I can do better than that. I hope I can."

"You realize," Marae says, "without Phydus, this may mean mutiny."

I nod.

I know that.

I've known it all along.

30
AMY

I STARE AT THE PRINTED LIST AND CURSE ORION ALOUD. Another puzzle.

I glance behind me, but Victria's still in the gen lab. Orion's clue was simple: *1, 2, 3, 4. Add it up to unlock the door.* I run my finger down the list, counting. Twenty-seven people on the list. The doors on this level are locked with a keypad—maybe punching in 27 will unlock one of them.

My hand goes immediately to the wi-com on my wrist. I know Elder would want to open the door with me. But I don't push the button. All I can think about is the anger in his voice when he ordered a curfew. And—I cringe—I promised him I'd go straight to my room and lock the door. How mad will he be if he finds out I came here instead?

Still clutching the list, I rush past the rest of the cryo chambers and head to the hallway on the far side of this level. There are four doors here—each made of thick, heavy steel and sealed shut with its own keypad lock. The hatch that leads out to space is through the second door—the keypad is smeared with red paint, a reminder of Harley's last night. There's one door to the left of it, one door to the right. At the end of the hallway is another door, the largest of all.

I start with the door to the left of the hatch. The keypad has both letters and numbers. I try typing in 27 first, but an error code flashes across the screen—**ERROR: PASSCODE MUST BE FOUR DIGITS OR MORE**. I try 0027 next, and when that doesn't work, I spell it out: *t-w-e-n-t-y-s-e-v-e-n*. Nothing.

I move to the right, past the hatch, and try the password on each of the other two locked doors.

Still nothing.

Frustrated, I recount the number of the people on the list, but it's still twenty-seven. I run back to the elevators and grab a floppy from the table there, checking the official record of frozens against Orion's list. Twenty-seven.

The significance of who Orion listed isn't lost on me—he's trying to remind me that the number of frozens in the military indicates trouble for those born on the ship. He thought this was a good enough reason to try to kill them all, including my father. And while, yes, twenty-seven military personnel out of a hundred frozens may be large, Orion's still a psycho to think my father would be okay with enslaving anyone.

I try the stupid doors one more time, but they still stay locked. Whatever the passcode is for opening the doors, it's not 0027 or *t-w-e-n-t-y-s-e-v-e-n*.

Frustrated, I take the elevator back up to the Hospital and—after locking my door, just as I promised Elder—I stare at the wrinkled paper until I fall asleep.

For the first time in a long time, I dream about Jason, my old boyfriend back on Earth. In my dream, Jason and I are at the party where we met. Even though in my memory, the party is full of laughter and dancing and fun, in my dream all I see is cigarette smoke and jocks who splash their red plastic cups of beer on me. When Jason and I meet outside, it starts to rain—but it's not romantic warm summer rain. It's spitty, cold, sharp rain. My father would have called it "pissing rain," and it stings my skin and gets in my eyes.

When we pull apart, Jason says, "I love you now that I can't have you."

And I say, "You were my first everything."

But Jason shakes his head. "No, I wasn't."

And before I can figure out what he wasn't my first of, he kisses me.

It's sloppy and wet and awkward and our teeth clack together and his tongue feels like a dying fish in my mouth, flopping around.

I pull back—but it's not Jason kissing me, it's Luthor.

"You'll never escape," he says.

I want to run away, but my muscles are frozen as Luthor steps closer. His mouth opens in a wide grin, and his teeth are all black and rotten. I open my mouth to scream, but before I can, his lips crash against mine.

I wake up, struggling against my tangled quilt. My face is damp—with sweat or tears, I can't tell. As soon as I escape my bed, I run to the bathroom and splash cold water on my cheeks, still gasping from the scream I never sounded in my nightmare.

I grip the sides of the sink with both hands, unable to stop shaking. I don't recognize the girl in the mirror. Eyes red, lips cracked, fear spilling out. I don't like admitting how much Luthor scares me. I wrap my arms around myself, squeezing them tight against my body. Why should I be so afraid of him when he hasn't even *really* done anything? Is *almost* a good enough reason for fear?

Yes.

The room caves in around me. What I want to do is run, but I'm too afraid of what lurks in the dark, in the places where there's nothing but cows and sheep and no one to hear me shout for help.

And that pisses me off.

It's not just Luthor, though he's the biggest part of it. It's the eyes that glared at me in the City. It's the way some of them, like Harley's mother, Lil, still flinch when they see me. It's the fact that it will be this way for the rest of my life, and there's nothing I can do to stop it, no more than I could jumpstart the ship's engine. I can't change what I am or where I came from, and because of this, they're never going to accept me.

I dress quickly—so quickly that I mess up my hair wrap and have to do it over again. I doubt anyone's awake yet, it's so early, but I don't want to risk it. I make sure the paper I found last night is tucked securely in my pocket and then I am out the door, through the silent Hospital, and racing down the path. When I reach the grav tube dais, the solar lamp clicks on, momentarily blinding me. I press the wi-com on my wrist and activate the grav tube.

The winds start up, and for a minute I think about jumping out, just comming Elder and asking him to come get me. A few strands of my hair float up. Then the winds accelerate and even more hair escapes from my scarf, reaching up like thousands of tiny arms. For one instant my toes are on the ground but my heels are lifted, and then *whoosh!* I'm sucked up into the tube. I shut my eyes. I don't want to see the Feeder Level shrink away as I soar higher and higher. I don't open them again until the winds die down and I step out onto the Keeper Level.

I try to smooth the scarf over my hair, then give up and rip it off, stuffing it into my jacket pocket. I don't have to hide my hair from Elder anyway.

I open my mouth to call for him, then snap it shut, realizing something.

For the first time in three months, I didn't start my day by talking to my parents on the cryo level.

When I woke up sad and lonely and empty inside . . . I came straight here.

Straight to Elder.

Just like Victria went straight to Orion.

Orion was wrong about me. It's Elder who's my safe place. Elder's my home.

The Keeper Level is silent. I'm going to feel like an idiot if I've come all the way up here and Elder's not around. But as I cross the Great Room, I can hear soft snoring. Elder's bedroom door is open. I lean through the doorway.

He looks younger asleep, the exact opposite of the fierce aging that yesterday's chaos spread across his face. The room is messy in a way only a boy's room can be messy: clothes everywhere, despite the fact that he's got a "hamper" that automatically cleans clothes *right there*. There's a musky scent in the room, something that doesn't exactly smell like Elder, but that reminds me of him even more. You could drop me anywhere in the universe, blindfolded, and I'd know this was his room just from the smell.

I step over piles of clothes and sit on the edge of his bed, near his feet. Elder's bed dips, and his eyes flutter open.

"Amy," he says in a sleep-heavy voice, warm and smiley, drawing the syllables out so that my name ends with "meeee."

"Amy!" he shouts, sitting straight up in bed. "What the frex—how'd you—why are you here?"

I grin. "I found this," I say, tossing the folded paper I found in my cryo chamber at Elder's lap. He reaches for it, stretching in a way that reminds me of a cat.

"What is it?" he asks as he reads the page.

"It's a list of everyone in the military who's frozen on the cryo level. I double-checked it against the official records." Elder looks confused, but then I add, "It's the next clue Orion left for me . . . for us."

Elder stares at the paper, brow furrowed in thought. "The last clue was about adding things up."

"Yeah," I say. "I counted—there are twenty-seven people on that list. But I tried twenty-seven—the number, spelling it out—it didn't work. None of the doors opened."

I don't know what I expected from Elder—for him to suddenly remember *another* locked door somewhere on the ship or for him to magically add up the list to something other than twenty-seven, but all he does is say "Hmmm," and toss the paper back to me. He slides out of bed, and once he's past the covers, I see that he's not wearing pants. In fact, all he has on are a pair of boxer shorts—made of thin white linen and considerably shorter and tighter than the boxers boys wore on Earth. I stare openly. When I'd raced up here and plopped onto his bed, I hadn't thought about what he'd be wearing—but now—

Elder laughs, and I notice his smirk.

"Oh, shut up and put some pants on!" I say, throwing a pillow at him.

I'm still blushing as Elder—now fully clothed—leads me back to the grav tube in the Learning Center. He pushes his wi-com to start the tube, then turns and holds his hand out to me.

Wait, what?

"I'll go after you," I say, stepping back.

Elder raises an eyebrow, a hint of a smile playing on his lips. "Come on, just ride with me."

We'd done it once before, of course. But that was when I was half-drugged with Phydus, and before . . . before I'd started thinking about how life stuck on a ship wouldn't be so bad if Elder walked around pantsless more.

Before I can protest again, Elder pulls me closer, the warmth of his body wrapping around me. He holds me loosely, knowing that I still don't know what to do with his touch, but his grip is firm enough to make me certain that he'd never let me fall. Elder moves closer to the grav tube opening in a sort of sidestep-twirl. He uses his free hand to touch his wi-com.

"Ready?" he whispers. The words float around my face like a summer breeze.

I nod, because I can't find any of my own words.

The grav tube comes alive, the cool winds rushing and swirling in and around, making my hair flutter and our clothes cling to our bodies. Elder tightens his grip around me, takes one step forward, and plunges us into thin air.

We fall for a moment, in darkness between the levels, and my heart beats in my throat—not only from the exhilarating pull of the grav tube, but also from the way Elder's arms encircle me, holding me closer than he's ever done before. We're not free-falling—we're being sucked down, fast, faster than a person should fall. I cower against Elder's grasp, clutching my hands around his neck and burrowing my face into his shoulder, but his hold on me doesn't falter. He's the only stable thing in the swirling chaos.

A burst of light—we've gone through the entire Shipper Level and are already being sucked down into the Feeder Level. The tube bends—the Feeder Level has a curved roof, and the angle makes me feel as if I'm not just falling down, but falling on top of Elder. I think about wiggling away, but my body doesn't want to abandon the safety of Elder's arms.

I glimpse past his shoulder, once, and see the Feeder Level stretched out before me. I don't feel anything seeing it, not hate or love, and so I don't watch the fields and buildings zoom closer as we near the ground.

And then the winds calm, my hair floats down—an impossible tangled mess now—and we bob next to each other in the air for a minute before the winds stop and we're standing on the platform on the Feeder Level.

"See?" Elder says, tucking my hair behind my ears. "Not so bad."

I step back, off the platform, resisting the urge to smooth his hair down.

As we step onto the trail, our shoulders brush. I step away and walk a little in front of him.

"Come on," I say, unable to meet his eyes.

31
ELDER

AMY LEANS AGAINST THE CRYO-LEVEL WALL, WATCHING AS I approach the keypad by the locked door to the left of the hatch.

"I told you," Amy says, "twenty-seven doesn't work."

"Let me see the list again," I say. Amy thrusts the wrinkled paper into my outstretched hand. My wi-com beeps, but I ignore it.

"They look like submarine doors." The catch in Amy's voice makes me look up at her.

My mind races, trying to remember what a submarine is. One of those underwater things. I didn't think they were real. But then again, I used to think the ocean couldn't possibly be as big and deep as Amy said it was.

"They're all seal locked," I say. "The door to the Bridge is that way, too, and the hatches that connect the different levels. In case there's damage to the ship and one level's exposed, we can seal it off and . . ." I drift off, my attention turning back to the list.

"My father took me to see the USS *Pampanito* when I was kid—I only remember it because the name was so ridiculous that I sang it about a million times as I raced through the tiny hallways. *Pampanito! Pampanito! Pam-pa-NITO!* My dad tried to catch me, but he hit himself on the head trying to crawl through one of the small doorways. Almost knocked himself out." She gives a tiny laugh, but the sound dies quickly. I glance up from the list—Amy's staring at the wall, her eyes glassy.

I will do anything to make her happy again, so I give her the stars. I type the key code in quickly—*Godspeed*—and the hatch door flies open, exposing the millions of glittering dots in the sky.

I remember the first time I saw the stars. I thought they changed everything. I thought they changed me, like I'd become a different person just by seeing shining specks of light a million miles away. Now when I stare at them, I feel nothing. I don't believe in them anymore. When I first told everyone on the ship that I was giving them the freedom to be themselves, I took those interested in seeing the stars—the real stars—here. Some came. Far fewer than I'd expected. And then I realized: when you've lived your entire life within ten square miles surrounded by steel, it's easier to forget the outside. It makes it less painful to be trapped on a ship if you tell yourself it's not a trap.

That's the whole reason why I can't tell everyone about the stopped engine.

My gaze shifts to the red paint by the keypad. Maybe one day the smears of paint Harley left throughout *Godspeed* will fade, and maybe the stars never will, but I'd rather have Harley's colors.

Harley died for . . . well, I don't know what he died for. I just know he's not here anymore, and I miss him. But Kayleigh died for a truth, according to Orion.

His words echo in my mind, and I'm grateful. I don't want to think about hollow stars and Harley.

Instead, I think about Orion's puzzle. Orion seems to have known more about the ship's engine than anyone else. If I can figure out his frexing clue, I might actually figure out *why* the engine's stopped, maybe get us going again. *Add it up . . .*

I turn back to the list Amy found. Beside each of those twenty-seven names is their cryo-chamber number. What if I add those numbers together . . . ?

1,270.

"What are you doing?" Amy asks.

I try 1270 on all four doors, starting with the biggest door at the end of the hall.

The last door opens.

Everything is darkness. The room smells of dust and grease. I think about what Orion said, just before I froze him. *The frozens plan to work us or kill us.*

I want to see these weapons for myself.

Amy finds the light switch before me. It flickers on reluctantly, spluttering as if unwilling to show what the room contains.

And I can see immediately what made Orion fear that, when we land, we'll be made into soldiers or slaves.

You know what's really going to twist you? Orion had said just before I spun the dial to freeze him. *The fact that Elder sort of agrees with everything I'm saying.*

Pistols, rifles, larger guns than that. Blister packs of mustard bombs. Missiles—most about the size of my forearm, three that are bigger than me. Everything's sectioned off in compartments, sealed in heavy red plastic bags that are stamped with labels and FRX symbols.

"We don't know what's going to be on Centauri-Earth," Amy says, already defensive. "It could be aliens, or it could be nothing. It could be monsters or dinosaurs. We could be giants on the new world. Or we could be mice."

"Better to be armed mice, huh?" I say, picking up a filmy bag that protects a revolver.

"I know this looks bad."

"It looks like everything Orion said before was true," I say.

"It's *not*," Amy says immediately, but how does she know? I can see her thoughts warring—on the one hand, she believes absolutely that her father and the rest of the people from Sol-Earth would never use the weapons spread before us, but on the other hand, she can't deny that the weapons *are* here. And they seem so much more . . . I don't know, *violent* than I expected.

I head to the other side of the room, where the largest weapons are stored. I recognize torpedoes and missiles and bazookas from the vids of Sol-Earth discord Eldest showed me. A shelf lines the back of the room, cluttered with small round things, small cakes of compressed powder carefully packaged in clear plastic.

Amy picks one of the powder cakes up. "These look like toilet bowl cleaners we'd use on Earth, the kind you'd drop in the back of a tank." She turns it over in her hands, the heavy plastic package crinkling. Then she notices my confused expression. "Oh, yeah, the toilets here don't have tanks."

On the bottom of the heavy, clear, thick-plastic packaging is a warning label etched into the container:

Anti-agricultural Biological Chemical

For use with Prototype Missile #476

Range: 100+ acres

To employ: See Prototype Missile #476

FRX

FRX . . . Financial Resource Exchange. The group that funded *God-speed's* mission in the first place.

On the next shelf is a similar cake-tablet, but this one is black, and the label on the bottom calls it an Anti-Personnel Biological Chemical.

I put the things back on the shelf cautiously, careful not to set anything off. It takes all the strength I have not to throw them away, hurtle them as far as I can, shove them all out the hatch.

"Don't tell me you still think this is all for self-defense," I say. I don't want to pick a fight with Amy, but surely she can see these weapons are extreme. "This is chemical warfare. It's preparation for genocide."

"My mother's a geneticist and every bit as important as my father in the military," Amy counters immediately, but her voice is guarded, and I don't know if it's because she doesn't want me to question her beliefs further or if it's because she can't bear to let herself doubt them. "If the FRX was intent on wiping out all life on Centauri-Earth, then why would they enlist a biologist to help? Why have a scientist who studies life if all they want to do is kill everything? There are twenty-seven people in the military—but seventy-three who aren't."

I nod at her. She's right. Of course she's right. But that doesn't mean Orion's wrong.

Amy turns her back to me, surveying the armory. She gasps.

"What is it?" I ask.

Instead of answering me, Amy bends down and slides a mustard-colored blister pack off the shelf. "This thing looks like half a softball," she says, handing it to me. I turn the blister pack over and read the warning label on the bottom.

Warning: explosive; mild irritant
Explosive Compound Formula M
Range: 10 feet
To detonate: depress top center;
detonation time: three minutes
FRX

I put it back on the shelf as gently and quickly as I can, turning to see what Amy found under the blister pack.

"Look!" Amy says excitedly, waving a floppy. "The next clue!"

I lean over Amy's shoulder, wondering if this new vid will be about the weapons we've just discovered or if it will help us fix the ship. "Why did he use a floppy instead of a mem card this time?" I ask idly.

She shrugs. It doesn't matter—here's the next clue, and we're one step closer to finding what Orion hid before we froze him. And one step closer—I hope—to discovering just what that secret is.

And if it has anything to do with bringing the engine back to life.

I barely dare whisper the thought in my mind—but—there's no denying the fact that Orion knew much more than any of us thought he did, and it somehow revolves around the stopped engine. This giant secret he keeps hinting at—it *must* be the key.

"Ready?" Amy asks, swiping her fingers across the screen.

Instead of seeing Orion sitting on stairs and talking, though, the screen remains black. I lean closer. Amy's grip tightens, making the floppy curve.

"Why isn't there a video?" she asks. "Did I do something wrong?"

I shake my head just as white words start to scroll across the black screen.

You've made it this far. That's good. I expected nothing less from you.

First, I have a question for you. Why do we have these kinds of weapons?

"That's exactly what I've been wondering," I mutter.

"Mm?" Amy asks, her eyes bouncing from word to word.

"Nothing," I say.

There has to be a reason for it. You have to be asking yourself the same thing I asked Eldest: If we are on a peaceful, exploratory mission like Eldest said—why are we armed for war?

Eldest never really answered me. It's for when we land. That's all he'd tell me. That the frozens have a reason for needing this kind of weaponry. But you don't have guns like these unless you plan on killing something. It's either us or them—whoever, whatever is on Centauri-Earth.

Either way, we—all of us born on the ship—are going to be caught in the middle when we land.

The last words fade to nothing but black, and then static fills the screen, quickly replaced with an image of Orion on the bottom of the big staircase. This video is different from all the other videos—not just because it was prefaced with scrolling text, but because Orion is much younger here, maybe twenty or so. The camera films at a crooked angle, and Orion reaches out and readjusts it. He keeps looking around, as if nervous to be discovered.

ORION: I just learned the secret. The big one.

"He's younger here," Amy says.
"He looks like me," I say.
"No, he doesn't."
He does.

Orion leans forward on the steps, closer to the camera.

ORION: This is bigger than the cloning, bigger than Phydus. It's the reason for Phydus.

"He sounds like me too."
Orion swallows hard. A few moments pass before he speaks again. Amy casts a worried look in my direction, but I ignore her, focusing on the way Orion chews on his bottom lip.

ORION: Eldest doesn't want anyone to know this secret. I don't think he even wanted me to notice, but . . .

Orion speaks in a hurried voice now, low and urgent. We both lean forward too, neither of us breathing as we strain to hear.

ORION: . . . the outside of the ship needed maintenance. He told me to send First Shipper Devyn, but instead, I did it. I—I saw what he wanted me not to see. He's angry. Angrier than I've ever seen him. I've thought before that he might . . . But this time, I really think . . . I might have to . . .

The camera pans to the left, behind the staircase. A bundle of supplies lies open on a makeshift cot, along with a few sealed boxes.

ORION: I've been preparing for a while. Ever since I first saw the icy hell in the cryo level. Ever since I learned about the cloning. I know I can be replaced. It won't take much for Eldest to follow through with his threats.

The camera pans back to Orion, who looks defiant. *He looks,* I think, *like me.*

ORION: I may know Eldest's secrets, but he doesn't know mine. He hasn't figured out where I'm hiding or how. He's been watching me on the wi-com system, but I've figured out how to trick the signal, make it look like I'm at the Hospital when I'm not.

Orion raises a hand to his left ear and gently touches—but doesn't depress—the button there.

ORION: He doesn't know about this place. But it's not enough. I might have to . . .

Orion's fingers seize over the wi-com, his nails scratching the skin and leaving pink welts in their wake. I glance at Amy as she touches the bracelet wi-com on her wrist with one finger, a worried frown on her lips.

ORION: But the secret . . . it should stay a secret. No one should know this. Not even me. It's . . . too much.

Orion stands and begins pacing. His feet come off camera and on camera; his voice fades in and out.

ORION: I don't know what's frexing right anymore. Do I tell the truth? Or is the lie better? . . . And what about . . . ?

Muffled sounds echo as Orion moves away from the camera.

ORION: I can't cover it up. Someone may need to know—there might be a time when we have to . . . But the floppy network's not safe . . .

I strain my ears to make out the indistinguishable sounds in the background—Orion's muttering something, words I can't make out over the sound of his footsteps marching back and forth in front of the camera. He picks up the camera, and a jumble of images wash over the screen. After a moment, he turns the camera back to his face, now cast in shadows.

ORION: I'm leaving this for whoever finds it. If something happens to me . . . if Eldest . . . you know. Well. If something happens to me, I figured someone ought to know.

Orion takes a deep breath, then opens his mouth to speak. The video cuts off abruptly.

"That's it?" Amy asks.

"No, look—there's more."

Scrolling words fill the screen again.

That was a long time ago, but it doesn't make it any less true. Amy, you've seen the truth for yourself. You've seen the weapons. You know—you must know—that if we need weapons like this, then whatever's on Centauri-Earth isn't worth it. Lock up the armory, forget the passcode, and walk away.

3 2
A M Y

"WELL, *FREX*," ELDER SAYS, LEANING AWAY AND LOOKING AT the blank floppy in disgust.

I look up at him inquiringly.

"All that floppy did was prove that he was paranoid—and that this whole clue-chasing thing has been pointless."

"Pointless?" I pick the floppy up and stand as well.

Elder nods. "Pointless. I was hoping to learn how to restart the engine, but all we get from this vid is some big secret that Orion decided not to share with us. He sent us on a chase all over the ship to find clues that lead to a door that he *just tells us to lock again.* You don't get much more pointless than that."

I nod, folding the floppy and slipping it into my pocket. "There is definitely something sketch about this," I say as soon as the last words fade to black.

"Sketch?"

"You know, weird."

A wry grin slides across Elder's face. "Every time I think I know you, you say something so . . . strange."

"Ha!" I punch him on the arm. "I thought we've been over this before: you're the one who speaks *sketch*."

Elder pushes the heavy submarine-like door closed, and I make sure the door does lock behind us—but I'm not going to forget the code.

"I think Orion was scared," I say, following Elder down the hall.

"He was loons." Elder's voice is bitter. "That was filmed around the time Eldest tried to kill him, and it's clear he'd already lost it. Orion was paranoid—"

"He had a right to be paranoid." I can't help it; I touch the smooth skin behind my left ear, remembering the way Orion had scratched his skin in the video. What did it take for him to dig deeper into his skin, to rip the wires from his own flesh? I glance at the wi-com encircling my wrist and swallow back bile at the thought of how it was *those* wires, dripping in gore and blood, and . . . *ew.*

"It's weird, though." I pause, thinking. "All the rest of the videos have been on that mem card thing. This one was already loaded on a floppy, sitting in the armory. None of the other ones had text. And none of the other ones were that old. That video was made just before Orion faked his own death. Maybe someone, I don't know, messed with it."

"Maybe. Maybe not." Elder frowns at the video. "Look, I get that Orion made these vids for you, and you feel like you have to solve his frexing riddle. But we're going to have to figure out how to live on this ship without whatever stupid message he left for us." He runs his fingers through his hair. He usually does this when he's thinking, but there's anger in the way he does it now, as if he's only doing it to stop himself from punching something. "We have *serious* problems to deal with—and this was just a frexing waste of time. The engine isn't going to fix itself. Orion's just distracting us from the *real* problems."

I bite my lip. Orion didn't leave a message for us; he left it for *me*. And it was something about getting off the ship, I know it. The key to fixing the engine, the reason for the delay—something. Something important.

Besides. How much longer can we go on like this?

"Hold on," Elder growls, and then turns away from me, jabbing his wi-com button on the side of his neck with such force that it looks like it hurts. He speaks in a low voice for a moment, then shouts, "What?!"

"What is it?" I ask softly, putting my hand on his arm.

Elder jerks away from me. "What?" he says again into the wi-com. "I'll be right there." He presses the button behind his ear again and glances at me before taking off down the hallway toward the elevators. "I've got to go," he says.

"Why? What's wrong?" I have to jog to catch up. "Elder, what's wrong?"

"Bartie's causing more trouble." Elder slams his fist into the elevator call button. "I can't waste my time with this anymore," he says.

"It's not a waste," I say softly.

The elevator doors open, and Elder holds his arm out to prevent them from closing without him. He searches my eyes. "I'm not angry at *you*," he says, his voice sincere. "But these 'clues' aren't going to fix the ship."

Elder steps into the elevator, leaving me alone on the cold, empty cryo level. Part of me wishes he could stay, but I know he's needed on the other levels. As I walk slowly back to the locked doors, I wonder how things would be different if Elder didn't have to be in charge of *Godspeed*. I would never ask him to give up the leadership he's longed for all his life . . . but maybe if he didn't have to care about the ship first, I could believe him when he said he cared about me.

I pull the floppy we found out of my pocket. Maybe Elder is right. Maybe this is nothing but a wild-goose chase.

But . . . it's all I have right now. It's all I've had for three months. It's the first spark of hope I've had since waking up, and I have to cling to it. I have to. I have to believe something, *something* will come of this.

I play the video file again, skimming over the words and straining my ears to pick up some nuance in Orion's tone, something that will give me a clue.

Orion's voice—so much like Elder's—fills the hall. "Eldest doesn't want *anyone* to know this secret. I don't think he even wanted me to notice, but . . . the outside of the ship needed maintenance. . . . I—I saw what he wanted me not to see."

"Whatever you found," I tell Orion's face, "you saw it outside the ship."

We can't go outside the ship. There's the vacuum of space, waiting to suffocate us or turn our lungs to mush or pop our eyeballs or whatever. We'd die. Unless . . . unless behind one of the two remaining locked doors are *space suits.*

I stare up at the hatch that shows the stars. Well, *of course* there'd be something to enable people to safely go out the hatch. Surely the makers of the ship realized that in centuries of travel, the ship would need maintenance. That's what Orion called me in the first video, his contingency plan—this must be theirs. Four locked doors on this hall. One leads to the armory, one leads to an evacuation hatch . . . one must store space suits.

The possibility of what I'm thinking hits me so hard that I don't breathe for a minute. Then I remember the other thing Orion said.

But the secret . . . it should stay a secret.

No. I want—I need—to follow this through to the end. I need to know what Orion knows. Because if it's something that will get the ship going again, that will get us to the planet—it's worth it. And if it's proof that the ship will *never* move again—that's worth it too. It's the not knowing that's killing me. Not knowing if there's a chance that something can change, not knowing if there's hope at all.

I play the video again.

The thing is—there's something different about this clue. It feels off. It was on a floppy, not a mem card. The scrolling text, the fact that Orion was so much younger—it's as if someone found this video and cobbled it together from an old film. Which means . . . Orion didn't make this.

Someone else has the real video—the real clue.

33
ELDER

"FREX," I MUMBLE AS MARAE RUNS DOWN THE LIST OF EVERY
thing that's happened so far today. I've only been with Amy for two hours,
tops, but I should have known better than to ignore my coms.

First there was the meeting Bartie held at the Recorder Hall as soon as
the solar lamp clicked on. Second Shipper Shelby had been there already
and commed Marae, who tried to com me. By the time Marae had gotten to the Recorder Hall with the rest of the first-level Shippers, Bartie
had already presented his ideas for what the ship's leadership should be
like in the future, with an added note that I was too inept to rule. Thirty
people had pressed their thumbprints on his petition, giving it their mark
of approval.

Then Marae tried to "arrest" Bartie, but I don't think she really even
understood what the word meant, even though we've all been reading up
on police forces and civil conflicts. I think she thought if she just shouted
"I arrest you!" really loudly that would mean he'd quit, but instead he
uploaded the petition to the floppy network and everyone on the ship had
it by lunch.

Not that I had lunch. By midday, I was back in the City, standing up on the table at the Food Distro, explaining that, for some reason, wall food production was delayed. The whole time, the Food Distro manager, Fridrick, was staring at me, smirking, and I kept remembering how Bartie said that you could start a revolution if you took away people's food. I did an all-call explaining that extra portions would be delivered for supper, but no one was really satisfied with that answer.

It wasn't until now, with the workday nearly done, that Doc bothered to summon me to the Hospital and explain that someone had broken into his office and stolen his supplies of Phydus med patches.

"Why the frex didn't you tell me this sooner?" I shout.

Doc cringes. "You looked busy."

I roar—an inarticulate sound with no words. The stolen patches explain a lot—as I was running from one end of the ship to another, I'd noticed surreptitious looks and veiled comments, but I'd thought it was people passing around Bartie's manifesto. Now I see they were also passing around the Phydus patches. The people who've been depressed—and many who weren't—are trading anything they have for them.

"The worst thing," Doc tells me as I stare at his disheveled office, "is that this must have happened yesterday. I haven't been back to my office since early last morning. Whoever killed Stevy must have pocketed the patches after I left."

Doc's lips curl in disgust. I don't know which part he hates the most: that someone stole med patches, or that whoever it was turned his office into a mess.

"I made the concentration of Phydus in the patches high on purpose," Doc says, "so that one patch could quickly placate a person. But the problem is, with such a high concentration—"

"It only takes three patches to kill a person."

"Yes. It's very concentrated—two patches, and . . . It slows everything down. The organs. It's too much for the body to handle. Three is death. I should have diluted the drug, but I thought . . ."

"You thought you'd be the one administering it."

"Me or Kit. Someone who knew the dangers and could regulate it." He sounds guilty, sad. But I'm as much to blame as he is. I approved the use of the patches.

We both stare silently at his trashed office for a moment. Everything is normally so neat and organized. But now it's a chaotic mess. The desk shoved to one wall. The locking cabinet smashed open, with med patches spilling out in all colors, but none of them pale green.

Kit runs into the office. "There're reports," she says breathlessly.

"Of what?" Doc snaps.

"Dead. Someone dead. From the patches."

We immediately spring into action. Doc drives the electric cart across the Feeder Level, with me riding behind him. As the level flies past us, all I can think of is how much worse everything has been since I took over.

"You're going to have to do something," Doc calls back to me over the roar of the electric cart. "Something to really make the Feeders see you as leader. Use this problem to show your strength!"

Yeah. Right.

When we get to the City, Doc stops the cart in front of the weaving district. "Why are we stopping here?" I ask, my heart sinking.

Before Doc can answer, someone yanks me off the back of the cart and throws me onto the street. I stumble, almost losing my balance.

"You frexing chutz!" Bartie bellows.

I step back, surprised.

"What are you—?" I start.

Bartie shoves me, hard, with both hands on my chest. I stagger back, hitting the cart with the back of my legs. He hurls a handful of square, pale green med patches at my face.

"Did you do this?" Bartie shouts. He towers over me.

"I don't know what you're talking about."

"Those 'special' med patches are full of *Phydus*, you chutz." Spit flies in my face as he growls the words at me.

"I—I know," I say, looking over his shoulder where the patches he threw at me lie scattered on the ground.

"You *know?* You're not even going to deny it? You *know?* How could you let *Phydus* back on the ship? You—*you*—swore that you wouldn't use it again! You stupid frexing chutz!"

"How did you get any?" I shout back. I don't like the way he's in my face, the way he won't back up, give me room to breathe. I try to lean up, but he doesn't back down.

"How could you?" Bartie sneers. "You prance around here, talking about how great you are for letting the people all get off Phydus, and then you just slather some frexing med patches on them and call it done! Anyone get in your way—anyone cause too much trouble—just slap a frexing patch on them!"

Bartie spins away from me. But just as I take a step toward Doc, who's standing on the curb, too shocked to do anything, Bartie turns back and shoves me hard so that I slam against the side of the cart again.

"You're *worse* than Eldest, you know that? At least he treated us all the same. You're just picking us off as you choose."

He turns to go, shaking his fist out.

"Wait a frexing minute!" I shout. Bartie stops but doesn't turn; his back is stiff and straight, and his fingers curl into fists again. "I didn't do anything wrong!"

"Didn't do anything wrong?" Bartie sneers without turning around. "Tell that to Lil."

He strides off. The people on the street are silent, watching us. As soon as Bartie turns the corner, they start whispering.

"Lil?" I ask Doc as I gather up the patches from the ground, stuffing them into my pockets. They may be scattered throughout the rest of the ship, but at least I can make sure these don't fall into the wrong hands.

Doc's face is creased in a dark frown, but he's glowering at where Bartie walked off, not at me. "She's the one Kit found dead."

I rush up the stairs to Harley's childhood home. I don't know what I expect to find there—his mother is already dead. Lil's trailer is exactly as it was before—messy and slightly smelly. When I enter her bedroom, Lil's just where Amy and I left her, sprawled on the bed.

Across her forehead are three pale green patches. One word on each patch.

Follow the leader.

"You know what that means, don't you?" Doc asks. When I don't answer, he adds, "This was murder. Someone killed Lil. For you."

"For me?" I can't take my eyes off her body. It seems to melt into the bed.

"Follow the leader. It's a warning to others—to those who don't."

"But Lil wasn't rebelling. She wasn't involved with Bartie's group, and she never spoke against me—"

"She wasn't working," Doc says. He sits beside Lil on the bed, peeling the patches off one by one. They cling to her skin, lifting it up a little and making a *schlick* sound as they pop off her. "Anyone not working, anyone not fulfilling the needs of the ship . . . they're not following you."

Doc waits until I tear my eyes away from Lil's body. "She was murdered for you," he says clearly, slowly, as if to make sure that I understand the weight of her death rests on my shoulders.

34
AMY

I CAN'T KEEP STILL. I MAY HAVE GIVEN UP RUNNING, BUT I can't think cramped up on the cryo level, with all the locked doors mocking me. I have to *move.* When I get to the Hospital lobby, though, I'm surrounded by shouting patients, angry nurses, and a crowd that seems to grow by the minute.

"It's safe!" Doc's apprentice, Kit, tells a woman loudly. "Just one is *fine!*"

"How do I know that?" the woman asks. Her voice is thick, like she's been crying.

"Well, look at yourself," Kit says, exasperated. "You're fine, aren't you?"

"I think so . . . but . . ."

Kit growls in frustration and marches off, nearly crashing into me.

"Sorry," she says.

"No prob. What's going on?"

"Those frexing med patches. People are worried they're dying, but if they'd had the overdose, they'd already be dead. Try to convince them of that, though."

"What med patches?"

Kit reaches into her lab coat and shows me a square green patch. "Doc developed them for the depressed patients. Works, too. If you have only one. Problem is, word's gotten out that three or more will kill you."

"What's in them?"

"Phydus." She says it matter-of-factly, but she waits for my reaction before continuing.

Phydus. I thought we were through with that.

Part of me is angry. Very, very angry. I thought Elder and I agreed. I *thought* he had *promised*. No more Phydus. But another part of me can't forget the crowd that turned into a mob in the City.

"We're all going to die!" the woman Kit had been arguing with shouts. She grabs Kit by the lapels of her coat, her knuckles turning white.

Kit wraps one hand around the woman's wrist, and, surprisingly, the woman easily releases her. Her arms drop to her sides, and her whole body relaxes.

"There, isn't that better?" Kit asks gently.

The woman doesn't answer. And then I notice the pale green patch on the back of her hand.

Kit leads the woman to a chair against the wall and deposits her there. She turns back to me with a satisfied look on her face. And—I can't help but smile back at her. That worked. Maybe if Elder had had some patches in the City yesterday, things wouldn't have gotten so out of hand. And maybe if I had had one in the fiction room when Luthor burst in . . .

"Can I have some of those patches?" I ask Kit.

She narrows her eyes at me. "Didn't you hear? They're not safe. We're trying to get all the ones that were stolen back. Only Doc, the nurses, and I are supposed to use them."

Interesting. The patches were stolen.

"Can I just have one, then?" I ask.

Something in Kit melts. I think she thinks I'm depressed about being the only freak on the ship—she's always been nice to me in the way that some people are super-nice in a suffocating sort of way to people who are handicapped.

"Don't tell Doc," she whispers, slipping me a patch. I hide it in my pocket, next to the floppy I found in the armory.

I pull my jacket hood up before I leave the Hospital, but, armed as I am with a Phydus patch, I don't bother with the scarf around my hair. I head directly to the Recorder Hall. It's a long shot, but Orion left the clues—the *real* clues—for me. Even if the last clue was tampered with, Orion's had a pretty solid plan to make sure I've gotten where I needed to go. So far, the clues have come from Harley's paintings or the Recorder Hall. Maybe the next one will too.

Yeah. Right. It's going to be so easy to find one clue out of all the book rooms, art galleries, and artifact rooms in the Recorder Hall—*if* the clue is even there. For the first time ever, *Godspeed* actually feels . . . huge. I've got a snowball's chance in hell to find this thing.

I can't help but smirk. After all, Dante's hell *was* made of ice.

As I approach the Recorder Hall, I see a group of people standing in a tight cluster on the porch. I pull my hood lower and slip my hand into my pocket, fingering the Phydus med patch.

"The ship needs guidance," a man says.

I stop near the handrail, hesitant to go up the steps. Instead, I turn around so, if the group looked at me, they'd only see the back of my jacket.

"Bartie?" a woman asks. "Maybe Luthor?"

"Maybe one of them. But not necessarily. Just someone . . . older. More experienced."

I try to look casual and uninterested as I strain to hear more.

"Elder's been training for this his whole life," a female voice says. I want to cheer—at least someone's sticking up for Elder.

The first man's laugh is harsh and mirthless. "Elder never *listened* to Eldest. They're too different."

I think of the giant cylinders hidden on the cryo level, filled with clones of Eldest. They're more alike than the man could guess. Part of me thinks that, perhaps, Elder should have told them about the cloning. It was one of the few things he kept secret, and I don't begrudge him this— after all, the only person this secret affects is him.

"Haven't you noticed how slim the rations are getting? There wasn't even lunch today. Elder thinks if he controls our food, he can control us. And if that doesn't work, he'll patch us. Those patches are dangerous— they've already killed."

"I'd like to know how those frexing patches got everywhere," a woman with a deep voice says. "I half think Elder did it after the trouble at the Food Distro. He might not be putting that frexing drug in our water any- more, but he's making sure the troublemakers get it somehow."

"Doc said the patches were stolen," the first woman, the only dissenter in the group, says.

"He *says*," the man shoots back. "But Doc's always brownnosed the Eldest. I bet Elder told him to make sure anyone causing trouble gets patched."

"Yes, but—" the woman starts to say.

I've had enough. "Are you really going to stand here and spread lies about Elder?" I demand, whirling around and striding up the steps toward the group. "You're going to start a rebellion, talking like that."

The man in the center of the crowd turns, but he doesn't seem to care much that I've overhead him. If anything, he's proud.

"This isn't about rebellion," he says gently, as if explaining something to someone very young. "Have you read Bartie's manifesto?" He waves the floppy at me, but I don't take it. "This is about doing what's best for the ship. About keeping everyone safe and happy." He pauses. "The ship is more important than any one person. Even Elder."

"Happy?" I shoot back. The kinder the man's voice is, the angrier I'm becoming. "What has Elder done to make you *unhappy*?"

The woman with a deep voice shakes her head. "It's not that Elder's *bad*. It's that he wasn't our choice."

"Bartie lists all kinds of books in the Recorder Hall," the man says, waving the floppy at me again. I still don't take it. "All those governments on Sol-Earth. They had systems. Voting and elections, things like that. Things where people could *choose* and have a voice."

"Taking the ship from Elder isn't the right thing to do," I insist. They seem so—I don't know, *logical*—that I think if I could just sit them down, show them how hard Elder's working, how much he really cares, maybe they wouldn't be so willing to trash him.

"I'm sorry," the man says. "But we can't trust you either."

"And why not? I live here too!"

He shakes his head. "But you're not one of us." His eyes drift down to my red hair spilling from the jacket. I try to stuff it back under the hood. The man smiles smugly. He looks perfectly at ease, as if he's in complete control. In contrast, I can already feel my face is hot. "All I know," he says, "is that we didn't need police before you. Everything was fine before you."

I back down the first two steps. "Maybe Elder would be the leader we need him to be if he didn't have any distractions," the deep-voiced woman says in a conversational tone, as if she's not talking about eliminating *me* as a distraction.

I back down the next two steps. "It did all start with her," the other woman says.

I'm gripping the Phydus patch in my pocket, deeply aware that one won't subdue everyone in the group. Why did I bother trying to say anything? I should have known better.

Orion's list brushes against the back of my hand.

No. I won't let them scare me away from the chance to find the next clue.

I storm up the stairs and shoulder past the woman with the deep voice. The man steps out of my way, but he does so with an eerie twist on his lips, watching me as I push open the doors to the Recorder Hall and enter. I don't like that look. It reminds me too much of the way Luthor looks at me, as if I'm a thing, not a person.

Inside, the Recorder Hall is mostly deserted. A single man, tall and skinny, reads an essay by Henry David Thoreau on the *Literature* wall floppy, and four people are bunched together, reading about the Boxer Rebellion. But no one's looking at the *Science* floppy at all. That's strange. This is the first time since Elder took the ship off Phydus that no one's analyzing the engine diagram, trying to improve efficiency, not knowing that the engine hasn't moved us forward in years.

I make my way quickly to the book rooms. I don't think the group on the porch is going to bother following me in here, but I'd rather get done as quickly as possible.

I bypass all the nonfiction rooms. Orion left this clue for me, and even if someone else has hidden it, I still think my best chance of finding it is either in fiction or art.

I have to have a chance of finding it. I have to.

Someone probably changed the last clue—deleted parts, probably added that text—but Orion left me a much more elaborate path. He's put so much care and planning into hiding each clue. There *has* to be something else, some way to figure out the next step.

I trail my fingers along the shelf, looking for something that might hint at Orion's next clue. I flip through Dante's *Inferno* again, and then *Paradiso* and *Purgatorio*. I look through everything by Lewis Carroll, including that stupid poem Ms. Parker made us diagram, "Jabberwocky."

This is useless. Orion may have left the next clue in a book, but he didn't leave it in a book he's already used.

I collapse into the chair in front by the metal table in the center of the room. A copy of Shakespeare's sonnets lies in the middle, just where I threw it after finding it misshelved by Dante a few days ago. I guess the new Recorder, Bartie, is too busy writing manifestos and trying to start an unneeded revolution to bother with doing his actual job.

Sighing, I snatch up the book and head for the *S* shelves. There's just enough room to squeeze the sonnets between *King Lear* and *Macbeth*.

I head for the door—might as well see if there's anything attached to any of the rest of Harley's paintings.

I pause. Orion had a contingency plan for everything—why not make sure the clues are close together, just in case someone tampered with one? I'm the only one who ever really bothers with the book rooms—and before me, there was only him. What are the chances of someone else putting a book on the wrong shelf—*right* next to the book that held the first clue?

I rush back to the *S* shelf, my hands shaking as I reach for the poetry book. The pages are glossy and thick, dotted with illustrations from the Elizabethan era. On the first page is a color portrait of Shakespeare. The Bard wrote about star-crossed love, but I doubt he ever realized his works would one day be soaring through the stars.

I frown. We're not exactly *soaring* now, are we?

I flip through the pages quickly, creasing them in a way that I know Elder would frown upon. But . . . there's nothing here. I force myself to slow down, reading each poem even though they make little sense to me.

I take a deep, shaking breath. Part of me wants to throw the book against the wall. I'd gotten my hopes so far up.

Maybe Elder's right. Maybe this whole thing is pointless.

Still, I take the book with me as I head back to my room in the Ward.

The Hospital's still busy even though it's nearly time for the solar lamp to turn off, but the third floor is almost empty. Only Victria sits in the common room, staring out the window. I start to say something to her, but I remember the angry look she gave me when she found me in Harley's room and in the cryo level, so I move straight to the glass doors leading to the hallway. She glances up at me as I pass, but not with an angry glare.

She's been crying.

I think of saying something to her, but I doubt she'd care to speak to me. I hear her sniffle as I reach for the door. *She hates me.* There's a muffled sound behind me, like she's holding in a sob. But I hear anyway.

I let the glass doors close and head over to the couch.

"Go away," she says, but there's no heart in her voice.

"What's wrong?"

She turns back to the window.

I lean into the seat cushion and cross my legs. "I'm just going to stay here until you tell me."

She waits a long moment, as if testing me. When I don't move, she finally speaks, her words fogging the glass of the window, "I just miss him. The worse things get, the more I think about what he might have done."

"Is this . . . is this about Orion?" I ask.

She chokes out a laugh, a wet sound marred by her angry tears. She swipes her arm across her face. "It's stupid really," she says, still talking to the window more than to me. "He . . . he was older than me. I was just some stupid little kid to him. But . . . I've always loved stories. Books. And I'd go to the Recorder Hall, and he'd be there."

My lips twitch up in a small smile, and I think back to what I knew of Orion before I discovered he was a murderer. He wiped my face and hands clean when I'd been crying once, and I sort of wish I could do the same for Victria now.

"The thing that makes me so upset," Victria continues, "is that I never had a chance to tell him. I mean, I think he knew, but I never actually said the words. I'd go to the Recorder Hall almost every day, and we'd talk and joke, but . . . I never said what I wanted to. And now it's too late."

It's sad how much Victria and I have in common—she wants to reveal her deepest secrets to people who are nothing but ice, too.

"I think," I say slowly, "that if you really loved him, he probably knew, whether you said it or not."

She finally turns to look at me, and there's a hint of a smile on her lips. Her eyes are mostly dry now. "I just wish I had a choice," she says.

"A choice?"

"If I could, I'd make myself not care anymore."

We're both silent for a long moment.

If I could quit caring about my parents, frozen below, would I? It would make things easier. I wouldn't wake up every morning with a hollow ache inside of me.

And then I think of Elder. It's the question I ask myself every time he looks at me with those soft eyes of his, every time he jumps to do something just because I asked it: do I love him? I don't *know*. But I do know that I can at least tell myself I don't.

"I think love is a choice," I say. That's why I can't love Elder. Because I don't have anyone else to choose from.

"But who," Victria asks, "would choose this?"

We both look up when the elevator doors slide open.

Shit.

Really?

After all this, *he* has to walk in? What, does he have a stalking meter on me or something?

"Get out," I say.

Luthor grins.

"My two lovely carros, all in one room together."

"Get out," I say again.

He moves toward where we are sitting. I jump up, but Victria doesn't; she curls her legs up under her and wraps her arms around her stomach.

"You know," Luthor purrs, "I think it might be fate. To see the both of you, here, together."

I put my hand in my pocket, but I don't back up as he draws closer. There's nowhere to back up to, anyway—we're trapped in front of the windows.

He reaches out to touch me. He strokes my left arm in a sickeningly gentle way until his fingers brush against my elbow, then he grabs me and pulls me roughly to him. Victria chokes out a sort of sob-scream, but I jerk my right hand out of my pocket and slap him full across the face.

It's a strong slap—but not strong enough to make a full-grown, well-muscled man fall to the ground. Not without a little help, anyway. He crashes down, his fingers still wrapped around my elbow. My shirt rips before I can shake him off. He lies on the floor, looking up at me passively.

"What the frex?" Victria whispers. She's still curled in on herself, but she leans forward to stare at Luthor's body.

"Kit gave me one of those new med patches," I say. I nudge Luthor's face with my foot, showing her the pale green square outlined by my handprint on Luthor's cheek.

"You were pretty fast to get that out."

"Yeah, well," I say, "I don't exactly trust Luthor."

"Yeah." Pause. "Me either."

I look at her, really look at her, past the hard shell she always wears. Luthor spoke to both of us with that purr in his voice. And, even now with Luthor on the floor, she holds her arms around her stomach. In protection, but not for herself.

"Are you pregnant?" I whisper.

Stupid question. Nearly all the women on board the ship are pregnant—the Season did most of that, and Doc's needles did the rest. But the ones not on Phydus, people like Harley and Luthor and Elder and Victria, chose whether to participate in the Season or not.

She nods.

I step over Luthor's immobile body and sit down on the couch next to her. "What did he do to you?" The words come out as a whisper.

She stares at Luthor. He blinks at the ceiling. The Phydus patches are stronger than when the drug was in the water. He'd do anything I told him to, I think. He would walk off the roof of the Hospital if I led him to the edge. Nice thought.

Before, Victria was crying. Now, her eyes are dry, even though I can see the still-damp tracks of tears snaking down her cheeks. Now she keeps the tears inside her, controlling them in a way she can't control the past.

She curls tighter, her knees under her chin.

"It was him," she says, eyes shut.

I'm afraid of what she means, but I've already guessed the truth. I touch her shoulder. Her whole body shifts into me, but she doesn't let go of her knees, of the way she's made herself into a tight bundle around her stomach. Because she lets me, I wrap my arms around her.

"It was him," she says again. Her voice sounds like a faraway echo. "During the Season."

"Luthor?" I whisper. My voice catches in fear of what she's saying.

"I didn't want to," she says. "He was so *violent*." She glances up at me, her eyes wet and red. "He mentioned you. Because he didn't get you . . ."

Because he didn't get me, he went to her.

"I tried to . . ." Her voice cracks. It doesn't matter what she tried to do, or didn't. I understand.

I remember that moment when I gave up. When I waited for it to be over.

For me, though, it stopped.

But not for her.

No wonder she hates me: because I was spared, and she was not.

And now, with her body curled up in protection around her baby, I realize that it's not stopped, at all, during the past three months.

What lasted for minutes for me is still with her, growing inside of her, a thing she must hate and love all at the same time.

I wrap my arms tighter around Victria and pull her closer to me. "It's over," I whisper, even though I know it's not. It never will be.

I tug at Victria's left hand until she releases the death grip she has on her knees. She looks at me curiously as I flatten her fingers. Her hand is cold and clammy, but it's no longer shaking. I wrap my pinkie finger around hers.

"This is a promise," I tell her, squeezing her pinkie with mine. "A promise that you don't have to be alone with this secret and pain anymore."

Her finger lies still in mine—she doesn't believe me. She stares at Luthor's immobilized form.

I think we both get the same idea at the same time. Our eyes meet. Luthor can't move—he's helpless.

For the first time, we have the ability to take back a little bit of what he took from us, months ago.

So we're going to.

Victria uncurls from the couch. She's hesitant at first, but then she gets up slowly, deliberately. She stands over Luthor's body.

And she kicks him as hard as she can, right in the stomach.

He gives out a sort of breathless *Oof!* but doesn't move.

She kicks him again, and again. Water leaks from his eyes, but he doesn't protest or move to defend himself, even when Victria kicks him in the groin, hard.

She drops to her knees, beating his chest with her fists. "How could you," she gasps. "I *knew* you!"

I squat down next to her. "Let it go," I say, "Come on." I touch her shoulders to pull her away, but she jerks back—not to hit him, but to bury her face in her arms, sobbing.

I can't stand to see her break like this. I can't stand to know that when the patch wears off, he'll blame her, he may still try to hurt her, or me.

I drop to my knees near his face. His eyes still stare straight up, but I can tell by the way they twitch that he knows I'm here.

"I want you to know something," I whisper in his ear softly. "I want you to know that I know where I can find a gun. If you don't know what a gun is, look it up in the Recorder Hall. My father taught me how to hold a gun steady, how to breathe out as I squeeze the trigger, how to group my shots in a target so that even if the first bullet doesn't stop you, the next will. When I was fourteen, my father took me hunting with him, in Colorado, and I killed an elk. He did this so that I would know what it is to take a life, so that I would not hesitate to do it when I needed to. I am telling you this, now, so that you know I won't hesitate to kill you."

Luthor's eyes dance back and forth; he's trying to get the power to turn—away from me or toward me, I don't know.

I lean closer to him, so close I can smell his skin, and when I speak, I can see how the little hairs near his ear move with my breath. "I also want you to know that I won't kill you right away. But that you'll wish I had."

I stand up and offer Victria my hand. She takes it, but as we head to the door, she breaks away from me and delivers one last vicious kick to Luthor's face.

We leave him, broken and bleeding, on the floor.

3 5

E L D E R

THE NEXT MORNING, I WAKE TO A COM.

"Are you up yet?" Amy's voice is excited.

"I am now," I say, stretching. "Is anything wrong?"

"Nope," she says. "Come down to the cryo level."

"Amy, is this about Orion and his frexing clues?" I ask, pulling on pants. "I don't have time for that. I've got to focus on the engine and keeping the ship going—look at what happened yesterday while I was on the cryo level."

"Don't get sassy. Just come down here."

"Sassy?"

"Come on!" she says. "You're going to want to see this!"

"Oh, really?"

"Elder, remember the video last night?"

"The vid that got cut off? Amy, either Orion was loons or someone else messed with that video. Either way—"

She cuts me off. "That's beside the point. There was still enough information for me to figure it out. Remember when Orion said Eldest started to scare him? He said it happened after he got off the ship."

"Off the ship?" I say, so surprised that I pause on my way to the grav tube.

"Whatever he found, he saw it outside the ship."

"Which means . . ." I say, not daring to finish my thought aloud. I start running to the tube entrance.

"That the next locked door must contain spacesuits."

Amy's pacing in front of the elevator by the time I reach the cryo level. "What took you so long?" she demands. Before I have a chance to answer her, she grabs my arm and starts dragging me to the hall in the back.

"I read the whole thing last night," she says, tossing me a slender book.

"What's this?" I turn it over, reading the title.

"Shakespeare's sonnets. Keep up. Anyway, I read the whole thing—actually, I had to read it twice—but I finally noticed something *very* interesting."

"Interesting how?"

"Turn to page 87."

Balancing the book in one hand, I carefully turn the pages. Amy taps her foot impatiently, but I don't want to risk damaging this treasure from Sol-Earth. I turn over page 85. And—

"Where's page 87?" I ask. I flip page 85 back and forth—but the book jumps straight to page 89.

"Exactly," Amy says, a huge grin spreading across her face. "It's so neatly cut out of the book that you'd never notice that page was gone unless you were looking for it."

"This is the clue?" I ask, handing the book back to Amy.

"I think the clue was on page 87," Amy says. "Someone altered whatever clue Orion left in the armory, trying to make us give up and quit looking. Whoever did that also cut the page from the book."

"How did you find it?" I ask. I'm trying to remember what any of Orion's videos said that indicated Shakespearean poetry.

"It was in the fiction room," Amy says. *"Anyway,"* she continues when I open my mouth to question her further, "the point is—that missing page. It had a sonnet on it." She turns back to page 85 and shows me the book. "This page has Sonnet 29 on it." She turns to page 89. "This page has Sonnet 31. Which means that page 87 must have had Sonnet 30 on it."

Amy tosses the book to the ground and my eyes go wide to see a treasure of Sol-Earth treated so casually. Amy doesn't notice, though, as she spins around to the largest door at the end of the hall. "Codes have to be at least four digits long," she says. "So try 0030." She jerks her head to the door on the right of the hatch.

"This is never going to work," I say.

In answer, Amy punches 0030 in the keypad by her door.

"Told you," I say when nothing happens after I punch the code in my door too.

Amy picks the book back up and examines it again. "But . . . I was so sure."

I look over her shoulder. "I don't know why you think those sonnets are numbered. They have letters beside them, not numbers."

"It's Roman numerals," Amy says dismissively. Then she lowers the book, meeting my eyes. "It's *Roman numerals.* We shouldn't use 0030 as the code—we should use XXX. And a zero in front, since there needs to be four digits."

She rushes to the keypad and tries 0XXX.

Her door doesn't unlock. "Why did the Romans use letters instead of numbers?" I ask.

She ignores my question. "Try that lock," she says, moving closer to the door I'm at.

"You're getting your hopes up for nothing. Orion was loons. This whole clue chase is loons."

"Just. Try. It."

I roll my eyes and tap out 0XXX on the keypad.

Beep! Click.

"Frex," I say in awed surprise.

.

3 6
AMY

THE DOOR SWINGS OPEN, AND IT'S NOT UNTIL I TAKE A HUGE
gasp of air that I realize I'd been holding my breath. For all my confidence,
I can't believe that worked.

There are ten cubbyholes built into the wall, one suit in each compartment. Cords and tubes are coiled at the base around heavy boots, and
shelves over the suits display helmets that, despite a fine layer of dust, still
retain some of their mirror-like shine.

Elder rushes inside and runs his hands over the nearest suit. It looks
like a painted paper bag but drips from his hand like silk. Behind the silk-
like body suit, I can see harder pieces that look like plastic armor.

"Do you know how to use these?" Elder turns, asking me with shining
eyes.

"Why would I?" I say.

"You're from Sol-Earth. These were made there."

I laugh, a short, bitter bark. "The whole ship was made on Sol-Earth;
that doesn't mean I know anything about it!"

"But—"

"There's a manual," I say. A thick metal-and-glass screen connected to a
coiled cord hangs on the wall. Maybe it once worked as video instructions

or an interactive guide, but the cord is frayed and the glass cracked. Under the monitor, though, is a thick black book. Good thing it's pretty hard to break a book. I pick it up and flip to the first page. Two-thirds of it isn't even in English. The part that *is* in English is so complicated it makes my eyes cross. At the end of the book, though, is a step-by-step illustrated guide of what to do to operate the space suits. I guess the builders of the ship made sure the people on the ship could use the suits even if their language somehow evolved or something else went wrong.

As I hand the manual to Elder, I notice that it had been resting on another book.

"What's that?" Elder asks me, but he's more interested in the manual than the slender book I found beneath it.

"*The Little Prince*," I say, reading the title aloud. It's such a small book that the huge manual hid it completely. Could this be another hint from Orion? One page is dog-eared, and I turn to it. The colors are faded, but it's still possible to decipher the illustration in front of me: a giant king dressed in a robe embroidered with stars sits atop a tiny planet.

Below the illustration, a line of text is circled and recircled, over and over.

"I," replied the little prince, "do not like to condemn anyone to death."

"Well, that's ominous," I mutter. The text reminds me of the threat I made last night. Clearly the little prince never met someone like Luthor. I glance up at Elder. I should tell him. But . . . now is not the time.

I lift up a folded piece of paper that's been slipped inside the book. My hands shake as I unfold it—I recognize the feel of this paper, thick and glossy.

Sonnet XXX, the clue that was lost. Or stolen.

The text on this page is riddled with lines and a note. "Look at this," I say, turning to Elder.

Whatever interest Elder had in discovering the next clue is now gone. His entire attention is focused on the space suits. I grin at him; he looks like a kid who's been told he can get whatever flavor of ice cream he wants from the shop.

I carefully tuck the ripped page into my pocket and turn to the operating manual. It's obvious Elder couldn't care less about old books and hidden clues while we're looking at space suits.

"There are two kinds of suits—one for extended exposure and one for moderate exposure. The brown ones are smaller and easier to use, but you're only supposed to use them for about two hours or less."

"That's fine," Elder says, going to the cubbyholes. He picks up a body suit, and it's not so much brown, as in the picture, but bronze. It sparkles in the dim light of the room, and when he shakes it out, dust mingles with glitter.

"The moderate suits have an underlayer of protection against outside elements and hazardous temperatures," I continue. "Then you put on the outer suit over that, for insulation and more protection. The outer suit seems to just snap on, then you connect gloves and boots over that. This looks crazy simple," I say. "I thought a space suit would be really complex."

"The other ones, the ones for long exposure, do look more complicated. But if Orion's right and the problem is obvious, I should only need the short-exposure suit," Elder says. "A little help?"

He's already discarded his own clothes—they lie in a heap on the floor—and he's zipped himself into the bronze underlayer.

"Uh—no. No," I say, striding over to him.

"What?" he asks.

"*NO*. You are *not* going out there. No way. Not with a flimsy suit you only know how to use because of an illustrated guide. *No*."

"Amy, it—"

"NO."

"But—"

"Don't you remember what happened to Harley? Space isn't a field on the Feeder Level! It. Will. *Kill*. You. And this?" I pinch the silky underlayer with my finger and let it snap back against his body. "This isn't good enough. You can't just throw on a suit and jump off the ship!"

Elder looks at me doubtfully, like a child frustrated with an overprotective mom. I don't care. I lean in closer to him. "You're too important to risk."

"The vid," Elder says, his voice low. "It's the only way to figure out what Orion meant."

"You were the one who said Orion was loons."

"Yeah, but—"

"Besides, that last clue was probably tampered with. Most likely someone didn't want us finding this room or the suits, and—"

"But *Amy*," Elder says. "Space suits!" Elder can't keep down his excitement about going out into the stars—but I can't keep down my fear.

"The suits don't change anything!" But I'm wrong. They change everything. "Let me go," I whisper. "Let anyone else. We can't risk you."

Elder smiles—a huge, carefree grin, and I really do feel like a mother watching her baby totter off into a fire. "I'm touched. You actually do care about me."

My mouth drops open. "You idiot. Of *course* I care about you."

He leans forward quickly and pecks me on the forehead. "Then help me get the suit on."

I growl—but I can't stop him. At least I can make sure he's as safe as possible. I pick up two halves of the breastplate. I feel like a lady dressing her knight in his armor, just like a movie I saw a long time ago on Sol—on Earth. The lady tucked a token—a small scarf—into the knight's armor to remind him of her love for him. I don't have a scarf, and I'm not even sure if I love Elder, but I strap him so hard into the breastplate that he grunts in protest.

I keep checking the manual. It doesn't seem right that all it takes to go into space is a set of bronze long johns and a plastic shell. I knew space suits had come a long way from the puffy white marshmallow-like suits of the twentieth century, but this thin suit doesn't seem adequate. Still, when I watched videos of men and women working in the space of *Godspeed* before it launched, their suits looked exactly like this.

Elder steps into the boots one at a time. They go halfway up his calves, and when I push a button on them, they shrink against his legs. Elder hobbles to the center of the room, then turns around, letting me inspect him.

"Looks solid," I admit.

"All that's left is the helmet and the backpack," Elder says, reaching for the helmet.

"This first." I help pull Elder's arms through the straps of the pack, and it snaps into the hard shell pieces of the suit.

I plug the wires from the pack into their connectors on the shoulder of the suit. "This is a PLSS, a primary life support subsystem," I say as I connect a tube to the base of the helmet. "Basically, it has all the stuff you need to live—brings in oxygen, takes out carbon dioxide, regulates pressure, all that."

I snap on a metal-enforced cable to a hook at the front of Elder's suit. "And this," I say, "is your lifeline back to me—to the ship. I'm attaching the other end to the hatch. The book says there's a special hook there just for this."

Elder nods. He looks pale, and there's a sheen of sweat on his face.

I think about kissing him then. Just in case.

Instead, I cram his helmet onto his suit and lock it into place. The PLSS has only two modes—on and off—so I open the latch door, flip the switch to on, and secure the door back in place.

"That's pure oxygen," I say loudly. "Get used to it now, before you're in space."

Elder nods, but he's got so much on that his whole top half bends back and forward. I bite my lip, worried.

Elder follows me, clomp-hobbling, to the hatch. Inside, I latch the end of his lifeline to a hook on the floor.

"Come back to me," I whisper to Elder's helmet, but I don't know if he can hear me.

I step back into the hallway. The hatch closes behind me. I look through the bubble window. Elder raises one hand.

I punch the code into the keypad slowly, hesitating before the last digit. Should I do this? Is it worth it to find Orion's big secret if it risks Elder?

The door in front of me seals shut, a grinding metal-on-metal noise as it locks. Through the window, I have one last look at Elder in his bronze suit. I am overcome with an insane urge to rip the controls out of the wall beside me and keep the hatch from opening.

But it's too late. It opens.

And Elder's gone.

37
ELDER

MY ARMS AND LEGS FEEL SLOGGED DOWN AS IF WALKING through muddy water. Everything's muffled in the suit. Amy shuts the door that leads into the ship; I can see her pensive face through the window, the worry exaggerated by the rounded glass. The lock creates a dull, almost-imperceptible click that nevertheless reverberates.

Then I'm alone with just the sound of the life-support system strapped to my back, a soft *whoo-sh-whoo* swirling in my ears.

The back hatch opens, and the universe explodes around me. I'm launched through the doorway backward, my arms and legs jerking painfully as my body flies out into space. The movement winds me, and I can't breathe. Just as I start to panic, I feel cool oxygen flowing through my helmet.

The cord tethering me to the ship pulls taut, and my body bobs against it, my arms and legs no longer stiff in the suit. I look up. And I am *surrounded* by the universe.

and stars

A million suns stretch out beyond me, their light piercing the darkness. The ship seems to glow. I scan it, looking for whatever massive secret Orion told me I would find.

The ship itself is mostly egg-shaped, with a horned beak protruding from the bridge. A honeycomb of glittering glass covers the arching protrusion. Beneath that, then, must be the Feeder Level. I stare at the smooth exterior of the ship, marveling how only a few moments ago I was on the other side, running my fingers over dusty rivets. There's a line of thick, dark metal rimming the bottom of the ship, about where the cryo level starts, and a pointed ridge sticks out from the front, like a smaller version of the bridge's beak. There's glass there, too—an observatory must be hidden behind the last locked door on the cryo level.

There's nothing here that stands out as unusual, except maybe the as yet unseen observatory. I recline in space, my eyes roving over the hull— there are no strange cracks or marks; the thrusters in the back of the ship aren't working, but I already knew that. Was that the great secret Orion wanted me to find out? That the ship isn't moving?

It would be disappointing to learn that after all this, that was Orion's great mystery. But how can I be disappointed in space?

I stretch out my arms and legs, knowing that there are no walls here that can contain them. I look past *Godspeed* and forget about whatever pointless mission Orion's video sent me on. I gaze out, to the stars. I remember the first time I saw real stars, through the hatch window. They were beautiful then, but now, seeing them here, all around me, *beautiful* feels like an inadequate word. I see the stars as a part of the universe, and having spent my life behind walls, suddenly having none fills me with both awe and terror. Emotion courses through my veins, choking me. I feel so insignificant, a tiny speck surrounded by a million stars.

A million suns.

Centuries away is Sol. Circling around it is Sol-Earth, the planet Amy came from. And one of these other stars is the Centauri binary system, where the new planet spins, waiting for us.

And here we are, in the middle, surrounded by a sea of stars.

A million suns.

Any of them could hold a planet. Any of them could hold a home.

But all of them are out of reach.

The thought makes me queasy-dizzy, a sick feeling that starts in my stomach and blurs my vision.

The stars don't look like suns anymore. They look like eyes.

Laughing eyes. Winking eyes that mock me, forever dancing away from my reach.

I swat at them, my arms feeling funny.

My body feeling funny.

And then I hear it. Soft, barely audible.

Boop . . . boop . . . boop.

An alarm. A warning, piped directly into my helmet.

I breathe deeply—or I try to—but I can't. The air is thinner now, and even though my nostrils flare and my mouth is open, black spots dance before my eyes. I can't get enough air. Something's wrong with the PLSS strapped to my back—something's wrong with the oxygen.

My first instinct is to call for help—I raise a gloved hand to my neck and bump up against the solid helmet before I realize that, of course, I can't reach my wi-com.

My tether to the ship isn't more than twenty yards long, but *Godspeed* feels as far away as the millions of stars around me. I start pulling myself closer to the ship, hand over hand, swimming through nothing to reach the safety of the open hatch.

I can hear my heart beating in time with the alarm.

The more I think about *not* breathing, the more I want to breathe.

I tug on the tether, and my hands slip from it. The movement spins me off, away from the cord, jerking me around.

I have spent the whole time facing the ship, looking back at the path we have taken. But now I see behind me, toward where the ship is facing. And I realize why *Godspeed* seemed to glow. This . . . I never expected this. How did Orion keep *this* secret? How could anyone keep this secret? It's—it's everything—it's—

There, hanging in the sky, right in front of me—

Is a planet.

38
AMY

I STARE OUT THE OPEN HATCH, MY EYES NOT ON THE STARS, but on the tether that ties Elder back to me.

I count down the seconds. The tether twitches. And I know:

Something's wrong.

3 9
ELDER

I CAN'T BREATHE, BUT IT'S NOT BECAUSE OF THE LACK OF oxygen. It's because everything about me—my lungs, my heart, my brain—stopped when I saw that blue and green and white orb floating in the sky.

In the distance, far larger than the millions of stars around me, I can see Centauri A and Centauri B, the two stars that make up the center of this solar system. They're so bright and so big compared to the other stars that they melt in my eyes like blurry, glowing orbs of ice.

But I don't stare at them.

I stare at the planet.

That—*this*—is Orion's secret. It's not that the ship isn't working, that we're never going to make it.

It's that the ship has already *arrived.*

We're already here! There—*there*—is the planet that will be our home!

It floats, so bright that it hurts my eyes. Giant green landmasses spread out across blue water, with swirls and wisps of clouds twirling over top. At the edge of the planet, where it turns away from the suns and starts to darken, I can see bright flashes of light—bursts of whiteness in the darkness—and I think: *Is that lightning?* In the center, where the light of the suns makes the planet seem to glow from within, I can see, very distinctly, a continent. *A continent.* On one edge, it's cracked and broken like an egg, dark lines snaking deep into the landmass. Rivers. Lots of them. Maybe something too big to be rivers if I can see it from here. Fingers of land stretch out into the sea, and dots of islands are just out of their grasp. *That area will be cool all the time,* I think. *Boats can go along the rivers, up and down. We can swim in the water.*

Because already, I can see myself living there. Being there.

On a planet that looks up at a million suns every night, and at two every day.

I want to scream, shout with joy. But the air is so thin now.

Too thin.

I've spent too long looking at Orion's secret.

The *boop . . . boop . . . boop . . .* fades away. There's nothing to warn about now.

Because there's no air left.

My sight is rimmed with black. My head pulses with my heartbeat, which sounds as loud to me as the alarm once did. I turn from the planet— *my planet*—and start pulling, hand over hand, against the tether, toward the hatch. The ship bobs in and out of my vision as my whole body jerks. I'm panicked now and fighting to stay awake. I try to suck in air, but there's nothing there to suck. I'm drowning in nothing.

Closer.

My hands slip, and I'm afraid—if I lose my grasp, if I fall all the way back to the end of the tether—I'll never make it back to the ship. I'll never make it back to Amy.

But if I have to die, I think, *at least I can die looking at the planet.* Is this what Harley thought? Did he see Centauri-Earth before he died? Was his last thought one of regret—that he threw himself to the stars when the planet was almost within his grasp?

I look down at my hands wonderingly. When did I forget to put one hand over the other as I pull myself along the tether? I'm still floating in the direction of the ship—the lack of gravity ensures that—but I have to keep pulling myself along the rope or I'll never make it back to *Godspeed*—to oxygen—in time. I force my arms to move, drag my body closer to the ship. I pull harder than before. Desperation fills my muscles. My mouth hangs open, sucking at nothing. My throat convulses.

I've got to get to the ship.

My muscles are shaking, but I don't know if it's from exertion or suffocation. Just—one more tug—there. The hatch. My fingers scramble, trying to grip the edge of the opening. On the other side of the door is Amy. I crane my head up and, through my watery eyes, I can see her pressed against the glass. I heave, once, and my body propels up, floating through the zero gravity. I bounce against the ceiling of the inside of the hatch. Black spots dance before my eyes.

The hatch door grinds closed . . . so slowly . . .

I turn in time to see the planet, just barely out of sight, only visible here, at the rim between the ship and space—

—The hatch door locks into place.

And I see nothing but black.

40
AMY

AS SOON AS THE HATCH DOOR SHUTS, I REACH FOR THE handle, but it has to re-pressurize before it can open. Through the window of the hatch, I see Elder's body thunk against the floor as gravity returns. I pound on the door with both fists, but he doesn't so much as twitch. He lies there, motionless, his face obscured by the helmet.

An eternity later, the lock clicks and I fling the door open. I drop to my knees at Elder's side and turn his body over so he's flat on his back. His arms and legs are limp; the shell of his suit is clunky and in the way.

The helmet first. Elder's head pours out of it and thunks on the metal floor.

"Elder," I say. "ELDER." I slap him, hoping for something, but—

I jab my wi-com and com Doc. "Get down to the cryo level!" I scream into my wrist as I attack the shell armor of the suit, ripping at the latches and stays around Elder's torso, breaking it open to reveal his chest.

"What's wrong?" Doc asks. His voice is breathless over the wi-com, as if he's already running.

"It's Elder!" I shout.

"I'm on the Shipper Level, but I'll be there as soon as I can."

"Hurry!"

I bend down to Elder's chest—he's not breathing. My hair falls across his face, into his slightly open mouth, but he doesn't flinch.

I don't know if this will work—I pray it will, but I don't know—I tip Elder's head back—his skin is so cold—pinch his nose, and breathe into his mouth. I did this on a dummy once after swim lessons in Florida when I was a kid, but the dummy was plastic and an unrealistic mix of hard and soft—nothing at all like the warm wet of Elder's mouth. I do two short bursts of breaths—*Puff! Puff!* Then I lean back on my knees, fold my hands over each other, and press down on his chest.

Push, push. Push, push. Push, push. Push, push. Push, push. Push, push.
Push, push. Push, push. Push, push. Push, push. Push, push.
Push, push. Push, push. Push, push.
Push, push.

Puff! Puff!

Push, push.
Push, push. Push, push. Push, push.
Push, push. Push, push. Push, push. Push, push. Push, push.
Push, push. Push, push. Push, push. Push, push. Push, push. Push, push.

Nothing.

Pushpushpushpushpushpushpushpushpushpushpushpushpushpush.

God, why isn't this working?! Am I doing it right? I can barely remember that one hour of CPR training so long ago—what if I'm *hurting* him?

I lower my head to breathe into his mouth again. I have to swallow back a sob. I won't cry.

He's not dead. I won't let him be dead.

Puff!

I lean up to take some more air—and I feel, just barely—a whiff of breath coming from Elder. I lean down, my cheek next to his lips—and I can feel it. Air. His chest rises and falls, rises and falls. I move down, pressing my face against his body.

I can feel the thud of his heartbeat, weak, but beating, beating, beating with life.

I rest my head on his chest, relishing in the warmth of him, in the sound of his body, still alive.

41
ELDER

"UHHRRR," I GROAN. MY CHEST FEELS AS IF SOMEONE CRACKED it open and then taped it shut again.

"Elder!" Amy leans over me.

"What happened?" My voice is alien to me, high. My nose is cold on the inside—there's a tube blowing air up into it.

"I think you died a little bit," Amy says. She tries to laugh, but the sound fades on her lips. Her eyes are red, as if she's either been crying too much or needs to cry but hasn't yet.

I lie still for a moment, assessing myself. I'm in the Hospital. "I feel like shite," I conclude.

"Yes, that's what happens when you die for a little bit."

Amy starts to head to the door, but I grab her wrist. "Don't go."

"I should get Doc," she says. "He's been waiting for you to wake up."

"Not yet," I say. I slip the tube under my nose off my face.

"Don't do that," Amy says. "It's oxygen."

"I've got enough now, see?" I take a big, obvious breath and disentangle myself from the tube.

Her brows furrow, but she allows me to pull her down so she's sitting on the edge of the bed. I bite my lip, then release it—my lips are sore and feel bruised. I can taste copper along the soft flesh.

"I thought I was going to lose you," Amy whispers. Her fingers trail down the side of my cheek, lightly brushing the place where my face is still bruised from Stevy's punch a few days ago. Her fingers are cool, her touch so soft I barely feel it.

"I'm fine." I smile wryly. "Better than fine."

"Are you really okay?" she asks, moving a piece of hair off my face.

"Amy," I say, taking a deep breath and relishing the taste of air. "Amy, we're here. We're *at* the planet. We've made it."

Her brow crinkles.

"That's what I saw when I went outside. I saw Centauri-Earth."

She shakes her head, as if making my words rattle around inside her skull.

"We're going to land. *Soon.*"

Something snaps. Her eyes go out of focus. "We'll be able to wake my parents up," she says slowly. "I won't have to spend my whole life on this ship. I'll be able to go outside again. I'll see the sun."

"Suns," I correct. "Centauri-Earth has two suns."

"Suns. *Suns.*" And the light in her eyes reminds me of the two shining orbs hanging over the planet.

"Now aren't you glad I went outside?" I ask, grinning at her. "All I had to do was die a little, and you get a new planet!"

I expected her to laugh, or at least smile. I did not expect her to slap my arm. "You stupid idiot!" she says, smacking me again. "I don't want the new planet without you!"

Her eyes round as she realizes what she just said. Anytime we'd gotten this close to talking about *us* before, Amy has shied away from the topic. But now, instead of drawing away from me, she leans closer. Her hair spills over her shoulders, brushing my chest as she leans down. Her fiery joy at learning about the planet is replaced with something else, something warmer, like a slow-burning but steady flame.

"It wouldn't be worth it without you," she says, her voice low.

My arm snakes out, wrapping around her waist and pulling her closer so that she's practically lying on top of me. I can feel every inch of her; her heartbeat is crashing about so hard that I'm surprised it's not making the bed shake.

She looks terrified, but she doesn't pull away.

Her kiss is soft and gentle, barely pressing against my bruised lips. There is sweetness in it, and innocence, and a promise.

Doc clears his throat.

I get one glimpse of Amy's surprised face, and then she scurries back to the chair against the wall, her face bright red.

"How are you feeling, Elder?" Doc asks as he approaches the bed. He frowns at the discarded oxygen tube. He checks my pulse, waves a light in front of my eyes.

"I'm fine," I insist.

Finally, he seems to agree with me and sits down in the chair next to Amy. "Now," he says, an edge to his usually even voice, "would you like to tell me just what the frex you were thinking?"

I open my mouth, but no answer comes out. My eyes dart to Amy's—how much does Doc know?—and she shakes her head subtly.

"Don't try to hide things from me," Doc says, his voice going up a notch. "It's obvious what you two were doing."

"It . . . is?"

Doc glares at me. "I know what that suit was. It was for going outside the ship. Orion did it once, when the ship needed an external repair. And you two found the suits and thought, 'Oh, let's just go outside *in space* and *play!*'"

"It's not like—" I start, but Amy widens her eyes at me, silencing me.

"Elder, I understand, I do," Doc says, his voice dipping back down to a low monotone, the same sort of voice he'd use when asking how I was, just before offering me a med patch to calm down. "You wanted to see what it was like out there. But you should have realized. Those suits are ancient. I doubt any of them are truly safe." He pauses, not meeting my eyes. "Elder—you're too valuable. With Orion frozen and the ship off Phydus—we can't take any chances. Not with you."

Doc covers his face with his hands, and I'm surprised—I've never seen him overcome with emotion like this before.

Beep, beep-beep.

I move to silence the wi-com.

"Are you getting a com?" Doc asks. "You better take it." He glares at me, his worry replaced with anger. "Just because you do something loons doesn't excuse you from your duties."

"I know," I say, wounded. I press my wi-com.

Doc's scowl softens, and he looks like he's about to apologize to me, but I put one finger up, listening to the com.

When I disconnect the link, I stand up. Amy looks as if she'd like to push me back into the bed, but I ignore her.

"Amy." I try to put the words I cannot say into the look I give her. "We need to talk later. About the *thing*."

She nods.

"But I've got to go now," I say.

Amy grabs me by my elbow before I make it out of the room. "What is it?" she asks, and even though she's only said three words, the tone of her voice begs me to stay with her.

But I can't.

"Marae's dead."

42
AMY

THE ROOM FEELS HOLLOW WHEN ELDER LEAVES. I TRY TO remember Marae—I knew she was the First Shipper, a title something like being second in command to Elder. She was tall and all business, with a severe haircut and piercing eyes, but I don't really know anything about her other than her appearance.

And now it's too late.

And too late for her to see the new planet too.

Guilt tugs at my navel. I shouldn't be so happy, not when someone else has been killed. But—we're here! The ship is going to actually land! As I pass by the common room in the Ward, I stop to stare out of the huge windows. In my mind, I replace the perfectly even rolling hills and boxed-up trailers of the distant City with forests and oceans and sky.

We're here.

I grin in satisfaction as I drift back to my room. I may hate Orion for all he did to me after I woke up, but I can't deny that his clues led Elder and me straight to Centauri-Earth.

And nearly killed him, I think.

My hands raise of their own volition, and I touch my lips with my fingers. That kiss . . . I hadn't thought about what I was doing, I just did it.

And now I can't forget the way his lips felt against mine. Had I meant what I said, that the new planet would be pointless without him?

Yes.

But . . . if—no, *when*—the ship lands, everything will be different.

That is just as true as our kiss.

I shake my head. I can't think about this now.

I lock my bedroom door and pull out the Shakespearean sonnet I found in the room with the space suits. Part of me wants to go back to get the copy of *The Little Prince* that was down there as well, but I can't bear the thought of going back to the cryo level just yet. I can't think about the hatch without also seeing Elder's crumpled body on the floor. I remember that brief moment when I thought it was already too late.

I run my finger along the smooth edge of the page. I doubt Orion cut it from the book of Shakespeare's sonnets. Someone's tampering with the clues, I'm sure of it. I toss the sonnet on my desk as I start pacing around my room. If Orion's big secret was the planet, we don't even need this clue. Isn't the planet the answer to the mystery?

He said there was a choice, though. He said I would have to make the decision. There must be something else—something bigger even than the planet.

I feel a bit like a puppet, with Orion pulling the strings to make me move. Some of the strings, though, are getting tangled.

And some cut.

I take a deep breath and try to forget the lifelessness in Elder's lips as I tried to breathe life into him again.

Was Elder's accident even an accident? If someone's tampering with the clues, how hard would it have been for them to puncture the suit's air tubes? If I were to go to the cryo level right now and check all the

suits, would I find that they were all damaged in some tiny, unnotice-
able way?

I collapse into my desk chair and open up the folded sonnet. I'm going
to keep playing Orion's game. Even if someone is trying to stop me.

This sonnet, just like all the others in the book, makes no sense at all.
But unlike the other sonnets, this one's marked up.

*O*XXX

When to the sessions of sweet silent thought
I summon up remembrance of things past,
I sigh the lack of many a thing I sought,
And with old woes new wail my dear time's waste:
Then can I drown an eye, unus'd to flow,
For precious friends hid in death's dateless night,
And weep afresh love's long since cancell'd woe,
And moan the expense of many a vanish'd sight:
Then can I grieve at grievances foregone,
And heavily from woe to woe tell o'er
The sad account of fore-bemoaned moan,
Which I new pay as if not paid before.
But if the while I think on thee, dear friend,
All losses are restor'd, and sorrows end.

TUBE

I sit up straighter, staring at the handwritten annotations. They're all
about something hidden and forgotten. And tube? The only tube I know
is the grav tube, and nothing could be further from a Shakespearean

sonnet than a futuristic device that sucks people up to different levels of a spaceship.

I trace my finger over the weird lines near the bottom of the poem. They almost look like stairs.

My eyes widen. *Stairs.* Like the staircase Orion has been sitting on in every video he left for me!

The grav tube was invented on the ship after the launch, which means that there had to be *some* way for the first generations on *Godspeed* to go between the levels. Like a staircase . . . a *hidden* staircase that everyone has since forgotten because of the grav tube! I scan the lines of the poem Orion underlined—*hid* and *vanish'd sight* must mean that these stairs are *very* well hidden. In the videos, the stairs are always dark. Orion felt safe there, even from Eldest, who didn't know about them.

But . . . where are they?

43
ELDER

MY MIND WHIRLS AS THE WIND IN THE GRAV TUBE BEATS against my skull as I fly up to the Shipper Level. Amy has never kissed me like that before, has never looked at me that way.

I want to replay what just happened over and over in my mind, but when I reach the Bridge and see Second Shipper Shelby's solemn face, I force myself to forget about everything else but Marae.

"We found her in here," she says, moving to open the door. Although the Engine Room is crowded and the Shippers appear to be working, all eyes are on Shelby and me as we enter the Bridge, our footsteps echoing across the metal floor. The only light comes from a lamp near Marae's still hand.

I look away—I don't want to face the fact of her dead body yet. My eyes drift to the metal ceiling, high and rounded. On the other side of the steel plates is a planet. Marae had no idea how close she was. And it was always just right there.

She lies sprawled across the table, her body dripping off the chair. Her eyes are open and empty, staring at nothing. Floppies with diagrams and charts flash under her face; a printed schematic of the engine lies crushed under one arm.

At the base of her neck, just under her shortly cropped hair, are three pale green med patches. One word in black ink on each patch.

Follow.

The.

Leader.

"This doesn't make sense," I whisper. If someone's killing people who disobey me, why kill Marae? She's been my staunchest supporter from the start. She's unswervingly faithful, and she's led the rest of the Shippers in that attitude as well. She jumped at the chance to lead my police force. If Doc was Eldest's greatest adviser, Marae was mine.

"Who did this to you?" I whisper, but of course she's not going to tell me. But it has to be someone of high rank, doesn't it? Someone who either has access to the Bridge or who knows Marae well enough that she'd be persuaded to open the door. Besides the Shippers, a few of the scientists, Doc and Kit, technicians, even Fridrick, as foreman of food distribution, could also come to this level. And with the med patches stolen, any of them could have done this.

Shelby makes a small noise behind me. She's staring resolutely at the ceiling of the Bridge, her jaw tight.

I want to say something to comfort her, but all that comes out is, "You're First Shipper now." She nods once. She will not dishonor Marae by showing weakness. She will make a fine First Shipper.

The ceiling of the Bridge is domed, much like the ceiling in the cryo level and the Great Room on the Keeper Level. When I was outside—I smile a secret smile, *when I was outside*—it had looked as if there were glass windows over the Bridge. Well—not glass, surely. Glass is too fragile for the ship's entry into the atmosphere or other dangers of space—asteroids, comets, meteors. But some other clear, strong material, maybe a thick polycarbonate, would work. Something that sparkled, reflecting the light of the planet, shining from the dual suns.

But this roof is metal.

Just like the roof on the Keeper Level. Eldest hid the false stars under a metal roof there . . . one with panels and hinges, just like this one . . . with hydraulic controls on the sides. . . . My eyes trail all the way down to the wall, to the switch near the door that's controlled by a biometric scanner. I grind my teeth. I don't know why I'm surprised that secrets have been hidden here too, just like the rest of the ship.

And I am frexing sick of secrets and lies. It's one thing to not tell everyone that the ship's engine is dead—it would have been the end of all hope—but the planet changes everything.

"Lock the Bridge door," I order Shelby.

She hesitates a fraction of a second, then turns and silently pulls the heavy metal door closed.

"Lock it," I repeat.

"These are above standard lockdown-grade seals," Shelby says. "They completely seal the Bridge from the rest of the ship."

"I know," I say.

Shelby scans her thumb and the locks click into place. She flicks another switch, and lights cascade on like dominoes. But rather than illuminating Shelby's face, the lights cast shadows over her. She looks doubtful—even scared. Scared to be locked in a room with me.

And with what's left of Marae.

"Today I went outside." I speak to Shelby, but my eyes are locked on Marae's open, empty ones.

"I don't understand, sir," Shelby says.

"Outside. In the stars. Through the hatch."

Shelby gasps.

"Amy and I found some space suits, and I went. And I saw . . . well, let me show you what I saw."

I start to move toward the far wall but stop, turn, and bend over Marae's still body. Carefully, as respectfully as I can, I tilt her cold, stiff face up so that her empty eyes can see the ceiling. This is my last gift to her.

I go behind Shelby and roll my thumb over the biometric scanner on this wall, the one just like the scanner by Eldest's door on the Keeper Level. This—like the roof over the navigational chart in the Keeper Level—must have been retrofitted into the ship's design. Not part of the original, no— this must have been the Plague Eldest's way of covering up the truth.

"Command?" the computer's voice asks in a pleasant tone once it accepts my authority.

"Open," I say, unable to keep from smiling.

And the metal roof splits apart.

Shelby screams and drops to her knees, covering her head. She thinks the ship itself is splitting open, just as I did when the roof on the Keeper Level opened up to reveal the light bulb stars. She thinks the Bridge will tear apart in explosive decompression and we'll be sucked out into space, our deaths quick but painful as our bodies succumb to anoxia, our skin turning blue and our organs bursting.

I walk over to Shelby—my calm pace makes her quake more—and crouch down beside her. "Get up," I say over the *whirr* of grinding gears as the roof folds out of the way. "You don't want to miss this."

I offer her my hand. I can feel her trembling in my palm, but she stands anyway. She searches my eyes at first—looking for something, I don't know what—but I tilt my head up, and I see her do the same out of the corner of my eye.

Because the universe is there, above us, glittering through the honeycomb windows that cover the Bridge. The universe—the stars, the blackness between them—and the planet.

44
AMY

AT LUNCHTIME, I PRESS THE BUTTON IN MY WALL, BUT NO food comes out. I punch it again. It does no good.

My first instinct is that the food delivery system in my wall is broken, but when I step outside my room into the hallway, I can hear Doc shouting, even though his office door is shut.

"I don't care if you think the people in the Ward don't count, Fridrick!" Doc bellows. "They still deserve food!"

I slip back into my room and snatch the sonnet from my desk, but my heart's sinking. This is more trouble for Elder—and for the ship. I think about comming him and warning him that no food's been delivered to the Hospital, but his dead friend takes priority over lunch.

Instead, I make my way down to the grav tube to search for the stairs. There are two tubes, one near the City, one on this side of the level. My stomach twists at the idea of going into the City by myself, but considering how close this tube is to the Recorder Hall, I think I've got a better chance of finding the hidden stairs near it than the other one. *If there even are stairs,* I can't help but think. I just hope I've got this clue figured out correctly.

The Hospital lobby is crowded as usual, but I keep my head down and my hood up as I weave through the people complaining about med patches. A few people look really sick—one woman is dangerously thin, with sunken eyes and hollowed cheeks. Another man keeps throwing up, holding a pail in his lap.

I take a deep breath of the recycled air as soon as I leave the Hospital— then immediately put my head back down. A group of people, among them the crowd that was arguing for Elder's removal yesterday, are gathered down the path near the pond.

"And, once again, no food deliveries for lunch," a voice echoes from the crowd. I glance up; Bartie's in the center of the group, standing on the bench.

I resist the urge to run over and knock him into the pond. Bartie had always seemed nice and even quiet before this week, but as the ship spins more and more out of control, all I can see is him standing in the center of the storm.

As I hurry along the path, I keep my head down. Which is, perhaps, why I bump right into a couple heading toward Bartie and the group at the pond.

"Sorry!" the woman says pleasantly.

"Where are you going?" the man asks. I hesitate—just a moment. I recognize that voice.

Luthor.

I should have started running, but my brief pause has given Luthor time to touch my shoulder. I peek at him under my hood, careful to keep my face down. The bruises Victria and I inflicted on him are a nasty greenish purple. His left eye is still swollen; a dark red scab covers his split lip.

"Come with us," he says, still not recognizing me. "Bartie's talking about how we could move the ship to a system that's more fair."

He pulls me around by my shoulder. I try to jerk away, and my hood slips down. For a moment, I see surprise in Luthor's face; then his eyes narrow to malicious slits.

The woman gasps as if I'm Quasimodo or something, but Luthor grins with all his teeth. The cut in his lip cracks open, shiny red, but he doesn't seem to care. His grip on my shoulder tightens, and I hiss in pain.

"Come on," the woman says. "The freak isn't invited."

Luthor releases me suddenly, pushing me at the same time, and I stumble on the path. Laughing, the two of them continue down toward the pond.

"It's not like I wanted to go anyway!" I yell. The pair pause, their backs to me. Before they turn around, I race down the path toward the grav tube.

Fortunately, since this grav tube can only be used by Elder, no one else is out this way. I lean back, looking at the clear plastic tube that goes all the way up, through the ceiling, to the Keeper Level.

It's stupid, but the first thing I want to do is push the wi-com on my wrist and fly up to Elder. I can't get the taste of his kiss off my lips.

I shake my head, forcing myself to focus on the wall behind the grav tube. I usually avoid the ship's walls. From a distance, you can squint and blur out the rivets that hold it together, pretend that the sky-blue paint is sky. But when you're up close, you can smell the metal, the same sharp taste in the back of your throat as blood, and when you touch it, it's cold and immovable.

I rap my knuckles against the steel wall the same way my father tapped on the drywall in our house to find a stud before hanging a picture. Maybe the sound will clue me in to whatever's behind the wall. For a moment, I flash back to the other time I beat against the walls, when I was crying and screaming and clawing at the metal, desperate to find a way out. Orion found me then, one of the only welcoming faces on the ship, and I thought I'd found a friend in him. Not a murderer.

I focus on the sound of my knuckles against the wall. *Tap-tap. Tap-tap. Tap-tap.* There's nothing here. *Tap-tap. Tap-tap. Tap-tap.* What am I doing? I look like an idiot. *Tap-tap. Taaap-taaaap.*

My hand stills. Just to the right, a little off center from the grav tube dais, the wall echoes hollowly. I lean closer.

And then I see it. Faint, dusty, almost invisible.

A seam in the wall.

I run my fingers along the outline of what I now know is a door. There's no handle or hinges that I can see, so the door must open inward. I push against it, but it doesn't give. I lean in with all my weight, my shoes sliding on the ground, digging scar marks into the earth.

The door opens.

It's dark inside.

The door doesn't want to open more than a crack, and I have to squeeze myself inside. With the sliver of light from the Feeder Level pouring into the darkness, I can see a bigger handle on the side of the door, a stamped metal floor, a covered box on the wall at eye level.

And stairs.

I push against the inside of the door with all my weight, and the three-inch thick door crashes shut. For a moment, I panic and tug against the giant handle until the door opens back up a crack, allowing me to catch a whiff of grass and dirt from the Feeder Level. I can get back out. I sigh in relief and push the door shut again.

It's empty and silent here. I breathe deeply, and notice the sound of my presence more than the taste of dust and stale air.

I can see nothing through the inky darkness. I fumble in the dark, patting the cool metal wall until I stub my fingers against the raised plastic of the covered box I saw embedded in the wall before I shut the door. The cover lifts up on hinges at the top, and under that I find a light switch similar to the ones I remember from Earth. I should have assumed that the lights would operate like this—this whole area is part of the ship's original design.

But it's not an overhead light that flicks on; instead, the stairs start to glow. My feet thud hollowly on the metal floor as I draw closer. Tiny LED lights race up the railings on either side of the stairs, and a thin row of lights mark the front of each step. The lights are encased in plastic tubing, almost like outdoor Christmas lights.

My mind stops.

Before, if I thought *Christmas*, I would have remembered my past on Earth and would have succumbed to the aching sadness for a life I can never have again.

Now, I can think the word and not feel anything but a dull ache, a phantom pain for a part of my life that's been amputated.

I shake my head and place my hand on the railing. My fingers glow pink from the tube of lights. I mount the first step and look up—the stairs climb higher and higher, zigging up like levels in a parking deck. I try to count how many times the stairs twist and turn, but the lights jumble together at the top. *Godspeed* is as tall as a skyscraper. The last time I was in New York, I tried to climb the stairs of the Empire State Building. My parents and I raced to see who could get to the top quickest. I made it to forty flights before I gave up, and that wasn't even halfway. These stairs are twice as big, reaching up all the way from the Feeder Level to the Keeper Level, where Elder is.

But what about the cryo level? Where are the stairs that go down there?

I wander away from these stairs to the wall. On the other side is space—and past that is the planet. It's odd. The Feeder Level wall is clearly thinner—I can feel residual warmth through the metal, and the door leading out isn't too heavy; it's the same thickness as the wall. On the other hand, the exterior walls seem massive. Steel beams arch up, following the curve of the ship at a smaller angle than the rounding roof of the Feeder Level. The rivets in this wall are much, much thicker, about the diameter of my palm.

I press my hand against the metal, and it comes away with a reddish-brown-colored dust. The metal here is cooler, and there's a sense of stoic, strong weight behind it.

Inside the Feeder Level, where it's airy and bright and warm, I feel caged in and trapped. But here, beside thick, heavy walls, in a narrow, curving corridor, in dim light with nothing but the smell of metal and dust—here, I feel closer to the outside.

To freedom.

I find a second set of stairs soon after, a narrow hole leading down in this space between the heart of *Godspeed* and the universe. These stairs are narrower and steeper, and they go down into what must be the cryo level. I long to explore—the only place I can imagine the stairs open up on the cryo level is in the last locked room. But I can't do this without Elder. It's not right to explore the ship without him.

I meander back around to the door leading to the Feeder Level. Orion said he lived here, in hiding from Eldest. I can't imagine what it would take for someone to willingly cage himself into a narrow dark hall without even the fake sun of the solar lamp to warm him. How many days passed before he couldn't bear the darkness anymore and crept back into the Feeder Level under the guise of being a Recorder? Did he spend his time leaned up against the outside wall of the ship or against the inside wall that surrounded the Feeder Level?

Whatever he did, this was the perfect hiding place. No one else knows the stairs even exist.

Once, I stayed at a fancy hotel in Atlanta when my mom was giving a lecture at a genetics conference. I spent most of my time in the hotel's pool. On the last day, I attempted to go back to my room and pack, but the elevator was broken. It took me half an hour to find the stairs, and when I did, they were hidden behind a door marked with a four-inch square metal placard. I'd gone an entire week not knowing where the stairs were, not even thinking about them, even though I knew, logically, that the hotel had to have stairs, somewhere.

The people of *Godspeed* have gone *years* without knowing about the stairs. And I can't help but think: if they've forgotten stairs, what else have they forgotten?

45
ELDER

I SLIDE MY THUMB OVER THE BIOMETRIC SCANNER AGAIN, and the metal panels over the ceiling start to close. Shelby's eyes stare as hard as they can until the metal clicks back into place.

"We're there," she says, her voice alight with music and tears. "We're here."

"We're here."

For a moment, we share a smile. Then her gaze slides down to Marae's murdered body. I'm filled with regret that even though her eyes stare unblinkingly up, she'll never see the planet.

"I will take Marae's body to the stars myself," I say. "But I need you to get the remaining first-level Shippers here, on the Bridge, and start whatever process we need to begin planet-landing."

She nods. "All the first-level Shippers are trained for this. There are simulators, and the information has been passed down since . . ."

"Since the ship left Sol-Earth."

"We were always ready for planet-landing, even when it was centuries beyond us."

"How much time will you need?"

Shelby stares at the control panel, thinking. "The First Shipper runs scans. . . ."

Her eyes shoot to mine. She'd forgotten. She's First Shipper now.

"I'll run scans. The first level is to ensure that the planet is habitable."

"I thought we always knew the planet was habitable."

Shelby nods. "Before the mission, the probes from Sol-Earth indicated the planet's environment was stable and could support life, but the first stage of planet-landing is to ensure that's actually the case. I'm, well, to be honest, I'm a little worried. If the ship's engine has been diverted for this long because we've been in orbit . . . why haven't we landed already?"

My wonder at seeing the planet has slowly been replaced by this very question. It's possible we've been in orbit since the Plague—perhaps the rebellion that sparked the Eldest system came about as long ago as that. Why *didn't* the ship land before?

"Before we even think about landing, I want to make sure it's possible," I tell Shelby.

"I'll do the scans myself. They should take several hours. I'll know more then."

"First," I say, "we have to say goodbye."

Shelby's eyes drop to Marae's body, still staring at the ceiling. She nods silently.

Shelby brings me a transport—a folded-up black box lined with electromagnets that work with the controls under the metal of the ship's floors to easily carry heavy objects. She snaps the box open. It automatically spreads out, locking into shape, a large, deep rectangle with a circuit board on the side to communicate with the grav tube. This transport has been used for some piece of machinery—it's dirty, scratched, and smeared with mechanical grease. I try to run my sleeve over it, but all I do is spread the dirt around. I don't want to treat Marae's body like a piece of broken machinery to be thrown away, but I can't bear the idea of prolonging her funeral among the stars. I rush back into the engine room and grab some machinery towels to lay out on the transport.

And then it's time to move Marae.

I lift her body by the shoulders; Shelby picks up her feet. We have to bend Marae's knees and curve her back so that she fits completely in the box. We end up curling her into the fetal position.

Shelby's slight body seems massive beside the shell of Marae's. I didn't know life took up so much space. Shelby bends down over Marae's body, and it reminds me of the pictures of scavenger beasts from Sol-Earth, the ones that feed on the rotting flesh of carcasses.

"I don't know how to do this without you," Shelby whispers to Marae. "But I'll try."

And she doesn't look like a scavenger anymore; she looks like an orphan.

She bends swiftly, and I don't know if she's kissing Marae's flaxen cheek or whispering in her ear, but either way, it's not like Marae can feel it.

The Shippers gather around as we pull the transport out. For most of them, this is the first death they've seen. When Eldest was in charge, death was a methodical, scheduled product of the Hospital.

They stare at Marae's body as I pass; I stare at the floor. The hard lines of the metal blur. I rub my face angrily with my hands.

I force my shoulders down, my back straight.

I look directly ahead of me and only allow my clenching jaw to show how much this hurts.

46
AMY

WITHOUT ELDER, THERE'S LITTLE POINT IN ME EXPLORING the stairs further. Instead, I go to the garden behind the Hospital. Bartie and his crowd have left, including Luthor. The smashed grass around the bench is the only remnant of the impromptu meeting. I peel the moccasins off my feet and pad through the cool grass to the water's edge. I think about com-ing Elder, but I'm afraid of bothering him when he's doing something important. I sit on the bank, my knees drawn up under my chin, and stare at the pond's perfectly still surface. I try to see through its depths—the water's clear, and not very deep, but my eyes bore past the dangling roots of lotus flowers to the green-brown murkiness that shadows my view.

I lean back, and grass tickles my neck. My feet slip down the bank until my toes touch the cool water. I slide my feet into the pond and close my eyes. The solar lamp above me beats down warmth and light, but behind my eyelids, it looks like the same bright reddish blur that the Sun looked like on Earth when I'd lie down outside.

A shadow crosses over me, and the brightness dims—like the sun covered by clouds. I open my eyes, and Elder's face is rimmed with light as he leans down over me.

"Hey," I say, suddenly breathless. All my thoughts of dragging him off to the stairs and exploring the ship disappear as he collapses beside me, exhaustion etched on his face.

"What's wrong?"

Elder makes a noncommittal noise.

I want to reach out to him, let him know that I'm sorry for his loss, but I know no words will ever be enough.

Elder leans back in the grass, staring at the metal ceiling of the Feeder Level. If we were outside on Earth, this would be nice. Lying in cool grass next to a pond, staring up at clouds the way little kids do. But this isn't Earth and the clouds are paint and even if there is a planet past this ship, it still seems a very long way away.

"Marae was murdered. Like Stevy. The same phrase on the med patches."

"I'm sorry," I say, the two most inadequate words in the English language.

"I want to know who's doing this."

"Maybe the same person who tried to hide Orion's last clue," I say. Before Elder has a chance to speak, I add, "And maybe the same person who sabotaged your space suit."

"Sabotaged the suit?" Elder asks.

I twist my head to stare at Elder through the bright green grass. "Whoever tampered with the clues and tried to throw us off the trail could have easily punctured the PLSS tubing or something. If you died, you couldn't tell anyone what you saw. And look how close it came to working."

Elder starts to respond, but as soon as he opens his mouth, he turns to answer a com. "Doc says Bartie's causing trouble at the Food Distro. Again," he says, sighing, leaning up.

I touch my hand to his face, just over the purple-green bruise on his jaw. He leans into my hand—not a lot, just enough so that I'm suddenly aware of the pressure of his skin against mine.

"Elder," I say, "you can't keep on doing everything yourself."

"Who else is going to stop Bartie? Who else is going to get the Food Distro back on track? Who else is going to help the Shippers get ready for planet-landing—after the scans show whether or not we even *can* planet-land?"

There's a note of panic in his voice, and pain. I want to tell him everything will be okay, but I don't want to lie. I lean forward a fraction of an inch, and he leans forward, and I catch his eyes just as he starts to close in.

I think, *He's going to kiss me.*

I think, *Good.*

His lips bruise mine in their need, and when my mouth parts in a tiny *o* of surprise, his kiss deepens. His arms are strong; he's lifting the whole of my upper body up and against him. His body speaks for him; he *needs* me.

My arms slide from the ground up his arms, my fingers trailing through the tiny hairs along his forearms. His muscles tighten under my graze; his biceps are like rocks, pulling me even closer against him. My hands dance across his shoulders and meet at the base of his neck, and I swirl my fingers in his hair.

There's something deeply satisfying in touching him—it reminds me that he's real, despite how close I came to losing him earlier today.

My hands tighten, and I use my grip to lift my body up against his. One of his arms slides down my back, pulling my hips closer to him.

Elder breaks the kiss, and he peers into my eyes. I can only imagine what we look like—rolling around in the grass by the pond. Just like the Season. But I don't care. This isn't like that. The Season was just mindless, emotionless, loveless movements. But this is—

Elder reaches up and brushes a stray strand of hair from my face. I close my eyes and relish the touch. His fingers clench against my scalp—I feel the pressure of his hand, pulling me into another kiss.

And I go to him.

Sweeter, this time. Slower. Softer. I feel his lips this time, not the hunger.

I become aware of his body next to mine. I let my hand rest just above his heart, pounding away in his chest, so violent I can feel it mirroring my own heartbeat.

Then my hand slips lower, down his side. The bottom of his tunic has pulled up, and my fingers slide over the bare skin just above his hip.

Elder moans, a low guttural sound from deep inside him. His hands slide down my mussed hair to my shoulders, and he gently pushes me away. Our feet still touch under the pond's surface, though.

"Augh!" he says suddenly, smashing his hand into the side of his neck. "I don't have time for this!"

I scoot away from him, stung, then notice the way his head tilts. Someone is trying to com him.

"I'm sorry," Elder says immediately, leaning back up and staring into my eyes. "Stars, Amy, I'm sorry," he adds. "It's just—with Marae's death, and the planet, and—*frex!*"

My eyes widen, but Elder just punches the wi-com in the side of his neck. "What?" he barks into it.

I sit up slowly, no longer comfortable lying in the grass. As Elder listens to his com, I stare at the still surface of the pond.

I have no idea what I want. I told Victria that love is a choice, and I told myself that I didn't have to choose Elder, but I can't forget the way my heart stopped when his did.

47

ELDER

SHE LOOKS SO SAD AND ALONE, SO *ABANDONED*—AND I'M
the one who abandoned her, even though I'm still sitting by the edge of
the pond beside her. I shouldn't have kissed her. It's like tasting dessert
before supper is served; it's only made me want more. But I couldn't help
it. I don't know what it is about Amy. I couldn't help it.

But I should have. With everything that's happening now, the last thing
I should be trying to do is kiss Amy. I need to focus on the planet—and she
needs to figure out what she wants. I can see the questions in her eyes, the
way she won't quite name what's between us.

Now she sits quietly, not meeting my eyes, her cheeks almost as pink
as her lips.

Her lips.

No.

I look away from her. And her lips.

"What happened?" she asks quietly.

A beastly roar rises up in me, and I force myself to swallow it down.

What happened? I can't control myself around her, that's what happened. I want her so much that it overrides everything else, every other thought in my head, every instinct, every restraint. My want is consuming—and I'm afraid it won't just consume me, but her too.

"With the Shippers, I mean," she adds when I don't answer her. "When you told them about the planet."

I frown. It's obvious Amy would rather ignore everything that just happened—or I've scared her off between my frustration and impatience. Frex. I run my fingers through my hair, tugging at the strands, hard, trying to pull some coherent thoughts up through the roots.

"They're running scans," I say. "If everything indicates that Centauri-Earth is habitable, then we might begin planet-landing in a matter of days."

Amy narrows her eyes. "Might?" she asks.

If she could, she'd land this ship right now. "Amy," I say, warning already creeping into my voice, "we can't just land the ship on Centauri-Earth. We have to make sure it's safe."

"Who cares if it's safe?" she says, throwing up her hands.

"I care. And I care about everyone else on this ship."

"It's just going to take a couple of days, right?" she asks.

Maybe. If we're lucky. "Of course," I say.

"Okay, then," Amy breathes. "I've been worried about . . . The sooner we land, the better."

"It's not all bad here," I think, put off by the disgust in her voice.

Amy looks at me incredulously. "People are angry. Marae was *murdered.*"

"Without Phydus," I say, "the people—they're thinking . . . they're doing . . ."

"Shut up." There's cold anger in Amy's voice. "Some people are good. Some people are bad. Phydus doesn't fix anything. It just hides the good and bad under a haze of nothing."

"But—" I start, but I keep it to myself. But maybe it really *is* worth hiding the good if it distorts the bad, too.

Marae would have thought so.

"The water's very still," Amy says.

I don't try to contain the disbelief on my face. Frex, really? We've gotten to the point where I can kiss her breathless, then we can talk about murder, and all she can comment on is the frexing pond?

"Aren't there any fish?" she asks.

Fish. Frexing fish. We're not painting charts on walls or setting up guards or trying to track down a murderer. I guess when it's my people being killed, not hers, she doesn't care so much.

"No fish," I growl, standing up. "Not anymore."

Amy looks up at me, questions in her eyes. "You're really upset."

"Frex, Amy, of course I am!" I shout. She flinches from my voice. "I'm sorry." I run my fingers through my hair. "Sorry. It's just—yes. I'm upset."

She reaches for my hand and opens her mouth to speak, but before I can find out whatever it was she wanted to say, a voice interrupts us.

48
AMY

"OH, I'M SORRY," LUTHOR SAYS. "I DIDN'T MEAN TO *INTERRUPT*."
While his face is impassive, his eyes linger on the inch of exposed skin above my waistband. I tug my tunic down with such violence I'm afraid my fingers will poke through the handwoven material.

"What do you need, Luthor?" Elder asks. I'm not sure if the impatience in his voice is because Luthor interrupted us or because Elder knows how close Luthor is to Bartie's plans for a revolution. Elder twists around to look up at the man. "Stars, Luthor, what happened to you?!"

Now it's my turn to smirk at his black eye and busted lip.

"Nothing of importance," Luthor tells Elder. "Nothing I can't . . . *handle* . . . myself.*"

I don't let my face betray my fear.

Luthor sneers down at me, but when Elder glares at him, he shrugs, chuckling softly to himself as he meanders down the path away from us.

"That man is a frexing nuisance," Elder says. "The only reason he's been helping Bartie is because he likes trouble for trouble's sake."

"Yeah," I say in a hollow voice. Before Luthor interrupted, I was going to tell Elder about the stairs and everything else I'd found out this morning. But Luthor's very good at silencing my words.

Elder turns his full attention to me. "What's wrong?" When I don't answer, he adds, "Amy, do you know something? About Luthor? Did Luthor do something?"

A hand wrapped around my wrist, pushing me down into the ground, cutting off the circulation in my hand, fingers digging into that little space over the blue veins under my palm. But when I look down, it's my hand wrapped around my wrist, not Luthor's.

I open my mouth.

"Tell me," Elder says.

I can't.

It's too late. I can't change the past, and it will only upset him. I can't explain why I never told him before—a combination of being afraid to put what happened into words and being worried about what his reaction would be. I let too much time pass. Part of it was my fault—I shouldn't have gone outside during the Season. And even though I know, logically, it's not my fault, it's his, I still can't forget—

His body straddling mine. Holding me down. His eyes, laughing—knowing what he was doing. The way he watches me even now. The way his gaze lingers on all the wrong places. The way his thumbs rub against his fingers, as if imagining my skin under his touch.

Elder touches my hand.

I flinch away.

But then I remember how Victria shied away from me.

And if I can't speak for myself, I can at least speak for her.

I talk to the pond, because it's easier to talk to water than to Elder's rigid face. I start at the end, telling him about how Victria and I used the med patches to exact something of revenge on Luthor. I tell him that Victria's pregnant, and explain how it wasn't her choice. I know I shouldn't betray her trust, but I also know that Elder, more than anyone else on the ship, needs to know the full extent of Luthor's evil. I add my fear that Luthor did the same to the girl in the rabbit fields.

And then I tell him how Luthor has been threatening me. I try to be emotionless as I describe the way he chased me across the field, the way it excited him when I tried to escape, but my voice still cracks.

To his credit, Elder doesn't interrupt, not once.

"It was his eyes, Elder. I could tell," I say. "He *knew* what he was doing. He knew, and he was enjoying himself." I think of the way he slowly licked his lips. "He still is. We're a game to him. We're just mice, and he's a cat, and he loves toying with us."

For the first time since I started speaking, I glance at Elder. There are scars in the earth, claw marks. Elder loosens his fists when he sees me staring, and two clumps of dirt fall from his hand.

"Thank you for telling me this, Amy." His voice is so cold that he reminds me of Eldest.

I reach out to him and grab his forearm. His muscles are taut and hard.

"I've been so fixated on Bartie and whatever revolution he thinks he can cook up," Elder says, "that I forgot the evil one man can do on his own."

I try to draw Elder's gaze to me, but his narrowed eyes are focused on the ground. "It was Luthor the other day in the Recorder Hall." I say. "He's the one who said he could do whatever he wanted. Maybe Bartie even got the idea from him."

He stands. "Thank you for telling me this, Amy," he repeats.

"Elder?"

He walks away, fists still clenched and stained brown and green from the ground.

49
ELDER

"ELDER, THERE'S—YOU NEED TO COME TO THE CITY."

Doc's com arrives just when I don't need it to. I'd gone to confront Luthor as soon as Amy had told me everything he'd done. I'd never been so mad in my entire life. I can still feel the rage coursing through my blood, although it's somewhat cooled now.

"Frex!" I shout. "All I've done is run across the ship from one place to another! I'm frexing tired of this!"

Doc's silent on the wi-com a moment. "You won't be doing that soon."

For a moment, I think he's talking about the planet, but no—I've not told him about that yet. Only Amy and the first-level Shippers know.

"What's that supposed to mean?"

"Elder, it's chaos. It's—mutiny."

"Frex!"

"I think it's Bartie, but—look, you've got to come out here."

It takes me a while to get from the cyro level to the City, but I race as fast I can, driven by the urgency in Doc's voice. I can tell before I'm at the

City that something is very, very wrong. I hear it first—or, rather, I *don't* hear it. I don't hear the regular noises of the City, the undercurrent of sound that is always there during the day merely from the people living. Instead, muffled voices and footsteps reverberate.

That's when I see it.

The Food Distro is at the end of the main street, and that's where everyone's pressing together. They're all looking at one thing.

Fridrick, dead.

His body is plastered with so many med patches that they cling to his skin like scales. Someone's taken a great swath of cloth, probably from a bolt in the weaving district, and hung it from the windows of the third floor of the Distro. Fridrick's body hangs from the center, sagging the cloth down precariously, his arms and head flopped over the front.

In big bold letters painted in black across the front of the impromptu banner: *Follow the leader.*

"This is a message!" a voice roars. My eyes drop from the banner and the body down to the front of the Food Distro, where Bartie stands.

I realize that the people hadn't been silent in order to observe Fridrick's death. They had been silently waiting for Bartie to speak.

"Anyone who won't blindly obey the *leader*"—he sneers the word—"will be dealt with! Have we not seen it with Stevy? As soon as he protested against Elder—dead!"

"Protested against me" is a bit of an understatement—the man beat me across the face.

"And we all know Fridrick's protests! He was trying to save us all, keep the food stores in check—and look! Elder forced him to distribute food, and now there isn't enough! And Fridrick's protests"—he pauses dramatically, swooping his arm up to the body above him—"have been silenced!"

If Bartie's trying to stir up a revolution, it's not working that great. Although the front of the crowd cheers him on, I can't help but smile smugly at the fact that at least two-thirds of the crowd is silent—worried, but not ready to overthrow the only government they've ever known.

Still, I'm not going to let him stand there and frexing lie about me.

I push my wi-com and order an all-call.

"Attention, all residents of *Godspeed*," I say. The group at the front of the crowd stills. Many turn to look at me. "As you are well aware, the Eldest system has worked on this ship for countless gens. I chose to work a little differently from my predecessor. I chose to give you the ability to make choices for yourself."

Beep, beep-beep.

"Attention, all residents of *Godspeed*," Bartie's voice says in my wi-com. My head snaps up. Bartie's looking over the crowd, straight at me. "Elder is not the only one who can control the wi-com system. But he is right. He gave us a choice. And for that, I thank him." He bows his head a fraction of an inch in my direction. "Because he gave you the ability to choose someone other than him."

The crowd's attention is entirely on Bartie now. How the frex did he break into the wi-com system? Only a few select members of the crew— me, Doc, the First Shipper—have the permissions needed to do all-calls. Bartie must have hacked into the system.

I slam my hand into my wi-com. "System override," I order, then begin another all-call. "People of *Godspeed*," I say in as loud a voice as I can. "Calm down. This is not the time for mutiny and dissent. This morning, I discovered we are much closer to Centauri-Earth than we ever thought. We will begin planet-landing—soon. Very soon. You only have to—"

"LIES!" Bartie roars, not through his wi-com, but from his perch at the Food Distro. His face is twisted, enraged, and the word expels from him like a rock thrown into the crowd.

"It's not a lie," I insist, my voice crackling over the wi-com. "Please, everyone, calm down. The mission—"

Beep, beep-beep.

"Frex the mission!" Bartie roars into the wi-com all-call system. "This is just one more way that Elder wants to manipulate you! Look around you, friends! This—*this*—is all we have! *Godspeed* is our home, there's no point in trying to reach Centauri-Earth anymore! There is only this—and freedom!"

"I gave you freedom!" I shout, then remember to use my wi-com. Before I can, though, Bartie overrides me.

"He may say he's given you freedom, but think about how much he still controls. He makes all the decisions. He controls who eats, and how much. He controls who gets what meds—and he is the one who let the poison Phydus back on this ship. That was his decision, his choice, and you paid for it."

I remember that day I found him in the Recorder Hall. *Technical Instruction on Communication Systems.* And a history of the French Revolution. He was probably the one who hacked into the floppy system—but I wonder, if I had handled things differently, would his rebellion have stopped there rather than escalating into a mob gathered around Fridrick's dead body?

"What about the food?" someone calls from near the back.

Bartie pushes back the doors of the Food Distro. "Take what you can," he shouts. "There's little left."

And that does it.

The people stampede into the Food Distro. The windows in the front are smashed open and people start running through them. The mob swarms forward in a surge so fast that Bartie has to dive out of the way. People fight their way out of the building, rolling barrels or hefting heavy sacks of food on their backs. Others start fighting them, ripping open the sacks and brawling over the contents. In the rush, Fridrick's body flops out of its tenuous hold on the banner, crashing into the ground. The mob swells back, then washes over where he landed, ignoring the body in the rush for food.

Fighting breaks out. It starts out as shoving as people wrestle their way to the front of the crowd, closer to the food stores. Shoves turn into punches, punches turn into brawls. Food is forgotten as two men turn on each other. The larger man punches the smaller one in the mouth, and an arc of blood sprays out over the crowd. The smaller man's friends leap into the fight, and soon there are so many punching and kicking and shouting that I can't even find the original two fighters amid the fists and blood, the sound of flesh hitting flesh.

I've seen the chaos of Sol-Earth from vids and pics on the floppy network. But this is different. I'm in it here.

A woman shouts, "Get out of the frexing way!" as a barrel of milk rolls down the street. She chases after it, screaming at anyone who gets too close to it.

"The Greenhouses!" a man roars, leading a group of twenty or so off the main road toward the produce section. Shite. They're going to kill every crop we have.

I try to do another all-call. No one even notices.

A man shoves a woman out of his way; the woman crashes to the ground. Another man leaps to her defense, slamming his fist into the first man. Before I can even respond, two more men enter the fray. The woman scrambles out of the way as the fight grows. The bag of produce the man had been carrying crashes to the ground, spilling its contents—tomatoes and peppers—out onto the street. Some of the others pick up the smashed vegetables and start hurtling them at the fighters. The circle of fighting grows and grows.

And then one of them turns to me. I had lingered at the back of the crowd, away from the surging masses, when I should have run away.

"It's Elder!" he roars. "Get him!"

They turn as one, a multi-headed monster ready to strike.

"Fire!" someone screams. A trail of smoke rises through the windows, snaking out around the *Follow the leader* sign.

In the distraction, I run for it. As I turn down a side street, I press my wi-com.

"Amy," I say as soon as she answers. "Get to your room. Lock your door." I disconnect before she has a chance to respond.

I head straight to the grav tube. As I go, I see others running too, hiding, going for their homes or the fields, racing, like me, to some kind of shelter. A man pulls a woman behind him into the butcher's block. He grabs a cleaver and stands in the doorway, daring anyone to attack. Another woman collapses on the steps leading to her home, clutching her stomach and screaming.

As the grav tube sucks me up, I see the chaos spread out before me. The Food Distro is truly in flames now, the smoke heavy and black, already making the painted sky above it gray.

My eyes adjust slowly on the Shipper Level. It seems dark compared to the brightness of the solar lamp on the Feeder Level. And quieter.

While the Feeder Level was all boiling action, the tension here feels like a dense fog.

Shelby rushes to me; she'd clearly been waiting for my arrival.

"What do we do?" she asks.

The entire level seems to come to a standstill as everyone waits for me to answer.

"Get the first-level Shippers—meet me at the door to the Bridge," I say.

"But sir—what about the Feeder Level?"

"That's an order," I say. "Immediately."

I stare her down. I try to assume the cold, impassive face that Eldest wore so well, the look that demanded obedience. I don't know if I can make that face work, even though Eldest and I share the same DNA. I should be able to arrange my features—the same as his—into an identical look of power and command, but the more I think of it, the more I feel like a little kid trying on Daddy's shoes.

She does it, though. She pushes her wi-com, gives the orders to the First Shippers, and then strides down the hall toward the Bridge.

Before I follow her, I have some coms of my own to make.

"Com link req: Bartie," I say, pushing my wi-com.

A moment later, Bartie answers my com.

"You're going to destroy us all," I say.

"You opened the door." Bartie's voice is strained, as if he's running—running from the mob he himself created. "I just pushed them through it."

50
AMY

I HEARD THE WI-COMS FIRST.

Then I saw the smoke.

Then I could hear, far in the distance—the sound of the ship in revolt.

Elder coms me and at first I'm relieved—at least I know he's escaping the mob—but he sounds as if he's running—fleeing—and the com cuts out before I can say anything.

I run straight to the Hospital, to the elevator, to the cryo level.

It is silent here, and cold.

Above me there is rage, and fire, and chaos.

But here: stillness and ice.

I pull my parents out at the same time, relishing in the feel of cold metal on my skin, the *ch-thunk* sound the cryo chambers make as they settle on their stands.

"Today," I whisper, "I miss *you*."

I know it's stupid, I know it's pointless, but there is still within me a tiny part of my mind that believes my parents can fix anything. Even a mutinous ship, even people who are tearing apart the only home they've known. Even me, caught in the eye of this storm.

Elder said the ship would be landing soon, a voice whispers to the piece of me that still cries for them.

When the ship lands, they'll be woken up anyway. Why not wake them up now?

Why not?

Why not?

Why not?

5 1
ELDER

THE FREX AM I SUPPOSED TO DO WITH A SHIP IN REVOLT? IF they'd just *listen*, we could be discussing preparations for planet-landing. Instead, the people seem intent on ripping the ship apart at the seams.

I storm into the irrigation room first.

"Drop the strongest rain program we have," I order the Shipper on duty, Tearle.

"Elder," Tearle protests. "That has the potential to cause minor flash floods on the streets."

"Do it," I order.

"How long should the rain be?" He sounds reluctant, but he moves over to the water controls regardless.

"I'll tell you when to stop it."

I go across the hall to the solar lamp operations. The solar lamp is automated, but the level of heat is regulated by one Shipper, a mousy woman who looks as if she'd be more comfortable on one of the farms. Her name is Larin.

I take out a floppy and pull up the security vid feeds from around the City. The vids show the Food Distro—the rain is flooding it, and the fire is already turning into smoldering ruins. I swipe my hand across the screen to vids of the farms, the Greenhouses, the main street of the City. People are fighting and screaming through the rain. Although there's no sound on these vids, I don't need it. I know what a rebellion sounds like.

"I want you to cover the solar lamp," I tell Larin. She's been watching me, worried, waiting for my command.

"It's the middle of the day, Elder!" She looks at me as if I'm crazy.

I suppose I am. The solar lamp is never cut off, but a heavy metal screen covers it during the ship's version of night. It's all scheduled, so dark time lasts exactly eight hours and only happens when it's the proper time. Not now.

"Cover the lamp," I order again.

"But—"

"Cover it."

She stands up and crosses the small room to the control panel. Larin's fingers hover over a switch. She mutters something.

"What was that?" I demand.

"Maybe Bartie is right," she says clearly.

I stride across the room and slam my hand against the switch. Beneath us, the Feeder Level is plunged into darkness. But here we're not. I lean in close to Larin's face. If Marae were here—frex, if Eldest were here . . .

She stares back defiantly.

Then looks away.

"Uncover the lamp," I order.

Her hand shoots forward, flicking the lamp back on. She stares back at me, hoping that I'm about to leave. But I don't. Instead, I wait another minute.

On the floppy, the vids show the people staring at the sky, trying to peer through the torrential downpour to see the solar lamp. It has never gone dark other than at scheduled nighttime. At least I've shocked them enough to stop the fighting.

"Cover the lamp again," I say.

She hesitates, but doesn't protest this time.

I watch the screens black out once more.

And I push my wi-com and do an all-call. "Attention, all residents of *Godspeed*. Everyone on board the ship—every single person—is to report to the Keeper Level Great Room this evening at dark time."

"Bring back the lamp," I tell the Shipper when I disconnect the wi-com.

She flips the switch immediately, but she doesn't take her eyes off me.

I press my wi-com button one more time. It won't take Bartie long to come up with his own sort of all-call, something about how I have no right ordering everyone to come to me or something like that.

"Wi-com, Eldest override," I say. "Authorization code: 00G. Disable all communication; exception: Eldest device."

I turn around and leave the solar lamp room, order Tearle to stop the rain, and then head down the hall. Now Bartie can't com anyone. None of them can but me. At least Amy's safely locked in her room.

As I cross the Shipper Level, I can feel them all watching me. The Shippers stop their work until I pass, eyes following me down the hall.

Before, I would have felt that their eyes contained questions and doubt, and that would have made me crumble.

But now, I don't care. I'm taking the authority that should have been mine from the start.

For the first time in my life, I feel as if I am truly Eldest.

• • •

Shelby and the first-level Shippers are waiting for me at the Bridge. I stride straight to them and lock the door behind me.

"What have the scans shown?" I demand. If it's going to take a planet-landing to stop this shite from Bartie and his so-called revolution, I'll land the frexing ship. But I won't do it unless I know the ship can make it.

While Shelby brings up the scans on a floppy, I seethe. It's irrational, but I can't help but blame Orion for some of this. Maybe there really is something in his frexing clues that would get us to the planet easier, but the man was so loons he hid the information.

Shelby hands me the floppy. "All the scans indicate that the planet's environment is habitable. The planet has water, breathable air, vegetation. . . . There's nothing to indicate that we can't land," she says.

There's a catch in her voice.

"What's wrong?"

"Our records indicate that there are supposed to be a set of deeper-level probes on the Bridge," she says. "We've looked everywhere and can't find them."

"Why do we need probes if the scans are clear?"

"We don't *technically* need them. But—it's in our records that the probes should be deployed. Besides, I'm worried. . . . Why have we been here, in orbit, all this time? Why didn't we planet-land when we got here? And . . . not only are the probes missing, but so are the communication boxes."

"The what?"

"There was a system set up to communicate with Sol-Earth. In our records, we have diagrams and manuals for operation and how to fix them if they break . . . but they're not there. It's not just that we lost communication with Sol-Earth—it's that our only method of communicating with them is entirely gone."

The other first-level Shippers all look nervous behind Shelby; they're worried too. Something's not right.

"Whatever the reason," I say, "it doesn't matter now. Now we're at a point where we need to land. And we can. So we will."

Shelby nods.

"Are you all prepared for planet-landing?" I ask.

Shelby straightens her shoulders. "I've gone over several sims with the first-level Shippers. We are good to go."

I glance at the elaborate control panels at the front of the Bridge. "It looks complicated."

"It's not. Actually, there's an autopilot—" Shelby finally leans up and points to the center of the long control panel, where there are only a few controls. "The ship is designed to land itself when directed. The rest of the controls are for if something goes wrong. This?" She points to a large black button. "Initiates the planet-landing launch."

"But you said the engine's thrusters weren't working."

Shelby laughs, and there's relief in the sound of it. "They're not—but we don't need those. There's a different set of thrusters with a separate fuel system for planet-landing—short, high-powered burst thrusters just for breaking orbit. It doesn't matter at all that the main thrusters are out. We'll . . . never need them." There's wonder in her voice. She's only just realizing just how much has changed with the introduction of this planet.

"So, I just push this button," I say, pointing to the big black one, "and we land?"

"Technically. But it's not as simple as that," Shelby explains. "You'd need that throttle to help direct where the ship goes after re-entry. And there's always the chance that the re-entry doesn't go smoothly; then you need—" She indicates the rest of the Bridge. "But don't worry. Me and the other Shippers know how. And the controls work. Our records indicate that we've had to use the Bridge controls at least six times throughout the flight—we crossed an asteroid belt many gens ago, and our ancestors before the Plague had to adjust the flight plan."

She meets my eyes and, despite herself, a grin spreads across her face. "We're going to land this thing, aren't we?"

"Oh, yes," I say. "But before we do that, I'm going to show everyone what they almost lost."

5 2
AMY

WHEN I CLOSE MY PARENTS BACK UP IN THE CRYO CHAMBER, I think about everything I wish I could tell them, but all I say is: "Soon."

I think about returning to my room—my grumbling stomach would appreciate it if I got something to eat—but I doubt there's any wall food at the Hospital, and I can't reach Elder on my wi-com.

Part of me wishes that instead of coming here by the elevator, I'd explored the stairs I'd found with Orion's clues. I'm desperately curious about where they lead—surely they go to the last locked door—but even though no one but me knows about the stairs, I'm half afraid to go down them without Elder.

Instead, I go to the hatch that leads to the stars. Maybe I can see the planet through the bubble-glass window if I look just right.

That's odd.

The code for the door is *Godspeed*, or, on the numbered pad, 46377333. But the little window over the keypad already shows numbers: 46377334. The numbers fade to an error message: INCORRECT CODE. As the message changes back to the wrong numbers, I look inside the hatch.

Someone's lying facedown on the floor.

My eyes widen. I clear out the incorrect code and type in the right one, opening the hatch door.

My heart drops. I know who this is. My hand flies immediately to my wi-com, and I try first for Elder, but the stupid thing just beeps uselessly. I stare at the body on the floor, my stomach churning. I can't seem to catch my breath.

"Luthor?" I ask tentatively.

I try to com Doc too, but I can already tell from the stench that it's too late.

I roll the body over. Green patches line his arms from wrist to elbow.

I look for the message Elder told me had been written across some of the victims, *follow the leader.* But there's nothing here. Just patches and death.

His eyes are open, glassy. They stare straight ahead.

His body is stiff. Cold. He's been dead awhile.

He died down here, probably before Elder gave his announcement about planet-landing. He died without knowing hope. He died cold and alone, blocked from the light of the stars, on a hard metal floor, surrounded by walls.

There's nothing I can do. He's dead.

I glance back at the keypad by the door. Whoever dumped his body in the hatch meant to type the code and open the outer door, sending the body out into the vacuum of space. They messed the code up on the last number and left the body by accident.

I bite my lip, trying to think who would do this—and what I should do if I figure it out. Does Luthor's murderer deserve punishment? He tried to rape me, he *did* rape Victria, and he would do it again, given the chance. He's been pushing for a rebellion not because he believes in any ideal of democracy, but because he thrills in causing chaos. He never showed any remorse. He didn't make a mistake—he was evil, and he knew, and he relished in it.

I remember the rage in Elder's eyes when I told him what Luthor had done, and how he went away for so long after.

No. *No.*

I force my mind to think of the future.

Planet-landing.

Fresh air.

My parents, awake and with me.

No more walls.

I turn my back very deliberately on the body and walk to the hatch door. I shut it, trying as hard as possible not to catch sight of the body through the bubble window.

I start to type the correct code into the control panel by the door.

G-o-d.

I pause.

Under my tunic, the gold cross necklace weighs heavily against my neck, as if it would like to pull me down, down. I feel the disapproving gaze of my parents, frozen and locked away in their cryo chambers. This— this is covering up a murder.

A murder of a horrible man who deserved to die.

But a man, nonetheless.

But he deserved it.

I think about Victria's tear-streaked face.

I can't do anything; he's already dead.

I could tell Elder.

But what if I'm right and Elder—

Very quickly, I type out the rest of the code.

The door flies open; Luthor's body flies out.

He's gone.

Forever.

53
ELDER

I GET TO THE KEEPER LEVEL ONLY A FEW MINUTES BEFORE the solar lamp is due to click off—at its proper time—and I rush straight to Eldest's room, swing open the door of his closet, and pull out the Keeper Robe. Stars are sprinkled across the shoulder, a planet along the hem. This robe symbolizes every hope and dream my people have ever known. And I'm going to make those dreams come true tonight.

I push my wi-com and do an all-call. "Everyone on board *Godspeed* is to come immediately to the Keeper Level," I say, then disconnect the link. I don't want to waste time on words.

I slide the robe off the hanger and slip it over my shoulders. Before, it felt like the robe was too big for me. Tonight, I stand straight and tall, my chest puffed out, and the robe fits perfectly.

In a few minutes, I can hear people start to arrive. Amy won't be here; there's no way she'd come among a crowd of this many people—and while I'm glad she'll be safe in her room, I wish I could walk away from all the other residents of *Godspeed* and take her to the Bridge myself, just the two of us.

The people's footsteps are heavy on the metal floor, and their talk is loud, totally unlike the quiet, polite whispers that filled the Great Room the last time Eldest called a group meeting.

It will take a while for everyone to arrive. I can hear Shelby and the other Shippers organizing the group, making sure there is enough room for everyone. The Shippers are also, I know, stationing themselves among the people most likely to cause trouble. In the meantime, I sit down on Eldest's bed. I breathe in. I breathe out. I don't want to have to speak, not to everyone, but words will be required. I will have to do this.

There's a knock on the door. I walk across the room and open it. Shelby slips inside and shuts the door. I wonder how she knew I'd be here rather than in my room, then realize—she probably always assumed I'd be here. This is the Eldest's room, and whether I take his name or not, I'm still him now.

"I—oh," she says when she sees me.

"Yes?"

"Um . . . Is that wise?"

"What?" I follow her gaze. "The robe? Eldest wore it."

"Yes, but . . ."

"What did you need me for?"

"I think everyone's here now, sir," she says, squaring her shoulders.

For a moment, the robe seems to swallow me. I force my spine straighter and head to the door. It zips open.

A wave of silence washes over the entire crowd—those standing nearest the door cease talking immediately, then those behind them follow suit. And it is a *crowd*. I'd never realized how big over two thousand people looked when they were all looking at you.

Their eyes all follow me as I cross the short distance to the dais the Shippers have set up for me.

"You *chutz!*" a voice bellows across the crowded room.

The people in the room seem to move as one to make a path—and marching through that path is Bartie.

"What right do *you* have to wear that robe?" he shouts. His face is red, even the tips of his ears.

"I'm—" I stop. I can't say I'm Eldest—I never claimed that title. And the robe is for an Eldest only.

In the end, it doesn't matter that I didn't have anything witty to say to Bartie, because once he gets close enough to me, he knocks me aside so forcefully that I stagger back against the wall.

"The frex?" I say, but my words are drowned out by Bartie's voice.

"Are we going to put up with this?" Bartie roars, turning to the crowd. "How can this *child* dare call us all together and parade in Eldest's robe? He's no Eldest—he's no leader!"

And they cheer him.

Not all of them, certainly, but enough. Enough to make the sound of their support swirl inside my brain, soaking into my memory like water into a sponge.

"We deserve a new leader. One chosen by us!"

I grab Bartie by the elbow and spin him back around to face me. "What the frex do you think you're doing?"

"Your job," he sneers.

"I can do it myself!" I shout back.

"Oh, really?" He pushes me, hard, and I stumble back into the wall. Bartie's talking in a quieter voice now—and everyone is listening to him. He's evoked a truer silence than I did. When they quit talking for me, that's all they did, but now they're not just quiet, they're listening to him. Listening to his every word. "What have you done since Eldest died? Nothing."

"I took you all off Phydus!"

"Not everyone wanted to be off Phydus! What did you do for them? Let them huddle in their homes, scared. Let them die in the streets. Did you even notice how many of us aren't here? Have you noticed how many people don't work? How many have broken down, are scared, are alone? Do you even care?"

"Of course I care!"

Bartie takes a step back, looking me up and down, measuring me. "You can't be Eldest if you're still Elder," he says finally in a voice calm and quiet, but still loud enough for everyone to hear. "And," he adds in a voice so low only I can hear, "you can't be Eldest if you care for Amy more than *Godspeed*."

I don't know if it's because of his sneer or because a part of me is afraid he's right, but I rear back and slam my fist against his face with all the force I have in me.

Bartie looks shocked for a second, but then he recovers and throws an uppercut that catches me under my chin. My head jerks back so hard my neck pops, and my teeth snap over my tongue. I taste blood inside my mouth, and droplets of dark red stain the top of the Eldest Robe.

The entire crowd surges forward, and the silence they held before is broken. A chant erupts near Bartie and me as his closest supporters shout, "Lead yourselves! Lead yourselves!" Shelby's voice screams out over the chanting, directing orders to the other Shippers. I move to help her, but Bartie nails me in the stomach. I double over as Shelby jumps into the fight to defend me. Unfortunately, it doesn't do much good. As she's blocking Bartie, one of his lackeys rushes forward and slams me against the wall. My elbow cracks against the metal, and I hiss in pain as I draw my leg up and knee him in the stomach.

I race to the dais and leap over the small step.

"Enough!" I roar.

Apparently it's not.

This is what I'm king of: a whirling mass of humans who either hate me or ignore me.

I jab my finger into my wi-com—wincing, because the sudden movement makes my elbow hurt more. "Direct command: Tonal variation. Level two. Apply to entire ship."

Now they look at me, some of them with the same look they reserved for Eldest.

"End tonal variant." I disconnect the wi-com link. "I didn't call you here to lord over you!" I shout. "I called you here—oh, frex, just follow me."

I shove my way through the crowd and throw open the hatch in the floor that leads to the Shipper Level. I lead the way down the ladder and head directly to the Engine Room. Shelby calls after me, but I ignore her—she's going to tell me that this is a forbidden area, that I shouldn't do this—but they deserve to see. They have to see.

I open both Bridge doors, and the people pour inside. I hear shouts of wonder and amazement from many just at seeing the engine—only the first-level Shippers have ever come this far. Not everyone will fit on the Bridge, and Shelby and the first-level Shippers man the room, directing people where to stand, cutting off the entrance when the Bridge becomes too crowded. Other Shippers jump in to help, sending the message down the crowd that everyone will get a chance to see.

I roll my thumb over the biometric scanner and open the covering that hides the windows. The metal panels fall away slowly, revealing first a sprinkling of stars that soon give way to the glow of the planet spilling its light over the edges of the windows, brimming with promise and hope. I forget about the crowd. I see only the swirling white over blue and green. This is the world, the whole world, and it's *ours*.

"We're going *home!*" I shout.

For one second there is ringing silence throughout the Bridge.

Then the chaos returns—but instead of fighting and shouting, there is cheering and screams of joy. Some of the people surge forward, their arms outstretched. They can't even reach the window, but they're straining up, as if they think touching it will make the planet more real. The Shippers rush forward to create a barrier and protect the control panel.

Shelby organizes the group to move out in rotation, and the Shippers have to use force sometimes to get the crowd to continue on, seizing those who linger too long at the window by their arms and dragging them away. Some of the people don't react with joy. Victria looks at the planet for only a moment, then bursts into tears and runs from the Bridge. I see another woman slip a pale green patch from her pocket and place it on the inside of her wrist, over her dark blue veins. The intelligence slips from her eyes as the drug takes effect. Others talk, casting suspicious, dark looks at me and the Shippers. They have seen the false stars Eldest gave them; do they really think I could engineer a false planet? Perhaps they simply refuse to believe that a world exists outside the ship.

Bartie's one of the last to go.

"Tomorrow we'll be there?" he asks, facing the planet.

"Yes."

He shakes his head, and with each slow turn, I can see the incredulity shift to belief. He was raised with the idea that the ship would land when he was an old man, then told he'd never see the planet. If it were not in front of him now, he still wouldn't believe in it.

Bartie clenches his fists, then releases them. "When we land . . . who will lead?"

"I—what?"

"Are you still going to be the leader, or will it be one of the frozens on the cryo level?" Bartie asks.

This is a new question. No one else has thought past the actual planet-landing—including me. "I—er—I don't know. No—I'll lead. It'll be me, still."

Bartie raises his eyebrow. "But leading the colony will be different from leading the ship," he says. "Maybe we'll need a new leader."

I stop fully now. "What are you saying?"

"I want you to think—really think," Bartie says slowly, not meeting my eye, "if you're the best leader. If you're what we all need."

"Of course I am!"

"Why?"

It should be such a simple question, but I find I don't have an answer. The best I can come up with is that I was born to this job. But that's not enough. Amy's shown me enough history for me to know that princes born to kingdoms aren't always the best leaders.

I'd like to say that there's just me to lead.

But that's not true. Bartie's right in front of me.

54
AMY

I IGNORE THE ALL-CALL ELDER SENT INVITING EVERYONE TO the Keeper Level. He couldn't have meant that I should go too. My support would hurt him more than help, and I can think of nothing more dangerous than being crammed into a close-fitting room with every other person on the ship. Instead, I've spent the last hour with my face pressed against the bubble window in the hatch door, thinking about how, just beyond my vision, there's a planet waiting for me.

I don't move until I hear footsteps and the sound of a door zipping open on the other side of the cryo level.

My first instinct is to freeze, but then I remind myself of how few people have access to this level, and so I creep forward until I get to the main room. The door to the genetics lab is open.

"Hello?" I call out.

I can hear shuffling noises from inside. I step through the door. Victria kneels in front of Orion's cryo chamber. Her dark hair clings to the skin on the back of her neck, and her hands shake as she tucks a strand behind her ear. The chair that usually stands beside it is knocked over, as if she's slid from the seat to get closer to him.

"How do you stand it?" she asks in a hollow voice.

"Stand what?"

"Your parents are still frozen, right? How do you stand not waking them up? They're so close."

I don't say anything. There's something strange in her voice, scary.

"I could do it," she says. "I could do it right now. It can't be that hard to unfreeze someone. *You* were unfrozen."

I stop.

"What does it matter, anyway? The ship's landing soon. I can just unfreeze him."

So, Elder's told them about the planet.

"I need him!" Victria says, her voice raising an octave. "I need him!"

"Why?" I ask gently.

"Because I'm frexing scared, all right? I'm terrified!" Victria screams. Her hands are shaking; she reaches into her pocket and pulls out a square green med patch.

"Doc said those were dangerous," I say.

"Everyone has them; everyone uses them." Victria's voice sounds like a chant. "Just not more than one, only one."

"How did you get this?" I ask warily. Kit had told me they were stolen.

Victria shrugs as she tries to rip one open, but the package twists instead of tears, and she throws it down. She sits down fully on the tile floor, and more green patches spill from her pockets, at least a dozen. I raise my eyebrows but don't comment, although I do want to know why she has so many. Ignoring the patches completely, Victria wraps her arms around her legs and buries her head into her knees.

"Why are you so scared?" I ask, scooping up the med patches and slipping them into my own pocket, out of Victria's reach.

"It was so *huge*."

"What was?"

"The planet."

My heart sinks. Elder showed everyone else the planet? Why didn't he tell me he was going to? Maybe it would have been worth the risk, if I could have finally seen it for myself. Or . . . he could have shown me before.

"It was pretty," Victria says. Her eyes rove over me, lingering on my red hair. "But it was different. *Strange.*"

"You'll like the new planet," I say.

"How do you know?"

"Well—there won't be walls."

"But I like the walls," Victria whispers.

And I realize, to her, the metal isn't a cage, crushing her into a claustrophobic existence. No—to her, the walls are the walls of a comfortable home. It's the outside—the vast, never-ending outside—that terrifies her.

"Orion used to say we don't know what's down there. It could be anything."

"The probes and scans all say the planet is habitable," I start, but she cuts me off. She drops to her knees and leans forward, her panicked eyes meeting mine.

"Orion used to show me stuff, forbidden records. There were dinosaurs on Sol-Earth. Monsters that eat you. Animals bigger than people. Sinkholes and volcanoes and tornados and earthquakes."

"Lions and tigers and bears, oh my," I say softly, but Victria doesn't see it as a joke—she nods in agreement. These are monsters to her too.

She's rubbing her stomach so much that she reminds me of the shiny-bellied Buddha at the Chinese restaurant Jason took me to for our first date, back before I even knew what *Godspeed* was.

"I can't breathe, I can't breathe," Victria chants. Her hand clutches convulsively against her chest.

"Let's get you in the chair," I say, offering her my hand to help her stand. Victria shakes her head so violently that her entire torso turns. She jerks away from me. Her arms are seizing and shaking, and I can see beads of sweat building on her face, trembling down her neck. She rocks back and forth, clutching her legs closer to her chest, gasping for breath.

"I'm dying, I'm dying!" Victria chokes out.

"You're *not*," I insist, forcing my voice to remain calm. "You're having a panic attack. Victria, you've got to calm down. The baby—"

"Oh, stars, the baby!" Victria wails, rocking faster. "I can't have a *baby*! Not here! Not there!" She wheezes, trying to drag air back into her.

"Victria. Victria! Calm down, please, calm down. Tell me what's wrong," I say, desperately. "What's making you so scared?"

All I can make out of her response is "dying" and "Orion" and "planet" and "no."

I shove my hand into my pocket, withdrawing the same med patch Victria tried to rip open earlier. Beneath the wrapper, I can feel the oddly squishy patch—but it's so thin that it's hard to believe this little square can knock someone out. That three will kill. I smack it onto the top of her hand.

Her rocking stills. Victria's arms slacken, and her legs sprawl out in front of her.

"Are you okay?" I ask quietly.

Victria blinks.

"Come on," I say, standing. I offer Victria my hand, and she pulls herself up. She's upright now, but her shoulders are slouched and her eyes vacant. Her hair, sweaty and bedraggled, clings to her face. I reach over and swipe it off her forehead, tucking the loose strands behind her left ear, next to her wi-com. She doesn't flinch when I touch her; she doesn't even seem to notice.

"Victria?" I say. Then, louder: "Victria?"

Victria blinks.

I lead her to the elevator.

When we get to the Hospital lobby, it's more crowded than I've ever seen it. Two hassled nurses are trying to contain a group of people trying to push their way farther in, and apprentices are dashing about from patient to patient. A man near me grips the armrests of the chair he's sitting in so hard that he bends the metal.

"What's wrong with them all?" I ask Kit as she rushes by. "Was there some sort of accident?"

She shakes her head.

Doc sees Victria and me from across the lobby and makes his way over to us, dropping a single green med patch in the hands of every patient who gets to him first, their arms reaching out to him in supplication.

"What is going on?" I ask him. "Is this from the riot today?"

Doc shakes his head. "Elder doesn't think. He never thinks first. You can't give them everything at once. People can't handle this sort of thing." He diverts his attention to the man gripping the chair beside us. Then he reaches into the pocket of his lab coat and pulls out a pale green packet. He rips the backing off it and slaps it on the man's arm. The man's grip slackens, and an empty, expressionless sort of peace washes over him.

"I'll take her to her room," Kit offers, steering Victria by the elbow down the hall.

I think of returning to my room but instead go the other way, toward the door. I need fresh air, even if the air is just recycled oxygen. Outside, it's pitch black, but I don't need lights along the path to the Recorder Hall. Everything's muddy from the heavy rain, but mud or not, I know this path better than any of the courses I ran back at home. I know the feel of it under my feet—the thicker mulch near the Hospital doorstep, the flowers that brush my legs as the path winds through the garden, the cool scent of water as I turn around the pond, the slight incline as I approach the Recorder Hall.

I begin to see why those people in the Hospital are freaking out, and I'm overwhelmed with a sense of wonder that there's anything more than this. Even I, who once breathed air on top of the Rocky Mountains, who once swam in the Atlantic Ocean, have come to feel like there's nothing beyond these walls.

I forgot about Earth.

5 5
ELDER

I DIDN'T MEAN TO FALL ASLEEP—I MEANT TO JUST TAKE A quick nap, then get Amy and give her a private viewing of the planet on the Bridge. Instead, I awake the next morning with a smile on my lips but a foul taste in my mouth.

This is it.

This is finally it.

I dress quickly, but before I rush out of my room, I look behind me.

I've lived in this room over three years, ever since Eldest took me from the Feeder Level and began training me to be his successor. I have hated this room, when Eldest would lock me inside after I did something stupid, or later, after his death, when it reminded me of how alone I was. But I have loved this room, too. I smile, remembering the way Amy bounced on my bed when she woke me up here. I can't wait to hand her the one thing she's always wanted, the one thing I thought I'd deprived her of forever.

But—as eager as I am to move forward, I can't help but think of all I'm leaving behind.

I remember:

The first night I was here, lying awake, scared. And Eldest came in, sat on the edge of the bed, right there, and he told me he remembered feeling the same way the first night he started his training.

I remember:

Eldest and I got in a fight once—this was early on, when I was angry at Eldest but not yet afraid of him—and he yelled at me and I yelled back, and he raised his hand and struck me across the face. I'd run from the Learning Center to my room—it felt like I'd put miles between us—and hid between the bed and the nightstand for over an hour, until the smell of roast chicken and mushroom leaked into the room and up my nose. When I eventually crawled out, Eldest let me eat supper on the floor of the Great Room, using a projector to show me an old movie from Sol-Earth.

I remember:

When I was four or five or six, the family I was living with then, they were canners, decided to throw me a party. It was a going-away party—I was moving to another family the next day, but I was young enough to not really understand what that meant.

The mother of the family, Evie, she must not have been on Phydus, because she was funny and charming and she always knew what to say and do to make everything wonderful. Very different from the way I know her now, barely surviving with a green patch on her arm.

The day before I left her family, there was a feast in celebration—lamb and mint jelly, roast corn, biscuits and honey, baked sweet potatoes with brown sugar, berries sprinkled with sugar. And in the end, a cake.

It was a giant cake, so dense that Evie had to use both hands to cut it. The whole thing was iced in thick, crusty white icing, and Evie had written across the top *We love you, Elder!* She cried when she handed me the piece with my name on it.

An old man walked into the kitchen just as I was about to take the first bite. I didn't know who he was, but everyone else seemed to, and they all slowly put their forks down and pushed away from the table. I did the same, even though I didn't know why.

"I'm not here to interrupt!" the old man had said, laughing, and the tension broke like glass.

Evie cut a piece of cake for the old man—he got the piece that said *love*. Then he pulled up a chair beside mine. He was kind and funny—he acted like he didn't know how to use a fork and let me show him how. He kept dropping it, or using the wrong end of it, or trying to balance the cake on the handle instead of piercing it with the tines.

I remember everyone at the table laughing—true, hooting, uncontrollable laughter—as the old man just gave up and ate the cake with his fingers.

He nudged me. I grinned—there was icing on his nose, I recall—and I scooped up a handful of cake in one hand and crammed it in my face.

And then we were all eating cake with our hands, not even bothering with plates as we reached for more. Crumbs and icing were everywhere—smearing the tablecloth, in our hair, under our fingernails—and no one cared at all.

It was the happiest day of my life.

The next morning, Evie woke me up and helped me pack my few belongings in a bag. I would be spending the next year with the butchers, and there would be no cake at all that year.

"Who was that man who came yesterday?" I asked.

Evie was crying as she folded my clothes, but she laughed at my question. "Silly! That was Eldest, of course!"

• • •

I close my eyes and think of the way my teeth cracked the paper-thin crust on the top of the creamy icing, the way the cake filled my mouth as I chewed.

I glance at my bed, at the threadbare old blanket I had as a child that Eldest kept for me—or for himself. I pick up the blanket from the edge of my bed, press it against my face, and think about all Eldest was, and all he wasn't. All this ship has been, and all it will never be.

For a moment, I forget that today is the day I leave the ship, shut my eyes, and breathe in the scent of a thousand dreams.

Before heading to the Shipper Level, I re-activate the wi-com system for the rest of the ship. Within sconds, Shelby coms me.

"We're prepped and ready to begin planet-landing, sir," she says in my ear.

I smile as I walk away from my room. "Let's go home."

56
AMY

I WAKE UP EARLY. AFTER I DRESS, I THINK ABOUT SENDING Elder a com or even going up to the Keeper Level to see him. I want to see Elder. But—he has a ship to land.

To land. On the new planet. I release a shaky breath, full of relief and joy. Nothing else matters. Not Orion's stupid clues or Bartie's ridiculous revolution—we have the *planet.*

I head straight to the cryo level. It feels strange to do this now, even though I've done it every day for the last three months. I did it then because I believed I'd never see my parents alive again. Now, with my back to one row of cryo chambers and facing my parents' frozen bodies, it feels false.

Maybe it's because I know how close we are to waking them up for good.

I have so much I want to tell them—about how I'm stronger than I was before. About Harley and Luthor and Elder. I want to spill out every memory and every worry and every thought.

But I also know that I don't have to. We're there.

In the distance, I hear the unmistakable sound of a heavy door slamming shut. It's not the gen lab behind me. It's one of the doors down the hall past the cryo chamber . . . one of the *locked* doors.

This is it. This is whoever's tampering with the clues. It has to be.

I tear off down the hall, determined to catch whoever it is.

But no one's here.

Then I notice a crack of light seeping from the armory door.

I catch my breath. The armory door . . . that means whoever's in there has all the weapons. I, on the other hand, have none . . . unless you count the pocket-full of Phydus med patches I took from Victria.

I creep forward. The smart thing would be to run. But if I can just get an idea of *who* has been playing with us . . .

The door creaks loudly. Of-freaking-course it would creak loudly.

But no one's inside. Just in case, I step over to the closest rack, where the smallest guns are stored. At the top are tiny pistols. I wasn't kidding when I taunted Luthor. My father raised me to know what a gun is and how to use it. I pick up one of the red protection plastic bags and slide my finger through the seal. Gun oil wafts around me as I tip the bag open and the revolver falls into my hand. It has a small frame and a snubbed barrel, but it can hold .38 caliber bullets. The bullets are stored in a separate box, sealed with plastic. I press the grip into my palm as I load the gun. My hand's too small to fit it comfortably, but the gun's a double action, and all I've got to reach is the trigger.

I look closer, behind the shelves, the gun firmly in my hand. But no one is here.

Then I remember—I came here because I heard a door slam *shut*. Whoever was here may have started in the armory, but he slammed another door—on this hallway full of doors that are supposed to be locked.

I go back out and check the hatch through the bubble window, then open the room with the space suits. Nothing. I press my ear against the big door at the end of the hall, the last locked door, but it's too heavy for me to hear anything.

What's behind that door anyway? I briefly consider staying here to guard it. Whoever went in will have to go out. No one passed me as I raced through the hallway, and the only doors that can slam shut rather than zip open are these. Whoever it is has to be here.

Except . . . if this person knows how to unlock the doors, then whoever it is must also know about the stairs I found behind the walls . . . they go down too. They must reach the cryo level. And since there are no stairs here—they have to come out behind this last locked door. If I go up to the Feeder Level right now and run down the stairs, maybe I can catch whoever's been tampering with Orion's clues *and* discover what else is behind the locked door! If only Elder were here with me. . . .

I'm halfway down the hall when I remember the armory's still open, and even with a gun in hand, it's still not safe. I turn back and start to shut the door when I notice something: a floppy flashing near the shelf of explosives. I set the gun down and pick up the floppy.

Orion's face fills the screen.

<<begin video feed>>

This video wasn't done on the staircase. Instead, Orion sits in a chair bolted to the floor in front of a long, curved control panel. The room is dark, but I can see something glittering in the background.

This must be the Bridge, although it's much smaller than I would have expected.

ORION: Amy, you're nearly at the end. You're nearly at the choice you need to make. Have you seen it yet? The planet?

No. Not yet. But I know it's there.

ORION: Do you see now why I need you to decide? Because
you've been on a planet; you're the only one on *Godspeed* who's
been on a planet. And so you're the only one who'll be able to
judge whether or not it's worth it.

Orion touches his neck, his fingers sliding against the bumpy scar
where his wi-com used to be.

ORION: Before—before Eldest, and everything else . . . before
this [indicates scar] . . . I thought that the truth was an important thing. I'm not so sure now. Maybe it's better if we all remain
ignorant. I know I would be happier not knowing.

And to think, I'd nearly allowed myself to forget about Orion's clues in
the face of Elder's discovery. The planet just seemed so much more important than this mystery. Now I'm filled with curiosity.

ORION: But, perhaps, there are reasons why you need to
know the truth. This ship is old. Eldest sent me outside to help
with repairs, and I know that *Godspeed* is showing her age. So—
maybe it's time. Time to get off the ship.

Orion leans forward and picks up the camera. The image wobbles,
scanning the cramped, small area and the solid metal floor before spinning
around toward the control panel.

The camera focuses on the window. The image, blurry and bright, adjusts into focus. Through the honeycombed glass window, a curving, glowing ball of green and blue crests over the horizon of the ship.

I touch the small screen, making the blue and green of the planet on the screen look like an ocean's wave heaving and flowing.

ORION: When I first discovered *Godspeed* was in orbit around Centauri-Earth, I wanted the whole ship to know the truth. I tried to tell them. I tried to tell them everything. And because of this, Eldest tried to kill me.

Orion turns toward the window and stares at the planet. His scar is prominent on the screen.

ORION: He didn't kill me, though. I escaped. I hid for . . . for a long time . . . and then I snuck into the Recorder Hall. I integrated myself back into the ship. But it was in the Hall that I found even more secrets and lies. And it's because of this that I've decided to hide the truth, just like Eldest.

Orion's face turns back to the screen.

ORION: There's still the contingency plan. That's still here. If the ship has to land, it can. If you haven't figured it out, the last thing you need can be found in *Godspeed*.

Orion pauses, staring straight at the screen, as if he's given me some enormous clue. But *Godspeed* is huge, and everyone is already making preparations to leave. How am I supposed to find one tiny clue in the whole ship?

ORION: But if it doesn't have to . . . if there is any way to survive without landing the ship. You must. You must. I can't protect this truth forever, I know that. You have to. If there's any possible way for this ship to survive, you must do whatever it takes to stop the planet-landing.

What is Orion saying? I thought the whole point of his messages was to bring me to a point where I could make some big important choice. But now it's like he's saying the opposite.

ORION: No matter how bad things are on the ship, if you're not dying out, if the solar lamp still works . . . stay here. And make sure the ship stays too. Amy, you're my little contingency plan—but that's just it. You must only lead the ship to the planet as a last res—

Orion doesn't even get the last word out before his face disappears into loud static. I'm so surprised that I almost drop the floppy. The abrupt cut-off makes my stomach twist with dread, a feeling that doesn't go away when the static fades to black. Heavy white letters scroll over the dark background, spelling out a phrase I've come to fear.

Follow the leader.

The video cuts off.

That phrase—*follow the leader*. The static. The fact that this video was on a floppy, not a mem card. This clue must also have been tampered with. I don't know if Orion's message continued—maybe he was going to tell me the code to get behind the locked door?—but I'm certain he wasn't the one who left those words.

I look up now, carefully examining the armory. Before, I'd rushed in there looking for someone. Now, I look for something . . . and I find it. An empty shelf, a row of missing explosives.

"Oh, God," I whisper, my hand unconsciously going to the cross at my neck.

I race out of the armory, straight to the elevator.

I've got to get to the Shipper Level. *Now.* I've got to get to Elder. If I'm sure of anything, it's that whoever's telling us to "follow the leader" doesn't mean Elder—and those explosives are going to wipe out anyone who tries to land the ship.

57

ELDER

ALTHOUGH IT IS BARELY TIME FOR THE SOLAR LAMP TO TURN
on, the Shipper Level is crowded. I look around, half-expecting to see
Amy's bright red hair peeking out through the throng of Shippers, but no,
she's not here. Of course she's not. Even if she's the one I want to share this
with the most, it's loons of me to think of her now, when I need to focus on
planet-landing. I haven't seen her since I almost died—and so much has
changed since then. Amy was the first person I told about Centauri-Earth,
but she may very well be the last person I see once we land.

I shake my head to clear my mind. This isn't the time to get sentimen-
tal; it's time to land the ship.

The Shippers cheer as I walk down the corridor toward the Bridge, my
feet clanging against the metal grate floor. They reach for me—to shake my
hand, to slap me on the back, to just touch me in awe and thanks. When
I push through the Energy Room into the Engine Room, the scientists and
Shippers give me a standing ovation.

I beam at them.

It's everything I dreamed it would be.

First Shipper Shelby and the rest of her cadre stand in a line in front of the giant decorated doors that lead to the Bridge. They all salute me when I approach.

"I—uh," I say, and it's not until I'm uh-ing that I realize the room is completely silent and they now all want me to make a speech. A speech that consists of more than "uh."

Frex.

"I—uh—I mean . . ." I swallow, shut my eyes.

"This is not our home," I say. "We have lived on *Godspeed* all our lives, but it is not our home. We didn't choose to be born on a ship, trapped by the walls that keep us safe. But we do choose to be the ones who decide it is time to land. We choose to take the risk, to leave behind this shell, and to see what the rest of the universe has to offer.

"We choose our future. Let's go home."

"Home!" Shelby booms, and everyone repeats her word and cheers.

And then it's time.

Shelby opens the huge doors. She stands to the side, letting her crew—the remaining first-level Shippers—go first. There's an air of ominous gravity to the whole production; we're making history, and we're all aware of it.

I watch them enter the Bridge solemnly, and it feels so wrong that Amy's not among them. I knew when I first saw her, frozen, that she would change me forever. But she's changed the whole ship too, the fate of everyone on board.

As the last Shipper enters the Bridge, Shelby turns to me, and she smiles, and I step forward.

"Sir!"

I turn. One of the Shippers runs up to me. "Sir," he says, "the girl, the red-haired girl—she's here."

"Amy?"

He nods. "She's beating on the Energy Room door, yelling for you."

"Elder?" Shelby asks, her hand on the Bridge door.

I step back, away from the Bridge and toward the Energy Room door.

And then—

—an explosion rips open the ship.

It feels as if my eardrums have burst, and I lose my footing, crashing to the ground. My head cracks against the solid metal floor, but I'm moving—sliding toward what remains of the Bridge. Someone screams, and the sound is violently cut off. I twist around, and a chair soars across the room, the leg of it skidding across my shoulder, ripping my tunic and the skin underneath. There's shouting all around, but the sound is drowned out by the ringing metal crashes as tables and desks fly up from the ground. A stab of pain shoots up my leg—a screwdriver is embedded in my calf. I reach down and yank it out, but I'm still sliding across the floor.

I lift my head as high as I can—

The window on the Bridge is gone.

The metal seam that connected the honeycombed glass is twisted, ripped apart, scraggly at the ends like the paintings from Sol-Earth of creepy dead trees in winter. The vacuum of space is sucking the air out of the Bridge and the Engine room so violently that we're all caught up in its maelstrom, the chairs, desks, tables, tools—and people.

Shelby's crew is hit the worst—some have caught onto the control tables or the bolted-down chairs, but I don't see everyone. I do see blood and bone and organs at the front, near the hole—whatever blew apart the Bridge's window also blew apart the people sitting closest.

A Shipper—Prestyn—tries to stand but stumbles, lunges, and flies through the doors. His body catches on the metal fingers of the broken seams, ripping through him. Great globs of blood float off him in crimson spheres.

I slam into the wall by the Bridge's doors so hard my bones rattle, but the wall stops me from also flying out the window. I stand, pressing against the back wall for support, trying to breathe through the rushing wind. It won't take long—minutes maybe—for the vacuum of space to suck out all the air from both rooms.

Clutching the metal supports on the wall, I twist my head around to peer inside the Bridge.

It's too late—the gaping maw that was once the window has destroyed the Bridge. Shelby clings to a chair that's bolted to the floor. Her hair is plastered back, and her eyes are red and streaming.

"Don't!" she screams. *"Don't!"*

She means the button. This one, here, by my hand.

The one that would seal the Bridge doors.

The one that would protect us from space—but leave her in it.

She's reaching for me with one hand, *straining*, but she's too far away, she's just barely too far away, and I'll never be able to get to her, it's too late. Too late.

"No, no, no, no, no," she pleads.

She reaches toward me. Her fingers are almost within reach. If I reached out—maybe I could pull her to safety before I seal the doors shut?

But I can't take that chance. I can't risk the whole ship to save one person.

"No," she whispers.

But I push the button anyway.

The Bridge doors swing shut.

The violent winds die.

It takes a moment before everyone left can stagger back up. Some are bleeding—a few broken bones, a dislocated shoulder, a limp—from the debris that crashed into them. More than their physical injuries, though, is the horror that twists each face, a hollowed-out shocked expression that I doubt will ever fully fade.

It is silent here, but nowhere near as silent as the other side of the door.

5 8
A M Y

I HAVE NEVER RUN SO HARD OR SO FAST AS WHEN I RACED from the Hospital to the grav tube. Still, I knew I would be too late.

And I was.

When I finally got to the Engine Room, I could hear the explosion from behind the door.

And the screams.

Now, the Shipper Level—already packed from the events of the day— falls into a sort of hushed horror. People crowd around me in the Energy Room. The door to the Engine Room dents inward, like a monster is trying to claw it out, but the steel reinforcements hold. We fall back against the far wall anyway, and some people race out of the Energy Room, heading for cover, as if they think *Godspeed* will continue to protect them even as it's being ripped apart.

We all stare at the door, but it gives us no answers.

Red lights fade in and out along the edges of the floor and ceiling. The ship's computer announces, "Breached hull: Bridge," in a pleasant, cheerful sort of voice.

We wait. A woman opens her mouth to speak, but I quell her with a look. We're all listening to the silence. Wondering if anyone still lives on the other side of the door.

If Elder survived.

Something smacks against the door. A woman behind me screams, and a man near the hallway shouts, "Frex!" The door moves again—not with the force of a tornado, like before, but instead with a rattle and shake.

Fingers pop out at the door edges.

"They're alive!" shouts the same woman. And as one, we all rush to the door, prying our fingers into the open crack. Together we strain against the mechanics to slide the damaged door open. The door moves an inch. We all push harder. With a screeching metal-on-metal sound, the door finally, finally gives way.

I see the blood on him first—dripping from a gash in his shoulder, staining his dark skin red. Sweat makes his hair cling to his forehead. His arms strain to cast aside the remains of the door, and he staggers through.

"Elder," I whisper. My voice cracks in the middle. I feel tears stinging my eyes, but they don't fall. I almost lost him. Again. It wasn't until I saw his body on the hatch floor yesterday that I realized how much I cared about him, but even then I couldn't define my feelings.

A part of me has been holding back from him since I first started to see how devoted he was to me. That part of me wove words into my soul, words like *doubt* and *can't trust* and *lust* and *not worth it*. All those words break, all at once, like strings ripped from torn cloth.

Now, though, staring at his grief-stricken face, I don't think with words at all.

Beyond him, the Shippers are helping each other up. They cry in joy for those who lived and begin to mourn for those who died beyond the sealed Bridge door.

But I'm just looking at Elder, and he's just looking at me, and everything else disappears.

My hands are shaking. My legs are too—in fact, I'm shaking all over. I want to rush to him, but I can't. Instead, he's the one who makes a move. He barrels through the mangled doorway (although he's limping; why is he limping?) and wraps his arms around me. I collapse into him, but he supports me, lending me his strength when I don't seem to have any more of my own.

"Oh, God, Elder," I mutter into his chest, and it's not much, but it's the best prayer I've got.

He strokes my hair soothingly. The world continues around us—people rushing into or out of the Engine Room, more cries, more reunions—but we are a silent stalwart amid the chaos.

"How did you know?" Elder asks, his nose buried in my hair. The question is so the opposite of everything I am right now—logical words formed into a logical question—that it confuses me at first. I lean back and look up at him. Elder leads me past the remains of the door and through the crowd to a quiet corner in a room nearby. Beyond his shoulder I can still see the chaos of the explosion—Kit has arrived with a posse of nurses and taken charge, corralling the wounded to one area and commanding everyone else to leave. A group of engineers examines the seal-locked door of the Bridge, ensuring that there's no more danger of exposure.

"The explosion," Elder says, drawing me back to him. "You knew before, didn't you? You came here to warn me."

"I found another one of Orion's videos. In the armory."

"Orion—Orion did this?" Elder's eyes are befuddled; he's still reeling from the explosion.

"No, not Orion. But . . . someone else has his videos. Someone else knows the codes to the locked doors. I think Orion's been trying to tell us the way off the ship all along, but someone else found out his secret before we did and they've been trying to stop us."

I hand Elder the floppy with Orion's video. In the first video I found, Orion seemed certain that there was a choice to be made and that I would make it. But by this last video, he sounds the same way he did in the video of him just after he ran away from Eldest—scared and unsure. Whoever found these videos of Orion clearly agrees that the planet isn't worthwhile—and will murder anyone who tries to land the ship. The explosion on the Bridge is proof enough of that—it has ensured that even with Centauri-Earth so close, we'll never land.

I can't read Elder's face as he watches the short video—grief, anger, doubt, something else, something empty and painful. But when he looks up at me, all that's left in his eyes is a hollow sort of nothing.

"None of this matters," Elder says. "With the Bridge gone, we're going nowhere."

Once he says it, it becomes real for him. I see the sixteen years of his life trapped on the ship, and the decades of his future fall on him like a weight—he literally sags with the realization that *Godspeed* can't land. He's got everything on him now—the ship, the people, the deaths, the disappointment. And I realize: he has always had them. Always.

Elder looks behind him, to the Engine room, and beyond to the sealed doors. "Shelby was in there. In the Bridge."

And just like that, the terror's back. I push it down, try to drown it under the waters of my soul, keeping it under with both hands and watching it die.

"Why?" Elder's eyes search mine. He's not asking why someone would blow up the Bridge. He's asking why someone would let Shelby die for it.

5 9
ELDER

"NO, NO, NO, NO, NO," SHELBY SAID.

The words circle my mind, and I know they'll never leave.

Amy kisses me.

"No, no, no, no, no."

Amy tells me that someone did this because of a stupid video Orion made. That whoever did this just wanted to make sure that we would never, ever leave the ship. Ever.

"No, no, no, no, no."

Amy leads me to the grav tube and takes me to the Feeder Level. She shows me the hidden door and the stairs behind it.

"No, no, no, no, no."

Amy pushes open the door, and light fills the hidden space behind it. It creaks open, but all I hear is:

"No, no, no—"

BOOM!

Another explosion, this one deeper than the first, rumbles the ground and shakes the foundation of the Hospital. Shingles fall from the Hospital roof and clatter down the sides of the building, smashing against the ground. The doors fling open, and people stream out, a pillar of gray and brown smoke chasing after them. Emergency ladders flutter from the upper stories, and people start climbing down, dropping a few feet to the earth and racing toward the Recorder Hall for cover.

"The frex—" I start, as Amy grabs my arm. Even from here, we can feel the rumbling under our feet.

"Why would someone blow up the Hospital?" she asks. Her words are hollow, but her eyes are filled with fear.

Smoke drifts from the doors on the ground floor but nowhere else. There's no evidence of fire, no evidence of damage.

Amy's face drains of color, and she's paler than ever. "Oh, God. It wasn't the Hospital that exploded—"

"It was the cryo level," I finish for her.

"My parents," she whispers. Her eyes lose focus; her mouth is slack. "There are stairs; they go down to the cryo level. I know where they are. I could—"

"Go to them," I say, gripping her shoulders until she comes back to me. "Go now—but be careful. Whoever did this could still be there."

Amy swallows.

"I don't think that was a big enough explosion to destroy the cryo level." I shake my head, considering. "No, I'm sure of it. They're fine. They've got to be fine."

I can feel her pulling away, but she's still holding on to me, her fingers gripping my sleeve.

"Go," I say gently. "I can do this. I'll take care of the ship—you take care of your parents. But . . ." I pause. "If you see anyone . . . or anything—if it's not safe down there, come back to me. Right away."

She gives me a slight nod and runs to the stairs without a word.

I turn and face the ship.

60
AMY

MY HEART THUDS IN MY THROAT, AND IT MAKES ME WANT TO throw up. I've been so focused on everything else—Elder, the murders, the mystery—I'd nearly forgotten the most important thing.

My parents.

Trapped in ice, in the cryo level, sleeping.

Helpless.

I race down, down, using the handrails to leap the steps two at a time—and the deeper I go, the more the smoke wraps around me.

It's an acrid scent, like burning metal, a smell so sharp it cuts my tongue like a knife. A snot-yellow dust covers my skin. It's as fine as baby powder, but it stings like bites from fire ants, and I use my sleeves to beat it off. I tug my tunic up over my face so it covers my nose and mouth, and I let my hair down, hoping I can get at least a little protection on the back of my neck from it.

My foot slips, and—fortunately—I grab a handrail. Just in time. There are two more steps—and then nothing.

I lean down, gripping the handrail for support. The bomb was centered on the elevator that extends from the Hospital to the cryo level, just as I'd suspected. Shrapnel and the force of the explosion have ripped through the metal stairs here as easily as if they'd been made of paper.

We're cut off from the cryo level.

For one crazy moment, I consider jumping. How many feet could it be to get to the bottom? These steps don't go directly into the cryo level. I'm a couple of feet above a solid metal surface. There must be a hatch or something leading down to the cryo level. There's a pillar between the stairs and the elevator—maybe there's a door built into it. But the yellow smoke is heavy and impenetrable, and judging by the ragged edges of the metal on the stairs, I bet there's plenty of debris below that could kill me. I stare as hard as my watering eyes allow me to, but all I can see is a mangled mess of shattered metal, twisted beams, and blown rivets.

My throat burns, making me cough; the yellow powder must be affecting me in ways I can't even tell. I shiver; it's colder here than anywhere else on the ship. I creep back up the stairs. I can feel my heartbeat thudding in my ears, and I'm cold with sweat. I grasp at air. I remember the way Victria thought she was dying, overwhelmed by the idea of a world beyond the ship. I feel the same panic surging inside me, overwhelmed by the idea of *still* being trapped behind walls, forever behind walls.

When I get back to the top, I search through the crowd that's gathered around Elder at the Recorder Hall to tell him what I found. He's surrounded by people, and I don't bother being polite—I shove them out of my way, ignoring their angry cries, then I pull Elder by the arm until we're far enough away that no one else can overhear us.

"I can't get to the cryo level," I say. I describe what I saw between the levels.

He nods as if he expected it. His eyes are dead and empty. Elder gave up hope on the Bridge, but I didn't give it up until I could see no more in him.

61
ELDER

THE HOSPITAL'S NO LONGER SAFE, SO WE SET UP THE RECORDER Hall as a temporary infirmary. Doc, who'd been close to the elevator when it exploded, has his left arm in a sling and a deep gash on his cheek, under his eye. Still, he moves from person to person, quickly assigning pills and med patches and bandages. More often than not, he slips the patients a pale green patch. I pretend not to notice.

In truth, I sort of want one myself.

Kit and the nurses bring the Shippers who survived the Bridge explosion, and another panicked wave of activity follows their arrival—bandages here, stitches there, all wrapped up with a bright green patch on top.

There aren't that many injuries. Not on the outside, at least. But I can see a spark of desperation in people's eyes as they slowly become aware of the fact that the explosions did not just kill nine more of our people: they also killed any hope we had of planet-landing.

Later that afternoon, maintenance crews inspect the Hospital. Just as Amy told me, the elevator—the one that goes all the way to the cryo level—was destroyed. The cables broke and the elevator itself crashed at the bottom of the shaft, but that was the extent of the damage.

Once things settle down, I do an all-call, requesting that everyone meet in the garden behind the Hospital. Eldest would have ordered another ship-wide meeting on the Keeper Level, but I know the last thing people want is to be away from the familiarity of the Feeder Level, especially if it brings them closer to the now-destroyed Bridge. The statue of the Plague Eldest is traditional for the changing ceremonies from Elder to Eldest, and it seems appropriate, given what I plan on saying.

"Hey, wait up!" Bartie calls as I make my way from the Recorder Hall to the garden. I don't answer him, but I do slow my pace.

"Is it true?" Bartie asks when he catches up to me. "The Shippers in the Recorder Hall are saying the Bridge is gone."

"Yeah," I grunt.

"Are you going to tell them?" Bartie continues, matching my quick pace so he can walk beside me. "I think you should tell everyone about the Bridge. About how we can't leave now."

"Shite, Bartie, you think so?" I don't bother quelling the sarcasm in my voice. "Here I was just thinking I'd take a nice little break and then maybe get a bite to eat; stars, might as well go into the Hall and watch a vid or something."

Bartie raises his hands in peace, but his face is angry. "You never do anything without someone telling you to," he says. "How was I supposed to know that this was different?"

"You're such a frexing hypocrite," I spit. "You're so worried about all I'm doing wrong, you have no idea what I'm doing right."

Bartie snorts, and in that sound, I can hear all the contempt and derision that I've had to put up with from him—from everyone—who's been judging me since Eldest died. And I'm frexing sick and tired of it.

"You want to be Eldest?" I say loudly. "Fine. Be Eldest. Then you'll know what it's like when you have to watch your friends die. Know what I did while you were just frexing lying around here all day? I was on the Bridge; I was in the doorway when it exploded. I watched Prestyn and Hailee and Brittne and the others get sucked out into space. I watched Shelby hanging on to a chair, saw the tears in her eyes as she reached out to me. But I let her die so I could save the Engine Room. And the rest of the frexing ship."

I march to the railing and look out at the Feeder Level, my back to him.

"You let Shelby die?"

"I watched her beg for her life, and then I sealed the door anyway."

No, no, no, no, no.

Bartie pauses for a moment, staring at me. I keep walking. He rushes to catch up. "Maybe you're more of a leader than I gave you credit for."

"Go frex yourself."

"I'm trying to apologize here."

"For what? Why? Because I let some Shippers die, suddenly I'm a better leader? Shite. That's Eldest's logic. Not mine."

This time, I make sure to outpace him.

I stand under the statue of the Plague Eldest. His concrete arms are raised in mock benevolence, but I wonder now, looking at his weather-worn face, if there was ever a time when there was something of him in me. We are, supposedly, genetically the same, but . . . would we have made the same decisions? Would he do what I'm about to?

I don't think so.

The people arrive slowly. Most of them—I can tell by their forlorn faces, looks of fear and anger—already know what I'm about to say. Some—family and friends of the first-level Shippers—are among those that gather closest to me.

When as many people as possible are crowded near the statue, I jump up on the base so I'm a little above them. I can spot individual faces, despite the fact that the garden is so crowded. Bartie stands in almost the exact center of the crowd. Doc and Kit stand by the Hospital. Amy's near the pond, standing a bit away from everyone. She's wearing a jacket, the hood pulled up over her face, but I know it's her. She glances up just in time to meet my gaze, and the pride in her eyes gives me the strength to speak.

"Hello," I say, because I can't really think of anything else to open with. "I have terrible news," I add, raising my voice when I notice the people straining to hear me better. I turn on my wi-com instead of shouting—now I can speak like I'm having a normal conversation.

"I have terrible news," I repeat, my voice transmitting directly into their ears. "But I suspect that most of you have already heard about the devastating events I'm about to discuss." I take a deep breath, preparing myself. Rather than trying to look at everyone, I seek out Amy again. It's easier if I can pretend I'm only talking to her. "The Bridge was blown up today. We—I—don't know who did it, but the attack was done purposefully. It resulted in the deaths of nine Shippers, including First Shipper Shelby." Now I look away from Amy. "It also prevented us from ever being able to land *Godspeed*."

I pause. No one speaks. I let the silence stretch out to the edges of the ship.

"Since I have assumed leadership, I have abolished the practice of contaminating the water system with Phydus. I have attempted to work with you, to find a way for you to carry on your lives aboard the ship without the drug. When I discovered that Centauri-Earth was within our reach, I attempted to fulfill the mission of *Godspeed* and land the ship."

I swallow hard, forcing myself to look at the whole crowd.

"But in this—as in all aspects of my leadership—I have failed."

There are gasps of surprise, angry looks, confused looks, murmurs of questions. But as soon as I open my mouth, everyone's silent again.

"I'll be honest: I thought my leadership would be as strong as Phydus had been. Clearly I was wrong. Since I took on the role of Eldest, the ship has spiraled into chaos. People have died. Not just from today's bombing, which led to nine deaths, but murders done in my name, calling others to follow the leader. And before that—suicides I could not prevent, injuries, and worse."

Many of the people in the crowd are crying now. I can't help myself; I look to Amy. She stands straight and tall, her gaze unwavering. I straighten my spine and throw back my shoulders.

"This is why"—I take a deep breath—"I am offering now, before you all, to step down from my role as leader of *Godspeed*."

My words are met with stunned silence. They gape at me, shocked and unsure of how to respond. I let the silence grow. Slowly, one by one, everyone starts to turn, searching through the crowd to see who my gaze has shifted to.

Bartie.

But he stands wordless, watching me.

After a while, when nobody moves, I say, "If no one else wishes to lead *Godspeed*, I will continue to do my best to serve this ship. That is all."

I disconnect the wi-com link and walk away.

6 2
AMY

THE CROWD DISSOLVES SLOWLY. THIS ISN'T OVER; I KNOW that much. Bartie may not have seized power tonight, but I think that stemmed more from shock than anything else. That—or he had some other reason for not yet assuming control. I don't trust him. If we don't get off this ship soon, Bartie *will* take over—or destroy the ship trying to.

Once everyone else has left, I wander up the path toward the statue. I used to think Elder looked nothing like the water-streaked concrete statue of the Plague Eldest, but now I'm not so sure.

Elder emerges from the shadows and starts walking beside me.

"How did you know?" I ask him.

"Know what?"

"That Bartie wouldn't ask you to step down then? That he wouldn't take over leadership of the ship when you offered."

Elder meets my eyes. "I didn't."

I try not to show my surprise at his words.

Although the Hospital has been cleared for occupancy, I steer Elder the other way, toward the Recorder Hall.

"I've been thinking," I say as we plod up the path.

"About what?" Elder's voice sounds tired and weak.

"How different you are from Orion."

Elder huffs out a breath of air.

"No, really," I insist. "Orion had backup plans for his backup plan. You don't. You just do what you think is right at the time and wait to see what happens."

"Maybe I should have a plan," Elder says. "Things might work out better if I did."

"You can't plan for everything. Orion couldn't have known some nut job would blow up the Bridge." I steal a glance at Elder and notice his frown. "And neither could you," I add, but I don't think he quite believes me.

We don't speak again as we mount the stairs to the Recorder Hall. It's quiet here. The artifacts inside are just a reminder of everything we can't have, and no one wants to be reminded of that.

"I'm sorry," Elder says. Light spills into the dark Recorder Hall from the open doors, then fades to nothing as Elder silently pulls them shut.

"For what?"

"You've lost your chance to leave the ship, to have your parents awoken—all of it."

I can wake them up. I don't say this aloud, but I know it's true. If we really have no chance of landing the ship, I *will* wake my parents up, no matter what.

"I've still got you, haven't I?" I say, reaching for his hand. Elder snatches it away. He doesn't want to be comforted.

"It's all my fault. I didn't think any of this would happen. . . ."

"It's not your fault," I say immediately. "No one could have known. . . ."

My voice trails off. But someone did know. Someone did guess. Orion. He really did have a plan for everything. A *contingency* plan . . .

I point to one of the giant wall floppies. "Can you bring up the blueprints of the ship?"

"Why?" Elder just stands there, begging me with his eyes to stop, to not make him think there's any hope left.

Except there is.

I push Elder to the wall floppy and don't leave his side until he starts tapping on the screen to bring up the blueprint. Once he does, I rush off to the other side of the hallway and grab a chair resting against the wall. I slam it down under the clay models of the planets and the little replica of *Godspeed*.

"In the last video, the one that I found when I discovered the missing explosives," I say, climbing up onto the chair, "Orion told me that the last thing I need to find will be in *Godspeed*."

"*Godspeed* is huge," Elder says. The wall floppy behind him shows the giant diagram of the ship. Seeing it there, projected on the wall, I can appreciate just how huge this ship is.

"I know," I say, "but isn't it odd? That word choice. He didn't say 'on *Godspeed*.' He said 'in.'"

"So?" Elder asks. His voice is still flat, and I know that while he's physically in the Recorder Hall with me, he's really still in the garden, giving up, still on the Bridge, watching his people die. He doesn't care about Orion's clues anymore.

I strain, reaching for the tiny model of *Godspeed* hanging suspended between the two clay models of the Earths.

"In *Godspeed*," I say. "*In* it." The chair wobbles as I stand on my tiptoes on top of it, my fingers brushing the bottom of the small model ship.

I noticed before that it was on a hook, as if it could be taken down and inspected. I push against the bottom, and the hook slides off. The ship falls. I reach out, grabbing it with one hand. The chair topples, and I jump off before it clatters to the ground. Elder catches me around the middle, and I gasp in surprise. He sets me down gently on the ground.

The model's about as large as my head and caked in dust. I blow on it, and huge chunks of dust fly away and then drop to the floor, too heavy to float. There's more dust on the top of the ship, in the grooves of the tiny model honeycomb window on the Bridge. I turn the replica over so the ship's on its side. It almost looks like a broken winged bird—a beak for a nose and thrusters for tail feathers.

I hand it to Elder.

He weighs it in his hand as if it's an alien thing, not a replica of the only home he's ever known. His face is intense—a scowl so deep that the shadows seem like black marks on his face. The veins in his hand pop up, and his fingers tense. Very deliberately, he presses his thumb against the Bridge window until the tiny honeycombed glass breaks. I see a dot of blood on his thumb, but he shows no sign of pain.

"It's accurate now," he says, handing the model back to me.

I search his eyes, but they're hollow inside.

"There's more glass here," I say, pointing to the bottom of the ship.

Elder shrugs, a sort of one-shoulder careless motion. "I saw it when I was outside. An observatory or something."

"It has to be on the other side of the last locked door," I say. "Why lock an observatory?"

I step over to the wall floppy. Elder stays where he is, by the chair, but his eyes follow me. I place the now-broken model on the ground and zoom in on the blueprints on the floppy. I use both hands to manipulate the image on the screen, sliding over the cryo level until I get to the section that shows the locked doors. Not all the doors are marked—the armory isn't—but behind the last locked door on the level is one word.

Contingency

"He keeps calling me—this—his contingency plan," I say under my breath. I turn and meet Elder's eyes, and notice there's a spark in them again.

"This bit of glass here," I say, picking up the model of *Godspeed* and pointing to it. I run my fingers from the broken Bridge to the bottom level of the ship. It's the same basic shape, a beak protruding from the front of the ship. The only difference is that the cryo level beak is smaller.

On the replica ship, a tiny metal line runs along the bottom, all around in a circle.

"This isn't Orion's contingency plan," I say slowly, turning the model over in my hand, "it's *Godspeed*'s. I can't believe we didn't think of this before! What ship doesn't have a backup plan? What ship doesn't have an *escape shuttle?* It's so obvious—the answer has been right in front of us the whole time!"

I carefully pull against the metal line on the replica *Godspeed*. The bottom half breaks apart from the ship.

Elder's eyes widen. "The cryo level . . . the *whole frexing cryo level*—can break away from the ship? The entire level is an escape shuttle?"

I toss the bottom part of the replica—the escape shuttle—at Elder. It soars through the air in a graceful arc, free from the rest of the ship. Free to find a home on the new planet.

6 3
ELDER

I CATCH THE ESCAPE SHUTTLE REPLICA WITH ONE HAND. "This is impossible," I say, staring at it.

"Why?" Amy laughs. "Think of the design. The most important supplies are down there. The stairs I went down earlier today—they don't go straight into the cryo level. They stop on the roof of it, and there's a hatch you have to go down in order to get into the actual level. In fact," I add, trying to remember what the area looked like through the yellow-tinted smoke, "I could see what was left of the elevator shaft behind a pillar, and there was a seal-lock hatch there too. Why else would you need a sealed door there? The builders of *Godspeed* didn't waste any space."

When she sees the doubt in my eyes, Amy growls in frustration. "Elder, think! You know I'm right—that part of the ship can break away. And you know what this means! We can still get to the new planet, even if the Bridge is gone. We can leave behind *Godspeed* and take the cryo level down!"

The possibilities swirl around me. Amy grins, knowing she's won me over. "That level's big—bigger than it needs to be if it's just storage," she says. "The roof is high—it has a higher oxygen capacity. And the floor's large enough to hold everyone—"

My shoulders sag. "But how the frex are we going to be able to get there if the elevator and the stairs are both blown up?"

Amy's grin is so huge all her teeth show. "Let's go for a swim," she says.

I can barely keep up with her as she races down the path back toward the Hospital. No—not the Hospital. The pond in the garden behind the Hospital.

"It was the fish that gave it away. I couldn't get over how weird it was that there weren't any fish in the pond," Amy says. She's practically running now, and I have to jog to keep up with her.

"The fish?"

"The koi. Harley painted koi. That's what he was painting when I first met him, and that was one of the last things he painted, too. His room is filled with fish."

"So?" I ask.

Amy stops so suddenly I crash into her.

"He knew fish. He saw them. It's not like he could just look those images up. And you told me—*you told me*—that it's not that there were no fish, but that there were none 'anymore.'"

"Exactly," I say. "There *used* to be fish."

"So where are they? Fish don't just disappear."

I stop, thinking. It was so loons then, when Kayleigh died. I don't remember anything but her body in the water when we found her. But after that . . . Harley didn't go back to the pond for ages, and when we did, the fish had just . . . disappeared.

"There's something at the bottom of the pond," Amy says. "Think about the blueprint. You know what's right above the contingency area?"

"The pond?" Hope bubbles up inside of me. *Stars!* There's still a chance! We can still make it to Centauri-Earth . . . although it will mean leaving *Godspeed* behind.

"The pond."

It's all so simple—and now that Amy tells me about it, I can see the truth in it. If Kayleigh had drained the pond, the fish, of course, would have died. But before she could do anything, Eldest found her. Patched her up to make her immobile, then refilled the pond. To everyone else, it looked like Kayleigh had swum into the pond and let herself drown, but in reality . . .

Amy's off again, racing toward the pond. Orion said that Kayleigh's death was murder, not suicide. When Harley and I found her body, she was plastered in med patches. I remember the way Evie became so placated when Doc pressed a Phydus med patch into her skin. Kayleigh didn't have the new Phydus patch, but there are others, patches that make you sleep, for example. And with enough med patches, Kayleigh would have just stood in the pond and let herself drown while Eldest watched his secret sink beneath the surface along with her.

Amy kicks off her moccasins at the edge of the pond and strips off her jacket, tossing it on the ground. She unwinds the long strip of cloth that binds her hair up.

"Turn around," she says, and only then do I realize I'm staring.

"It's not like I—um—you know—uh," I stammer, feeling my face grow hot with embarrassment.

"Turn. Around," Amy says again, but she's smiling at me.

I spin around, staring at the ground and trying very hard not to listen to the rustle of cloth as Amy undresses.

A moment later, I hear a splash and turn back around. Amy's pants and tunic lie in a crumpled pile; she must be wearing only her underwear and tank top under the water. My face grows even hotter at the thought, and I wonder how strange it would look if I stuck my head under the water to clear my mind.

"What are you looking for?" I call out over the water to her.

"A way down!" she says. The water's clear, although a foggy brown rises up from the silty bottom of the pond near her feet.

She dives under the surface and is gone for nearly a full minute.

Then she bursts up from the surface, takes a huge gulp of air, and dives back down.

Huge bubbles burst along the surface.

My eyes scan the water. I see flashes of red, flicks of pale skin. I count the seconds.

Then Amy breaks through the surface, sucking in air and letting it all out in one long whoop of triumph.

"What's going on?" a voice calls from the garden path.

"Crap, crap, crap," Amy mutters behind me as she wiggles back into her pants. I risk a look over my shoulder as she tugs her tunic back into place. She steps forward just as Bartie and Victria come around the hydrangeas and down to the pond.

Her wet clothes soak through her dry ones, making everything stick to her curves in a way that I can't rip my eyes from.

"Hello!" Amy calls to them.

"What are you doing?" Victria asks quietly.

I search her face. Victria was always the quiet one of our group, but I never noticed how silent she'd become since the Season. Not until Amy told me about what had happened to her.

I feel my fists clenching as I think about what happened to her—and how I didn't stop it from happening. My fingernails press painfully into my palms. I hate what happened to Victria—what almost happened to Amy. I . . .

"I just went for a little swim," Amy says, laughing.

"I can see that," Victria says. I'm glad that it seems like Amy has been there for her at least. And, perhaps, Bartie. He might be a chutz and a traitor to boot, but at least he's been a friend to Victria. More than I've been.

"What's that?" Bartie asks, pointing to the ground.

"Oops." Amy bends over and picks up two pale green med patches and shoves them back into her pocket. They must have fallen out as she dressed.

"Why do you have Phydus patches?" I ask, frowning. My first instinct is anger—she's the one who's been so solidly against Phydus—but it immediately melts into concern. I think about Evie, clawing at the walls of the ship. Do the walls crush Amy in the same way? Is Phydus getting her through the nights, when I don't see her?

Amy's eyes shoot to Victria, and silent understanding passes between them. "I picked some up. I thought . . . if I needed them. . . ." She glances at me, takes in my scowl. "Not for me!" she protests.

My frown deepens. She means she intended to use them as a weapon, in case someone attacked her. Someone like Luthor.

"Whatever's done is done," Amy says, and something in her tone tells me that she knows more than she's saying. "So," she continues in her most charming voice, trying to distract me, "is there a way to drain the pond?"

I raise one eyebrow, and I can tell that Amy understands my unspoken question: should we be doing this in front of Victria and Bartie? She lifts her shoulders slightly, and I know she means that there's really no reason not to show them. If this works, everyone on the ship will find out about it anyway.

"What is going on?" Bartie says, half his voice demanding, half laughing.

"There's a way off the ship!" Amy shouts gleefully.

"In the pond?" Victria asks.

"Not *in* it. *Under* it."

Victria casts an incredulous look at Amy, as if wondering if Amy's as crazy as she sounds. "The way off the ship is underwater?"

"It can't *stay* underwater." Amy laughs. "That's why we have to drain the pond."

Victria looks over to me. "Am I the only person who thinks this whole conversation is loons?"

"If you want to drain the pond," Bartie says, "there's a pump over there." He points across the water to a small black box cleverly hidden by a hydrangea bush.

"It's for emergencies," I say, shifting my weight so I'm in front of Bartie. "In case the Hospital or Recorder Hall caught on fire, we could use the pond water to put it out."

"Can you operate it?" Amy asks with gleaming eyes.

I have no idea—I've never tried before. "Of course I can," I say.

I start toward the other side of the pond—and Bartie, unfortunately, follows. "You don't know how to operate the pump, do you?" he asks, grinning.

I glare at him. "You don't get to do that," I say.

"Do what?"

"Pretend like you're still my friend."

Bartie nods. "Fair enough."

"And . . . no."

"No?"

"No, I don't know how to use the pump."

Bartie smiles at me, his old smile, like he used to do when we raced rockers. I kneel down beside the pump. It doesn't look that difficult, but when I reach for the handle, Bartie says, "Don't do that."

"Why not?"

Bartie shrugs. "You'll just spray the water everywhere. Unless you want to waste it, you'll have to divert it."

I reach for a switch. "Nope," he says.

"Frex, fine!" I say, throwing up my hands. "*You* do it."

Bartie bends down and flips two switches, spins a dial, and starts up the pump. I can hear gurgling, churning sounds, but it takes a while before the water level seems to go lower. Once it does, though, the water drains out faster and faster. The lotus flowers float limply as the water level sinks, their pale pink petals stained brown from mud. Their long stems look almost like strands of hair caught in the mud. I swallow hard, remembering the way Kayleigh's hair floated in the pond.

"It's almost done!" Victria calls excitedly. This is the first time I've seen her really smile in . . . months. "Are we supposed to see something in the water yet?"

Amy jumps into the muddy hole before all the water's out. Her feet sink into the silt, staining the hems of her trousers. She sloshes forward to the center of the pond.

"It's here!" she calls, pulling the roots of a lotus plant out of the round handle sticking up from the top of the hatch. "It's *here!*" she squeals excitedly.

"Wow," Victria mutters.

"Is this something else you're going to use to coerce us? Another 'grand' scene like showing everyone the planet?" Bartie asks, and whatever in him that was friendly before is gone now.

"I've got nothing to hide," I say loudly. "Let's all go down."

Amy twists the handle to the hatch. I skid into the pond, fighting against the sucking mud to reach her side. The others follow me in. I'm worried about them—should we let them follow us down into the unknown? But when Amy sees my face, she nods, once, as if telling me that they should come too. We lift the lid up before the water's gone, and some of it sloshes down the hole. A ladder stretches into the darkness.

"Come on," Amy says, pulling one leg free from the murky pond bottom and stepping onto the ladder. Before I can say anything else, she's already climbing down.

I lower the hatch lid over my head. I don't like the feeling of being trapped in the narrow space—it's so tight I can reach out both arms and touch the sides—but the idea of leaving the hatch open is worse. If someone thinks to follow us down, at least we'll have some warning when the lid is raised again. . . .

We climb down quickly, eager to be out of the confined space. As we reach the area between the levels, it gets even colder.

My breath comes out heavy, and the warm air bounces around the enclosed space. Chilly sweat drips down my back, making me shiver.

"Where are we?" Victria asks wonderingly.

"On a ladder," Bartie says.

"I know *that*, chutz. I meant, in terms of the ship."

"We're going to find out," Amy says as her feet hit something solid. "We're here."

We all jump down beside her. There's another hatch—we spin it open, and a smaller ladder automatically drops down, stopping at the floor beneath. Amy goes down first, and I follow her.

This is a bridge.

It mirrors the one on the Shipper Level in miniature. The window is smaller, but it still faces the planet. Victria turns her back to the planet, but the rest of us all stand, still stunned speechless by the sight of the massive blue and green orb. It seems so achingly close. The control panel angles under the window, rows of desks behind it. I think about what Shelby told me, how—if all goes well, and if these controls work like the ones on the main Bridge—you can just hit the autopilot button on the front of the control panel, and the ship will land itself.

Propped up on top of the autopilot button is a floppy, already loaded with a mem card.

"The last vid," Amy says.

"What is it?" Bartie asks, picking up the floppy.

I snatch it from his hands. My eyes question Amy—should we show them?

"All in," she whispers, and even though I'm not sure what that phrase is about, the meaning is clear.

Everyone crowds around me as I swipe my fingers across the screen. I glance up once at the honeycombed glass window showing the planet, and the video begins.

`<<begin video feed>>`

"What is this?" Bartie asks, drawing closer.

Victria gasps. Amy puts her arm around her shoulders and squeezes as Orion's face fills the screen.

He sits on a chair in front of the bridge. I glance up, looking at the real chair, the one in the middle. That's where Orion sat as he filmed this, the planet cresting over his left shoulder, so bright that it cast Orion in silhouette.

ORION: Oh, Amy. I wish I didn't have to show you this. I really do. Because . . . now that you've seen the planet, how can I ask that you turn away?

Orion glances behind him at the planet and sighs. Victria sighs too.

ORION: Because that's what I have to ask you to do. If at all possible—I need you to turn away, lock this door, and never come back.

Amy's mouth drops open, but no sound comes out.

ORION: Did you think the big secret was that we were here? That the planet is just on the other side of that window?

Orion shakes his head. I notice that Victria, her eyes glued to Orion's face, shakes her head just barely too, the movement hardly noticeable.

ORION: That's not the secret.

Orion reaches behind him and pulls out a sheaf of papers.

"This is what he has," Bartie says, picking up a sheaf of papers from where they were resting on the control panel. The edges are curled and the pages are dusty, but these are the same papers Orion holds on the screen.

Orion clears his throat, then reads, holding the papers up so the camera can show the report.

We all lean over the sheaf of papers Bartie holds, reading along with Orion's gravelly voice.

Date: 328460

Ship Status: Arrival

Ship Record: Godspeed has arrived at Centauri-Earth 248 days prior to expected planet-landing. Preliminary scans indicate that the planet is life-supporting, with appropriate gravity, air quality with sufficient oxygen levels, and liquid water. However, additional scans have proven that the planet is already inhabited. Not by any creatures we can tell are sentient, but the life-forms seem . . . aggressive.

Date: 328464

Ship Status: Orbital

Ship Record: We have continued to scan the planet. The life-forms on the surface have been confirmed. Visual probes indicate that the planet is habitable but inhospitable. Our current weapons do not seem a sufficient enough defense against the creatures on the surface.

Date: 328467

Ship Status: Orbital

Ship Record: Crew is restless. It is the opinion of our top stat-
isticians and scientists that we should not fulfill our mission for
planet-landing at this point. The surface is too dangerous. Communication with Earth has been severed. We cannot expect aid
from other sources, and we cannot defend ourselves outside the
ship. We will conduct a vote with the crew, explaining the situation. It is my recommendation that the crew remains on board the
ship where it is safe. Our needs are provided for, and the ship's
external engines can be redirected to internal maintenance.

Date: 328518

Ship Status: Orbital

Ship Record: Mutiny. The ship's crew did not see the logic of
staying aboard, despite my protests. There has been significant
loss of life. My scientists, however, have developed a method
of influencing them to obedience.

Amy and I look up at each other. "This is the Plague, isn't it?" she
asks. "This is where Phydus came from. This—this 'captain'—he's the first
Eldest."

I nod.

"Shh," Bartie snaps.

Date: 328603

Ship Status: Orbital

Ship Record: A way of life has resumed with increasing stability. The crew is once more submissive. We will work on rebuilding our numbers. In the event that communication can be resumed with Earth or aid otherwise received, we can still commence with planet-landing. Until that point, with conservation and careful production, the internal functions of the ship should subsist for countless generations.

Orion sets the papers down on the control panel at the front of the bridge in the exact same spot Bartie found them.

ORION: So, that's why we can't land. I'm not a frexing chutz; I get what's going on here. The Plague Eldest was right to keep us on board the ship. I've seen the armory—you've seen it too. There are weapons there. . . .

Orion shakes his head in disbelief. My eyes are on Victria.

ORION: Amy, surely you know that those weapons aren't normal. . . . If the Plague Eldest says that there are monsters on Centauri-Earth that those weapons can't kill . . .

He shakes his head again.

ORION: And besides, think about it. Think about those weapons.

Orion leans forward, closer to the camera. All four of us lean in closer too.

ORION: You think those frozens in the cryo chambers are going to use 'em? Frex, no. That's what we're here for.

Orion stands up, walks to the window, stares a minute, comes back.

ORION: See this?

Orion picks up the camera and angles it to show ten empty circles on the floor. As one, all four of us look up, over to the far wall and the ten hollow depressions in the floor.

ORION: That's where the probes were. After all the ones the Plague Eldest sent, every Eldest after that sent down another probe. They've all come back with warnings, that we can't live on Centauri-Earth without a fight. A fight we'll probably lose. A fight the frozens will make us fight.

"That's when he decided to kill them," Amy says. "All the frozens, after I woke up—that's why he unplugged them. You were getting close to the truth, even if you didn't realize it, and he was afraid of what they'd do."

I meet her eyes. "That's what he told us. That's what he told us all along. He wasn't lying."

Amy scowls. "He was lying about some of it. I don't care what he says, my father wouldn't—"

"*Shh!*" Bartie shoots us angry looks.

ORION: We ran out of probes a couple of gens ago. I don't know how long the engines will last now, how long we can stay here, in *Godspeed*. This is the contingency plan.

He raises both hands, indicating the cryo level's bridge.

ORION: If the engines fail, if life support falters, if *Godspeed* can't protect us anymore, then—and only then—we can leave the ship.

Orion's eyes stare directly out of the screen.

ORION: Amy, I could tell from the start: the thing you cared most about was the truth. When I first met you, you were crying at the wall, remember, and I told you everything was going to be okay, and I could tell—you weren't going to just accept what I said. You were willing to face the truth, even if it hurt.

I glance up at Amy; she's even paler than usual.

ORION: Well, this is the truth. What you do with it is up to you. I don't know what choice should be made—Eldest thought I knew too much; he was scared of what I would do—and I was scared too. Still am. That leaves you. Now that you know the truth, Amy, you have to decide.

Orion takes a deep breath. Amy holds hers.

ORION: Is the ship so bad that you have to face the monsters below? Is it worth the risk of your life—of everyone's lives? If the answer is yes, then begin the planet-landing. Use this shuttle if you have to. But. But if *Godspeed* can still be your home, if it's possible to stay on board—do so.

Amy lets out a long, shaking breath. Almost as if he heard her, Orion glares down. She bites her lip, her whole body focused on Orion's next words.

ORION: This is the last resort.

The screen fades to black.

<<end video feed>>

64
AMY

I LET THE FLOPPY SLIDE FROM MY FINGERS AND WATCH AS IT wafts to the floor.

"Does this mean," Victria says slowly, "that we get to stay on the ship? Forever?" Her eyes flick to the windows behind us, the planet on the other side.

"No," I say, shaking my head. *"No."*

"The only part of the ship that's damaged is the Bridge. We could stay . . . here. . . ." Elder's voice trails off under my flashing glare.

"The monsters? You're worried about the monsters, or whatever it is that's on the planet?" I roll my eyes. "Look, *I've* seen the armory. I'm not worried one bit. That captain? He was just scared. Or he didn't want to let go of his power. Look at him—he just assumed it would be bad and then hid all the evidence about the planet and set himself up as king of the ship. What kind of nepotistic megalomaniac does that? He didn't care about landing, about escaping, as long as he kept his power. And he's had every single person on this ship convinced of the same thing, including you!"

I'm so worked up by this point that I'm heaving as I finish, but I won't back down. "I am getting off this damn ship. I don't care if the boogeyman jumps up as soon as the door opens and swallows me whole so long as I can step outside just *once*."

"No!" Elder snaps. "I'm sorry, but *no*. This is ridiculous. I don't care how impatient you are; this is something worth taking our time on. It's worth it to know if we're going to die the minute we step off this shuttle!"

Ringing silence fills the bridge when he's done shouting. My face burns; I can almost hear the others repeating Elder's words in their minds. Bartie stares at Elder with a sort of intense, furious wonder. I *am* being a spoiled little brat, throwing a temper tantrum.

But they can't show me a planet and then snatch it away.

"Can you really go on living in *Godspeed* after having seen this?" I ask in almost a whisper, sweeping my arm toward the window.

Elder doesn't look to the planet. His gaze doesn't leave my eyes. "No," he says. "No, I couldn't."

Bartie clears his throat. I can't tell if he's scared or if he's angry—he glares at Elder, but he shifts uncomfortably on his feet. "I say we take a vote. If people don't want to go . . ."

"They stay?" I ask incredulously. "Really?"

"We have a better chance of survival on the planet now anyway, monsters or not," Elder says. Bartie turns to him. "The food stores are gone."

"We can grow more—" Bartie starts, but he's interrupted by a loud *boom!*

"What was that?" Victria says.

It wasn't the same explosive thunder the bombs made; this sounded more like something heavy crashing to the floor in the distance.

But we're alone on this level.

We're supposed to be alone on this level.

We creep to the door leading out of the bridge—the last locked door on the cryo level. It opens from this side, but Elder's smart enough to cram a chair in the door so it doesn't lock again.

The hallway's empty, the other doors all closed and locked. My stomach lurches—what if someone's down here messing with the cryo boxes? What about my parents? I force myself to think despite my rising panic. My heartbeat is thrumming in my ears, urging me to race down the hall. But no—I take a deep breath. The chambers would make a glass-on-metal cracking sound, not that thunderous boom of metal-on-metal.

The cryo area is empty—except for the far wall. Black dirt and debris from the explosion litter the floor near the elevator. The doors have been blown off; they lie like fallen soldiers on the floor. But the elevator shaft is blocked off with another set of heavy, seal-locked doors.

"The gen lab door is open," Elder whispers.

I nod. The four of us creep forward slowly. Elder steps around in front of me when I reach the door. I want to yank him back—I don't need him to play the hero—but he stops dead in the doorway. I crash into his back.

"Doc?" he asks. His voice is surprised, but I notice the way his neck tenses and his fists clench.

Doc turns around slowly as Victria, Bartie, and I pile into the room behind Elder.

Behind Doc is the source of the crashing sound we heard earlier—Doc opened up the cryo tube Orion was frozen in, and the metal frame smashed against the floor.

"What are you doing?" Elder asks. I try to move around Elder so I can get a clearer view, but he throws his arm out, keeping me behind him.

"I knew you were here," Doc says, tossing a floppy at Elder. Elder scans it and hands it back to me; Victria and Bartie look over my shoulder.

The screen shows the wi-com locator map. Blinking dots indicate each of us on the level—Doc, Bartie, Victria, Elder . . . and Orion.

My mouth feels dry and tasteless. Orion. That's my wi-com. Doc gave it to me just so he could keep track of where I was going.

"What are you doing, Doc?" Elder asks again. His tone is even, unnaturally calm.

Doc turns back to the cryo chamber. The glass window in the cryo tube is foggy with condensation, but I can still see the red veins popping in Orion's eyes. I imagine myself mirrored in his pupils. His hand is pressed against the window in front of his face. This cryo tube was developed after the glass boxes my parents and I were frozen in. It's metal, insulated like a thermos, and operates much more simply. It's like a shower instead of a bath—instead of lying in a glass coffin, all you have to do is step inside, let the cryo liquid dump on you, and then initiate the freezing process: one big red button on the front. I stare at it now, remembering when Elder pushed the button.

"Doc," Elder says, his voice a warning.

Finally, Doc turns to Elder. "This ship needs a leader. And the only one we have left is Orion."

"We have a leader," I say, stepping in front of Elder.

Doc smiles at me in a sad, ironic sort of way. "He could have been a leader. Given a few more years and a lot less of you." I sputter in anger, but Doc just shakes his head. "We have to have control. We need a *real* leader."

I laugh, a harsh sound I don't even recognize coming from my own throat. "We *have* a leader, I told you. And Elder will *never* let you go back to the way things were."

Doc laughs now, a soft, low chuckle. "Oh, Amy," he says, "you're so slow. And so wrong."

I turn around to tell Elder to shoot Doc's idea down.

He stares blankly, emptily, back at me.

"Elder?" I say, fear making my voice crack.

Victria steps out from behind both boys. "I'm sorry," she says, letting the pale green wrappers drop to the floor. "I just want Orion back."

In her hands is a gun, a small revolver with large-caliber bullets. "How did you . . . ?" I ask.

"Doc gave it to me. He knew—he knew I wanted protection. And when he told me that he could get Orion back . . . I made sure I could help him."

My mouth drops open. I've come to know so many sides of Victria—the unrequited lover, the victim, the forgotten friend. I never thought I'd see her as a traitor.

She moves to stand between Doc and the cryo chamber holding Orion's frozen body. And she never once lowers the gun.

Elder and Bartie stare straight ahead. A single square green patch clings to each of their necks.

6 5
ELDER

"NO, NO, NO," AMY WHISPERS.

Her words remind me . . . of . . . *something*.

But everything's so . . . slow.

"Stay back," Doc says.

I struggle to hold on to the situation . . . to understand. . . .

"Are you okay?" Amy says.

Why wouldn't I be?

Doc. Holding something that looks like an orange cut in half. Mustard yellow.

"I'll blow us all up," Doc says. "If that's what it takes. We have to protect the ship. Or I could just have Victria shoot you. Yes. We'll do that. It would leave less of a mess."

"I . . . I don't know how," she says softly.

"It's very easy, dear," Doc says. "Just point and squeeze the trigger. At this distance, you won't miss her."

His words mean something. I'm sure of it.

But . . . what?

Amy's crying. Just one tear, on the edge of her right eye, but I notice it.

Can't do anything.

Words float around me. Loud. Angry. Pleading.

"If he's that much of a distraction," Doc says, "maybe we should kill him now."
"Not Elder!" Amy shouts, pushing me behind her.

I feel gray.
Fuzzy.

"Elder!" Doc commands loudly. "Show me what's in your pocket!"

I do.
Wires.
Pretty wires.
Red.
Yellow.
Black.
Wires.

"Put them back in the Phydus machine," Doc orders. "You know you want to."
I do.

I do want to.

I shuffle toward the Phydus machine.

Something stops me.

Something pulls me back.

I try to keep walking.

I go nowhere.

"Amy," Doc warns. "Don't try to stop him."

"Elder," Amy's voice whispers in my ear. "Elder, fight it. Fight it. You don't want to start the Phydus machine again. You don't have to rule with drugs. You're good enough the way you are. Fight it. Be yourself."

"Amy," Doc warns. "You know I'll kill you. Or him. You know I will."

My legs move up and down, and I move forward again.

To the Phydus machine.

To put back in the wires.

Like I always knew I'd have to.

6 6
AMY

ELDER STANDS NEXT TO THE PHYDUS MACHINE, THE WIRES in his hand, but he doesn't seem able to hook them up. He's motionless, staring at the console. I wonder how long he's carried those wires in his pocket. He must put them there every day when he dresses, the same way I put on my necklace or wrap my hair. Has he carried them around with him all this time because he wanted to remember the way things were and should never be again . . . or because he wanted to remind himself that he had the same power to control people that Eldest had, if he chose to use it?

Doc stares into the glass at Orion. "He entrusted me with everything. I let him live. I helped him escape. He kept himself hidden from me for a long time—I didn't know he was the Recorder; I didn't know he was right beside me all those years. But before you froze him, he gave me his secrets. And I will not betray his trust the way you betrayed him."

Doc moves over to stand by Elder. I start to lunge after him, but Victria steps in my way. Her hand is shaking; she's not used to the weight of the gun, and the grip sits uncomfortably in her palm. Not that it matters . . . all it would take is one squeeze of her trigger finger, and I'd be gone.

I eye her warily, taking in the fear in her face, the sweat trickling down her neck. She doesn't want to do this, she doesn't want to hurt me, but she's like a caged animal, and a caged animal will do anything if threatened. I stay still.

"Oh, Elder, I tried to warn you, I did," Doc says, gently plucking the wires from Elder's hands. "I told you each time—follow the leader."

"You're *insane*," I shout. "Elder *is* the leader!"

Doc turns and looks at me, as if he's evaluating my worth and finding that I come up just short. "I did hope he could become Eldest. I gave him three months. But as more and more people started to question him, it became clear he was hopeless. And then there was *Bartie*." He sneers the name.

My eyes flick to Bartie, the green patch on his neck.

"Bartie thought he could start a *revolution*." Doc rolls his eyes. "His attempts were clever—hacking into the floppies and the wi-coms was smart—but in the end he's such a feeble sort of person. He would never *really* have what it takes to lead a true revolution. And besides," Doc adds, "I wasn't going to let dissent evolve into rebellion. Once we have a real leader again, any question of a revolt will disappear."

I don't like the way he says "disappear" in a voice that holds so much finality.

Doc's gaze shifts to me. "I tried to help. I made the patches, and when Elder didn't use them, I did. He could have used those deaths to instill the proper amount of fear required to demand obedience. But did you?" he asks, turning to Elder's emotionless face. *"No."* He shoves Elder's body. Elder doesn't resist, and he crashes against the Phydus machine. "As time went on," Doc continues, "it became more and more obvious that what we needed was for him to step down. *He* was the one who needed to follow the leader. The warnings were for *him*." He pokes a finger in Elder's chest. Elder stares straight ahead, his body slack.

"And Marae?" I ask.

"I tried to talk to her. Of everyone on the ship, she should have been on Orion's side. But no. She was for Elder."

Doc places the wires on top of the Phydus pump. The drug is not his main concern. He strolls across the room, back to Orion's cryo chamber.

"It's too late anyway, Amy." Doc sighs, a sound filled with disappointment. "Whatever kind of leader Bartie thought he could be or Elder may one day become, Orion already is. His only mistake was in trusting you to make the choice about the shuttle. I let you find Orion's vids, but I should have destroyed them all."

My mind races. "Why did you even give me Orion's wi-com?" I ask. "You must have known it would lead us to the clues he left!"

Doc glances up at me. "I did it," he says, "because Orion asked me to."

And it really is as simple as that. Call him anything you want, but Doc's loyal. Not to Eldest, not even to Orion, and certainly not to Elder. He's loyal to the *system*. According to the system, Orion should be the next leader, and, therefore, the person Doc will blindly obey—even when he disagrees.

But—this doesn't make sense. "If you're the one who gave me the first clue, then who tampered with the sonnet book and the clue in the armory?"

"I did." Doc checks a dial on Orion's cryo chamber.

"*You?* But—*why?*"

He looks at me as if he can't quite believe how slow I am. "I didn't do it for me. This ship—everyone on board—we could all die if we land on Centauri-Earth. *Die*. But," he adds, "I'm not unreasonable. I'll let the Eldest make the final decision. If he says the shuttle should be launched, well, I will step aside. I just didn't think he was right in choosing you as his decision maker."

I finally understand—he altered the clue in the armory and cut out the page in the sonnet book because he didn't want me to succeed. But he still left the book so I could find it. He didn't want me to find the clue, but he couldn't disobey Orion all the way.

"Did you mess with the space suits?" I ask.

"I figured if you got in there, one of you would use them."

"And you didn't care which one of us died?"

"If it helps," Doc says, turning back to the dials on Orion's cryo chamber, "I'd hoped it would have been you."

It doesn't help, actually.

"You never did realize the thing I needed you to understand," Doc continues, adjusting another dial. "You got so obsessed with what Orion was showing you that you never saw what *I* was showing you."

"Yeah?" I say. "And what was that?"

"That the important thing wasn't getting off the ship. We *can't* get off the ship, Amy, we can't. Orion hoped that one day, far in the future, it would be possible, but no. The armory, the probes—it's too dangerous. We have to stay here. We have to maintain the same order we've always had since the Plague Eldest."

I can't help myself—I snort in disgust.

"I know you disagree, Amy," Doc says idly, as if we're having a casual conversation between friends. "But the Eldest system *works*."

"Eldest was twisted, sick," I say. "You saw him at the end. He was too desperate for power."

"Yes, yes," Doc says dismissively. "There are aberrations in every Elder and Eldest, that is well documented, and Eldest should have stepped down when Orion came of age. And Orion—not Elder—should have become Eldest."

"Orion was a psycho!" I shout. I start to move forward, knocking into Bartie's shoulder as I do. He stares blankly ahead.

This was the wrong thing to do. The gun tightens in Victria's hand—she loves Orion, after all—and Doc moves closer to the cryo chamber.

"He is neither a 'psycho,' nor is he Orion," Doc says, turning a dial on the chamber door. "He is Eldest." He looks back at Elder, still standing motionless by the Phydus machine. "You never wanted to be Eldest, did you? You always wanted to be *just* Elder. That's why you wouldn't change your name. You knew, didn't you, that you weren't good enough to be Eldest. You're still just a child, preoccupied more with your silly infatuation than responsibility."

Elder—patched and silent—nods in agreement.

"Don't talk about Elder like that!" I roar. "Orion was a coward who killed helpless people!"

Doc turns toward me. "Don't forget, it was Orion who gave you your precious planet, not Elder. Even when he was nothing but a block of ice, he still controlled you as you searched the whole ship for his clues. That's the power of a *real* leader."

He's so calm, so even and measured—just like he always is. Even in this—in murdering people in Orion's name, in staging a coup to overthrow Elder—even now, there's no fire in Doc's eyes. He's just quietly and steadfastly moving forward with what he thinks is so obviously right. He's putting us all in our assigned places. Orion as Eldest. Elder as Elder. And me—I'm still, as usual, the one he can't categorize. And that's the real reason why he's got Victria pointing a gun in my face.

And I know for sure now, I know it deep down inside me—I'm not going to get out of this. I don't fit in with Doc's plan because I don't fit in on *Godspeed*, and Doc can't stand to have something—someone—stick out. He needs everyone to be perfectly the same, perfectly calm, and perfectly obedient to the proper Eldest, and I never, ever, will be.

I am so certain that Doc won't let me out of this room alive that I half expect Victria to pull the trigger and end it all now. Instead, Doc punches a code into Orion's cryo chamber.

Doc turns back around. "Amy, I'm no leader. I know that. I only want to do what I've been trying to tell everyone else to do."

"Follow the leader," I say softly.

"Exactly. There's no hope anymore," Doc says. "We can't land on the new planet. And we can't survive up here without Orion. Don't you see? We need a *real* leader. Not Bartie, not Elder. We need our Eldest. It's our only hope."

Victria looks up at Doc, but he isn't looking at her; he's looking at me. "I just want Orion back," she says, but he doesn't pay any attention to her.

"We're not talking about hope," I tell Doc, but my eyes are on Victria. "We're talking about faith. Faith that the new world will be better than this. And faith that even if it's not, it will be worth the risk to go down there and see."

Orion's cryo chamber beeps, a loud echoing sound.

"There," Doc says, "the regeneration process is beginning."

"What?" I snap.

"Really?" Victria says, turning.

And that's my chance. Elder's not the only one who's been carrying things in his pocket—I still have Phydus patches of my own. In one swift motion, I rip one from its packaging, slap it on Victria's arm, and snatch the gun away from her unresisting fingers.

Doc eyes me, trying to determine if I'll shoot him.

"It's too late," he says, almost casually. "I've already begun the regeneration process." The light above Orion's face stays green. "Even if you shoot me, he'll still wake up."

I move slowly to my right, near Bartie, but even if I could rip the patch off him, the Phydus would still be in his system. No help there.

"Amy, you're being ridiculous," Doc says in the same sort of voice he used when we first met, when he threatened to drug me for the rest of my life. "You're not thinking straight."

"I am," I say. "I don't want Orion ruling this ship."

"There's a chance Elder won't use the escape shuttle, you know."

And he's right. I do know it. I saw the reluctance in his eyes, the way he protested my immediate reaction to land the ship.

"I have faith in him," I say. *And much more than that,* I think.

Doc shakes his head as if I'm a student who can't answer the homework question correctly.

"You don't think I put all my *faith* in Victria, do you?" he asks, sneering over the word. And he pulls out his own gun. It sits weirdly in his hand. Like Victria, he's unsure of how to hold it. Still, it's not like a gun is hard to figure out. The killing end's pointed at me, and that's enough.

I widen my stance, making my feet even with my shoulders. I was raised with guns like a proper military brat; my father made sure I knew how to protect myself, to treat weapons as tools, not toys. I've never been more grateful for the Saturdays at the target range than I am now. I breathe out and feel the cool metal of the trigger under my finger.

"You can't kill me," Doc says.

"You're right," I say, and pull the trigger.

|

67
ELDER

I SEE IT ALL IN SLOW MOTION, WITH EVERYTHING FUZZY around the edges. The bang from the gun bursts out; a cloud of acrid smoke evaporates quickly, leaving behind only the smell of copper and burning. Doc crumples, an explosion of red erupting from his leg. Amy dives forward, soaring through the air, smacking a pale green patch on Doc's arm.

Another bang. Another gun. Doc's gun.

Another burst of smoke and blood.

Amy crashes down, clutching her arm. Dark red blood seeps through her fingers.

She pulls her hand away, presses her wi-com. Shouts.

She staggers to Victria. Drops to her knees beside the body.

I see it all but can't move, can't react. Everything's so heavy and slow. I just stare as Amy screams, choking on her own sobs. Amy presses both hands into the blossoming red stain across the front of Victria's tunic. Blood leaks out of Amy's own sleeve, but she ignores it, intent on putting pressure on Victria's wound.

I move my head and stare impassively at Doc. His dull eyes meet mine. The green patch on his arm ensures that he just lies there, ignoring the bullet in his leg.

I turn back to Amy and Victria.

"NO!" Amy says.

Victria's hand reaches toward Doc. No. Toward Orion.

"NO!" Amy screams again.

She throws her weight against Victria. Blood pumps between her fingers, spurting out in bubbles of crimson.

"No," Amy whispers.

Victria's hand goes slack.

My face is wet. I raise my hand and touch my cheek. The tears drip from my fingers like the blood dripping from Amy's.

6 8
A M Y

MY HANDS ARE SOAKED IN BLOOD. IT'S STILL WARM, JUST LIKE Victria's body. I move to shut Victria's staring eyes, and some of her blood— or my blood, I can't tell which—drips on her face and slides down her cheek. I don't close her eyes. Let her stare at Orion.

I stand, wiping Victria's blood on my pants. I pull down the neck of my tunic, staring at the bleeding wound in my left arm, just below my shoulder. Doc fired the gun as he fell. The bullet grazed me—and killed Victria.

I shut my eyes, trying to block out the image before me, but all I can smell is gunpowder and blood. I push my wi-com again. Kit answers immediately. "I found the hatch," she says, breathless. "I'll be there soon."

I rip the green patch off Bartie, who is standing closer to me, but I don't wait for the light to return to his eyes. Avoiding Victria's body, I cross the genetics lab to reach Elder. When I peel the med patch from his neck, I leave a line of red on his skin.

I bury my head into the soft spot between Elder's chest and arm. My blood seeps through his shirt, but I don't care. I just stand there, willing myself to be as emotionless as he is, even if it's just because there are still trace amounts of Phydus in his system.

When I feel his arms raise and wrap around me, I break. I sob into his chest, wild, loud, uncontrollable sobs that leave me breathless but still aren't enough.

"What the frex happened?!" Kit shouts from the doorway. Her eyes are wide and shocked, jumping from Bartie to us to Doc and finally to Victria.

She drops to her knees beside Victria, ignoring the blood that seeps into her trousers.

"It's too late," I say.

Her eyes rove across the room, and at first I'm worried that she's too shocked to do any good. I realize, though, that she's evaluating all that's happened and all that needs to be done. She closes Victria's eyes. I've heard people say that dead bodies look like they're sleeping. But not Victria. She had peace and serenity when her eyes were focused on Orion, but now that they're shut, she looks well and truly dead.

Kit reaches into her pocket and tosses me two pale yellow patches. "Antidotes for Phydus," she says, moving immediately to Doc.

"Don't give him one," I warn. Kit opens her mouth to protest, but when she sees my look, she nods.

"Perhaps it would be best for him to stay on Phydus," she says in a worried voice. "He must be in a lot of pain, and the Phydus will dull it."

"I don't care about that," I say, my voice cold and hard. "But keep that patch on him."

Kit's hand hovers over Doc's wound, and she searches my eyes. Finally, she nods slowly, understanding my meaning. She cuts off Doc's pant leg and bends to examine the wound—right where I aimed, just below his knee. Blood pulses from the bullet hole.

I rip open one of the yellow patches and rub it into Elder's skin until I see him wince in pain. He blinks, his eyes clearer.

"Back again?" I whisper.

He nods, a grim expression filling his face. He eyes linger on Victria's body, and I wonder how much he saw and understood while under the influence of the Phydus patch.

"You shot him," he says, his eyes darting from Doc to me again.

I did. But if I hadn't—maybe he wouldn't have fired his gun either. Maybe Victria would still be alive.

"I had to shoot him," I say, hoping to convince myself of the fact too.

He nods again. I can't tell if he doubts me or not. Does he blame me for Victria's death?

"How bad is it?" he finally asks, jerking his head toward my arm.

"Are you hurt too?" Kit says, looking up from Doc as she sprays foam on his wound. The foam bubbles up and turns pink as it disinfects the wound. Kit starts to wrap Doc's leg in a large bandage.

"I'll be fine," I say.

"She's shot," Elder says. "In the arm."

He takes the other yellow patch from me and moves over to Bartie. Bartie's eyes are glued on Victria's body the whole time as he shifts from drugged to aware, and once the Phydus has truly left his system, he tries to say something but chokes on the words. He lunges toward Victria, but Elder catches him, and the two stand there, their arms wrapped around each other, all rivalry forgotten in the death of one of their last childhood friends.

"Here," Kit says.

I jump, surprised—I hadn't noticed that she'd finished with Doc. Kit cuts away the sleeve of my tunic and cleans the wound with the disinfect-ing foam.

"Is it bad?" Elder asks as he and Bartie break away.

Kit rips open a pale purple patch.

"No," I say immediately.

"It's for pain."

"No patches."

She shrugs and starts to wrap my arm. The bleeding hasn't quite stopped, but it's slower—I probably won't even need stitches. It's Victria who got the full force of the bullet.

"Come on," Elder says to Bartie.

"Where are you going?" I ask.

"We're sending Victria to the stars," Bartie says.

"Let me help." Kit tugs the bandage around my arm, tight, and I hiss in pain.

Bartie holds Victria by the shoulders, and Elder stoops to pick up her feet. "We can do this alone, Amy." Elder's voice is kind, and his eyes beg me to understand. Bartie and Elder need to say goodbye together. They need to remember Victria the way she was before Orion was frozen, and she drowned in her love for him. Before I was unfrozen.

The two men silently carry their friend's body out the door, toward the hatch, leaving only a bloodstain behind.

6 9
ELDER

BARTIE SLAMS THE HATCH DOOR SHUT, AND I PUNCH IN THE code. We both stand at the window and watch as we send our last childhood friend to the stars.

Through the bubble glass window, we see Victria's body fly up. The pull of the vacuum makes her rise and float backward, her face obscured by her black hair, her arms and legs reaching to me even as they are pulled farther and farther away.

And then she's gone.

Kit approaches us as the hatch door closes. Doc—with the green patch still on his arm—limps beside her. Kit tries to use her weight to support Doc, but he's much bigger than she is.

"Let me help," Bartie says, taking Kit's place under Doc's arm. His voice is gravelly with unshed tears. When I meet his eyes, I know—what's happened in the last three months cannot overshadow what's happened in the last thirty minutes. We're friends again.

"Make sure that patch stays on," I say, and Bartie nods.

Kit and Bartie take Doc toward the hatch. I think about giving them a hand—it's going to be hard getting him up the ladder—but I don't want to help Doc. I don't ever want to see Doc again.

I go back to the gen lab. Amy, her arm swaddled in bandages, stands in front of Orion's frozen face.

The memories of what happened while I was patched are hard to sort out in my mind. It's the difference between swimming in water and swimming in syrup. But I do know one thing: Doc killed Marae and the others because I'm not as good a leader as Orion would have been.

Amy said Orion had a plan for everything, and I'm starting to think I should have one too. Because I don't know what I'm going to do now.

"You kept those wires," she says as I step beside her. "The wires to the Phydus machine. You had them the whole time. You went straight to the machine—"

"Doc had patched me," I say. "I don't think I could have helped but go to the machine."

"But you had those wires with you the whole time."

I did. "But," I say, "I think I deserve some credit for never using them, even if I did have them."

"Yeah," Amy says, offering me a hint of a smile. "You do."

We stare at Orion's cryo chamber.

"What do these numbers mean?" Amy asks, pointing to the LCD screen on the front of the box.

I watch the numbers tick down. "It's a countdown clock."

"I was afraid of that."

I bend down, examining the electronics. Apparently, Doc already started the regeneration process. Orion should be unfrozen within twenty-three hours and forty-two minutes. I try to stop the clock, but even though I turn the dial, the screen continues to tick away time.

"Just turn it off," Amy says, bending down to look at the electronics.

"We can't just unplug it," I say. I've definitely learned my lesson about that one.

"Well, make it stop."

"I can't," I say, fiddling with the dials some more. I notice the screen and keypad. "Doc's locked up the system."

"Reset it."

I hesitate. "That could be dangerous. If regeneration has already started, it could damage his body if we just stop it."

"It's only been going on for twenty minutes," Amy says. "It can't do that much harm."

But I'm remembering how I froze Orion without preparing his body. He's already damaged from that. Messing with the cryo tube now might kill him.

"I don't care if it's dangerous. He needs to stay frozen."

"Amy, it's not that simple. I *can't*. The cryo chamber is only pro-grammed to go one way."

"I don't want him to wake up," Amy says in a very quiet voice.

I look at Amy and bite my lip. Because I do.

I don't know if it's because of our shared DNA or because I understand the choices he's made. Maybe it's because of the guns in the armory or the ship records in the bridge. Maybe it's because I'm starting to think Doc was right, and Orion would be a better leader than me. But Orion doesn't seem as loons as before.

Amy puts her hand on my elbow, drawing my gaze away from the countdown clock and back to her. "I couldn't kill him."

I stare, unsure of how to respond.

"Doc. He had a gun on me. On you. I didn't know which of us he'd shoot."

I touch the bandage on Amy's arm—not firmly enough to put any pressure on her wound.

"It's just a graze. But when the gun was pointed at us, I thought, 'I have to kill him, or he'll kill one of us.' But I didn't. I couldn't."

"Why are you—"

"Elder," Amy says, "I believe in the bottom of my heart that Orion doesn't deserve to live. There are *some* people," she adds, emphasizing the word, "that *don't* deserve a second chance. I haven't forgotten what it was like to drown in my cryo box. A day doesn't go by that I don't remember."

I did that to her. Not Orion. Me.

"Two people are dead, and they died like I almost did. And *he* did that to them."

"Amy, I can't stop the regeneration process."

"He doesn't deserve to live."

"Would you kill him?"

Amy's eyes dance back and forth between mine. She couldn't kill Doc. But her hatred for Orion goes deeper.

"You're right. Some people don't deserve a second chance. But Orion—" I pause, unsure of how to explain. "Orion was wrong, yes. But it's not like he went on a murdering spree or something. He had a reason. He acted out of fear."

Amy bites her bottom lip, thinking. I know she's comparing Orion, who thought he was doing the right thing, to Luthor, who knew he was doing wrong.

I want to wrap my arms around her and erase the worry etched on her face, but I know it's not as simple as that. "Maybe," I say, turning back to the cryo chamber. "I can't stop the regeneration. . . . But I can delay it."

Amy steps aside and lets me focus on the controls on the chamber. I feel two sets of eyes on me: Amy's, begging me to keep Orion frozen, and Orion's, pleading to come back to life.

"I can do it," I say finally. "I can slow it down."

"Do it," Amy says.

I punch the numbers in, adjust the dial, and the countdown clock goes from one day to three.

"Can we keep doing this?" Amy asks. "Every time the countdown clock gets low, can we just add more time?"

I nod slowly.

"That's what we'll do, then," she says, her jaw set. "We'll just keep backing it up. He doesn't ever have to wake up."

Amy stares into Orion's bulging eyes with a sort of fierce intensity. But I stare at Amy, unable to recognize this girl with such hatred in her heart.

70
AMY

WHEN ELDER AND I EMERGE FROM THE HATCH, THERE'S already a crowd.

"Is it true?" someone calls out.

"Is what true?" Elder asks.

"Is there still a way off this ship?"

Bartie offers me a hand, pulling me up from the last rungs of the ladder in the hatch. "I had to tell them," he said. "It's not like they couldn't see the giant hatch in the middle of the pond."

"It's true!" Elder calls.

"Do we all have to go?" someone else shouts. I whirl around to see who asked this, but I can't tell. The crowd here seems divided. Those closest to the mud hole that used to be the pond are jubilant. They hug each other, happy tears staining their faces as they celebrate Elder's words.

But other people linger near the back. They look suspicious and worried, scowling and talking to each other behind their hands. Even from here, I see a few with pale green patches. Some hold the patches in their hands, squeezing the wrapper but not ripping it open. Others already have patches on their arms, already have glazed looks in their eyes.

"We're going to have another meeting," Elder shouts. "I'm calling everyone together now." He pushes his wi-com and does an all-call, telling all 2,296 passengers to come to the garden immediately.

No. Not 2,296. Not anymore. I count the number down in my head. Victria. Luthor. All the top-ranking Shippers. The people who died in the riot. The ones Doc slathered in patches. The population of *Godspeed*, which always seemed so inimitable to me before, now seems very fragile.

Bartie approaches Elder hesitantly. "Can I . . . would you mind if I said something too?"

Elder shoots him a wry grin. "Going to try to start another riot?"

"No," Bartie says. He's completely serious.

Elder looks up at me, and I take the hint, letting them have their privacy. The two men move away from me, talking in low quiet tones. I can see the strain in Elder's face as he listens to whatever Bartie is saying, and when they quit talking, they shake hands with a sort of finality that leaves me nervous.

It seems to take forever before everyone gathers at the pond. The people come slowly—I can see them crossing the fields toward us. I touch my hair—I'm not wearing my head wrap or even my jacket, but I don't care. I'm not afraid of them anymore. Today I shot a man and watched a woman die. Beneath my feet is a shuttle that will take me far away from here. Their opinion of me means nothing.

I stand on the edge of the pond, on the side nearest the wall. As everyone crowds around the edges of the silty muddy remains of the pond, some of them draw closer to me. Many still keep their distance or sneer, but most ignore me. One girl accidentally brushes my arm.

"Sorry," she says.

I can't help but stare in wonder. She didn't flinch away or look disgusted; she didn't snatch her arm back as if it were now contaminated.

Elder walks straight into the muddy remains of the pond and stands near the hatch. Victria said before that we can't choose who we love. I still don't know if that's true, but it doesn't matter anymore. Because, choice or no, my heart is his.

Everyone looks down at him—we all stand on the edge of the pond, towering above him. He's up to his ankles in muck, and he shifts uneasily as if he's nervous. Even from here I can see the pale purple-green of bruises on his face, but he's never looked stronger or more noble.

Elder taps into the wi-com system so that everyone can hear him clearly. He mumbles at first, something I can't discern, then speaks clearly and loudly.

"In the centuries of travel on *Godspeed*, much has been gained. But much has also been lost and forgotten. Including this." Elder sweeps his hand toward the open hatch.

"We thought that beneath our feet was another level of the ship. We were wrong. It's not a level. It's an escape shuttle. At the end of this hatch there is another bridge. The entire level can break away from *Godspeed*, and it will take us to our new home on Centauri-Earth."

I glance around me—every eye is on Elder.

He clears his throat and explains more about how the shuttle works. Although he hesitates, he also tells them about the possibility of danger, Orion's warnings.

"It's not ideal," he says, and this makes my head snap up. "When we launch the shuttle, we'll be leaving behind *Godspeed*. I know this ship has been your home. It's been mine too. But *Godspeed* isn't stable. It was never meant to be a permanent solution. The cryo level is large, and we'll pack it as tightly as we can. Focus on bringing essentials with you. Some things will have to be left behind."

Elder motions for Bartie to come closer. Elder steps away from the center of the pond, and everyone's attention shifts to Bartie.

"I wanted to say something too," Bartie says through the wi-com system. "What Elder has told you is true. I was in the shuttle today; I saw it myself. And what he says about leaving things behind is true too. And . . ." He swallows deeply. "And I am one of the things that will be left behind. *Godspeed* is my home. I don't want another. I'm staying here. And if you would like to stay here with me, you're welcome to."

My mouth drops open. I turn around, expecting the crowd to be shocked or skeptical, to think Bartie's lost it . . . but a lot of them . . . don't. They seem to agree.

They want the walls.

"Can we?" someone shouts.

"Is it safe?"

"It's suicide," I say under my breath, but I don't feel so safe that I can shout back.

Elder crosses the pond and motions for someone to talk to him. The young woman nods and speaks to him, shooting glances at Bartie and the crowd behind her.

Finally Elder speaks again. "The scientists agree that the internal functions of the ship could last for at least a generation, maybe indefinitely if the biosphere is maintained and energy conserved."

Conversation surges again through the crowd. Elder raises his arm— and they're all silenced immediately.

"This is an important decision. Whatever you decide now—there will be no going back. Stay or leave—your decision will be permanent."

He takes a deep breath.

"But your decision will be yours."

71
ELDER

AMY CORNERS ME IN THE KEEPER LEVEL AT THE END OF THE DAY.

"You can't be serious," she demands.

"I can't force people to go." I roll my shoulders back, trying to ease some of the tension within them.

"It's suicide! *Godspeed* can't last forever—in a few generations, everyone will die out!"

"I've talked to Bartie about this," I say, collapsing in one of the blue plastic chairs I've pulled into the Great Room from the Learning Center. "When the ship's no longer sustainable, they'll . . ."

"They'll what?" Amy demands. "Make a suicide pact? Drink the bad Kool-Aid?"

I have no idea what she's talking about. "Doc has an array of med patches. The black ones . . ."

"*Kill?*" She sounds disgusted.

"As humanely as possible."

Amy throws her hands down and starts pacing around the Great Room. "This is ridiculous," she says. "You can't let them stay here! You have to force them to come! They're killing themselves—"

I cut her off. "I've talked to the scientists. The ship isn't going to disintegrate overnight. There will be enough energy to last for a couple more generations at least."

"And then?" Amy demands.

And then black patches.

"It's what they want," I say.

"You're the leader! Make them come!"

I wait until she stops pacing and faces me. "Amy, I have to consider more than just your opinion."

She bites down as if she's chewing on her words, then sits down opposite me.

"How many are staying?"

"About eight hundred."

"Eight hundred?!" Amy jumps up again.

"About."

"That's . . ."

"More than a third of the ship," I say.

"They'd rather die in a cage than live on a planet?"

"This is their home, Amy," I say. "I know you can't understand how *Godspeed* is a home, but it is."

She sits back down, slowly. "You should *make* them go," she snaps. "But," she adds when I open my mouth, "I can see how they might want to stay. If they've never seen anything else . . ."

"Amy," I say, "we have to let them decide for themselves." I touch her knee, bringing her gaze back to me. "*We're* going."

A tentative smile spreads across her face. She leans forward, her elbows on her knees. "Oh, Elder," she says, and it comes out in a rush, like a breath of relief, "you're going to love it. Being on a world without walls.

There's so much . . . so much that you're going to see. Trees—great big, towering trees. That pond—it's tiny—there'll be an ocean on the planet. Clouds. The sky—the *sky*. You'll see birds. Birds!"

I laugh. "I've seen birds! We have chickens."

"No!" Amy's voice rings with music. "Those chickens aren't even proper chickens. I'm talking about real birds! Birds that tweet so loud you wake up in the morning before your alarm clock. Birds that soar and swoop and *fly!*"

With that, she jumps up, twirling with her arms raised. She ends her spin facing me, her eyes alight. "You have no idea how wonderful it's going to be!"

She sees birds and freedom and oceans.

I see the armory, with piles of explosives. I hear Orion saying, *If God-speed can still be your home, if it's possible to stay on board—do so.*

"Yeah," I tell her, smiling as best I can. "It'll be brilly."

Amy collapses in her chair. She's giving me this look that says, *You have no idea,* and all I can think is that neither does she. Centauri-Earth isn't the Earth she came from. She doesn't know what's down there, no one does, the only one who had a clue about it was Orion, and it scared the shite out of him.

"What if he's right?" I didn't mean to say it out loud, but she knows immediately who I'm talking about.

"It'll be worth it," Amy says immediately, not even pausing to question herself.

"But—"

"No. It will be. Whatever is down there . . . Maybe it's too danger-ous. Maybe we won't survive. I don't know. But I do know I'm leaving. I won't die on this ship. I cannot live surrounded by walls. Not now. Not anymore."

Not now that she's seen through the honeycombed glass. Not now that the planet is within her grasp.

"Maybe it's a good thing some are staying," Amy says, more serious now. "There will be less trouble."

I meet Amy's eyes.

She narrows hers.

"Orion is . . . he is going to be left here, right? We're not taking him to the new planet, are we?"

"Amy—I can't leave him here."

"*What?*"

"Orion's coming."

"If we left him here, he could be unfrozen. He could live here on the ship."

I hold myself very still. "He's going to be unfrozen anyway. The timer can't be stopped, just delayed."

She kicks her chair back and starts pacing. Her hair swings out every time she turns like an angry swipe of a red blade.

"Bartie and I talked about it. Doc will stay here and he *will* be punished, but Bartie's going to give him a tree-all."

"A trial," Amy corrects me automatically.

I didn't ask Bartie what Doc's punishment would be. Not death—they need a doctor, and Kit's coming with us to Centauri-Earth. But Bartie was closer to Victria than I was, and I know Doc's punishment will be severe.

"So, that's it?" Amy says, "You two are splitting up the bad guys? Bartie gets Doc and you get Orion?"

"Something like that," I say. Bartie needed Doc, but neither of us knew what to do with Orion. If he wakes up on the ship, Doc will support him and undermine Bartie. If he comes with us to the new planet, he'll still cause trouble. Neither of us was willing to unplug him or throw him out of the hatch. In the end, I volunteered.

"It's not *fair*," she says. "Why should he come? He's just going to cause more chaos. Can't you see that? He's *frozen*, and people are still being killed and blowing up all kinds of crap for *him*. Imagine what he'll do when he wakes up."

I shake my head. "It was always the plan. He would wake up with the other frozens, and they would judge him for his crimes."

"You don't have to make them judge," she shoots back. "You could just leave him here."

I could. I know I could. It would be far simpler. But I also know—because, no matter how much I want to deny it, we're bound—so I know, I *know* . . . he wants off. He left those clues for Amy to find, he left the decision for Amy to make . . . but the mere fact that he left clues, that he didn't destroy our hope of leaving shows that, ultimately, he—like me— wants off *Godspeed*.

I can't condemn him to a life behind the walls of *Godspeed*, even if he deserves it.

"I'll let the frozens judge him, and I'll stick by what they say," I tell Amy.

Her lips tighten; there's a narrow white line on the edge of them. "It won't be as simple as that, and you know it."

"He's going to the new planet," I say.

Amy stops in her tracks. "If you do this, things can't be the same between us. I can't believe you're even considering taking Orion with us."

"I can't believe you'd take away the planet from anyone, even Orion."

She looks at me as if my words have punched her, then runs to the grav tube without another word.

I go to Eldest's room in the dark, alone. The Keeper Robe lies on the floor, wrinkled.

I leave it there.

72
AMY

ON MY LAST DAY ABOARD *GODSPEED*, I PACK EVERYTHING I own in a small bag. The clothes that once belonged to Kayleigh, who died for the secret Orion couldn't keep. The notebook I wrote letters to my parents in, when I didn't think I'd see them again. My teddy bear.

I leave behind the maroon scarf. I won't have to hide myself on the new planet. As I fold the length of material and place it on the desk, I glance around this room that was mine for three months. I thought I would spend the rest of my life here. Or—maybe I'd move to the Keeper Level with Elder one day.

I swallow down the lump in my throat. Maybe Elder's right and Orion doesn't deserve to drown in his cryo box. But he doesn't deserve the new planet, either. I try to remember the things I thought I loved about Elder, but all I can see now is the stubborn set of his eyes, the tone of his voice when he refused to leave Orion on *Godspeed*.

I carry my bag in one hand and Harley's last painting in the other. There's not much room for art, but I will make room for this.

The solar lamp clicks on just as I reach the edge of the pond. The bottom is dry earth now, cracked under the heat of the solar lamp, and the lotus flowers are wilted strands of green and pink, already dead.

I'm the first one down. I tuck my bag and Harley's painting into an out-of-the-way corner on the bridge and then sit down in the chair opposite the honeycombed glass window. Past the bridge, the shuttle is packed nearly to the brim. The rooms are all unlocked, every square inch used for storage. Except for the armory—Elder has decided to keep that door locked, even if we could have used the space. I'm not sure if it's because he's afraid someone will try to steal a gun or if he wants to keep the extent of the armory hidden for now, but either way I think he made the right choice.

Every other room, though, is full of crates of food—enough to last us a month. Jugs of fresh water. Medicine. Clothing. Manufacturing tools. Shelves of tiny seedlings from the Greenhouses. Elder and Bartie divided the livestock. Several of the larger animals were slaughtered, the meat smoked and salted. Some of the smaller ones—rabbits and chickens—are crated. There's a mini-barnyard next to the cryo chambers.

All that's left now are the people.

They come in twos and threes. They bring with them only what they can carry. They come with pieces of handmade furniture, an old cradle, a rocking chair, a spindle. They come with bags of cloth, or butcher knives, or scientific equipment. They come with nothing in their hands, and they stare at the planet through the honeycombed window and they cry. They go straight to the cryo chamber, where the others were waiting, not bothering to turn their heads a fraction of an inch to see what they will be facing.

They see me and they smile, they hug me, they touch my pale skin and red hair with wonder. They see me and they scowl, they curse, they say they're only coming because their friend, their lover, their mother is going, and they'll risk a new world to stay with them.

They scurry down the ladder, they jump on the floor, they spin in the bridge, they go to the edge of the window and touch the glass. They sigh when they reach the floor, their shoulders slumping under the weight of their thoughts, their skin flushed and creased with worry, with sorrow, with fear.

But the important thing is simply: they come.

Elder arrives last.

"That's it," he says. "That's all of them."

All of them willing to go.

He hesitates, and I run to him, throwing my arms around his neck. I don't care about our disagreements, I don't care about our fight—not for this one moment. Elder wraps me in a hug that lifts me up, then sets me gently back on the ground. "I'm scared as shite," he whispers into my hair.

"Me too," I whisper back.

He searches my eyes. "What's wrong?"

I don't answer him, and after a moment, he looks away. He knows what's wrong.

"I have to take him," Elder says.

"You really don't."

Instead of answering me, Elder pushes his wi-com. "We will begin launch in a few minutes," Elder says. "We're relying on autopilot. I have had some training on the operation of the shuttle, but . . ."

He doesn't say that his training was little more than Shelby showing him the controls. Still, that's more knowledge than anyone else has; only the top-ranking Shippers—the ones killed in the explosion on the Bridge—had any real experience with these controls.

"You should stabilize your belongings and find a secure place during launch," Elder adds before disconnecting his wi-com.

We can hear the shuffle of movement from here. Elder closes the bridge door.

His face is hard, his shoulders squared.

He looks like a general about to go into battle, but without any armor or weapons.

He motions for me to follow him—we go to the control panel under the window.

"It's worth it, right?" he asks, staring at the planet.

I lean over the control panel, trying to see as much of the planet as I can. It's bright and blue and green, with swirls of stringy white clouds. I can make out lakes and mountains, a yellow-brown stretch that must be desert, a ribbon of green dots that are islands. It's the most beautiful thing I've ever seen.

But then I glance at Elder's face.

His worry infects me, and now as I look at the surface of Centauri-Earth, I wonder: what's down there?

Victria's staring eyes fill my memory.

Death is easy, and sudden, and can't be stopped. Maybe Centauri-Earth is just beginning to evolve, and dinosaurs will crush us. Or Centauri-Earth may be light-years ahead of Earth, my Earth, and the aliens there will laugh at our weapons as they kill us. It's obvious that plants grow on the planet—there is so much green amid the blue—but what if all the plants are poison? What if all the blue water is salt?

"It's worth it." I move to touch him, but he grabs my hand first, squeezes my fingers, then lets me go.

"What was it you said to Doc?" Elder asks. "About faith?"

"I don't remember," I say with a dry laugh. "I was too busy trying not to get killed."

"Well, whatever it was—you were right." His hand rests over the auto-pilot launch button.

"Ready?" he asks.

"Ready."

Acknowledgments:

This book quite simply would not exist without my amazing agent Merrilee Heifetz, who pushed me to come up with a better idea than my original one, and I'm forever grateful for that.

A book is more than an idea, and so my thanks go also to Ben Schrank and Gillian Levinson for helping me to see which words best told the story. I knew I was in good editorial hands when one of your notes said, "Don't be afraid to kill off more characters!"

When it comes to producing this book, I couldn't have a better team behind me than the one at Razorbill. Thank you Natalie Sousa and Emily Osborne for the beautiful cover designs for all the books; Emily Romero, Courtney Wood, Erin Dempsey, Erin Gallagher and Anna Jarzab for the amazing marketing and online programs; Casey McIntyre for organizing the Breathless Tour and working so diligently on publicity; and everyone else at Razorbill for being so brilly.

A special thanks to Cecilia de la Campa at Writers House for helping the series go around the world, and to Chelsey Heller for helping me navigate foreign contracts.

This book went through more drafts than I care to admit, but I'd like to thank Heather Zundel, Erin Anderson, and Christy Farley for reading the earliest version. And telling me to throw it away. Thank you Tricia Hoover, Christine Marciniak, Jodi Meadows, and Jillian Boehme for reading the next version . . . that I also threw away. Corinne Duyvis and Casey McCormick, thank you for reading first chapters until I'm sure you were sick of them. Elana Johnson, Lisa Roecker, Laura Roecker, Shannon Messenger, Lauren DeStefano, Michelle Hodkin, Stephanie Perkins, Saundra Mitchell,

Victoria Schwab, Myra McEntire, and all the Bookanistas, all the members of the League: thank you for listening to me prattle on about books and writing.

Kiersten White, Melissa Marr, and Carrie Ryan believed in me before *Across the Universe* was even a book, and I'm very grateful to them for that. Carrie, thanks also for always reading my long, rambling emails and giving me the best advice for every situation!

Thank you, Jennifer Randolph, for being one of my first supporters. Thank you, Laura Parker, for being so selfless and sharing in my joy. Thank you, Melissa Spence, for driving across the state just to celebrate with me. All of your friendships mean the world to me.

I'd like to thank the students at Burns High School who leant me their names for this story, particularly those of you who wanted to have the goriest, bloodiest ends. I hope you enjoyed being killed off!

Thanks to Village Coffee for keeping me caffeinated and Fireside Books & Gifts for keeping me well read.

And, of course, my deepest love and gratitude to my parents, Ted and JoAnne Graham, who are just as excited as I am about this whole endeavor, and to my husband, Corwin Revis, who read every draft, even the worst ones, and still loved me after all that.

Thank you all.

Your universe changed with book one.
Your heart stopped with book two.
And now in book three?

It's time to go home.

Coming January 2013

SHADES OF EARTH

Book III in the *Across the Universe* Trilogy
From *New York Times* Bestselling Author Beth Revis

The journey is just beginning . . .

2112